TRIBUTE

TRIBUTE

Nora Roberts

G. P. PUTNAM'S SONS / NEW YORK

PUTNAM

G. P. PUTNAM'S SONS
Publishers Since 1838
Published by the Penguin Group

Library of Congress Cataloging-in-Publication Data
Roberts, Nora.
    Tribute / Nora Roberts.
        p.   cm.
    ISBN 978-0-399-15509-3
    1. Child actors—Fiction.   2. Granddaughters—Fiction.   3. Motion picture
actors and actresses—Fiction.   4. Grandmothers—Fiction.   5. City and town
life—Fiction.   I. Title.
PS3568.O243T75   2008   2008000860
813'.54—dc22

Printed in the United States of America
10   9   8   7   6   5   4   3   2

BOOK DESIGN BY MEIGHAN CAVANAUGH

For Jason and Kat, as you start your life together.
May the garden you plant root strong, blossom with
the colors and shapes each of you brings, and both
of you tend, so the blooms flourish.

Part One

DEMO

The past cannot be presented;
we cannot know what we are not.
But one veil hangs over the past,
present, and future.

—Henry David Thoreau

ONE

According to legend, Steve McQueen once swam buck-naked among the cattails and lily pads in the pond at the Little Farm. If true, and Cilla liked to think it was, the King of Cool had stripped off and dived in post *The Magnificent Seven* and prior to *The Great Escape*.

In some versions of the legend, Steve had done more than cool off on that muggy summer night in Virginia—and he'd done the more with Cilla's grandmother. Though they'd both been married to other people at the time, the legend carried more cheer than disdain. And since both parties were long dead, neither could confirm or deny.

Then again, Cilla thought as she studied the murky water of the lily-choked pond, neither had bothered—as far as she could ascertain—to confirm or deny while they'd had the chance.

True or false, she imagined Janet Hardy, the

glamorous, the tragic, the brilliant, the troubled, had enjoyed the buzz. Even icons had to get their kicks somewhere.

Standing in the yellow glare of sun with the dulling bite of March chilling her face, Cilla could see it perfectly. The steamy summer night, the blue wash from the spotlight moon. The gardens would've been at their magnificent peak and stunning the air with fragrance. The water would've been so cool and silky on the skin, and the color of chamomile tea with pink and white blossoms strung over it like glossy pearls.

Janet would have been at her stunning peak as well, Cilla mused. The spun-gold of her hair tumbling free, spilling over white shoulders . . . No, those would have been spun-gold, too, from her summer tan. Gilded shoulders in the tea-colored water, and her Arctic-blue eyes bright with laughter—and most likely a heroic consumption of liquor.

Music darting and sparkling through the dark, like the fireflies that flashed over the fertile fields, the velvet lawns, Cilla imagined. The voices from the weekend guests who wandered over the lawns, the porches and patios as bright as the music. Stars as luminous as the ones that gleamed overhead like little jewels scattered away from that spotlight moon.

Dark pockets of shadows, streaming colored lights from lanterns.

Yes, it would've been like that. Janet's world had been one of brilliant light and utter dark. Always.

Cilla hoped she dove into that pond unapologetically naked, drunk and foolish and happy. And utterly unaware her crowded, desperate, glorious life would end barely a decade later.

Before turning away from the pond, Cilla listed it in her thick notebook. It would need to be cleaned, tested and ecologically balanced. She made another note to read up on pond management and maintenance before she attempted to do so, or hired an expert.

Then the gardens. Or what was left of them, she thought as she crossed through the high, lumpy grass. Weeds, literal blankets of vines, overgrown shrubs with branches poking through the blankets like brown bones, marred what had once been simply stupendous. Another metaphor, she supposed, for the bright and beautiful choked off and buried in the grasping.

She'd need help with this part, she decided. Considerable help. However much she wanted to put her back into this project, get her hands into it, she couldn't possibly clear and hack, slash and burn, and redesign on her own.

The budget would have to include a landscaping crew. She noted down the need to study old photographs of the gardens, to buy some books on landscaping to educate herself, and to contact local landscapers for bids.

Standing, she scanned the ruined lawns, the sagging fences, the sad old barn that stood soot gray and scarred from weather. There had been chickens once—or so she'd been told—a couple of pretty horses, tidy fields of crops, a small, thriving grove of fruit trees. She wanted to believe—maybe needed to believe—she could bring all that back. That by the next spring, and all the springs after, she could stand here and look at all the budding, the blooming, the business of what had been her grandmother's.

Of what was now hers.

She saw how it was, and how it once had been through her own Arctic-blue eyes shaded by the bill of a *Rock the House* ball cap. Her hair, more honey than gold dust, threaded through the back of the cap in a long, messy tail. She wore a thick hooded sweatshirt over strong shoulders and a long torso, faded jeans over long legs, and boots she'd bought years before for a hiking trip through the Blue Ridge Mountains. The same mountains that rolled up against the sky now.

Years ago, she thought. The last time she'd come

east, come here. And when, she supposed, the seeds for what she would do now had been planted.

Didn't that make the last four—or was it five—years of neglect at least partially her doing? She could've pushed sooner, could have *demanded*. She could have done something.

"Doing it now," she reminded herself. She wouldn't regret the delay any more than she would regret the manipulation and bitter arguments she'd used to force her mother to sign over the property.

"Yours now, Cilla," she told herself. "Don't screw it up."

She turned, braced herself, then made her way through the high grass and brambles to the old farmhouse where Janet Hardy had hosted sparkling parties, or had escaped to between roles. And where, in 1973, on another steamy summer night, she took her own life.

So claimed the legend.

THERE WERE GHOSTS. Sensing them was nearly as exhausting as evaluating the ramshackle three stories, facing the grime, the dust, the disheartening disrepair. Ghosts, Cilla supposed, had kept the vandalism and squatting to a minimum. Legends, she thought, had their uses.

She'd had the electricity turned back on, and had brought plenty of lightbulbs along with what she hoped would be enough cleaning supplies to get her started. She'd applied for her permits and researched local contractors.

Now, it was time to start something.

Lining up her priorities, she tackled the first of the four bathrooms that hadn't seen a scrub brush in the last six years.

And she suspected the last tenants hadn't bothered overmuch with such niceties during their stint.

"Could be more disgusting," she muttered as she scraped and scrubbed. "Could be snakes and rats. And God, shut up. You're asking for them."

After two sweaty hours and emptying countless buckets of filthy water, she thought she could risk using the facilities without being inoculated first. Chugging bottled water, she headed down the back stairs to have a whack at the big farmhouse kitchen next. And eyeing the baby-blue-on-white laminate on the stubby counters, she wondered whose idea that update had been, and why they'd assumed it would suit the marvelous old O'Keefe & Merritt range and Coldspot refrigerator.

Aesthetically, the room was over the line of hideous, but sanitary had to take precedence.

She braced the back door open for ventilation,

tugged rubber gloves back on and very gingerly opened the oven door.

"Oh, crap."

While the best part of a can of oven cleaner went to work, she tackled the oven racks, the burners, the stove top and hood. A photograph flitted through her memory. Janet, a frilly apron over a wasp-waisted dress, sunlight hair pulled back in a sassy tail, stirring something in a big pot on the stove. Smiling at the camera while her two children looked on adoringly.

Publicity shoot, Cilla remembered. For one of the women's magazines. *Redbook* or *McCall's*. The old farmhouse stove, with its center grill, had sparkled like new hope. It would again, she vowed. One day, she'd stir a pot on that same stove with probably as much faked competence as her grandmother.

She started to squat down to check the oven cleaner, then yipped in surprise when she heard her name.

He stood in the open doorway, with sunlight haloing his silvered blond hair. His smile deepened the creases in his face, still so handsome, and warmed those quiet hazel eyes.

Her heart took a bound from surprise to pleasure, and another into embarrassment.

"Dad."

When he stepped forward, arms opening for a hug, she tossed up her hands, wheeled back. "No, don't. I'm absolutely disgusting. Covered with . . . I don't even want to know." She swiped the back of her wrist over her forehead, then fumbled off the protective gloves. "Dad," she repeated.

"I see a clean spot." He lifted her chin with his hand, kissed her cheek. "Look at you."

"I wish you wouldn't." But she laughed as most of the initial awkwardness passed. "What are you doing here?"

"Somebody recognized you in town when you stopped for supplies and said something to Patty. And Patty," he continued, referring to his wife, "called me. Why didn't you tell me you were coming?"

"I was going to. I mean I was going to call you." At some point. Eventually. When I figured out what to say. "I just wanted to get here first, then I . . ." She glanced back at the oven. "I got caught up."

"So I see. When did you get in?"

Guilt pricked her conscience. "Listen, let's go out on the front porch. It's not too bad out front, and I have a cooler sitting out there holding a cold-cut sub with our names on it. Just let me wash up, then we'll catch up."

It wasn't as bad in front, Cilla thought when she settled on the sagging steps with her father, but it was bad enough. The overgrown, weedy lawn and gardens, the trio of misshaped Bradford pears, a wild tangle of what she thought might be wisteria could all be dealt with. Would be. But the wonderful old magnolia rose, dense with its deep, glossy leaves, and stubborn daffodils shoved up through the thorny armor of climbing roses along the stone walls.

"I'm sorry I didn't call," Cilla began as she handed her father a bottle of iced tea to go with half the sub. "I'm sorry I haven't called."

He patted her knee, opened her bottle, then his own.

It was so like him, she thought. Gavin McGowan took things as they came—the good, the bad, the mediocre. How he'd ever fallen for the emotional morass that was her mother eluded her. But that was long ago, Cilla mused, and far away.

She bit into her portion of the sub. "I'm a bad daughter."

"The worst," he said, and made her laugh.

"Lizzie Borden."

"Second worst. How's your mother?"

Cilla bit into her sub, rolled her eyes. "Lizzy's definitely running behind me on Mom's scale at the moment. Otherwise, she's okay. Number Five's putting together a cabaret act for her." At her father's quiet look, Cilla shrugged. "I think when your marriages average a three-year life span, assigning numbers to husbands is practical and efficient. He's okay. Better than Numbers Four and Two, and considerably smarter than Number Three. And he's the reason I'm sitting here sharing a sub with the never-to-be-matched Number One."

"How's that?"

"Putting the song and dance together requires money. I had some money."

"Cilla."

"Wait, wait. I had some money, and she had something I wanted. I wanted this place, Dad. I've wanted it for a while now."

"You—"

"Yeah, I bought the farm." Cilla tossed back her head and laughed. "And she's *so* pissed at me. She didn't want it, God knows. I mean, look at it. She hasn't been out here in years, in *decades*, and she fired every manager, every overseer, every custodian. She wouldn't give it to me, and it was my mistake to ask her for it a couple years ago. She wouldn't sell it to me then, either."

She took another bite of the sub, enjoying it now. "I got the tragedy face, the spiel about Janet. But now she needed seed money and wanted me to invest. Big no on that followed by big fight, much drama. I told her, and Number Five, I'd buy this place, named an amount and made it clear that was firm."

"She sold it to you. She sold you the Little Farm."

"After much gnashing of teeth, much weeping, various sorrowful opinions on my daughterly behavior since the day I was born. And so on. It doesn't matter." Or hardly mattered, Cilla thought. "She didn't want it; I did. She'd have sold it long before this if it hadn't been tied up in trusts. It could only be sold and transferred to family until, what, 2012? Anyway, Number Five calmed her down, and everyone got what they wanted."

"What are you going to do with it, Cilla?"

Live, she thought. Breathe. "Do you remember it, Dad? I've only seen the pictures and old home movies, but you were here when it was in its prime. When the grounds were gorgeous and the porches gleaming. When it had character and grace. That's what I'm going to do with it. I'm going to bring it back."

"Why?"

She heard the unspoken *How?* and told herself it didn't matter that he didn't know what she could do. Or hardly mattered.

"Because it deserves better than this. Because I think Janet Hardy deserves better than this. And because I can. I've been flipping houses for almost five years now. Two years pretty much on my own. I know none of them was on the scale of this, but I have a knack for it. I've made a solid profit on my projects."

"Are you doing this for profit?"

"I may change my mind in the next four years, but for now? No. I never knew Janet, but she's influenced almost every area of my life. Something about this place pulled her here, even at the end. Something about it pulls me."

"It's a long way from what you've known," Gavin said. "Not just the miles, but the atmosphere. The culture. The Shenandoah Valley, this part of it, is still fairly rural. Skyline Village boasts a few thousand people, and even in the larger cities like Front Royal and Culpepper, it's far and away from L.A."

"I guess I want to explore that, and I want to spend more time with my East Coast roots." She wished he'd be pleased instead of concerned that she'd fail or give up. Again.

"I'm tired of California, I'm tired of all of it, Dad. I never wanted what Mom wanted, for me or for herself."

"I know, sweetie."

"So I'll live here for a while."

"*Here?*" Shock covered his face. "Live here? At the Little Farm?"

"I know, crazy. But I've done plenty of camping, which is what this'll be for a few days anyway. Then I can rough it inside for a while longer. It'll take about nine, ten months, maybe a year to do the rehab, to do it right. At the end of that, I'll know if I want to stay or move on. If it's moving on, I'll figure out what to do about it then. But right now, Dad, I'm tired of moving on."

Gavin said nothing for a moment, then draped his arm around Cilla's shoulders. Did he have any idea, she wondered, what that casual show of support meant to her? How could he?

"It was beautiful here, beautiful and hopeful and happy," he told her. "Horses grazing, her dog napping in the sun. The flowers were lovely. Janet did some of the gardening herself when she was here, I think. She came here to relax, she said. And she would, for short stretches. But then she needed people—that's my take on it. She needed the noise and the laughter, the light. But now and again, she came out alone. No friends, no family, no press. I always wondered what she did during those solo visits."

"You met Mom here."

"I did. We were just children, and Janet had a party for Dilly and Johnnie. She invited a lot of local children. Janet took to me, so I was invited back whenever they were here. Johnnie and I played together, and stayed friends when we hit our teens, though he began to run with a different sort of crowd. Then Johnnie died. He died, and everything went dark. Janet came here alone more often after that. I'd climb the wall to see if she was here, if Dilly was with her, when I was home from college. I'd see her walking alone, or see the lights on. I spoke to her a few times, three or four times, after Johnnie died. Then she was gone. Nothing here's been the same since.

"It does deserve better," he said with a sigh. "And so does she. You're the one who should try to give it to them. You may be the only one who can."

"Thanks."

"Patty and I will help. You should come stay with us until this place is habitable."

"I'll take you up on the help, but I want to stay here. Get a feel for the place. I've done some research on it, but I could use some recommendations for local labor—skilled and not. Plumbers, electricians, carpenters, landscapers. And just people with strong backs who can follow directions."

"Get your notebook."

She pushed to her feet, started inside, then turned back. "Dad, if things had worked out between you and Mom, would you have stayed in the business? Stayed in L.A.?"

"Maybe. But I was never happy there. Or I wasn't happy there for long. And I wasn't a comfortable actor."

"You were good."

"Good enough," he said with a smile. "But I didn't want what Dilly wanted, for herself or for me. So I understand what you meant when you said the same. It's not her fault, Cilla, that we wanted something else."

"You found what you wanted here."

"Yes, but—"

"That doesn't mean I will, too," she said. "I know. But I just might."

FIRST, CILLA SUPPOSED, she had to figure out what it was she did want. For more than half her life she'd done what she was told, and accepted what she had as what she *should* want. And most of the remainder, she admitted, she'd spent escaping from or ignoring all of that, or sectioning it off as if it had happened to someone else.

She'd been an actor before she could talk because it was what her mother wanted. She'd spent her childhood playing another child—one who was so much cuter, smarter, sweeter than she was herself. When that went away, she'd struggled through what the agents and producers considered the awkward years, where the work was lean. She'd cut a disastrous mother-daughter album with Dilly, and done a handful of teen slasher films in which she considered herself lucky to have been gruesomely murdered.

She'd been washed up before her eighteenth birthday, Cilla thought as she flopped down on the bed in her motel room. A has-been, a what-ever-happened-to, who copped a scattering of guest roles on TV and voice-overs for commercials.

But the long-running TV series and a few forgettable B movies provided a nest egg. She'd been clever about feathering that nest, and using those eggs to allow her to poke her fingers into various pies to see if she liked the flavor.

Her mother called it wasting her God-given, and her therapist termed it avoidance.

Cilla called it a learning curve.

Whatever you called it, it brought her here to a fairly crappy hotel in Virginia, with the prospect of hard, sweaty and expensive work over the next several months. She couldn't wait to get started.

She flipped on the TV, intending to use it as background noise while she sat on the lumpy bed to make another pass through her notes. She heard a couple of cans thud out of the vending machine a few feet outside her door. Behind her head, the ghost sounds of the TV in the next room wafted through the wall.

While the local news droned on her set, she made her priority list for the next day. Working bathroom, number one. Camping out wasn't a problem for her, but moving out of the motel meant she required the basic facilities. Sweaty work necessitated a working shower. Plumbing, first priority.

Halfway through her list her eyes began to droop. Reminding herself she wanted to be checked out and on site by eight, she switched off the TV, then the light.

As she dropped into sleep, the ghosts from the next room drifted through the wall. She heard Janet Hardy's glorious voice lift into a song designed to break hearts.

"Perfect," Cilla murmured as the song followed her into sleep.

SHE SAT ON the lovely patio with the view full of the pretty pond and the green hills that rolled back to the blue mountains. Roses and lilies stunned the air with perfume that had the bees buzzing drunk-

enly and a hummingbird, bold as an emerald, darting for nectar. The sun poured strong and bright
out of cloudless skies to wash everything in the
golden light of fairy tales. Birds sang their hearts out
in Disneyesque harmony.

"I expect to see Bambi frolicking with Thumper
any minute," Cilla commented.

"It's how I saw it. In the good times." Young,
beautiful in a delicate white sundress, Janet sipped
sparkling lemonade. "Perfect as a stage set, and ready
for me to make my entrance."

"And in the bad times?"

"An escape, a prison, a mistake, a lie." Janet
shrugged her lovely shoulders. "But always a world
away."

"You brought that world with you. Why?"

"I needed it. I couldn't be alone. There's too much
space when you're alone. How do you fill it? Friends,
men, sex, drugs, parties, music. Still, I could be calm
here for a while. I could pretend here, pretend I was
Gertrude Hamilton again. Though she died when I
was six and Janet Hardy was born."

"Did you want to be Gertrude again?"

"Of course not." A laugh, bright and bold as the
day, danced through the air. "But I liked to pretend
I did. Gertrude would have been a better mother, a
better wife, probably a better woman. But Gertrude

wouldn't have been nearly as interesting as Janet. Who'd remember her? And Janet? No one will ever forget her." With her head tilted, Janet gave her signature smile—humor and knowledge with sex shimmering at the edges. "Aren't you proof of that?"

"Maybe I am. But I see what happened to you, and what's happened to this place, as a terrible waste. I can't bring you back, or even know you. But I can do this."

"Are you doing this for you or for me?"

"Both, I think." She saw the grove, all pink and white blossoms, all fragrance and potential. And the horses grazing in green fields, gold and white etched against hills. "I don't see it as a perfect set. I don't need perfect. I see it as your legacy to me and, if I can bring it back, as my tribute to you. I come from you, and through my father, from this place. I want to know that, and feel it."

"Dilly hated it here."

"I don't know if she did, always. But she does now."

"She wanted Hollywood—in big, shiny letters. She was born wanting it, and lacking the talent or the grit to get it and hold it. You're not like her, or me. Maybe . . ." Janet smiled as she sipped again. "Maybe you're more like Gertrude. More like Trudy."

"Who did you kill that night? Janet or Gertrude?"

"That's a question." With a smile, Janet tipped back her head and closed her eyes.

BUT WHAT WAS THE ANSWER? Cilla wondered about that as she drove back to the farm in the morning. And why did it matter? Why ask questions of a dream anyway?

Dead was dead, after all. The project wasn't about death, but about life. About making something for herself out of what had been left to ruin.

As she stopped to unlock the old iron gates that blocked the drive she debated having them removed. Would that be a symbol to throwing open again what had been closed off, or would it be a monumentally stupid move that left her, and the property, vulnerable? They protested when she walked them open, and left rust on her hands.

Screw symbols and stupidity, she decided. They should come down because they were a pain in the ass. After the project, she could put them back up.

Once she'd parked in front of the house, she strode up to unlock the front door, and left it wide to the morning air. She drew on her work gloves. She'd finish tackling the kitchen, she thought. And hope the plumber her father had recommended showed up.

Either way, she'd be staying. Even if she had to pitch a damn tent in the front yard.

She'd worked up her first sweat of the day when the plumber, a grizzle-cheeked man named Buddy, showed up. He made the rounds with her, listened to her plans, scratched his chin a lot. When he gave her what she thought of as a pull-it-out-of-his-ass estimate for the projected work, she countered with a bland stare.

He grinned at that, scratched some more. "I could work up something a little more formal for you. It'd be considerable less if you're buying the fixtures and such."

"I will be."

"Okay then. I'll work up an estimate for you, and we'll see what's what."

"That's fine. Meanwhile, how much to snake out the tub in the first bath upstairs? It's not draining right."

"Why don't I take a look-see? Estimate's free, and I'm here for that anyway."

She hovered, not so much because she didn't trust him but because you could never be sure what you might learn. She learned he didn't dawdle, and that his fee for the small task—and a quick check of the

sink and john—meant he wanted the job enough
that his estimate would probably come into line.

By the time Buddy climbed back into his truck,
she hoped the carpenter and electrician she'd lined
up for estimates worked out as well.

She dug out her notebook to tick her meeting
with Buddy off her day's to-do list. Then she hefted
her sledgehammer. She was in the mood for some
demo, and the rotted boards on the front porch
were just the place to start.

TWO

With her hammer weighted on her shoulder and her safety goggles in place, Cilla took a good look at the man strolling down her driveway. A cartoon-ishly ugly black-and-white dog with an enormous box of a head on a small, stocky body trotted be-side him.

She liked dogs, and hoped to have one eventu-ally. But this was one odd-looking creature, with bulbous eyes bulging out of, and little pointed devil ears stuck on top of, that oversized head. A short, skinny whip of a tail ticked at his behind.

As for the man, he was a big improvement over the dog. The faded, frayed-at-the-hem jeans and baggy gray sweatshirt covered what she judged to be about six feet, four inches of lanky, long-legged male. He wore wire-framed sunglasses, and the jeans had a horizontal tear in one knee. A day or two's worth of stubble prickled over his cheeks and jaw in a look she'd always found too studied to be hip. Still, it fit with the abundance of brown streaky hair that curled messily over his ears.

She distrusted a man who had his hair streaked, and imagined he'd paid for the golden boy tan in a flash parlor. Hadn't she left this type out in L.A.? While those elements added up to mostly harmless to her, and a casual how-ya-doing smile curved on a nicely defined mouth, she tightened her grip on the hammer.

She could use it for more than bashing out rotted boards, if necessary.

She didn't have to see his eyes to know they were taking a good look, too.

He stopped at the base of the porch steps while the dog climbed right up to sniff—though the sound was more of a pig snuffle—at her boots. "Hey," he said, and the smile ratcheted up another notch. "Can I help you?"

She cocked her head. "With what?"

"With whatever you've got in mind. I'm wondering what that might be, seeing as you're holding a pretty big hammer there, and this is private property." He hooked his thumbs in his front pockets as he continued in that same easy Virginia drawl. "You don't look much like a vandal."

"Are you a cop?"

The smile made the lightning strike to grin. "I don't look any more like a cop than you do a vandal. Listen, I hate getting in your way, but if you're thinking about bashing out some pieces of the house here, putting them up on eBay, I have to ask you to reconsider."

Because it was heavy, she lifted the hammer off her shoulder. He didn't move as she brought it down, then rested the head on the porch. But she sensed him brace. "EBay?"

"More trouble than it's worth. Who's going to believe you're selling a genuine hunk of Janet Hardy's house anyway? So, why don't you load it up? I'll close up behind you, and no harm, no foul."

"Are you the custodian?"

"No. Somebody keeps firing them. I know it looks like nobody gives a half a damn about the place, but you can't just come around and beat on it."

Fascinated, Cilla shoved her safety goggles to the top of her head. "If nobody gives a half a damn, why do you?"

"Can't seem to help myself. And maybe I admire the balls it takes to pick locks and wield sledgehammers in broad daylight, but, seriously, you need to load it up now. Janet Hardy's family may not care if this place falls over in the next good wind, but—" He broke off, sliding his sunglasses down his nose, peering over them before he took them off to swing them idly by one earpiece.

"I'm slow this morning," he said. "Chalk it up to only getting a swallow of coffee in before I noticed your truck here, and the open gate and such. Cilla . . . McGowan. Took me a minute. You've got your grandmother's eyes."

His were green, she noted, with the sun bringing out the rims and flecks of gold. "Right on both. Who are you?"

"Ford. Ford Sawyer. And the dog licking your boots is Spock. We live across the road." He jerked a thumb over his shoulder, drawing her gaze up and over to the rambling old Victorian on a pretty knoll across the way. "You aren't going to try to brain me with that if I come up on the porch?"

"Probably not. If you tell me why you showed up this morning, and didn't happen to see me here all day yesterday, or notice Buddy the plumber and assorted subcontractors leaving a half hour ago."

"I was still in the Caymans yesterday. Had myself a little vacation. I expect I missed assorted subcontractors as I was just rolling out of bed a half hour ago. Took my first cup of coffee out on the front veranda. That's when I saw the truck, the gate. Okay?"

Seemed reasonable, Cilla decided. And maybe he'd

come by the tan and sun streaks naturally. She leaned the hammer against the porch rail. "As one of the people who gives a half a damn and more about this place, I appreciate you looking out for it."

"No problem." He walked up until he stood on the step just below her. As they were eye level, and she hit five-nine, she decided her estimate of six-four was on the mark. "What're you planning to do with the hammer?"

"Rotten boards. The porch needs to be rebuilt. Can't rebuild until you demo."

"New porch, Buddy the plumber—who seems to know his stuff, by the way—assorted subcontractors. Sounds like you're planning to fix the place up."

"I am. You look like you've got a strong back. Want a job?"

"Got one, and I haven't found tools to be my friend. But thanks. Spock, say hello."

The dog sat, cocked his big box of a head and held up a paw.

"Cute." Cilla obliged by leaning down, giving the paw a shake while Spock's bulging eyes gleamed at her. "What kind of dog is this?"

"The four-legged kind. It'll be nice to look over here and see this place the way I imagine it used to be. You fixing to sell?"

"No. I'm fixing to live. For now."

"Well, it's a pretty spot. Or could be. Your daddy's Gavin McGowan, right?"

"Yes. Do you know him?"

"He was my English teacher, senior year of high school. I aced it in the end, but not without a lot of sweat and pain. Mr. McGowan made you work your ass straight off. Well, I'll let you get on bashing your boards. I work at home, so I'm there most of the time. If you need anything, give a holler."

"Thanks," she said without any intention of following through. She fit her goggles back in place, picked up the hammer as he started back down the drive with the dog once again trotting beside him. Then gave in to impulse. "Hey! Who names their kid after a car?"

He turned, walked backward. "My mama has a considerable and somewhat unusual sense of humor. She claims my daddy planted me in her while they were steaming up the windows of his Ford Cutlass one chilly spring night. It may be true."

"If not, it should be. See you around."

"More than likely."

FASCINATING DEVELOPMENTS, Ford mused as he took a fresh cup of coffee onto the veranda for his postponed morning ritual. There she was, the long drink of water with the ice blue eyes, beating the living crap out of the old veranda.

That hammer was probably damn heavy. Girl had some muscle on her.

"Cilla McGowan," he said to Spock as the dog raced after invisible cats in the yard, "moved in right across the road." Wasn't that a kick in the ass? Ford recalled his own sister had all but worshipped Katie Lawrence, the kid Cilla had played for five? six? seven years? Who the hell knew? He remembered Alice carting around an *Our Family* lunch box, playing with her Katie doll and wearing her Katie backpack proudly.

As Alice tended to hoard everything, he suspected she still had the *Our Family* and Katie memorabilia somewhere up in Ohio, where she lived now. He was going to make a point of e-mailing her and rubbing her face in who he'd just copped as a neighbor.

The long-running show had been too tame for him back in the day. He'd preferred the action of *The Transformers*, and the fantasy of *Knight Rider*. He remembered after a bitter battle with Alice over God knew what, he'd exacted his revenge by stripping Katie naked, gagging her with duct tape and tying her to a tree, guarded by his army of Storm Troopers.

He'd caught hell for it, but it had been worth it.

It seemed a bit twisted to stand here now, watching the adult, live-action version of Katie switch sledgehammer for some sort of pry bar. And imagining her naked.

He had a damn good imagination.

Four years, Ford thought, since he'd moved in across the road. He'd seen two caretakers come and go, the second in just under six months. And not once had he seen any of Janet Hardy's family before today. Subtracting the almost two years he'd lived in New York, he'd lived in the area the whole of his life, and seen none of them before today. Heard of Mr. McGowan's girl Cilla passing through a time or two, but he'd never caught a glimpse.

Now she was talking to plumbers, tearing down porches and . . . He paused when he recognized the black pickup turning into the drive across the road as belonging to his friend Matt Brewster, a local carpenter. When a second truck pulled in barely thirty seconds later, Ford decided to get himself another cup of coffee, maybe a bowl of cereal, and take his breakfast out on the veranda so he could watch the goings-on.

He should be working, Ford told himself an hour later. Vacation was over and done, and he had a deadline. But it was so damn interesting out here. Another truck joined the first two, and he recognized that one as well. Brian Morrow, former top jock and wide receiver, and the third in the pretty much lifelong triumvirate of Matt, Ford and Brian, ran his own landscaping company. From his perch, Ford watched Cilla make the circuit of the grounds with Brian, watched her gesture, then consult the thick notebook she carried.

He had to admire the way she moved. Must be all that leg, he supposed, that had her eating up the ground so efficiently while appearing to take her time. All that energy so tightly packed in that willowy frame, the glacier blue eyes and china-doll skin masking the muscle it took to . . .

"Whoa, wait a minute." He sat up straighter, narrowed his eyes and pictured her with the hammer hefted on her shoulder again. "Shorter handle," he muttered. "Two-sided head. Yeah, yeah. Looks like I am working."

He went inside, grabbed a sketch pad and pencils and, inspired, dug out his binoculars. Back on the veranda, he focused on Cilla through the glasses, studying the shape of her face, the line of her jaw, her build. She had a fascinating, sexy mouth, he mused, with that deep middle dip in the top lip.

As he began the first sketch, he rolled around scenarios, dismissing them almost as soon as he considered.

It would come to him, he thought. The concept often came from the sketches. He saw her . . . Diane, Maggie, Nadine. No, no, no. Cass. Simple, a little androgynous. Cass Murphy. Cass Murphy. Intelligent, intense, solitary, even lonely. Attractive. He looked through the glasses again. "Oh yeah, attractive."

The rough clothes didn't disguise that, but they played it down. He continued to sketch, full body, close-up face, profile. Then stopped to tap his pencil and consider. Glasses might be a cliché, but they were shorthand for smarts. And always a good mask for the alter ego.

He sketched them on, trying out simple, dark frames, rectangular lenses. "There you are, Cass. Or should I say, Dr. Murphy?"

He flipped a page over, began again. Safari shirt, khakis, boots, wide-brimmed hat. Out of the lab or classroom, into the field. His lips curved as he flipped the page again, and his mind raced as he sketched out who and what his newly minted Cass would become. The leather, the breastplate—and the very nice pair rising over it. Silver armbands, long bare legs, the wild swirl of hair with the circlet of rank crowning the head. Jeweled belt? he wondered. Maybe. The ancient weapon—double-headed hammer. Gleaming silver when gripped by the hand of the blood descendant of the warrior goddess . . .

And yeah, he needed a name for her.

Roman? Greek? Viking? Celt?

Celtic. It fit.

He held up the pad, and found himself grinning at the image. "Hello, gorgeous. We're going to kick some major ass together."

He glanced back across the road. The trucks were gone now, and while Cilla was nowhere in sight, the front door of the farmhouse stood open.

"Thanks, neighbor," Ford said, and, rising, went inside to call his agent.

SURREAL WAS THE best way to describe Cilla's view on finding herself sitting on the pretty patio of her father's tidy brick colonial, sipping iced sun tea fussily served by her stepmother. The scene simply didn't fit in with any previous phase of her life. As a child, her visits east had been few and far between. Work trumped visitations, at least in her mother's game.

He'd come to her now and then, Cilla remembered. And taken her to the zoo or to Disneyland. But at least during the heyday of her series, there'd always been paparazzi, or kids swarming her, and their parents snapping photos. Work trumps Fantasyland, Cilla thought, whether you wanted it to or not.

Then, of course, her father and Patty had their own daughter, Angie, their own home, their own lives on the other side of the country. Which, Cilla mused, equated to the other side of the world.

She'd never fit into that world.

Isn't that what her father had tried to tell her? A long way, and not just the miles.

"It's nice out here," Cilla said, groping.

"Our favorite sitting spot," Patty answered with a smile that tried too hard. "It's a little chilly yet, I know."

"It feels good." Cilla racked her brain. What did she say to this sweet, motherly woman with her pleasant face, dark bob of hair and nervous eyes? "I, ah, bet the gardens will be great in a week or two, when everything starts to pop."

She scanned the bed, the shrubs and vines, the trim swath of lawn that would fill with pockets of shade when the red maple and weeping cherry leafed out. "You've put a lot of work into it."

"Oh, I putter." Patty flicked her fingers over her short, dark bob, twisted the little silver hoop in her ear. "It's Gavin who's the gardener in the house."

"Oh." Cilla shifted her gaze to her father. "Really?"

"I like playing in the dirt. Guess I never grew out of it."

"His grandfather was a farmer." Patty sent Gavin a quick beam. "So it came down through the blood."

Had she known that? Why hadn't she known that? "Here, in Virginia?"

Patty's eyes widened in surprise, then slid toward Gavin. "Ummm."

"I thought you knew—your grandmother bought my grandfather's farm."

"I— What? The Little Farm? That was yours?"

"It was never mine, sweetie. My grandfather sold it when I was just a boy. I do remember chasing chickens there, and getting scolded for it. My father didn't want to farm, and his brothers and sisters— those living at the time—had mostly scattered off. So, well, he sold it. Janet was here, filming on location. *Barn Dance*."

"I know that part of the story. She fell in love with the farm they used and bought it on the spot."

"More or less on the spot," Gavin said with a smile. "And Grandpa bought himself a Winnebago—I swear—and he and Grandma hit the road. Traveled all over hell and back again for the next six, seven years, till she had a stroke."

"It was McGowan land."

"Still is." Still smiling, Gavin sipped his tea. "Isn't it?"

"I think it's a lovely kind of circle." Patty reached out, patted her hand over Cilla's. "I remember how the lights would shine in that house when Janet Hardy was there. And how in the summer, if you drove by with the windows open, you could hear music, and maybe see women in beautiful clothes, and the most handsome men. Now and then, she'd come into town, or just drive around in her convertible. A picture she made."

Patty picked up the pitcher again, as if she had to keep her hands busy. "She stopped by our house once, when we had a litter of puppies for sale. Five dollars. Our collie had herself a liaison with a traveling salesman of indeterminate origin. She bought a puppy from us. Sat right down on the ground and let those pups jump and crawl all over her. And laughed and laughed. She had such a wonderful laugh.

"I'm sorry. I'm going on, aren't I?"

"No. I didn't know any of this. I don't know nearly enough. Was that the dog that . . ."

"It was. She called him Hero. Old Fred Bates found him wandering the road and loaded him in his pickup, took him back. He was the one who found her that morning. It was a sad day. But now you're here." Again, Patty laid a hand over Cilla's. "There'll be lights and music again."

"She bought the dog from you," Cilla murmured, "and the farm from your grandfather." She looked at Gavin. "I guess it's another circle. Maybe you could help me with the gardens."

"I'd like that."

"I hired a landscaper today, but I have to decide what I want put in. I've got a book on gardening in this zone, but I could use some direction."

"It's a deal. And I've got a couple of gardening books that might give you more ideas."

"A couple?"

Gavin grinned at his wife's rolling eyes. "A few more than a couple. Who'd you hire?"

"Morrow? Brian Morrow?"

"Good choice. He does good work, and he's reliable. Was a football star back in high school, and never pushed himself to be more than a dead average student. But he's built up a good business and reputation for himself."

"So I hear. I met another of your former students today. Ford Sawyer."

"Of course," Patty put in. "He lives right across the road."

"Clever boy, always was." Gavin nodded over his tea. "Tended to daydream, but if you engaged his mind, he'd use it. He's done well for himself, too."

"Has he? How?"

"He writes graphic novels. Illustrates them, too, which isn't usual, I'm told. *The Seeker*? That's his. It's interesting work."

"*The Seeker*. Super-crime-fighter sort of thing?"

"Along those lines. A down-on-his-luck private investigator stumbles across a madman's plot to destroy the world's great art through the use of a molecular scrambler that renders them invisible. His hopes to stop them—and secure his own fame and fortune—result in the murder of his devoted girlfriend. He himself is left for dead, but he's also exposed to the scrambler."

"And is imbued with the power of invisibility," Cilla finished. "I've heard of this. A couple of the guys who worked on my flips were into graphic novels. God knows Steve was," she said, referring to her ex-husband. "They'd argue the Seeker versus the Dark Knight or X-Men as compared to the Fantastic Four half the day. When I said something about grown men and comic books, I got the fish eye."

"Gavin enjoys them. Well, Ford's in particular."

"Do you really?" The image of the quiet-natured high school teacher poring over superhero comics amused her. "Because he's a former student?"

"That's certainly a factor. And the boy tells a good, meaty story centered on a complicated character who seeks redemption by seeking out evil. He attempted to do the right thing, but for all the wrong reasons. To stop a madman but for his own personal gain. And that single act cost the life of the woman who loved him, and whom he'd treated carelessly. His power of invisibility becomes a metaphor—he becomes a hero but will never be seen. Interesting work."

"He's single," Patty added, and made Gavin laugh. "Well, I'm only mentioning it because he lives right across the road, and Cilla's going to be alone at the farm. She might want some company now and again."

Head that one off at the pass, Cilla thought. "Actually, I'm going to be spending my days on the rehab, and my evenings plotting out the phases of the job. I'll be too busy for much company for a while. In fact, I should get back to it. I've got a full day scheduled tomorrow."

"Oh, but can't you stay for dinner?" Patty protested. "Let's get a nice home-cooked meal into you before you go. I've got lasagna all made up and ready to pop into the oven. It won't take long."

"That sounds great." Cilla realized it did just that. "I'd love to stay for dinner."

"You sit right here, have another glass of tea with your father."

Cilla watched while Patty popped up, then bustled across the patio and into the house. "Should I go help her?"

"She likes to fuss with meals. It relaxes her, the way gardening does me. She'll like it better if you sit out here and let her."

"I make her nervous."

"A little. It'll pass. I can tell you she'd have been disappointed if you'd said no to dinner. Lasagna's Patty's specialty. She makes the sauce from my tomato harvest every summer and cans it."

"You're kidding."

His lips quirked at her quick and absolute surprise. "It's a different world, sweetie."

"I'll say."

In this world, Cilla discovered, people ate homemade lasagna and apple cobbler, and treated a meal as food rather than a performance. And a guest or family—she thought she fell somewhere in the middle—was given a plate of each covered in tinfoil to take home for leftovers. If the guest/family was driving, she was offered a single glass of wine with dinner, then plied with coffee afterward.

Cilla glanced at her watch, smiled. And could be walking in her own door by eight.

After stowing the two plates in her trusty cooler, Cilla planted her hands on her hips and looked around. The bare bulbs cast harsh light and hard shadows, spotlighted cracked plaster and scarred floorboards. Poor old girl, she thought. You're in desperate need of a face-lift.

She picked up her flashlight, switched it on before turning off the overhead bulbs and, using it to guide her way, started toward the steps.

A glance out the front window showed her the lights sparkling from homes scattered across the hills and fields. Other people had finished their home-cooked meals, she supposed, and were settled down to watch TV or finish up a little paperwork. Maybe kids were being tucked into bed, or being told to settle down and finish their homework.

She doubted any of them sat reading changes in the script for tomorrow's shoot, or yawned through another running of her lines. Foolish to envy them, Cilla thought, for having what she never had.

Standing there, she picked out the lights in Ford's house.

Was he crafting the Seeker's next adventure? Maybe

chowing down on frozen pizza, what she imagined the bachelor's version of a home-cooked meal might be? And what was a comic book writer—pardon me, graphic novelist—doing living in a beautifully restored old Victorian in rural Virginia?

A single graphic novelist, she remembered with a smirk, with an unquestionably sexy Southern drawl and a lazy gait that edged up toward a swagger. And an odd little dog.

Whatever the reasons were, it was nice to see the lights shining across the road. Close but not too close. Oddly comforted by them, she turned away to continue upstairs, where she intended to slide into her sleeping bag and work on her plans.

HER CELL PHONE woke her out of a dead sleep, had her eyes flashing open, then slamming shut again against the glare of the light she'd neglected to turn off before dropping off. Cursing, Cilla pried one eye partially open as she slid a hand over the floor for the phone.

What the hell time was it?

Heart pounding, she read the time on the phone—3:28 A.M.—and her mother's data on the display.

"Crap." Cilla flipped the phone open. "What's wrong?"

"Is that any way to answer the phone? You don't bother to say hello?"

"Hello, Mom. What's wrong?"

"I'm not happy with you, Cilla."

What else is new? Cilla thought. And you're drunk or stoned. Ditto. "Well, I'm sorry to hear that, especially at three-thirty in the morning, East Coast time. Which is where I am, remember?"

"I know where you are." Bedelia's voice sharpened even as it slurred. "I know damn well. You're in *my* mother's house, which you tricked me into giving you. I want it back."

"I'm in my grandmother's house, which you sold to me. And you can't have it back. Where's Mario?" she asked, referring to her mother's current husband.

"This has nothing to do with Mario. This is between you and me. We're all that's left of her! You know very well you caught me in a weak moment. You took advantage of my vulnerability and my pain. I want you to come back immediately and tear up the transfer papers or whatever they are."

"And you'll tear up the cashier's check for the purchase price?"

There was a long, brittle silence during which Cilla lay back down and yawned.

"You're cold and ungrateful."

The thin sheen of tears on the words was much too calculated, and too usual, to get a rise. "Yes, I am."

"After everything I did for you, all the sacrifices I made, all of which you tossed away. Now, instead of you willing to pay me back for all the years I put you first, you're tossing money in my face."

"You could look at it that way. I'm keeping the farm. And don't, please don't, waste my time or your own trying to convince either of us this place matters to you. I'm in it, I've seen just how much you care about it."

"She was *my* mother!"

"Yeah, and you're mine. Those are the crosses we have to bear."

Cilla heard the crash, and pictured the glass holding her mother's preferred nighttime Ketel One on the rocks hitting the nearest wall. Then the weeping began. "How can you say such a horrible thing to me!"

Lying on her back, Cilla swung her arm over her eyes and let the ranting, the sobbing play out. "You should go to bed, Mom. You shouldn't make these calls when you've been drinking."

"A lot you care. Maybe I'll do what she did. Maybe I'll just end it."

"Don't say that. You'll feel better in the morning." Possibly. "You need to get a good night's sleep. You've got your show to plan."

"Everyone wants me to be her."

"No, they don't." Mostly, that's just you. "Go on to bed now, Mom."

"Mario. I want Mario."

"Go on to bed. I'll take care of it. He'll be there. Promise me you'll go up to bed."

"All right, all right. I don't want to talk to you anyway."

When the phone clicked in her ear, Cilla lay as she was a moment. The whining snub at the end signaled that Dilly was done, would go to bed or simply lie down on the handiest surface and pass out. But they'd passed through the danger zone.

Cilla pushed the speed-dial button she'd designated as Number Five. "Mario," she said when he answered. "Where are you?"

It took less than a minute to recap the situation, so she cut off Mario's distress and hung up. Cilla had no doubt he'd rush home and provide Dilly with the sympathy, the attention and the comfort she wanted.

Wide awake and irritated, she climbed out of her sleeping bag. Carting her flashlight, she used the bathroom, then trudged downstairs for a fresh bottle of water. Before going back to the kitchen, she opened the front door and stepped out onto the short section of porch that remained.

All the pretty sparkling lights were gone now, she noted, and the hills were utterly, utterly dark. Even with the thin scatter of stars piercing through the clouds overhead, she thought it was like stepping into a tomb. Black and silent and cold. The mountains seemed to have folded in for the night, and the air was so still, so absolutely still, she thought she could hear the house breathing behind her.

"Friend or foe?" she asked aloud.

Mario would rush into the house in Bel Air, murmur and stroke, flatter and cajole, and ultimately sweep his drunken wreck of a wife into his toned (and younger) Italian arms to carry her up to their bed.

Dilly would say—and say often—that she was alone, always so alone. But she didn't know the meaning of it, Cilla thought. She didn't know the depths of it.

"Did you?" she asked Janet. "I think you knew what it was to be alone. To be surrounded, and completely, miserably alone. Well, hey, me too. And this is better."

Better, Cilla thought, to be alone on a quiet night than to be alone in a crowd. Much better.

She stepped back inside, closed and locked the door.

And let the house sigh around her.

THREE

Ford spent two full hours watching Cilla through his binoculars, sketching her from various angles. After all, the way she moved jump-started the concept every bit as much as the way she looked. The lines, the curves, the shape, the coloring—all part of it. But movement, that was key. Grace and athleticism. Not balletic, no, not that. More . . . the sort of grace of a sprinter. Strength and purpose rather than art and flow.

A warrior's grace, he thought. Economical and deadly.

He wished he could get a look at her with her hair down and loose instead of pulled back in a tail. A good look at her arms would help *and* her legs. And hell, any other parts of her that might pop into view wouldn't hurt his feelings any.

He'd Googled her, and studied several photographs, and he'd NetFlixed her movies, so he'd have those to study. But the last movie she'd done—*I'm Watching, Too!*—was about eight years old.

He wanted the woman, not the girl.

He already had the story line in his head, crammed in there and shoving to get out. He'd cheated the night before, taking a couple hours away from his latest Seeker novel to draft the outline. And maybe he was cheating just a little bit more today, but he wanted to do a couple of pencils, and he didn't want to do those until he had more detailed sketches.

The trouble was, his model had too many damn clothes on.

"I'd really like to see her naked," he said, and Spock gave a kind of smart-assed snort. "Not that way. Well, yeah, that way, too. Who wouldn't? But I'm speaking professionally."

There came growlings and groanings now, with Spock rolling to his side. "I *am* a professional. They pay me and everything, which is why I can buy your food."

Spock snagged the small, mangled bear he carted around, rolled again and dropped it on Ford's foot. Then began to dance hopefully in place. "We've been through this before. You're responsible for feeding him."

Ignoring the dog, Ford thought of Cilla again. He'd pay another "Hi, neighbor" call. See if he could talk her into posing for him.

Inside, he loaded up his sketch pad, his pencils, tucked in a copy of *The Seeker: Vanished*, then considered what he might have around the house to serve as a bribe.

He settled on a nice bottle of cabernet, shoved that into the bag, then started the hike across the road. Spock deserted the bear and scrambled up to follow.

SHE SAW HIM COMING as she hauled another load of trash and debris out to the Dumpster she'd rented. Inside the house she'd started piles of wood and trim she hoped to salvage. The rest? It had to go. Sentiment didn't magically restore rotted wood.

Cilla tossed the pile, then set her gloved hands on her hips. What did her hot-looking neighbor and appealingly ugly dog want now?

He'd shaved, she noted. So the scruffy look might've been laziness rather than design. She preferred laziness. Over one shoulder he carried a large leather satchel, and as he came down her drive, he lifted a hand in a friendly greeting.

Spock sniffed around the Dumpster and seemed happy to lift his leg.

"Hey. You've had a lot going on here the last couple of days."

"No point wasting time."

His grin spread slow and easy. "Wasting time can be the point." He glanced at the Dumpster. "Are you gutting the place?"

"Not entirely, but more than I'd hoped. Neglect takes longer to damage than deliberation, but it does the job just as well. Hello, Spock." At the greeting the dog walked over, offered a paw. Okay, Cilla thought as they shook. Ugly but charming. "What can I do for you, Ford?"

"I'm working up to that. But first, I brought you this." He dug into the satchel, came out with the bottle of red.

"That's nice. Thanks."

"And this." He drew out the graphic novel. "A little reading material with your wine at the end of the day. It's what I do."

"Drink wine and read comic books?"

"Yeah, actually, but I meant I write them."

"So my father told me, and I was being sarcastic."

"I got that. I speak sarcasm, as well as many other languages. Do you ever read them?"

Funny guy, she thought, with his funny dog. "I crammed in a lot of Batman when they were casting Batgirl for the Clooney version. I lost out to Alicia Silverstone."

"Probably just as well, the way that one turned out."

Cilla cocked an eyebrow. "Let me repeat. George Clooney."

Ford could only shake his head. "Michael Keaton *was* Batman. It's all about the I'm-a-little-bit-crazy eyes. Plus they lost the operatic sense after the Keaton movies. And don't get me started on Val Kilmer."

"Okay. Anyway, I prepped for the audition by studying the previous movies—and yes, Keaton was fabulous—reading some of the comics, boning up on the mythology. I probably overprepped."

She shrugged off what had been a major blow to her at sixteen. "You do your own art?"

"Yeah." He studied her as she studied the cover. Look at that mouth, he thought, and the angle of her chin. His fingers itched for his pad and pencil. "I'm territorial and egotistical. Nobody can do it the way I do it, so nobody gets the chance."

She flipped through as he spoke. "It's a lot. I always think of comics as about twenty pages of bright colors and characters going BAM! ZAP! Your art's strong and vivid, with a lot of dark edges."

"The Seeker has a lot of dark edges. I'm finishing up a new one. It should be done in a few days. It would've been done today, probably, if you hadn't distracted me."

The wine tucked in the curve of her arm took on another level of weight. "How did I do that?"

"The way you look, the way you move. I'm not hitting on you on a personal level." He slid his gaze down. "Yet," he qualified. "It's a professional tap. I've been trying to come up with a new character, the central for another series, apart from the Seeker. A woman—female power, vulnerabilities, viewpoints, problems. And the duality . . . Not important for today's purposes," he said. "You're my woman."

"I beg your pardon?"

"Dr. Cass Murphy, archaeologist, professor of same. Cool, quiet, solitary woman whose heart really lies in the field work. The discovery. Prodigy. Nobody gets too close to Cass. She's all business. That's the way she was raised. She's emotionally repressed."

"I'm emotionally repressed?"

"I don't know yet, but she is. See." He pulled out his sketchbook, flipped to a page. Angling her head,

Cilla studied the drawing, studied herself if she wore conservative suits, sensible pumps and glasses.

"She looks boring."

"She *wants* to look boring. She doesn't want to be noticed. If people notice her, they might get in the way, and they might make her feel things she doesn't want to feel. Even on a dig, she . . . See?"

"Hmm. Not boring but efficient and practical. Maybe subtly sexy, given the mannish cut of the shirt and pants. She's more comfortable this way."

"Exactly. You've got a knack for this."

"I've read my share of storyboards. I don't know your field, but I can't see much of a story with this character."

"Oh, Cass has layers," he assured her. "We just have to uncover them the way she uncovers artifacts at a dig. The way she'll uncover an ancient weapon and symbol of power when she's trapped in a cave on a mythical island I have to create, after she discovers the dastardly plans of the billionaire backer of the project, who's also an evil sorcerer."

"Naturally."

"I've got some work to do there, but here she is. Brid, Warrior Goddess."

"Wow." It was really all she could think of. She was all leather and legs, breastplate and boobs. The boring and practical had become the bold, dangerous and sexy. She stood, legs planted in knee-high boots, masses of hair swirling and a short-handled, double-headed hammer lofted skyward.

"You might've exaggerated the cup size," she commented.

"The . . . Oh, well, it's hard to tell. Besides, the architecture of the breastplate's bound to give them a boost. But you hit on what you can do for me. Pose. I can get what I need from candid sketches, but I'd get better with—"

"Whoa." She slapped her hand over his as he flipped to a page covered with small drawings of her. "Those aren't character sketches. That's me."

"Yeah, well, same thing, essentially."

"You've been over there, watching me over here, making drawings of me without my consent? You don't see that as rude and intrusive?"

"No, I see it as work. If I snuck over here and peeked in your windows, that would be rude and intrusive. You move like an athlete with just a hint of dancer. Even when you're standing still there's a punch to it. That's what I need. I don't need your permission to base a character on your physicality, but I'd do a better job with your cooperation."

She shoved his hand away to flip back to the warrior goddess. "That's *my* face."

"And a great face it is, too."

"If I said I'm calling my lawyer?"

At Ford's feet, Spock grumbled. "That would be shortsighted and hard-assed. And your choice. I don't think you'd get anywhere, but to save myself the hassle, I can make a few alterations. Wider mouth, longer nose. Make her a redhead—a redhead's not a bad idea. Sharper cheekbones. Let's see."

He dug out a pencil, flipped to a fresh page. While Cilla watched, he drew a quick freehand sketch.

"I'm keeping the eyes," he muttered as he worked. "You've got killer eyes. Widen the mouth, exaggerate the bottom lip just a hair more, diamond-edge those cheekbones, lengthen the nose. It's rough, but it's a great face, too."

"If you think you can goad me into—"

"But I like yours better. Come on, Cilla. Who doesn't want to be a superhero? I promise you, Brid's going to kick a lot more ass than Batgirl."

She hated feeling stupid, and feeling her temper shove at her. "Go away. I've got work to do."

"I take that as a no on posing for me."

"You can take that as, if you don't go away, I'm going to get my own magic hammer and beat you over the head with it."

Her hands curled into fists when he smiled at her. "That's the spirit. Just let me know if you change your mind," he said as he slid the sketchbook back into his bag. "See you later," he added and, tucking his pencil behind his ear, headed back down her driveway with his ugly little dog.

SHE STEWED ABOUT IT. The physical labor helped work off the mad, but the stewing part had to run its course. It was just her luck, just her *freaking* luck, that she could move out to what was almost the middle of nowhere and end up with a nosy, pushy, intrusive neighbor who had no respect for boundaries or privacy.

Her boundaries. Her privacy.

All she wanted was to do what she wanted to do, in her own time, in her own way—and largely by herself. She wanted to build something here, make a life, make a living. On her own terms.

She didn't mind the aches and pains of hard physical labor. In fact she considered them a badge of honor, along with every blister and callus.

Damned if she wanted her steps, her movements documented by some pen-and-ink artist.

"Warrior goddess," she muttered under her breath as she cleaned out clogged and sagging gutters. "Make her a redhead and give her collagen lips and D cups. Typical."

She climbed down the extension ladder and, since

the gutters completed her last chore of the day, stretched right out on the ground.

She hurt every damn where.

She wanted to soak herself limp in a Jacuzzi, and follow it up with an hour's massage. And top that off with a couple glasses of wine, and possibly sex with Orlando Bloom. After that, she might just feel human.

Since the only thing on that wish list at hand was the wine, she'd settle for that. When she could move again.

With a sigh, she realized the stewing portion of the program was complete, and with her mind clear and her body exhausted, she knew the core reason for her reaction to Ford's sketches.

A decade of therapy hadn't been wasted.

So she groaned, pushed herself up. And went inside for the wine.

WITH SPOCK AND his bear snoring majestically, Ford inked the last panel. Though the final work would be in color, his technique was to approach the inking as a near completion of the final art.

He'd already inked the panel borders, and the outlines of the background objects with his 108 Hunt. After completing the light side of his foregrounds, he stepped back, squinted, studied, approved. Once again, the Seeker, shoulders slumped, eyes downcast, face half turned away, slipped back toward the shadows that haunted his existence.

Poor sap.

Ford cleaned the nib he'd used, replaced it in its section of his worktable. He chose his brush, dipped it in India ink, then began to lay in the areas of shadow on his penciling with bold lines. Every few dips he rinsed the brush. The process took time, it took patience and a steady hand. As he envisioned large areas of black for this final, somber panel, he filled them in partially, knowing too much ink too fast would buckle his page.

When the banging on the door downstairs—and Spock's answering barks of terror—interrupted him, he did what he always did with interruptions. He cursed at them. Once the cursing was done, he grunted a series of words—his little ritual incantation. He swirled the brush in water again and took it with him as he went down to answer.

Irritation switched to curiosity when he saw Cilla standing on his veranda holding the bottle of cab.

"We're cool, Spock," he said, to shut up the madly barking dog trembling at the top of the stairs.

"Don't like red?" he asked Cilla when he opened the door.

"Don't have a corkscrew."

This time the dog greeted her with a couple of happy leaps, and an enthusiastic rub of his body against her legs. "Nice to see you, too."

"He's relieved you're not invading forces from his home planet."

"So am I."

The response had Ford grinning. "Okay, come on in. I'll dig up a corkscrew." He took a couple steps down the foyer, stopped, turned back. "Do you want to borrow a corkscrew, or do you want me to open the bottle so you can share?"

"Why don't you open it?"

"You'd better come on back then. I have to clean my brush first."

"You're working. I'll just take the corkscrew."

"Indian giver. The work can wait. What time is it anyway?"

She noticed he wasn't wearing a watch, then checked her own. "About seven-thirty."

"It can definitely wait, but the brush can't. Soap, water, corkscrew and glasses all conveniently located in the kitchen." He took her arm in a casual grip that was firm enough to get her where he wanted her.

"I like your house."

"Me too." He led the way down a wide hallway

with lofty ceilings framed in creamy crown molding. "I bought it pretty much as it stands. Previous owners did a good job fixing it up, so all I had to do was dump furniture in it."

"What sold you on it? There's usually one or two main hooks for a buyer. This," she added as she walked into the generous kitchen with its wide granite serving bar opening into a casual family room, "would be one for me."

"Actually, it was the view, and the light from upstairs. I work upstairs, so that was key."

He opened a drawer, located a corkscrew in a way that told her his spaces were organized. He set the tool aside, then stepped to the sink to wash the brush.

Spock executed what looked like a bouncing, nail-tapping dance, then darted through a doorway. "Where's he going?"

"I'm in the kitchen, which sends the food signal to his brain. That was his happy dance."

"Is that what it was?"

"Yeah, he's a pretty basic guy. Food makes him happy. He's got an autofeeder in the laundry room and a dog door. Anyway, the kitchen's pretty much wasted on me, and so was the dining area they set up over there since I don't actually dine so much as eat. I'd be a pretty basic guy, too. But I like having space."

He set up the cleaned brush bristles in a glass. "Have a seat," he invited as he picked up the corkscrew.

She sat at the bar, admired the stainless steel double ovens, the cherry cabinets, the six-burner range and grill combo under the shining stainless hood. And, since she wasn't blinded by end-of-the-day fatigue, his ass.

He took two red wineglasses from one of the cabinets with textured glass doors, poured the wine. He stepped over, offered her one, then, lifting his own, leaned on the bar toward her and said, "So."

"So. We're going to be across the road from each other for quite a while, most likely. It's better to smooth things out."

"Smooth is good."

"It's flattering to be seen as some mythical warrior goddess," she began. "Odd but flattering. I might even get a kick out of it—the Xena-meets-Wonder-Woman, twenty-first-century style."

"That's good, and not entirely off the mark."

"But I don't like the fact that you've been watching me, or drawing me when I wasn't aware of it. It's a problem for me."

"Because you see it as an invasion of privacy. And I see it as natural observation."

She took a drink. "All my life, people watched me, took pictures. *Observed* me. Take a walk, shop for shoes, go for ice cream, it's a photo op. Maybe it was usually set up for that precise purpose, but I didn't have any control over that. Even though I'm not in the business, I'm still Janet Hardy's granddaughter, so it still happens from time to time."

"And you don't like it."

"Not only don't like it, I'm done with it. I don't want to bring that by-product of Hollywood here."

"I can go with the second face, but I've got to have the eyes."

She took another drink. "Here's the sticky part, for me. I don't want you to use the second face. I feel stupid about it, but I like the idea of being the inspiration for a comic book hero. And that is something I never thought I'd hear myself say."

Inside, Ford did a little happy dance of his own. "So it's not the results, it's the process. You want something to eat? I want something to eat." He turned, opened another cupboard and pulled out a bag of Doritos.

"That's not actual food."

"That's what makes it good. All of *my* life," he

continued as he dug into the bag, "I've watched people. Drawn pictures—well, I drew pictures as soon as I could hold a crayon. I've observed—the way they move, gesture, the way their faces and bodies are put together. How they carry themselves. It's like breathing. Something I have to do. I could promise not to watch you, but I'd be lying. I can promise to show you any sketching I do, and try to keep that promise."

Because they were there, she ate a Dorito. "What if I hate them?"

"You won't, if you have any taste, but if you do, that would be too bad."

Contemplating, she ate another chip. His voice had stayed easy, she noted—over the rigid steel underlying it. "That's a hard line."

"I'm not what you'd call flexible about my work. I can pretzel about most anything else."

"I know the type. What comes after the sketching?"

"You've got to have a story. Graphics is only half of a graphic novel. But you need to . . . Bring your wine. Come on upstairs."

He retrieved his brush. "I was inking the last panel on *Payback* when you knocked," he told her as he led her out of the kitchen and to the stairs.

"Are these stairs original?"

"I don't know." His forehead creased as he looked down at them. "Maybe. Why?"

"It's beautiful work. The pickets, the banister, the finish. Someone took care of this place. It's a major contrast with mine."

"Well, you're taking care now. And you hired Matt—pal of mine—to do some of the carpentry. I know he worked on this place before I bought it. And did some stuff for me after." He turned into his studio.

Cilla saw the gorgeous wide-planked chestnut floor, the beautiful tall windows and the wide, glossy trim. "What a wonderful room."

"Big. It was designed as the master bedroom, but I don't need this much space to sleep."

Cilla tuned into him again, and into the various workstations set up in the room. Five large, and very ugly, filing cabinets lined one wall. Shelves lined another with what seemed to be a ruthless organization of art supplies and tools. He'd devoted another section to action figures and accessories. She recognized a handful of the collection, and wondered why Darth Vader and Superman appeared so chummy.

A huge drawing board stood in the center of the room, currently holding what she assumed to be the panels he'd talked about. Spreading out from it on either side, counters and cubbies held a variety of tools, pencils, brushes, reams of paper. Photographs, sketches, pictures torn or cut out of magazines of people, places, buildings. Still another leg of the counter held a computer, printer, scanner—a *Buffy the Vampire Slayer* action figure.

Opposite that, to form a wide U, stood a full-length mirror.

"That's a lot of stuff."

"It takes a lot of stuff. But for the art, which is what you want to know, I'll do a few million sketches, casting my people, costuming them, playing with background, foreground, settings—and somewhere in there I'll write the script, breaking that into panels. Then I'll do thumbnails—small, quick sketches to help me decide how I'm going to divide my space, how I want to compose them. Then I pencil the panels. Then I ink the art, which is exactly what it sounds like."

She stepped over to the drawing board. "Black and white, light and shadow. But the book you gave me was done in color."

"So will this be. I used to do the coloring and the lettering by hand. It's fun," he told her, leaning a hip on one leg of the U, "and really time-consuming. And if you go foreign, and I did, it's problematic to change hand-drawn balloons to fit the translations. So I digitized there. I scan the inked panels into the computer and work with Photoshop for coloring." ·

"The art's awfully good," Cilla stated. "It almost tells the story without the captions. That's strong imaging."

Ford waited a beat, then another. "I'm waiting for it."

She glanced over her shoulder at him. "For what?"

"For you to ask why I'm wasting my talent with comic books instead of pursuing a legitimate career in art."

"You'll be waiting a long time. I don't see waste when someone's doing what they want to do, and something they excel at."

"I knew I was going to like you."

"Plus, you're talking to someone who starred for eight seasons on a half-hour sitcom. It wasn't Ibsen, but it sure as hell was legitimate. People will recognize me from your art. I'm not on the radar so much anymore, but I look enough like my grandmother, and she is. She always will be. People will make the connection."

"Is that a problem for you?"

"I wish I knew."

"You've got a couple days to think about it. Or . . ." He shifted, opened a drawer, drew out papers.

"You wrote up a release," Cilla said after a glance at the papers.

"I figured you'd either come around or you wouldn't. If you did, we'd get this out of the way."

She stepped away, walked to the windows. The lights sparkled again, she thought. Little diamond glints in the dark. She watched them, and the dog currently chasing shadows in Ford's backyard. She sipped her wine. Then she turned her head to look at him over her shoulder. "I'm not posing in a breastplate."

Humor hit his eyes an instant before he grinned. "I can work around that."

"No nudity."

"Only for my personal collection."

She let out a short laugh. "Got a pen?"

"A few hundred of them." He chose a standard roller ball as she crossed the room.

"Here's another condition. A personal, and petty, requirement. I want her to kick a *lot* more ass than Batgirl."

"Guaranteed."

After she'd signed the three copies, he handed her

one. "For your files. How about we pour another glass of this wine, order a pizza and celebrate the deal?"

She eased back. He hadn't stepped into her space; she'd stepped into his. But the tingle in her blood warned her to mark the distance. "No, thanks. You've got work and so do I."

"Night's young." He walked out of the room with her. "Tomorrow's long."

"Not as young as it was, and tomorrow's never long enough. Plus I need extra time to fantasize about putting in a Jacuzzi."

"I've got one."

She slid her eyes toward him as they came down the stairs. "I don't suppose you have a massage therapist on tap, too."

"No, but I've got really good hands."

"I bet you do. Well, if you were Orlando Bloom, I'd consider this a sign from God and be sleeping with you in about ninety minutes. But since you're not"—she opened the front door herself—"I'll say good night."

He stood, frowning after her, then stepped onto the veranda as she hiked toward the road. "Orlando Bloom?"

She simply lifted a hand in a kind of brushing-off wave, and kept walking.

FOUR

She had a couple of good, productive days. She'd
lined up her plumber, her electrician, her head carpenter, and had the first of three projected estimates on replacement windows. But her luckiest
find, to her way of thinking, had been connecting
with an ancient little man named Dobby and his
energetic grandson Jack, who would save and restore the original plaster walls.

"Old man McGowan hired my daddy to do these
walls back around 1922," Dobby told Cilla as he
stood on his short, bowed legs in the living room
of the little farm. "I was about six, came around to
help him mix the plaster. Never saw such a big
house before."

"It's good work."

"He took pride in it, taught me the same. Miz
Hardy, she hired me on to do some pointing up,

and replastering where she made some changes. That'd be back around, 'sixty-five, I guess."

Dobby's face reminded Cilla of a piece of thin brown paper that had been balled tight, then carelessly smoothed out. The creases deepened like valleys when he smiled. "Never seen the like of her, either. Looked like an angel. Had a sweet way about her, and didn't put on airs like you'd reckon a movie star would. Signed one of her record albums for me, too, when I got up the gumption to ask her. My wife wouldn't let me play it after that. Had to frame it up for the wall, and buy a new one to listen to. It's still hanging in the parlor."

"I'm glad I found you, to keep the tradition going."

"Not hard to find, I expect. Lot of people, in Miz Hardy's day, and with her wherewithal, woulda put up the Sheetrock." He turned his deep brown eyes on Cilla. "Most people'd do that now instead of preserving it."

"I can't save it all, Mr. Dobby. Some of it has to change, and some just has to go. But what I can save, I intend to." She ran a fingertip along a long crack in the living room wall. "I think the house deserves that kind of respect from me."

"Respect." He nodded, obviously pleased. "That's

a fine way to look at it. It's right fitting to have a McGowan here again, and one who comes down from Miz Hardy. My grandson and I'll do good work for you."

"I'm sure you will."

They shook hands on it, there where she imagined his father might have shaken hands with her great-grandfather. And where Janet Hardy had signed an album that would stand in a frame.

She spent a few hours off site with a local cabinetmaker. Respect was important, but the old metal kitchen cabinets had to go. She planned to strip some of them down, repaint them and put them to use in the combination mud- and laundry room she'd designed.

When she got home again, she found the open bottle of cabernet topped with a goofy, alien head glow-in-the-dark wine stopper, and a corkscrew sitting on the temporary boards at her front door.

The note under the bottle read:

Sorry I didn't get this back to you sooner, but Spock chained me to my desk. Recently escaped, and you weren't home. Somebody could drink all this selfishly by herself, or ask a thirsty neighbor to join her one of these nights.

Ford

Amused, she considered doing just that—one of these nights. Glancing back, she felt a little poke of disappointment that he wasn't standing out on his porch—veranda, she corrected. And the poke warned her to be careful about sharing a bottle of wine with hot guys who lived across the road.

Considering that, considering him, made her think of his studio—the space, the light. Wouldn't it be nice to have that sort of space, that sort of light, for an office? If she pushed through with her long-term plans of rehabbing, remodeling homes, flipping houses, she'd need an attractive and efficient home office space.

The bedroom she'd earmarked for the purpose on the second floor would certainly do the job. But imagining Ford's studio as she set the wine down on the old kitchen counter (slated for demo the next day), her projected office came off small, cramped and barely adequate.

She could take out the wall between the second and third bedrooms, she supposed. But that didn't give her the light, the look she now imagined.

Wandering the first floor, she repositioned, projected, considered. It could be done, she thought, but she didn't want her office space on the main level. She didn't want to live at work, so to speak.

Not for the long term. Besides, if she hadn't seen Ford's fabulous studio, she'd have been perfectly content with the refit bedroom.

And later, if her business actually took off, she could add a breezeway off the south side, then . . .

"Wait a minute."

She hustled up the stairs, down the hall to the attic door. It groaned in cranky protest when she opened it, but the bare bulb at the top of the steep, narrow stairs blinked on when she hit the switch.

One look at the dusty steps had her backtracking for her notebook, and a flashlight, just in case.

Clean attic. Install new light fixtures.

She headed up, pulled the chain on the first of three hanging bulbs.

"Oh yeah. *Now* we're talking."

It was a long, wide, sloped-roof mess of dust and spiderwebs. And loaded, to her mind, with potential. Though she'd had it lower than low on her priority list for cleaning and repair, the lightbulb was on in her head as well as over it.

The space was huge, the exposed rafter ceiling high enough for her to stand with room to spare until it pitched down at the sides. At the moment, there were two stingy windows on either end, but that could change. Would change.

Boxes, chests, a scarred dresser, old furniture, old pole lamps with yellowed shades stood blanketed with dust. Dingy ghosts. Books, probably full of silverfish, and old record albums likely warped from decades of summer heat jammed an old open bookcase.

She'd come up here before, taken one wincing look, then had designated the attic to Someday.

But now.

Go through the junk, she thought, writing quickly. Sort the wheat from the chaff. Clean it up. Bring the stairwell and the stairs up to code. Enlarge window openings. Outdoor entrance—and that meant outdoor stairs, with maybe an atrium-style door. Insulate, sand and seal the rafters and leave them exposed. Wiring, heat and AC. Plumbing, too, because there was plenty of room for a half bath. Maybe skylights.

Oh boy, oh boy. She'd just added a *ton* to her budget.

But wouldn't it be fun?

Sitting cross-legged on the dusty floor, she spent a happy hour drawing out various options and ideas.

How much of the stuff up here had been her great-grandfather's? Had he, or his daughter or son, actually used the old white bowl and pitcher for washing up? Or sat and rocked a fretful baby in the spindly rocker?

Who read the books, listened to the music, hauled up the boxes in which she discovered a rat's nest of Christmas lights with fat, old-fashioned colored bulbs?

Toss, donate or keep, she mused. She'd have to start piles. More boxes revealed more Christmas decorations, scraps of material she imagined someone had kept with the idea of sewing something out of them. She found three old toasters with cords frayed and possibly gnawed on by mice, broken porcelain lamps, chipped teacups. People saved the weirdest things.

She bumped up the mice quotient on discovering four traps, mercifully uninhabited. Curious, and since she was already filthy, she squatted down to pull out some of the books. Some might be salvageable.

Who read Zane Grey? she wondered. Who enjoyed Frank Yerby and Mary Stewart? She piled them up, dug out more. Steinbeck and Edgar Rice Burroughs, Dashiell Hammett and Laura Ingalls Wilder.

She started to pull out a copy of *The Great Gatsby*, and her fingers depressed the sides. Fearing the pages inside had simply deteriorated, she opened it carefully. Inside, in a depression framed by the raw edges of cut pages, sat a stack of letters tied with a faded red ribbon.

"Trudy Hamilton," Cilla read. "Oh my God."

She sat with the open book on her lap, her palms together as if in prayer, and her fingertips pressed to her lips. Letters to her grandmother, sent to a name Janet hadn't used since childhood.

The address on the top envelope was a post office box in Malibu. And the postmark . . .

Reverently, Cilla lifted the stack, angled it toward the light.

"Front Royal, Virginia, January 1972." A year and a half before she died, Cilla thought.

Love letters. What else could they be, tied with a ribbon, hidden away? A secret of a woman who'd been allowed precious few under the microscope of fame, and surely concealed by her own hands before, like Gatsby, she died young, tragically.

Romanticizing it, Cilla told herself. They could be chatty letters from an old friend, a distant relative.

But they weren't. She knew they weren't. Laying them back in the book, she closed it and carried it downstairs.

She showered first, knowing she didn't dare handle

the treasure she'd unearthed until she'd scrubbed off the attic dirt.

Scrubbed, dressed in flannel pants and a sweat-shirt, her wet hair pulled back, she poured a glass of Ford's wine. Standing in the hard fluorescent light—and boy, did that have to go—she sipped the wine, stared at the book.

The letters were hers now, Cilla had no qualms about that. Oh, her mother would disagree—and loudly. She'd weep about her loss, her right to anything that had been Janet's. Then she'd sell them, auction them off as she had so many of Janet's possessions over the years.

For posterity, Dilly would claim. For the public who adored her. But that was so much crap, Cilla thought. It would be for the money, and for the reflected glow of fame, the spread in *People* with photos of Dilly holding the stack of letters, her eyes sheened with tears, with inserts of her and Janet.

But she'd believe her own spin, Cilla thought. That was one of Dilly's finest skills, as innate as her ability to call up those tear-sheened eyes on cue.

What should be done with them? Should they be hidden away again, returned to sender? Framed like a signed record and hung in the parlor?

"Have to read them first."

Cilla blew out a breath, set the wine aside, then dragged a stool to the counter. With great care, she untied the faded ribbon, then slipped the top letter out of its envelope. The paper whispered as she unfolded it. Dark, clear handwriting filled two pages.

My Darling,

My heart beats faster knowing I have the right to call you that. My darling. What have I done in my life to earn such a precious gift? Every night I dream of you, of the sound of your voice, the scent of your skin, the taste of your mouth. I tremble inside as I remember the sheer glory of making love to you.

And every morning I wake, afraid it's all just a dream. Did I imagine it, how we sat by the fire on that cold, clear night, talking as we had never talked before?

Only friends, as I knew what I felt for you, what I wanted with you, could never be. How could such a woman ever want someone like me? Then, then, did it happen? Did you come into my arms? Did your lips seek mine? Did we come together like madness while the fire burned and the music played? Was that the dream, my darling? If it was, I want to live in dreams forever.

My body aches for yours now that we are so far from each other. I long for your voice, but not only on the radio or the record player. I long for your face, but not only in photographs or on the movie screen. It's you I want, the you inside. The beautiful, passionate, real woman I held in my arms that night, and the nights we were able to steal after.

Come to me soon, my darling. Come back to me and to our secret world where only you and I exist.

I send you all my love, all my longing in this new year.

> I am now and forever,
> Only Yours

Here? Cilla wondered, carefully folding the letter again. Had it been here in this house, in front of the fire? Had Janet found love and happiness in this house in the final eighteen months of her life? Or was it another fling, another of her brief encounters?

Cilla counted out the envelopes, noting they were all addressed the same way and by the same hand, though some of the postmarks varied. Forty-two letters, she thought, and the last postmarked only ten short days before Janet took her life in this house.

Fingers trembling a bit, she opened the last letter.

Only one page this time, she noted.

This stops now. The calls, the threats, the hysteria stop now. It's over, Janet. The last time was a mistake, and will never be repeated. You must be mad, calling my home, speaking to my wife, but then I've seen the sickness in you time and time again. Understand me, I will not leave my wife, my family. I will not endanger all I've built, and my future, for you. You claim you love me, but what does a woman like you know about love? Your whole life is built on lies and illusions, and for a time I was seduced by them, by you. No longer.

If you are pregnant, as you claim, there's no proof the responsibility is mine. Don't threaten me again with exposure, or you will pay for it, I promise you.

Stay in Hollywood where your lies are currency. They're worth nothing here. You are not wanted.

"Pregnant." Cilla's whispered word seemed to echo through the house.

Shaken, she pushed off the stool to open the back door, to stand and breathe and let the chilly air cool her face.

CULVER CITY
1941

"To understand," Janet told Cilla, "you have to start at the beginning. This is close enough."

The hand holding Cilla's was small and soft. Like all her dreams of Janet, the image began as an old photograph, faded and frayed, and slowly took on color and depth.

Two long braids lay over the shoulders of a gingham dress like ropes of sunlight on a meadow of fading flowers. Those brilliant, cold and clear blue eyes stared out at the world. The illusion of it.

All around Cilla and the child who would become her grandmother people bustled, on foot or in the open-sided jitneys that plowed along the wide avenue. Fifth Avenue, Cilla realized—or its movie counterpart.

Here was MGM at its zenith. More stars than the heavens could hold, and the child clutching her hand would be one of its brightest.

"I'm seven years old," Janet told her. "I've been performing for three years now. Vaudeville first. I wanted to sing, to perform. I loved the applause. It's like being hugged by a thousand arms. I dreamed of being a star," she continued as she led Cilla along. "A movie star, with pretty dresses and the bright, bright lights. All the candy in the candy shop."

Janet paused, spun into a complex and energetic tap routine, scuffed Mary Janes flying. "I can dance, too. I can learn a routine with one rehearsal. My voice is magic in my throat. I remember all my lines, but more, I can *act*. Do you know why?"

"Why?" she asked, though she knew the answer. She'd read the interviews, the books, the biographies. She knew the child.

"Because I believe it. Every time, I believe the story. I make it real for me so it's real for all the people who come to watch me in the movie show. Didn't you?"

"Sometimes I did. But that meant it hurt when it stopped."

The child nodded, and an adult sorrow clouded her eyes. "It's like dying when it stops, so you have to find things that make it bright again. But that's for later. I don't know that yet. Now, it's all bright." The child threw out her arms as if to embrace it. "I'm younger than Judy and Shirley, and the camera loves me almost as much as I love it. I'll make four movies this year, but this one makes me a real star. 'The Little Comet' is what they'll call me after *The Family O'Hara*'s released."

"You sang 'I'll Get By' and made it a love song to your family. It became your signature song."

"They'll play it at my funeral. I don't know that yet, either. This is Lot One. Brownstone Street." Just a hint of priss entered her voice as she educated her granddaughter, and tugged her along with the small, soft hand. "The O'Haras live in New York, a down-on-their-luck theatrical troupe. They think it's just another Depression-era movie, with music. Just another cog in the factory wheel. But it changes everything. They'll be riding on the tail of the Little Comet for a long time.

"I'm already a drug addict, but that's another thing I don't know yet. I owe that to my mama."

"Seconal and Benzedrine." Cilla knew. "She gave them to you day and night."

"A girl's got to get a good night's sleep and be bright-eyed and bushy-tailed in the morning." Bitter, adult eyes stared out of the child's pretty face. "She wanted to be a star, but she didn't have it. I did, so she pushed, and she pushed, and she used me. She never hugged me, but the audience did. She changed my name, and pulled the strings. She signed me to a seven-year contract with Mr. Mayer, who changed my name *again*, and she took all the money. She gave me pills so I could make more. I hated her—not yet, but soon. Today, I don't mind," she said with a shrug that bounced her pigtails. "Today I'm happy because I know what to do with the song. I always know what to do with a song."

She gestured. "That's the soundstage. That's where the magic happens. Out here, we're just ghosts, ghosts and dreams," she continued as a jitney full of actors in evening dresses and tuxes passed right through them. "But in there, it's real. While the camera's on, it's all there is."

"It's not real, Janet. It's a job."

The blue eyes filled with warmth. "Maybe for you, but for me, it was my true love, and my salvation."

"It killed you."

"It made me first. I wanted this. That's what you have to understand to figure out the rest. I wanted this more than anything I wanted before, or anything I wanted ever again, until it was nearly over. Those few moments when I do the scene, sing the song, and even the director's eyes blur with tears. When, after he yells 'Cut,' the crew, the cast all break into applause and I *feel* their love for me. That's all I wanted in the world, and what I'd try to find again and again and again. Sometimes I did. I was happy here, when I was seven especially."

She sighed, smiled. "I would've lived here if they'd let me, wandering from New York to ancient Rome, from the old West to small-town USA. What could be a better playground for a child? This was home, more than I'd had. And I was pathetically grateful."

"They used you up."

"Not today, not today." Frowning in annoyance, Janet waved the thought away. "Today everything's perfect. I have everything I ever wanted today."

"You bought the Little Farm, thousands of miles from here. A world away from this."

"That was later, wasn't it? And besides, I always came back. I needed this. I couldn't live without love."

"Is that why you killed yourself?"

"There are so many reasons for so many things. It's hard to pick one. That's what you want to do. That's what you'll need to do."

"But if you were pregnant—"

"If, if, if." Laughing, Janet danced over the sidewalk, up the steps of a dignified brownstone façade, then back down. "*If* is for tomorrow, for next year. People will play *if* about my whole life after I'm dead. I'll be immortal, but I won't be around to enjoy it." She laughed again, then swung Gene

Kelly style on a lamppost. "Except when you're dreaming about me. Don't stop, Cilla. You can bring me back just like the Little Farm. You're the only one who can."

She jumped off. "I have to go. It's time for my scene. Time to make magic. It's really the beginning for me." She blew Cilla a kiss, then ran off down the sidewalk.

As the illusions of New York faded, as Cilla slowly surfaced from the dream, she heard Janet's rich, heartbreaking voice soaring.

I'll get by, as long as I have you.

But you didn't, Cilla thought as she stared at the soft sunlight sliding through the windows. You didn't get by.

Sighing, she crawled out of the sleeping bag and, scrubbing sleep from her face, walked to the window to stare out at the hills and mountains. And thought about a world, a life, three thousand miles west.

"If that was home, that was what you needed, why did you come all the way here to die?"

Was it for him? she wondered. Were you pregnant, and they covered that up? Or was that just a lie to stop your lover from ending your affair?

Who was he? Was he still alive, still in Virginia?

And how did you keep the affair off the microscope slide? Why did you? was a keener question, Cilla decided.

Was he the reason you unplugged the phone that night, then chased the pills with vodka, the vodka with more pills until you went away? Not because of Johnnie then, Cilla mused. Not, as so many theorized, over the guilt and grief of losing your indulged eighteen-year-old son. Or not only because of that.

But a pregnancy so close to a death? Was that overwhelming or a beam of light in the dark?

It mattered, Cilla realized. All of it mattered, not only because Janet Hardy was her grandmother, but because she'd held the child's hand in the dream. The lovely little girl on the towering edge of impossible stardom.

It mattered. Somehow she had to find the answers.

Even if her mother had been a reliable source of information—which Cilla thought not—it was hours too early to call Dilly. In any case, within thirty minutes, subcontractors would begin to arrive. So she'd mull all this, let it turn around in her head while she worked.

Cilla picked up the stack of letters she'd read, retied the faded ribbon. Once again she tucked them inside Fitzgerald. Then she laid the book on the folding table currently standing as a work area, along with her stacks of files and home magazines—and Ford's graphic novel.

Until she figured out what to do about them, the letters were her secret. Just as they'd been Janet's.

FIVE

As nervous as a parent sending her firstborn off to school, Cilla supervised the loading of her vintage kitchen appliances onto the truck. Once restored, they'd be the jewels in her completed kitchen. Or that was the plan.

For the foreseeable future, she'd make do with the under-the-counter fridge, hot plate and microwave oven, all more suited to a college dorm than an actual home.

"Get yourself brand-new appliances down at Sears," Buddy told her.

"Call me crazy," Cilla said, as she suspected he already did. "Now let's talk about putting a john in the attic."

She spent the next hour with him, the electrician and one of the carpenters in the musty attic outlining her vision, then adjusting it when their suggestions made sense to her.

With the music of hammers, drills, saws jangling, she began the laborious task of sorting and hauling the attic contents out to the old barn. There, where the ghostly scents of hay and horses haunted the air, she stored both trash and treasure. While spring popped around her, Cilla watched old windows replaced by new, and old ceramic tiles hauled to the Dumpster. She breathed in the scents of sawdust and plaster, of wood glue and sweat.

At night she nursed her blisters and nicks, and often read over the letters written to her grandmother.

One evening, too restless to settle after the various crews had cleared out, she hiked down to study and consider her iron gates. Or she used them as an excuse, Cilla admitted, as she'd seen Ford sitting out on his veranda. His casual wave as she stood on her side of the road, and Spock's wagging stunted whip of a tail, made it easy, even natural to cross.

"I saw you rebuilding your veranda," he commented. "Where'd you learn to use power tools?"

"Along the way." After greeting the dog, she turned, looked back at the farm. "My veranda doesn't look too bad from yours, considering mine's not finished or painted. The new windows look good, too. I'm putting bigger ones in the attic, and adding skylights."

"Skylights in an attic."

"It won't be an attic when I'm done. It'll be my office. That's your fault."

He smiled lazily. "Is it?"

"You inspired me."

"I guess that's tit for tat, so to speak." He lifted his Corona. "Want a beer?"

"I really do."

"Have a seat."

She slid into one of his wide Adirondacks, scratched Spock's big head between his tiny pointed ears while Ford went inside for the beer. It was a good perspective of her place from here, she thought. She could see where she needed new trees, shrubs, where it might be a nice touch to add a trellis to the south side of the house, how the old barn wanted to be connected to the house by a stone path. Or brick, she thought. Maybe slate.

"I imagine the sound carries over here," she said when Ford came back out. "All that noise must be annoying."

"I don't hear much when I'm working." He handed her the beer, sat. "Unless I want to."

"Superior powers of concentration?"

"That would be a lofty way of saying I just tune things out. How's it going over there?"

"Pretty well. Fits and starts like any project." She

took a pull of her beer, closed her eyes. "God, cold beer after a long day. It should be the law of the land."

"I seem to be in the habit of giving you alcohol."

She glanced at him. "And I haven't reciprocated."

He kicked out his legs, smiled. "So I've noticed."

"My place isn't fit for even casual entertainment at the moment. Neither am I. You see that iron gate?"

"Hard to miss."

"Do I have it restored, or do I have it replaced?"

"Why do you need it? Seems like a lot of trouble to be stopping the car, getting out, opening the gates, driving through, getting out, closing them again. Even if you put in something automatic, it's trouble."

"I told myself that before. Changed my mind." Spock bumped his head against her hand a few times, and she translated the signal, went back to scratching him. "They're there for a reason."

"I can see why she needed them, your grand-mother. But I haven't noticed you using them since you moved in."

"No, I haven't." She smiled a little as she sipped her beer. "Because they're too much trouble. They don't fit the feel of the place, do they? The rambling farmhouse, the big old barn. But she needed them.

They're just an illusion, really." God knew she'd needed her illusions. "Not that hard to climb over them or the walls. But she needed the illusion of security, of privacy. I found some old letters."

"Ones she wrote?"

She hadn't meant to say anything about them. Was it two sips of beer that had loosened her tongue, Cilla wondered, or just his company? She wasn't sure she'd ever met anyone so innately relaxed. "No, written to her. A number of them written to her in the last year and a half of her life. By a local, I'd say, as the majority of the postmarks are from here."

"Love letters."

"They started that way. Passionate, romantic, intimate." She angled her head, studied him over another sip of beer. "Why am I telling you?"

"Why not?"

"I haven't told anyone else yet. I've been trying to figure them out, figure him out, I guess. I'm going to talk to my father about it at some point, as he was friendly with Janet's son—my uncle. And the affair seems to have begun the winter before he was killed—and appears to have started to go downhill a few months after."

"You want to know who wrote them." Ford rubbed the dog lazily with his foot when Spock shifted to bump against him. "How'd he sign them?"

" 'Only Yours'—until he started signing them with varieties of 'up yours.' It didn't end well. He was married," she continued as Spock, apparently rubbed enough, curled up under Ford's chair and began to snore. "It's no secret she had affairs with married men. From flings to serious liaisons. She fell in love the way other women change their hairstyle. Because it seemed like a good idea at the time."

"She lived in a different world than most women."

"I've always considered that a handy excuse or justification for being careless, for being selfish."

"Maybe." Ford shrugged. "Still true."

"She craved love, the physical and the emotional. As addicted to it as she was to the pills her mother started feeding her when she was four. But I think this one was real, for her."

"Because she kept it secret."

She turned back to him again. He had good eyes, she thought. Not just the way they looked with that rim of gold around the green, the flecks scattered in it. But the way he saw things.

"Yes, exactly. She kept it to herself because it was important. And maybe Johnnie's death made it all the more intense and desperate. I don't know what she wrote to him, but from his letters I can feel her desperation, and that terrible need, as easily as I can read his waning interest, his concerns with being found out and his eventual disgust. But she didn't want to let go. The last letter in the stack was mailed from here ten days before she died."

Now she shifted, and her gaze focused on the farm. "Died in that house across the road. He told her, in very clear, very harsh words, that they were done, to leave him alone. She must've gotten on a plane right after getting the letter. She walked off the set of her last, unfinished movie, claiming exhaustion, and flew here. That wasn't her way. She worked, she loved the work, respected the work, but she flicked it off this time. Only this time. She must've been hoping to win him back. Don't you think?"

"I don't know. You do."

"I do." It hurt, she realized. A little pang in the heart. "And when she realized it was hopeless, she killed herself. Her fault. Hers," she said before Ford could speak. "Whether it was the accidental over-dose, as the coroner decided to rule it, or the suicide that seems much more realistic. But this man has to know he played a part in what she chose to do that night."

"You want the piece of the puzzle so you can see the whole picture."

The shadows were long now, she thought. Long

and growing longer. Soon the lights would sparkle through the hills, and the mountains behind them would fold up under the dark.

"I grew up with her like another person in the house, or wherever I went, whatever I did. Her life, her work, her brilliance, her flaws, her death. Inescapable. And now, look what I've done." She gestured with the bottle toward the farm. "My choice. I've had opportunities I never would have had if Janet Hardy hadn't been my grandmother. And I've dealt with a lot of crap over the years because Janet Hardy's my grandmother. Yeah, I'd like the whole picture. Or as much of one as it's possible to see. I don't have to like it, but I'd like, maybe even need, the chance to understand it."

"Seems reasonable to me."

"Does it? It does to me, too, except when it doesn't and strikes me as obsessive."

"She's part of your heritage, and only one generation removed. I could tell you all kinds of stories about my grandparents, on both sides. Of course, three out of four of them are still living—and two of those three still live around here. And will talk your ear off the side of your head given half the chance."

"And apparently so will I. I need to get back." She pushed to her feet. "Thanks for the beer."

"I'm thinking about tossing something on the grill in a bit." He rose as well, casually shifting in a way that boxed her between the porch rail and his body. "That and the microwave are my culinary areas. Why don't you have another beer, and I'll cook something up?"

He could cook something up, she thought, she had no doubt. Tall, sun-streaked and charming with a faint wash of nerd. Too appealing for her own good. "I've been up since six, and I've got a full day tomorrow."

"Ever take a day off?" He trailed his fingertips—just the fingertips—down her arm. "And this would be me officially hitting on you."

"I suspected that. I'm not actually scheduling any time off right now."

"In that case I'd better take advantage of the moment."

She expected smooth, a nice quiet cruise by the way his head dipped toward hers, by the lazy interest in those gold-rimmed eyes. Later, when she could think about it clearly, she decided she hadn't been entirely wrong. It was smooth, in the way a good shot of excellent whiskey, straight up, is smooth.

But rather than a nice, quiet cruise, she got a strong, hard jolt when his mouth closed over hers. The sort that bulleted straight to her belly. The hands that gripped her arms gave one quick, insistent tug that had her pressed against him. In another of those subtle moves, he had her back against the post, and her mouth completely captivated.

Zero to sixty, she thought. And she'd forgotten to strap in first.

She clamped her hands on his hips and let the speed take her.

Everything he'd imagined—and his imagination was boundless—paled. Her taste was more potent, her lips more generous, her body more supple. It was as if he'd painted this first kiss in the brightest, boldest colors in his palette.

And even they weren't deep enough.

She was a ride on a dragon, a flight through space, a dive into the deep waters of an enchanted sea.

His hands swept up from her shoulders to her face, then into her hair to tug the band tying it back. He eased away to see her with her hair tumbled, to see her eyes, her face before he drew her back again.

But she pressed a hand to his chest. "Better not." She let out a careful breath. "I've already hit my quota of mistakes for this decade."

"That didn't feel like a mistake to me."

"Maybe, maybe not. I have to think about it."

He ran his hands down to her elbows and back up as he watched her. "That's really a damn shame."

"It is." She took another breath. "It absolutely is. But . . ."

At her light nudge, he stepped back. "Here's what I need to know. There's persistence, there's pacing and there's pains in the ass. I'm wondering which category you'd consider it if I wander over to your place now and then or invite you over here, with the full intention of trying to get you naked."

The dog made an odd gurgling sound from under the chair, and Cilla watched one of those bulging eyes open. As if he waited for the answer, too.

"You haven't come close to the third yet, but I'll let you know if you do."

She sidestepped. "But I'm going to take a rain check on that offer of food and nudity. I've got a porch—veranda—to finish tomorrow."

"Oh, that tired old excuse."

She laughed, went down the steps before she changed her mind. "I do appreciate the Corona, the ear and being hit on."

"Come back anytime for any or all of the above."

He leaned on the rail as she walked across the road, returned the wave she sent him when she reached the open gates. And he bent and picked up the little stretchy band of blue he'd tugged out of her hair.

FORD DEBATED GIVING her some time, some space. Then decided the hell with that. His latest novel was on his editor's desk, and before he dove too deeply into Brid, he wanted some visual aids. Plus, since Cilla didn't appear to be put off by the persistent, he intended to be just that.

After he rolled out of bed at what he considered the civilized hour of ten, checked the backyard to see that Spock was already up and chasing his ghost cats, he took his coffee outside and watched her work on her front veranda.

He considered he could get some very decent shots of her, in action, with his long lens. But decided that edged over into the murky area of creepy. Instead, he poured himself a bowl of Cheerios and ate them standing up, studying her.

The body was great. Long, lean, lanky and on the athletic side rather than willowy and slight. Cass would be fit, he decided, but instinctively conceal her . . . attributes. Brid, well, she'd be right out there.

The hair, that deep blond like shadowed sunlight, he decided. An easy transition there, too. Cass would habitually keep hers restrained; Brid's would fly and flow. Then the face. He wished he could see Cilla's now, but it was blocked by the brim of the ball cap she wore as she worked. He had no problem conjuring it in his mind, the shape, the angles, the tones. It would be a face Cass played down, one made quiet and intellectual by the glasses, the lack of makeup.

Beauty restrained, just like her hair.

But Brid, for Brid, the beauty would be bold, luminous. Not simply released but wild with it.

Time to get started.

Inside, he packed up his satchel again, hung his camera around his neck by its strap. He considered another token, and shoved an apple into the bag.

The sound of her nail gun peppered the air like muffled gunshots. And made Ford think of battles. Brid would never use a gun—much too crass, too ordinary. But how would she defend herself against them? With sword and hammer, deflecting bullets like Wonder Woman's magic bracelets? Maybe.

As he walked closer, the echoey music from one of the workers' radio jangled out country. Why was it always country? he wondered. Was it some sort of construction law?

Country music (including selected crossover artists) must be played on portable radios on all sites.

He caught the buzz of a saw, the whine of what might've been a drill, and assorted bangs from inside. Adding them together, along with the decor of Dumpster, Porta Potti and pickups, he found himself grateful he'd bought his own place move-in ready.

Plus, he sincerely doubted any of the workers he might have hired otherwise would have owned an ass like the one currently snugged into dusty Levi's and happily facing his way.

He could've resisted, but why? So he lifted the camera, framed her in and took the shot as he walked.

"You know why they have those calendars of scantily clad women holding power drills and such in mechanics' shops?" he called out.

Cilla looked over her shoulder, sized Ford up through her safety goggles. "So men can imagine their dicks as a power drill?"

"No, so we can imagine women imagine it."

"I stand corrected." She shot in the last two nails, then swiveled around to sit. "Where's your faithful companion?"

"Spock? He's busy, but sends his best. Where'd you learn to shoot that gun?"

"On-the-job training. I've got more boards to cut and nail, if you want a turn."

"Tragic and terrible things happen when I pick up tools. So I don't, and save lives." He reached in his bag. "Brought you a present."

"You brought me an apple?"

"It'll help keep your strength up." He tossed it to her, cocking a brow when she caught it neatly, and one-handed. "I had a feeling."

She studied the apple, then bit in. "About what?"

"That you'd field what comes at you. Mind if I take some pictures while you're working? I want to start some more detailed sketches."

"So you're going forward with the warrior goddess idea."

"Brid. Yeah, I am. I can wait until you take a break if the camera bothers you while you work."

"I spent more than half my life in front of cameras." She pushed to her feet. "They don't bother me."

She tossed the apple core into the Dumpster before stepping over to her lumber pile. Ford snapped away while she selected, measured, set the piece on the power saw. He watched her eyes as the blade whined, as it cut through wood. He doubted the camera could capture the focus in them.

But it captured the cut of her biceps, the ripple of

toned muscle when she hefted the planks and carried them to the finished decking.

"Living in California, I expect you're a woman who spends regular time at a gym."

Cilla set the plank on her marks, braced the distance with spacers. "I like a good gym."

"Let me say working out's worked out for you."

"I tend toward skinny otherwise. Rehab work helps the tone," she continued, driving in the first nail. "But I miss the discipline of a good gym. Do you know any around here?"

"As it happens, I do. Tell you what, you come on over when you're finished up for the day. I'll take you to see the gym, then we'll have dinner."

"Maybe."

"You're not the coy type. 'Maybe' means . . . ?"

"It depends on when I finish up."

"Gym's open twenty-four/seven."

"Seriously?" She flicked him a glance, then worked her way down the board with her nail gun. "That's handy. I'll adjust the maybe to probably."

"Fair enough. On the dinner end, are you vegetarian or fruititarian or some other 'tarian that requires restrictions on the menu?"

Laughing, she sat back on her heels. "I'm an eatitarian. I'll eat pretty much what you put in front of me."

"Good to know. Mind if I take a look inside, see what all the banging and sawing's about? It'll also give me the chance to rag on Matt about whatever comes to mind."

"Go ahead. I'd give you the tour, but my boss is a bitch about unscheduled breaks."

"Mine's a pushover." He stepped up, then bent down, sniffed at her. "First time I ever realized the smell of sawdust was sexy."

He stepped inside and said, "Holy shit."

He'd expected a certain amount of chaos, activity and mess. He hadn't expected what struck him as a kind of maniacal destruction. There had to be a purpose behind it all, he thought, as Cilla struck him as firmly sane, but he couldn't see it.

Tools scattered over the floor in what hit his organized soul with dismay. How did anyone find anything? Cords snaked and coiled. Bare bulbs dangled. Sections of wall gaped where for reasons that escaped him someone had cut or hacked them out. The wide planks of the floor were patchworked with stained cloths and cardboard.

Baffled, and slightly horrified, he wandered through, observing the same sort of mad bombarding in every room.

He found Matt in one of them, curling blond hair under a red ball cap, tool belt slung, measuring tape at the ready. He gave Ford an easy smile, said, "Hey."

"You make this mess?"

"Pieces of it. Boss lady's got ideas. Good ones. That's a woman who knows what she's doing."

"If you say so. How's Josie?"

"Doing good. We got a picture of the Beast."

Ford knew the Beast was the baby Josie was currently carrying. Their two-year-old son had been the Belly.

He took the sonogram shot Matt pulled out of his pocket, studied it, turned it and finally found the form. Legs, arms, body, head. "He looks like the other one did. Midget alien from Planet Womb."

"She. We just found out. It's a girl."

"Yeah?" Ford glanced up at his friend's huge grin, found his own spreading. "One of each species. Nice going."

"She's not dating till she's thirty." Matt took the picture back, looked at it with love, then slipped it back into his pocket. "So, you up for poker night at Bri's?"

Ford thought he'd rather face a root canal than poker night. But he, Matt and Brian had been friends just about all their lives. "If there's absolutely no escape."

"Good. I need the money. Hold that end of the tape a minute."

"You know better than that."

"Right." Matt set the tape himself. "If you touch it, it's likely to explode in my hand. I could lose a finger. Have you been through the place yet?"

"I just started."

"Take a look around. It's going to be a hell of a thing."

"It already looks like hell."

Unable to resist, he backtracked, went upstairs. It didn't get any better. What had been a bathroom was now a bare box with stripped walls and skeletal pipes, with raw holes in the floor and ceiling. Two bedrooms stood doorless, their windows still bearing the stickers of the manufacturer, their floors covered with ratty carpet.

But when he opened the door to the next bedroom, astonishment clicked up to temper. What the hell was she thinking? An air mattress and sleeping bag, cardboard boxes and an old card table?

"I take back the sane," he muttered, and headed back down.

He found her standing in front of the newly planked veranda guzzling water from a bottle. The warming temperatures and the labor combined to lay a dark sweat line down the center of the white T-shirt she wore with the jeans. It only added to his annoyance that he found a sweaty, possibly unstable woman so damned appealing.

"Are you crazy or just stupid?" he demanded.

Slowly, she lowered the bottle. And slowly, she tipped her head down until those glacial blue eyes met his. "What?"

"Who lives like that?" He jerked a thumb back toward the house as he strode down to her. "The house is torn to pieces, you're down to a hot plate in the kitchen, and you're sleeping on the floor and living out of a cardboard box. What the hell's wrong with you?"

"I'll take that one at a time. I live like this because I'm in the middle of a major project, which is why the house is torn up, though hardly to pieces. I'm down to a hot plate because I'm having the appliances rehabbed. I'm sleeping on an air mattress, not the floor, because I haven't decided what kind of bed I want. And there's nothing wrong with me."

"Go on up and get what you need. You'll take my spare room."

"I stopped taking orders a long time ago. From my mother, from agents, managers, directors, producers and all manner of others who decided they knew what was best for me, what I wanted, what I should do. I'm afraid you're too late."

"You're living like a squatter."

"I'm living as I choose."

He caught the flare of heat in the icy blue, but pushed anyway. "There's a bedroom over there with a perfectly good bed, one with sheets."

"Oh, if it's got actual sheets . . . no. Go away, Ford. My break's over."

"Your bitch of a boss'll have to give you another couple minutes. You can see this damn place from mine, and you can walk over every morning in about ninety seconds—after you've had a decent night's sleep in an actual bed, and used a bathroom that isn't the black and blue of a psychedelic bruise, and about the size of a quarter."

For some reason his obvious fury banked any embers of her own. Amused now, she laughed outright. "The bathroom's hideous, I'll give you that. But doesn't persuade me to pull up stakes. I get the impression you're a lot more fastidious than I am."

"I'm not fastidious." Temper veered sharply into insult. "Old men in cardigans are fastidious. Wanting to sleep in a bed and piss in a toilet that was manufactured sometime in the last half century doesn't make me fastidious. And your hand's bleeding."

She glanced down. "Must've scraped it." She wiped the shallow cut carelessly on her jeans.

He stared at her. "What the hell's wrong with *me*?" he wondered, and grabbed her.

He jerked her up to her toes. He wanted those ice-blue eyes level with his, wanted that gorgeous, tasty mouth lined right up. He didn't think any further than that before he swooped in and plundered.

She was sweaty, covered with sawdust and possibly had any number of screws loose. And he'd never, never wanted anyone more in his life.

He ignored her jump of shock. The bolt of lust that slammed into him blasted away any thought of niceties. He wanted, he took. It was as elemental as that.

The water bottle slipped out of her hand and bounced on the ground. For the first time in too long to remember she'd been caught completely by surprise. She hadn't seen this move coming, and even the potency of the kiss they'd shared the evening before hadn't prepared her for the punch of this one.

It was raw, and it was randy, and plowed straight through her to leave her muscles quivering and nerve ends quaking. She wanted, for one mad moment, to be gulped down in one greedy swallow, wanted him to throw her over his shoulder and drag her off to some dark cave.

When he jerked her away again, her head actually spun.

"Fastidious, my ass."

As she stared at Ford, she heard Buddy the plumber call her name from behind. "Don't mean to interrupt," he continued, "but you might take a look at what I'm fixing to do in this bathroom. When you get a minute."

She lifted a hand, wagged it vaguely in the air without looking around. "You're a dangerous man, Ford."

"Thanks."

"I don't know how I missed that. I'm usually good at spotting dangerous men."

"I guess I wear it well, since I've missed that my entire life myself. There's a lock on the spare bedroom. I can give you my word not to kick the door down, unless the house is on fire. Even then, since I've never kicked one down, you'd probably have plenty of warning."

"If and when I sleep at your house, it won't be in the spare room. But for now, I'm staying put. You're a dangerous man, Ford," she repeated before he could speak. "I'm a determined woman. I not only like living here, I need to. Otherwise, I'd be staying at the closest motel. Now, I've got to get inside. I'm putting in a basin-style sink with exposed pipes and wall-hung fixtures. Like you, Buddy doesn't understand my line of thinking."

He looked over her shoulder at the house, shook his head. "Right now, I'm not sure anyone understands your line but you."

"I'm used to that."

"Come on over when you're done, we'll check out that gym." He picked up his satchel and camera. Then the water bottle. "Your shoes are wet," he told her, then headed home.

Cilla looked down at her feet. Damned if they weren't. She squished her way into the house to talk to Buddy.

SIX

Cilla spent the bulk of her afternoon looking at toilets. And choosing sinks. She debated the advantages of travertine tile and granite, limestone and ceramic. In her last incarnation of flipping houses, budget had been king. She'd learned to stick to one, to select the best value and look at the neighborhood as well as the house itself. Too much over, too much under, and profit would be sucked away like dust bunnies in a Dyson.

But this time things were different. While budget could never be ignored, she was making choices for home, not for resale. If she intended to live on the Little Farm, to build a life and a career there, she'd be the one living with those choices for a long time to come.

When she'd stumbled into the real estate game, she learned she had a good eye for potential, for color, texture, balance. And she discovered she was fussy. A slight difference in tone, shape or size in bathroom tile *mattered* in her world. She could spend hours deciding on the right drawer pull.

And she'd discovered doing so, and finding the *right* drawer pull, made her absurdly happy.

On her return to the now empty construction zone of a house, she grinned at the new planks of her veranda. *She'd* done that, just as she'd build the rail, the pickets, then paint it a fresh farmhouse white. Probably white, she corrected. Maybe cream. Possibly ivory.

The sound of her feet slapping down on those planks struck her like music.

She hauled the samples she'd brought with her up to the bathroom, spent time arranging, studying. And basking in her vision. Warm, charming, simple. Exactly right for a guest room bath.

The oil-rubbed bronze fixtures she'd already bought and had planned this room around would be wonderfully complemented by the subtle tones in the tile and old-fashioned vessel sink.

Buddy, she thought, would eat his words when this was done.

She left the samples where they were—she wanted to take another careful look at them in natural, morning light—then all but danced to the shower to wash off the day's work.

She sang, letting her voice boom and echo off the cracked, pitiful and soon to be demolished tiles of her own bathroom. No playback from a recording studio or soundstage had ever pleased her more.

WHEN FORD OPENED THE DOOR, Cilla held out the traveling bottle of cabernet. He took it, held it up and estimated there was nearly half a bottle left.

"You lush."

"I know. It's a problem. So how about a drink before we go scout out this gym?"

"Sure."

She'd left her hair down, he noted, so that it spilled, ruler straight, inches past her shoulders. Her scent brought a quick, vivid sensory memory of the night-blooming jasmine that rioted outside his grandmother's house in Georgia.

"You look good."

"I feel good. I bought three toilets today."

"Well, that certainly deserves a drink."

"I picked out bathroom tile," she continued as she followed him back to the kitchen, "cabinet knobs, light fixtures and a tub. A really wonderful classic slipper-style claw-foot tub. This is a big day. And I'm thinking of going Deco in the master bath."

"Deco?"

"I saw this fabulous sink today, and I thought, yeah, that's it. I could do a lot of chrome and pale blue glass in there. Black-and-white tiles—or maybe black and silver. A little metallic punch. Jazzy, retro. Indulgent. You'd be tempted to wear a silk robe with marabou feathers."

"I always am. As I've always wondered what is a marabou, and why does it have feathers?"

"I don't know, but I may buy that robe just to hang in there and finish it off. It's going to rock."

"All this from a sink?" He handed her a glass of wine.

"That's how it usually works for me. I'll see a piece, and it gives a tug, so I can see how the rest of the room might work around it. Anyway." She lifted her glass in toast. "I had a good day. How about you?"

She sparkled, he thought. A trip to Home Depot, or wherever she'd been, and she sparkled like sunlight. "Well, I didn't buy any toilets, but I can't complain. I've got a good handle on the book, the story line, and managed to put a lot of it on paper." He studied her as he sipped. "I guess I understand your sink, after all. I saw you, you gave a tug. And the rest works around you."

"Can I read it?"

"Sure. Once I get it smoothed out some."

"That's awfully normal and untemperamental. Most of the writers I've known fall into two camps. The ones who plead for you to read every word as it's written, and the ones who'd put out your eyes with a shrimp fork if you glimpsed a page of unpolished work."

"I bet most of the writers you've known are in Hollywood."

She considered a moment. "Your point," she conceded. "When I was acting, script pages could come flying at you while you were shooting the scene. I actually liked it that way. More spontaneous, keeps the energy up. But I used to think, how hard can it be? You just put the idea down in words on paper. I found out how hard it can be when I started to write a screenplay."

"You wrote a screenplay?"

"Started to write. About a woman who grows up in the business—an insider's view—the rise and the fall, the scrambling, the triumphs and humiliations. Write what you know, I thought, and boy, did I know. I only got about ten pages in."

"Why did you stop?"

"I failed to factor in one little element. I can't write." She laughed, shook back her hair. "Reading a million scripts doesn't mean you can write one.

Even a bad one. And since of that million scripts I've read, I've read about nine hundred thousand bad ones, I knew a stinker. With acting, I had to believe—not make believe, but believe. Janet Hardy's Number One Rule. It struck me it's the same with writing. And I couldn't write so I could believe. You do."

"How do you know?"

"I could see it when you started telling me about this new idea, about this new character. And it shows in your work, the words and the art."

He pointed at her. "You read the book."

"I did. I confess I intended to flip through it, get the gist so I wouldn't fail the quiz if and when you asked me about it. But I got caught up. Your Seeker is flawed and dark and human. Even when he's in superhero mode, his humanity, his wounds show through. I guess that's the point."

"You'd guess right. You just earned yourself another drink."

"Better not." She put a hand over her glass when he reached for the wine. "Maybe later, over dinner. After you show me the gym. You said it was close."

"Yeah, it is. Come take a look at this."

He gestured, then opened a flat-panel cherry door she'd admired. Lower level, she assumed and, since touring houses always appealed, started down with him.

"Nice stairs again," she commented. "Whoever built this place really . . . Oh. Man."

Struck with admiration and not a little envy, she stopped at the base. The slope of the hill opened the lower level to the rear of the house through wide glass doors and windows, and a small and pretty slate patio beyond, where the dog currently sprawled on his back, feet straight up, sleeping.

But inside, on safety mats over the wide-planked oak floor, stood the machines. In silence, she wandered, studying the elliptical trainer, the weight bench, the rack of weights, the recumbent bike, rowing machine.

Serious stuff, she mused.

An enormous flat-panel TV covered one wall. She noted the components tucked into a built-in, and the glass-front bar fridge holding bottles of water. And in the corner where the wood merged with slate rested a whirlpool tub in glossy black.

"Matt's work?"

"Yeah. Mostly."

"I'm more and more pleased with my instinct to hire him. You never have to leave here."

"That was sort of the idea. I like to hole up for long stretches. It was designed as a family room, but since my family doesn't live here, I figured why haul myself to a gym when I can bring the gym to me? And, hey, no membership fee. Of course, it cuts out being able to ogle toned and sweaty female bodies, but you've got to make some sacrifices."

"I have a basement," Cilla mused. "An actual underground basement, but it's big. I gave some thought to finishing it off eventually, but more for storage and utility. But with the right lighting . . ."

"Until then, you're welcome to use this."

Frowning, she turned to look at him. "Why?"

"Why not?"

"Don't evade. Why?"

"That wasn't an evasion." And wasn't she an odd combination of caution and openness, he thought. "But if you need more specifics, I only use it a few hours a week. So you're welcome to use it a few hours a week, too. Call it Southern hospitality."

"When do you generally work out?"

"No set time, really. More when the mood strikes. I try to make sure the mood strikes five or six days a week anyway, otherwise I can start to resemble Skeletor."

"Who?"

"You know, Skeletor. Masters of the Universe? Archenemy of He-Man. And, no, you don't know. I'll get you a book. It doesn't fit anyway, because despite the name, Skeletor's ripped. Anyway, you can use those doors there, when your mood strikes. I won't even know you're here. And I might get lucky, have my mood match yours—then I'd be able to ogle a toned, sweaty female after all."

She narrowed her eyes. "Pull up your shirt."

"I thought you'd never ask."

"Keep your pants on. Just the shirt, Ford. I want to check out the abs."

"You're a strange woman, Cilla." But he pulled up his shirt.

She poked a finger into his stomach. "Okay. I just wanted to be sure you actually use this equipment, and the mood striking is a side benefit rather than a purpose."

"I've got a purpose when it comes to you."

"Which I get, and which is fine. But I'd really like to take you up on your offer and do that without strings or expectations. I appreciate the hospitality, Ford. I really do. Plus you have Matt's seal of approval, and I like him."

"It's a good thing because I pay him five hundred a year for that seal."

"He loves you. It came across when I subtly and cleverly pumped him about you."

He felt a quick and happy twinge. "You pumped him about me?"

"Subtly," she repeated. "And cleverly. And he's a nice guy, so . . ." She scanned the room, the equipment again, and he could almost feel her longing. "How about we barter? I'll happily take advantage of your equipment, and if you have something around the house that needs fixing or dealing with, I'll take care of it."

"You're going to be my handyman?"

"I'm pretty damn handy."

"Will you wear your tool belt, and a really short skirt?"

"Tool belt, yes. Skirt, no."

"Damn it."

"If I can't fix it, I'll send one of the guys over. Maybe one of them will wear a really short skirt."

"I can always hope."

"Deal?"

"Deal."

"Great." Smiling, she studied the room again. "I'm going to take advantage first thing tomorrow. Why don't I take *you* out to dinner to seal the deal?"

"I'll rain-check that as I've got the menu planned up in Chez Sawyer."

"You're going to cook."

"My specialty." He took her arm to turn her toward the steps. "I only have the one that doesn't involve nuking. It involves tossing a couple steaks on the grill, stabbing a bunch of peppers on a skewer and baking a couple of potatoes. How do you like your steak?"

"So I can hear it faintly whisper moo."

"Cilla, you're a woman after my own heart."

SHE WASN'T. She wasn't after anything but the pursuit of her own goals, and the satisfaction of finding them. But she had to admit, Ford made it tempting. He engaged her mind, putting it at ease and keeping it on alert. It was, Cilla thought, a clever skill. She enjoyed his company, more than she felt was altogether wise, particularly since she'd planned to spend more of her time alone.

And he looked damn good standing over a smoking grill.

They ate on his back veranda, with the well-fed Spock snoring in table-scrap bliss. And she found the down-to-basics meal exactly right. "God, it's so beautiful here. Peaceful."

"No urges for club crawls or a quick foray down Rodeo Drive?"

"I had my fill of both a long time ago. Seems like fun at the time, but it goes sour fast if it's not really your place. It wasn't mine. What about you? You lived in New York for a while, didn't you? No urges to take another bite out of the Big Apple?"

"It was exciting, and I like going back now and then, soaking up that energy. The thing was, I thought I was supposed to live there, given what I wanted to do. After a while, I realized I was doing more work when I came down to visit my parents for a few days, hang with friends, than I was in the same stretch of time up there. I finally figured out there were just too many people thinking up there, all hours of the day and night. And I thought better down here."

"That's funny," she replied.

"What is?"

"In an interview once, a reporter asked my grandmother why she bought this little farm in Virginia. She said she could hear her own thoughts here, and that they tended to get drowned out with everyone else's when she was in L.A."

"I know exactly what she meant. Have you read many of her interviews?"

"Read, reread, listened to, watched. I can't remember a time she didn't fascinate me. This brilliant light, this tragic icon, who I came from. I couldn't escape her, so I needed to know her. I resented her when I was a kid. Being compared to her, and always falling short."

"Comparisons are designed to make someone fall short."

"They really are. By the time I was twelve or thirteen, they actively pissed me off. So I started to study her, very purposefully, looking for the trick, the secret. What I found was a woman who was stupendously and naturally talented. Anyone compared to her would fall short. And realizing that, I didn't resent her anymore. It would be like resenting a diamond for sparkling."

"I grew up hearing about her, because she had the place here. Died here. My mother would play her records a lot. She went to a couple of parties at the farm," he added. "My mother."

"Did she?"

"Her claim to fame is kissing Janet Hardy's son, that would be your uncle. A little odd, isn't it, you and me sitting out here like this, and back years, my mother and your uncle made out in the shadows across the road. Might be odder still when I tell you my mama did some of the same with your daddy."

"Oh God." On a burst of laughter, Cilla picked up her wine, took a quick drink. "You're not making that up?"

"Pure truth. This would be, of course, before she settled on my father, and your father went out to

Hollywood after your mother. Complicated business, now that I think about it."

"I'll say."

"And mortifying for me, when she told me. Which was with some glee, when I ended up in your father's class in high school. The thought that my mother had locked lips with Mr. McGowan was damn near traumatizing at the time." His eyes lit with humor. "Now, I like the synchronicity that my mother's son has locked lips with Mr. McGowan's daughter."

Circles, Cilla thought. She'd thought of circles when she'd come to rebuild her grandmother's farm. Now here was another circle linked to that. "They must've been so young," she said softly. "Johnnie was only eighteen when he died. It must've been horrible for Janet, for the parents of the other two boys—one dead, one paralyzed. She never got over it. You can see in every clip, every photo of her taken after that night, she was never the same."

"My mother used to use that accident as a kind of bogeyman when I got old enough to drive. You'd see Jimmy Hennessy around town from time to time in his wheelchair, and she never missed the opportunity to remind me of what could happen if I was careless enough to drink or get high, then get behind the wheel or into a car with someone who'd been using."

He shook his head, polished off his steak. "I still can't go to a bar and guiltlessly enjoy a single beer if I've got to drive myself home. Mothers sure can screw things up for you."

"Does he still live here? The boy—well, not a boy now—the one who survived the wreck?"

"He died last year. Or the year before. I'm not sure."

"I didn't hear about it."

"He lived at home his whole life. His parents looked after him. Rough."

"Yes. His father blamed Janet. Blamed her for bringing her Hollywood immorality here, for letting her son run wild, for buying him the fast car."

"There were two other boys in that car. Nobody forced them into it," Ford pointed out. "Nobody poured beer forcibly down their throats or pumped pot into their systems. They were young and stupid, all three of them. And they paid a terrible price for it."

"And she paid them. According to my mother—and her bitterness over it tells me it's true—Janet paid each of the families of those boys a considerable sum of money. Undisclosed amount, even to my mother. And again, according to the gospel of Dilly, Janet only kept the farm as a kind of monument to Johnnie, and tied it up in trusts for decades after her own death for the same reason. But I don't believe that."

"What do you believe?"

"I believe Janet kept it because she was happy here. Because she could hear her own thoughts here, even when those thoughts were dark and dreadful." She sighed, sat back. "Give me another glass of wine, will you, Ford? That'll make three, which is my absolute personal high-end limit."

"What happens after three?"

"I haven't gone over three in years, but if history holds, I go from relaxed, perhaps mildly and pleasantly buzzed, to drunk enough to have yet one or maybe two more. Then I'd be very drunk, jump you, and wake up tomorrow with a hangover and only blurred memories of our encounter."

"In that case, you're cut off after this." He poured the wine. "When we encounter, your memory's going to be crystal."

"I haven't decided on that yet, you know."

"That's okay, I have." He propped his chin on his fist, stared at her. "I can't get myself out of your eyes, Cilla. They keep pulling me in."

"Janet Hardy's eyes."

"No. Cilla McGowan's eyes."

She smiled, sipped her last glass of wine. "I was

going to make up an excuse—or not even bother to make one up—about not coming tonight."

"Is that so?"

"That is so. Because you got bossy about my living arrangements."

"Defining 'bossy' as 'sensible.' Why did you come?"

"Buying the toilets put me in a really good mood. Seriously," she said when he choked out a laugh. "I've found my thing, Ford. After a long time looking."

"You found your thing in toilets."

It was her turn to laugh. "I found my thing in taking something broken down or neglected, or just a little tired, and making it shine again. Making it better. And doing that's made me better. So because I was in a good mood, I walked across the road. I'm really glad I did."

"So am I."

SHE DIDN'T SEE him or Spock when she let herself in his home gym the next morning. Cilla plugged in her iPod and got down to business. She gave herself a solid hour, and at some point during it the dog strolled out into the backyard and lifted his leg a number of times. But there was still no sign or sound from Ford when she let herself out again, with one wistful glance at his hot tub.

No time for jets and indulgence, she told herself. But as Spock raced over, so obviously thrilled to see her, she spent a good ten minutes rubbing him while he gurgled and grunted in what seemed to be some form of communication. The workout, the silly dog, just the day itself put her in a fine mood as she jogged back across the road. She showered off the workout sweat, downed coffee and a blueberry yogurt. By the time she strapped on her tool belt, her crews and subs began to arrive.

It took time, every morning, but Cilla was happy to spend it. Talking, evaluating, brainstorming away problems.

"I'm going to expand the bathroom, Buddy," she told him, and, as she expected, he let out a windy sigh.

"The one I'm using now, not the one you've roughed in."

"That's something anyway."

"I've already talked to Matt," she said. "Come on up, and I'll show you what we're going to do."

He hemmed and he hawed, but that was expected, too. In fact, she'd come to look forward to it. "Now that we're putting my office upstairs instead of in this bedroom, I'm going to use this space to make it a master suite. We'll be taking out this wall," she began.

He listened, he scratched, he shook his head. "Gonna cost you."

"Yes, I know. I'll draw it up in more detail later, but for now, here's the idea." She opened her notebook to the sketch she'd drawn with Matt. "We'll keep the old claw-foot tub, have it refurbished and set here. Floor pipes and drains. Double sinks here, and I'm thinking undermount."

"Guess you'll be putting a slab of granite or whatnot."

"No, zinc."

"Say, what?"

"Zinc countertop. And over here, I'm putting in a steam shower. Yes," she said before he could speak. "Hollywood ideas. Glass block here, to form the water closet. In the end, it's going to reflect and respect the architecture, pay homage to retro, and, Buddy, it will rock."

"You're the boss."

She grinned. "Damn straight."

The boss moved outside, to build her rail and pickets in the April sunshine.

When her father pulled in, Cilla had her sides run, and had worked up a fresh sweat.

"Doesn't that look nice," he commented.

"It's coming along."

He nodded toward the house, and the cacophony of construction noise. "Sounds like more's coming along inside."

"First-stage demo's done. I've changed some things, so we'll have more demo on the second floor later. But the inspector's coming tomorrow." She lifted her hand, crossed her fingers. "To approve the rough plumbing and electric. Then we'll boogie."

"It's the talk of the town."

"I imagine so." She gestured toward the road. "Traffic's increased. People slow down, even stop, to look. I had a call from the local paper for an interview. I don't want pictures yet. Most people can't see what it's going to be while it's at this stage, so I gave the reporter a quick hit over the phone."

"When's it going to run?"

"Sunday. Lifestyle. Janet Hardy still has the switch." Cilla pushed back her cap to swipe the back of her hand over her forehead. "You knew her, Dad. Would she approve?"

"I think she loved this place. I think she'd be pleased you love it, too. And that you're putting your mark on it. Cilla, are you building that railing yourself?"

"Yeah."

"I had no idea you could do that. I thought you had the ideas, then you hired people to work them out."

"Some of that, too. Most of that, I guess. But I like the work. Especially this kind. I'm going to go for my contractor's license."

"You . . . Well, how about that?"

"I'm going to start a business. This house? Talk of the town, and that's going to turn into revenue for me down the road. I think people might like to hire the woman who rebuilt Janet Hardy's little farm, especially if she's Janet's granddaughter. And after a while?" Her eyes narrowed and gleamed. "They'll hire me because they know I'm good."

"You really mean to stay."

So he hadn't believed it. Why should he? "I mean to stay. I like the way it smells here. I like the way I feel here. Are you in a hurry?"

"Nope."

"Do you want to walk around a little, play land-scape consultant?"

He smiled slowly. "I'd like that."

"Let me get my notebook."

Walking with him, listening to him as he gestured to an area, described the shrubs and groupings he suggested, Cilla learned more about him.

His thoughtful way of listening, then responding, the pauses between while he considered. His ease with himself, the time he took.

He paused at the edge of the pond, smiled. "I swam in here a few times. You're going to need to get these lily pads and cattails under control."

"It's on the list. Brian said maybe we'll do some yellow flags."

"That would be a nice choice. You could plant a willow over there. It'd make a pretty feature, weeping over the water."

She scribbled. "I thought a stone bench maybe, somewhere to sit." Remembering, she looked up at him. "So, is this where you kissed Ford Sawyer's mother?"

His mouth dropped open in surprise, and, to Cilla's delight, a flush rose up into his cheeks. He chuckled, and began to walk again. "Now how'd you hear about that?"

"I have my sources."

"I have mine. I hear you kissed Penny Sawyer's son out in the front yard."

"Buddy."

"Not directly, but he'd be the root of it."

"It's a little weird."

"A little bit," Gavin agreed.

"You haven't answered the question."

"I guess I'll confess I did kiss Penny Quint—which she was in those days—more than a few times, and some of those times here. We went steady for a number of months in high school. Before she broke my heart."

He smiled when he said it, and had Cilla smiling in return. "High school is hell."

"It sure can be. The heartbreaking took place here, too, as it happens. And back there, near the pond. Penny and I had a fight—God knows about what—and we broke up. I admit to having been torn between wooing her back and making a play for your mother."

"You dog."

"Most boys are dogs at eighteen. Then I saw Penny, near the pond, kissing Johnnie." He sighed, even now, remembering. "That was a blow. My girl—or I still half thought of her as my girl—and one of my friends. It broke the code."

"Friends don't move in on exes," Cilla said. "It's still the code."

"Johnnie and I had words about it. Then and there, and Penny gave me a piece of her mind. About that time, your mother came along. She's always been drawn to drama. I went off with her, soothed my heart and ego. That was the last time Johnnie and I spoke. The last words we spoke to each other were hard ones. I've always regretted that."

There was no smile now, and in its place, Cilla saw old grief. "He died two days later. And so did another of my friends, and Jimmy Hennessy was paralyzed. I was supposed to go with them that night."

"I didn't know that." Something squeezed inside her. "I've never heard that."

"I was supposed to be in that car, but Penny kissed Johnnie, Johnnie and I had hard words. And I didn't go."

"God." A shudder snaked down Cilla's spine. "I owe Ford's mother quite a bit."

"I went off to college the next fall, like I planned— then a couple of years in, I dropped out, went off to Hollywood. Got myself a contract. I think it was, at least in part, because I was another kind of reminder of her brother, her mother, that had your mother giving me another look. She was too young when the look turned serious. We both were. We got engaged secretly, broke up publicly. Back and forth, back and forth for years. Then we eloped.

"We had you hardly a year later." He draped his

arm around Cilla's shoulders. "We did our best. I know it wasn't very good, but we did our best."

"It's hard, knowing so much of what happened, what was done, was rooted in death at worst, on mistakes at best."

"You were never a mistake."

She didn't respond. How could she? She'd been called one often enough. "You were still in college when Janet died?"

"I'd finished my first year."

"Did you hear anything about a man, someone out here, she was involved with?"

"There was constant speculation, constant gossip about Janet and men. I don't recall anything out of the ordinary, or any talk of someone from here. Why?"

"I found letters, Dad. I found letters written to her from a lover. They're postmarked from here, or a lot of them are. She hid them. The last one, bitter, after he'd broken off the affair, was mailed only ten days before her death."

They'd walked back to the house, stood now at the edge of the back veranda. "I think she came back here to see him, to confront him. She was desperately unhappy, if even half of the accounts from the time are true. And I think she was in love with this man, this married man she'd had a passionate, tumultuous affair with for over a year before it cooled."

"You think he was local? What was his name?"

"He didn't sign them by name. She—" Cilla glanced over, noticed how close they stood to the open window. Taking her father's arm, she drew him away. "She told the man she was pregnant."

"Pregnant? Cilla, there was an autopsy."

"It might have been covered up. It might not have been true, but if it was, if it wasn't a lie to get him back, it could've been covered up. He threatened her. In the last letter, he told her she'd pay if she tried to expose their relationship."

"You don't want to believe she killed herself," Gavin began.

"Suicide or not, she's still dead. I want the truth. She deserves that, and so do I. People have talked murder and conspiracies for decades. Maybe they're right."

"She was an addict, sweetheart. An addict who couldn't stop grieving for her child. An unhappy woman who shone in front of the cameras, on the stage, but who never really found her happiness away from them. And when Johnnie died, she lost herself in grief, and smothered the grief with pills and alcohol."

"She took a lover. And she came back here. John-nie kissed your girl, and as a result, you lived. Small moments change lives. And take them. I want to find out what moment, what actual event, took hers. Even if it was by her own hand."

SEVEN

LAS VEGAS
1954

Janet held the sleeveless, full-skirted dress up, and did a twirl in front of the wall of mirrors. "What do you think?" she asked Cilla. "The pink's more elegant, but I really want to wear white. Every girl should be able to wear white on her wedding day."

"You'll look beautiful. You'll look beautiful and young, and so incredibly happy."

"I am. I'm all of those things. I'm nineteen. I'm a major movie star. My record is number one in the country. I'm in love." She spiraled again, and again, spun-gold hair flying in gleaming waves.

Even in dreams, her sheer joy danced in the air, fluttered over Cilla's skin.

"I'm madly in love with the most wonderful, the most handsome man in the world. I'm rich, I'm beautiful, and the world—right this moment—the world is mine."

"It stays yours for a long time," Cilla told her. But not long enough. It's never long enough.

"I should wear my hair up."

Janet tossed the dress onto the bed where the pink brocade suit already lay discarded. "I look more mature with my hair up. The studio never wants me to wear it up. They don't want me to be a woman yet, a real woman. Always the girl next door, always the virgin."

Laughing, she began to fashion her sleek fall of hair into a French twist. "I haven't been a virgin since I was fifteen." Janet met Cilla's eyes in the mirror. And with the joy layered amusement, and a thin coat of disdain. "Do you think the public cares if I have sex?"

"Some do. Some will. But it's your life."

"Goddamn right. And my career. I want adult roles, and I'm going to get them. Frankie's going to help me. Once we're married, he'll manage my career. He'll handle things."

"Yes," Cilla murmured, "he will."

"Oh, I know what you're thinking." Standing in her white silk slip, Janet continued to place pins in her hair. "Within the year I'll be filing for divorce. Then a brief reconciliation gets me knocked up with my second child. I'm pregnant now, but I don't know it. Johnnie's already started inside me. Only a week or so, but he's begun. Everything changes today."

"You eloped to Vegas, married Frankie Bennett, who was nearly ten years older than you."

"Vegas was my idea." Janet picked up a can of hair spray from the dressing table, began to spray suffocating clouds of it. "I wanted to stuff it down their throats, I guess. Janet Hardy, and all the parts she plays, wouldn't even know Vegas exists. But here I am, in the penthouse of the Flamingo, dressing for my wedding. And no one knows but me and Frankie."

Cilla walked to the window, looked out.

A pool sparkled below, lush gardens flowing back from its skirting. Beyond, the buildings were small and on the tacky side. Colors faded, shapes blurred, like the old photographs Cilla supposed she'd pieced together to form the landscape for the dream.

"It's nothing like it will be, really. Vegas, I mean."

"What is?"

"You'll marry Bennett, and the studio will spin and spin to counteract the damage. But there won't be any, not really. You look so spectacular together, and that's almost enough. The illusion of two gorgeous people in love. And you'll take on your first true adult role with Sarah Constantine in *Heartsong*. You'll be nominated for an Oscar."

"After Johnnie. I have Johnnie before *Heartsong*. Even Mrs. Eisenhower will send a baby gift. I cut back on the pills." She tapped the bottle on her dressing table before turning to lift the dress. "I'm still able to do that, to cut down on the pills, the booze. It's easier when I'm happy, the way I am now."

"If you knew what would happen? If you knew Frankie Bennett will cheat on you with women, will gamble away so much of your money, squander more. If you knew he'd break your heart and that you'd attempt suicide for the first time in just over a year, would you go through with it?"

Janet stepped into the dress. "If I didn't, where would you be?" She turned her back. "Zip me up, will you?"

"You said, later, you'll say that your mother offered you like a virgin to the studio, and the studio tore the innocence out of you, piece by piece. And that Frankie Bennett took those pieces and shredded them like confetti."

"The studio made me a star." She fastened pearls at her ears. "I didn't walk away. I craved what they gave me, and gave them my innocence. I wanted Frankie, and gave what was left to him."

She held up a double strand of pearls, and understanding, Cilla took them to hook around Janet's neck.

"I'll do amazing work in the next ten years. My very best work. And I'll do some damn good work in the ten after that. Well, nearly ten," she said with a laugh. "But who's counting? Maybe I needed to be in turmoil to reach my potential. Who knows? Who cares?"

"I do."

With a soft smile, Janet turned to kiss Cilla's cheek. "I looked for love all of my life, and gave it too often, and too intensely. Maybe if I hadn't looked so hard, someone would have given it back to me. The red belt!" She danced away to snatch a thick scarlet belt from the clothes tossed on the bed. "It's just the right touch, and red's Frankie's favorite color. He loves me in red."

She buckled it on, like a belt of blood, and stepped into matching shoes. "How do I look?"

"Perfect."

"I wish you could come, but it's only going to be me and Frankie, and the funny old justice of the peace and the woman who plays the spinet. Frankie will leak it to the press without telling me, and that's how the photo of the two of us coming out of the tacky little chapel gets into *Photoplay*. Then the shit hits the fan." She laughed. "What a ride."

And laughed, and laughed, so that Cilla heard the echoes of the laughter as she woke.

BECAUSE SHE WANTED to let her thoughts simmer away from the noise and distractions, Cilla spent the majority of her time the next two days sorting out the dozens of boxes and trunks she'd hauled into the barn.

Cilla had determined on her first pass that her mother had already culled and scavenged whatever she deemed worthwhile. But Dilly had missed a few treasures. She often did, to Cilla's mind, being in such a rush to grab the shiniest object, she missed the little diamonds in the rough.

Like the old photo tucked in a book. A very pregnant Janet plopped on a chaise by the pond, mugging for the camera with a glossily handsome Rock Hudson. Or the script for *With Violets*—Janet's second Oscar nomination—buried in a trunk full of old blankets. She found a little music box fashioned like a grand piano that played "Für Elise." Inside, a little handwritten note read: *From Johnnie, Mother's Day, 1961,* in Janet's looping scrawl.

By the end of a rainy afternoon, she had a pile designated for the Dumpster, and a small stack of boxes to keep.

When she hauled out a load in a wheelbarrow, she found the rain had turned to fragile sunlight and her front yard full of people. Ford and her landscaper stood on the wet grass laughing at each other, along with a man with steel-gray hair who wore a light windbreaker. Crossing to them from a little red pickup was the owner of the roofing company she'd hired. A boy of about ten and a big white dog trailed after him.

After some posturing, and looking out from between Ford's legs, Spock tiptoed—if dogs could tiptoe—up to the white dog, sniffed, then plopped down and exposed his belly in submission.

"Afternoon." Cleaver of Cleaver Roofing and Gutters gave her a nod of greeting. "Had a job to check on down the road, and thought I'd stop on the way home to let you know we'll be starting tomorrow if the weather's clear."

"That's great."

"These are my grandsons, Jake and Lester." He winked at Cilla. "They don't bite."

"Good to know."

"Grandpa." The boy rolled his eyes. "Lester's my dog."

As Cilla crouched to greet the dog, Spock bumped through them to claim Cilla's hand. It was a clear: Uh-uh, you owe me first.

Cleaver hailed the trio of men walking toward them. "Tommy, you son of a . . ." Cleaver slid his gaze toward his grandson, smirked. "Gun. Don't think you can fast-talk this lady into selling. I've got the roof."

"How you doing, Hank? I'm not buying. Just checking up on my boy here."

"Cilla, this is my dad." Brian, the landscaper, gripped his father's shoulder. "Tom Morrow."

"He's a slick one, Miz McGowan," Hank warned her with another wink. "You watch out for him. Before you know it, he'll talk you into selling this place, then put up a dozen houses."

"This acreage? No more than six." Tom offered a smile and his hand. "Welcome to Virginia."

"Thanks. You're a builder?"

"I develop land, residential and commercial. You've taken on quite a project here. I've heard you hired some good people to work on it. Present company excepted," he said with a grin to Hank.

"Before these two get going," Brian interrupted, "I've got some sketches on the landscaping I wanted to drop off for you to look at. Do you want a hand with that haul?"

Cilla shook her head. "I've got it. I'm just going through the stuff I brought down from the attic, stowed in the barn. Rainy-day work, I guess."

Brian lifted a dented toaster out of the wheelbarrow. "People keep the damnedest things."

"I can attest."

"We cleaned out the attic when my mother passed," Hank put in. "Found a whole box of nothing but broken dishes, and another dozen or more full of papers. Receipts from groceries back thirty years, and God knows. But you want to be careful sorting through, Miz McGowan. Mixed all in there we found letters my daddy wrote her when he was in Korea. She had every one of our report cards—there's six of us kids—right through high school. She never threw a blessed thing out, but there're important things up there."

"I'm going to take my time with it. I'm finding it an interesting mix of both sides of my family so far."

"That's right, this used to be the McGowan farm." Tom scanned the area. "I remember when your grandmother bought it from old man McGowan, back around 1960. My father had his eye on this land, hoping to develop it. He brooded for a month after Janet Hardy bought it—then he decided she wouldn't keep it above six months, and he'd snap it up cheap from her. She proved him wrong.

"It's a pretty spot," Tom added, then gave his son a poke. "See that you make it prettier. I'd better get going. Good luck, Miss McGowan. If you need any recommendations on subs, just give me a call."

"I appreciate that."

"I'd better get on, too." Hank pulled at the brim of his cap. "Get my grandsons home for supper."

"Grandpa."

"They'll talk another twenty minutes," Brian commented when his father and Hank strolled toward the red pickup. "But I really do have to get going." He handed Cilla a large manila envelope. "Let me know what you think, what kind of changes you might want."

"I will, thanks."

After Brian tossed the toaster into the Dumpster, he shot a finger at Ford. "Later, Rembrandt."

On a short laugh, Ford waved. "Around and about, Picasso."

"Rembrandt?"

"Short story. Wait. Jesus." After she'd handed him the envelope and started to push the wheelbarrow up the Dumpster's ramp, Ford nudged her aside.

"Flex your muscles all you want, but not while I'm standing here holding paper and guys are around."

He shoved the envelope back at her, then rolled the wheelbarrow up to dump. "Brian and I could both draw, and somehow or other got into a sex-parts-and-positions drawing contest. We got busted passing sketches back and forth in study hall. Earned us both a three-day pass."

"Pass to what?"

He looked down as he dumped. "Suspension. I guess you didn't go to regular school."

"Tutors. How old were you?"

"About fourteen. I got my ears burned all the way home when my mother picked me up, and got grounded for two weeks. Two weeks, and it was my first and last black mark in school. Talk about harsh. Hmm."

"I bet they still have them," she said when he rolled the barrow down again. "And future generations will find them in the attic."

"You think? Well, they did show considerable promise and a very healthy imagination. Want to go for a ride?"

"A ride?"

"We can go get some dinner somewhere, catch a movie."

"What's playing?"

"Couldn't say. I'm thinking of the movie as a vehicle for popcorn and necking."

"Sounds good," she decided. "You can put the wheelbarrow back in the barn while I wash up."

WITH HER NEW wiring approved, Cilla watched Dobby and his grandson replaster the living room walls. Art came in many forms, she decided, and she'd found herself a pair of artists. It wouldn't be quick, but boy, it would be right.

"You do fancy work, too?" she asked Dobby. "Medallions, trim?"

"Here and there. Not much call for it these days. You can buy premade cheaper, so most people do."

"I'm not most people. Fancy work wouldn't suit this area." Hands on hips, she turned a circle in the drop-clothed, chewed-up living space. "But simple and interesting might. And could work in the master bedroom, the dining room. Nothing ornate," she said, thinking out loud. "No winged cherubs or hanging grapes. Maybe a design. Something Celtic . . . that would address the McGowan and the Moloney branches."

"Moloney?"

"What? Sorry." Distracted, she glanced back at

Dobby. "Moloney would have been my grandmother's surname—except *her* mother changed it to Hamilton just after Janet was born, then the studio changed it to Hardy. Gertrude Moloney to Trudy Hamilton to Janet Hardy. They called her Trudy as a girl," she added and thought of the letters.

"Is that so?" Dobby shook his head, dipped his trowel. "Pretty, old-fashioned name Trudy."

"And not shiny enough for Hollywood, at least when she came up in it. She said in an interview once that no one ever called her Trudy again, once they'd settled on Janet. Not even her family. But sometimes she'd look at herself in the mirror and say hello to Trudy, just to remind herself. Anyway, if I came up with some designs, we could talk about working them in upstairs."

"We sure could do that."

"I'll do some research. Maybe we could . . . Sorry," she said when the phone in her pocket rang. She pulled it out, stifled a sigh when she saw her mother's number on the display. "Sorry," she repeated, then stepped outside to take the call.

"Hello, Mom."

"Did you think I wouldn't hear about it? Did you think I wouldn't see?"

Cilla leaned against the veranda column, stared

across the road at Ford's pretty house. "I'm good, thanks. How are you?"

"You have no right to criticize me, to judge me. To *blame* me."

"In what context?"

"Save your sarcasm, Cilla. You know exactly what I'm talking about."

"I really don't." What was Ford doing? Cilla wondered. Was he writing? Drawing? Was he turning her into a warrior goddess? Someone who would face down evil instead of calculating how to stretch the budget to accommodate handcrafted plaster medallions, or handle a motherly snit long-distance.

"The article in the paper. About you, about the farm. About me. AP picked it up."

"Did they? And that bothers you? It's publicity."

" 'McGowan's goal is to restore and respect her neglected heritage. Speaking over the busy sounds of banging hammers and buzzing saws, she states: "My grandmother always spoke of the Little Farm with affection, and related that she was drawn to it from the first moment. The fact that she bought the house and land from my paternal great-grandfather adds another strong connection for me." ' "

"I know what I said, Mom."

" 'My purpose, you could even say my mission, is

to pay tribute to my heritage, my roots here, by not only restoring the house and the land, but making them shine. And in such a way that respects their integrity, and the community.' "

"Sounds a little pompous," Cilla commented. "But it's accurate."

"It goes on and on, a showcase during Janet Hardy's visits for the luminaries of her day. A pastoral setting for her children, now peeling paint, rotted wood, overgrown gardens through a generation of neglect and disinterest as Janet Hardy's daughter, Bedelia Hardy, attempted to fill her mother's sparkling footsteps. How could you let them print that?"

"You know as well as I do you can't control the press."

"I don't want you giving any more interviews."

"And you should know you can't control what I do, or don't. Not anymore. Spin it, Mom. You know how. Grief kept you away, and so on. Whatever happy times you spent here were overshadowed, even smothered, by your mother's death here. It'll get you some sympathy and more press."

The long pause told Cilla her mother was considering the angles. "How could I think of that place as anything but a tomb?"

"There you go."

"It's easier for you, it's different for you. You never knew her. She's just an image for you, a movie clip, a photograph. She was flesh and blood for me. She was my mother."

"Okay."

"It would be better, for everyone, if you vetted interviews with me or Mario. And I'd think any reporter who works for a legitimate paper would have contacted my people for a comment or quote. Be sure they do, next time."

"You're up early," Cilla said by way of evading.

"I have rehearsals, costume fittings. I'm exhausted before I begin."

"You're a trouper. I wanted to ask you something. The last year or so, before Janet died, do you know who she was involved with?"

"Romantically? She could barely get out of bed by herself half the time in the first weeks after Johnnie. Or she'd bounce off the walls and demand people and parties. She'd cling to me one minute, and push me away the next. It scarred me, Cilla. I lost my brother and my mother so close together. And really, I lost them both the night Johnnie died."

Because she believed that, if nothing else, that was deeply and painfully true, Cilla's tone softened. "I know. I can't imagine how terrible it was."

"No one can. I was alone. Barely sixteen, and I

had no one. She left me, Cilla. She chose to leave me. In that house you're so determined to turn into a shrine."

"That's not what I'm doing. Who was she involved with, Mom? A secret affair, a married man. An affair that went south."

"She had affairs. Why wouldn't she? She was beautiful and vital, and she needed love."

"A specific affair, during this specific period."

"I don't know." Dilly's voice clipped on the words now. "I try not to think about that time. It was hell for me. Why do you care? Why dredge that kind of thing up again? I *hate* the theories and the speculations."

Tread carefully, Cilla reminded herself. "I'm just curious. You hear talk, and she did spend a lot of time here in that last year, year and a half. She wasn't really involved with anyone back in L.A., that I've heard about. It wasn't like her to be without a man, a lover, for very long."

"Men couldn't resist her. Why should she resist them? Then they'd let her down. They always do. They make promises they don't keep. They cheat, they steal, and God knows they can't stand for the woman to be more successful."

"So how are things with you and Num—with Mario?"

"He's the exception to the rule. I've finally found the kind of man I need. Mama never did. She never found a man worthy of her."

"And never stopped looking," Cilla prompted. "She would have wanted the comfort, the love and support, especially after Johnnie died. Maybe she looked here, in Virginia."

"I don't know. She never took me with her back to the farm after Johnnie. She said she had to be alone. I didn't want to go back anyway. It was too painful. That's why I haven't been back in all these years. It's still a fresh wound in my heart."

And we come full circle, Cilla thought. "Like I said, I'm just curious. So if something or someone occurs to you, let me know. I'd better let you get to rehearsal."

"Oh, let them wait! Mario had the best idea. It's phenomenal, and such a good opportunity for you. We'll work a duet for you and me into the show, in the second act. A medley of Mama's songs with clips and stills from her movies on screen behind us. We'll finish with 'I'll Get By,' making it a trio, putting her onstage with us, the way they did with Elvis and Céline Dion. He's talking to HBO, Cilla, about broadcasting."

"Mom—"

"We'll need you back here next week for rehearsals, and costume design, choreography. We're still working out the composition, but the number would run about four minutes. Four spectacular minutes, Cilla. We want to give you a real chance for a comeback."

Cilla closed her eyes, debated sawing off her tongue, letting it fly—and settled on somewhere in the middle. "I appreciate that, I really do. But I don't want to come back, geographically or professionally. I don't want to perform. I want to build."

"You'd be building." Enthusiasm bubbled across the continent. "Your career, and helping me. The three Hardy women, Cilla. It's landmark."

My name's McGowan, Cilla thought. "I think you'd be better spotlighted alone. And the duet with Janet? That could be lovely, heart-wrenching."

"It's four minutes, Cilla. You can spare me four fucking minutes a night for a few weeks. And it will turn your life around. Mario says—"

"I've just finished turning my life around, and I like where it's standing. I've got to go. I've got work."

"Don't you—"

Cilla closed the phone, deliberately shoved it back into her pocket. She heard the throat clear behind her and, turning, saw Matt in the doorway. "They just got the grouting done on the tile in the bathroom upstairs. Thought you'd want to take a look."

"Yeah. We'll be installing the fixtures tomorrow then."

"That'd be right."

"Let me get my sledgehammer. We can start taking down that wall up there. I'm in the mood for demo."

THERE WAS LITTLE, Cilla decided, more satisfying than beating the hell out of something. It relieved frustration, brought a quick and wild rise of glee, and fulfilled all manner of dark fantasies. The fact was, it was—on several levels—every bit as therapeutic as good sex.

And since she wasn't having any sex—good or otherwise—at the moment, knocking down walls did the job. She could be having sex, she thought as she strode out of the house trailing plaster dust. Ford and his magic mouth had made that fairly clear.

But she was on a kind of moratorium there—as part of the turn-the-life-around program, she supposed. New world, new life, new style. And in there, she'd found the real Cilla McGowan.

She liked her.

She had the house to rehab, her contractor's license to study for, a business to establish. And a family mystery to unravel. Scheduling in sex with her hot neighbor wouldn't be the smartest move.

Of course, he just had to be standing out on his veranda when she walked out, thinking of sex. And the low-down tingle had her asking herself if it was really, completely, absolutely necessary to abstain. They were both adults, unattached, interested, so why couldn't she walk on over there and suggest they spend the evening together? Doing something more *energetic* than sharing a beer?

Just straight out. No dance, no pretenses, no illusions. Isn't that what the real Cilla wanted? She angled her head as she considered. And plaster dust rained down from the bill of her cap.

Maybe she should shower first.

"You're weak and pitiful," Cilla muttered and, amused at herself, started to circle around to the back of the house and the landscaping crew.

She heard the deep-throated roar of a prime engine, glanced back. The sleek black bullet of a Harley shot down the road and seemed to ricochet through her open gates. Even as it spit gravel, she ran toward it, laughing.

Its occupant jumped off the bike, landed on scarred combat boots and caught Cilla on the fly.

"Hello, doll." He swung her in one quick circle, then kissed her enthusiastically.

EIGHT

Who the hell was that? And why in the hell was she kissing him?

Ford stood holding his after-coffee-before-beer Coke and stared at the man Cilla was currently attached to—like, like sumac on an oak.

What was with the ponytail anyway? And the army boots? And why were the hands—the guy wore a bunch of rings, for Christ's sake—rubbing Cilla's ass?

"Turn around, buddy. Turn around so I can get a better look at your Wayfarer-wearing face."

At Ford's tone, Spock gave a low, supportive growl.

"Jesus, his whole arm's tattooed right up to the sleeve of his black T-shirt. See that? You see that?" he demanded, and Spock muttered darkly.

And that glint? Oh yeah, that was an earring.

"Move the hands, pal. You're going to want to

move those hands, otherwise . . ." Ford looked down at his own, surprised to see he'd crushed the can of Coke, and the contents were foaming over his own fingers.

Interesting, he thought. Jealousy? He wasn't the jealous type. Was he? Okay, maybe he'd had a couple of bouts with it in high school, and that one time in college. But that was just part of growing up. He sure as hell wouldn't get worked up about some over-tattooed earring guy kissing a woman he'd known for a month.

Okay, maybe she'd gotten under his skin. And Spock's, he conceded as his dog stood at full alert, snarling and grumbling. But a good part of that could be attributed to the work, and her starring role in it. If he felt territorial, it was just a by-product of the work, nothing more or less.

Maybe a little more, but a man didn't like to stand around and watch a woman slap her lips to some strange guy's when they'd been slapped to *his* a couple of days before. The least she could do was stop flaunting it in his face and take it inside where . . .

"Shit. Shit. They're going inside."

"I CAN'T BELIEVE YOU'RE HERE."
"I told you I'd swing down if I had time."

"I didn't think you'd have time, or remember to swing down."

Steve tipped down his Wayfarers and looked at Cilla over them with his deep and dreamy brown eyes. "When have I ever forgotten you?"

"Do you want a list?"

He laughed, gave her a hip bump as they crossed the veranda. "When it counted. Whoa." He stopped just inside the doorway, scanned the living area, its pockets of drying plaster, the patchwork of scarred floors and splattered drop cloths. "Excellent."

"It is, isn't it? And it will be."

"Nice space. Floors'll clean up. Walnut?"

"They are."

"Sweet." He wandered through, passing casual how's-it-goings to the workers still on-site cleaning up for the day.

He walked lightly, and looked slight. Looks, Cilla knew, were deceiving. Under the T-shirt and jeans, he was ripped. Steve Chensky honed his body with the devotion of an evangelist.

Cilla thought if he'd worked half as hard on his music, he'd have made it from struggling artist to serious rock star. Or so she'd told him, countless times. Then again, if he'd listened to her, their lives might have turned out very differently.

He stopped in the kitchen, took his measure of the place with his sunglasses hooked in his T-shirt. "What's the plan here?"

"Take a look." She flipped through the notebook sitting on the one remaining counter, found her best sketch of the concept.

"Nice, Cill. This is nice. Good flow, good work space. Stainless steel?"

"No. I'm having the fifties appliances retrofitted. Jesus, Steve, they rock. I'm looking at faucets. I'm thinking of going copper there. Kind of old-timey."

"Cost ya."

"Yeah, but it's a good investment."

"Granite countertops?"

"I toyed around with doing polished concrete, but for this? You've got to go with granite. I haven't picked it out yet, but the cabinets are in the works. Glass fronts, see, copper leading. I nearly went white there, but I want the warmth, so they're cherry."

"Gonna have something." He gave her an elbow bump this time. "You always had an eye."

"You opened the door so I could use it."

"I opened it. You knocked it down. I drove by the Brentwood house before I headed to New York. Old time's sake. It still looks fine. So, gotta beer?"

She opened the mini fridge, pulled out a beer for each of them. "When do you have to head back to L.A.?"

"I got a couple of weeks. I'll trade labor for digs."

"Seriously? You're hired."

"Like old times," he said, and tapped his beer to hers. "Show me the rest."

Ford bided his time. He waited a full hour after the crews headed out for the day. No harm in wandering over, he told himself. Paying a friendly visit. He scowled at the Harley, and after Spock peed copiously on its front tire, crouched down to exchange a quick high five with his loyal best friend.

It wasn't as if he'd never driven a motorcycle. He'd taken a few spins in his day. Okay, one spin. He just didn't like bugs in his teeth.

But he *could* drive one if he wanted to.

He jammed his hands in his pockets and resisted giving the Harley a testing kick. He heard the music—ass-kicking rock this time—and instead of going to the front, followed the sound around back.

They sprawled on the steps of the veranda with a couple of bottles of beer and a bag of Doritos. His flavor of Doritos, Ford noted. With her head tipped back against the post, Cilla laughed so the sound of it poured right over the music. And straight into Ford's gut.

Tattoo Guy grinned at her, in a way that spoke of love, intimacy and history.

"You never change. What if you'd . . . Hey, Ford."

"Hey."

Spock stiff-walked over to Tattoo Guy. "Steve, this is Ford, my neighbor across the road. And that would be Spock. Steve detoured down from New York on his way back to L.A."

"How you doing? Hey, guy, hey, pal." He ruffled Spock's big head with his ringed hand. Ford's lips curled in disgust when his dog—his loyal best friend—dropped his head lovingly on Steve's knee.

"Want a beer?" Steve offered, giving Spock a full-body rub.

"Sure. Are you driving the Harley cross-country?"

"The only way to travel." Steve opened a beer, passed it to Ford. "My girl out there, she's my one true love. Except for Cill here."

Cilla snorted. "I notice you still put the bike first."

"She'll never leave me, like you did." Steve clamped a hand on Cilla's knee. "We used to be married."

"You and the bike?"

The cool remark had Steve tossing back his head

and laughing. "We're still married. Cill and I only were."

"Yeah, for about five minutes."

"Come on. It was at least fifteen. Pull up a step," Steve invited.

The polite thing to do, the sensible thing to do would be to back off, back away. But Ford was damned if he'd be polite or sensible. He sat. And the brief sour look he sent Spock had the dog hanging his head. "So you live in L.A."

"That's my town."

"Steve got me into flipping. Houses," Cilla added. "He needed some slave labor on a flip one day, drafted me. I liked it. So he let me go into the next one with him."

"When you were married."

"God no, years after that."

"You were writing a script when we were married."

"No, I was doing voice-overs and recording. I started the script after."

"Right, right. I worked on a session with Cilla, picking up some change and contacts while I was trying to get my band off the ground."

"You're a musician." It just figured.

"Right now I'm a licensed contractor who plays guitar on the side, and does the HGTV thing."

"*Rock the House,*" Cilla supplied. "Home-improvement type show that takes the viewer through stages of a rehab, remodel, a flip. Named after Steve's construction company."

TV guy, Ford thought. *That* just figured.

"Construction was my day job, back in rock-star-hopeful days," Steve continued. "And I talked Cill into bankrolling my first flip when I saw how the real estate market was heading and when the band flushed away. Hit that mother in the sweet spot. Is that your Victorian across the street?"

"Yeah."

"Nice. So do you know where we can get a pizza around here?"

Pizza was a key word for Spock, who lifted his shamed head and did his happy dance. "Eat in or delivery?"

"Delivery, man. I'm buying."

"I've got the pizzeria's number," Cilla told him. "Do you want the usual?"

"Stick with a winner."

"Ford?"

"Whatever you want's fine."

"I'll call it in."

When Cilla went in, Steve tipped back his beer. "Did you rehab the place yourself?"

"No, I bought it that way."

"So what's your line? What do you do across the street?"

"I write graphic novels."

"No shit." Steve bumped Ford in the arm with his beer. "Like *The Dark Knight* and *From Hell?*"

"More Dark Knight than Campbell. You into graphic novels?"

"Ate comic books for breakfast, lunch and dinner when I was a kid. But I didn't discover the graphics until a few years ago. Maybe I've read some of yours. What . . . damn, are you Ford Sawyer?" The brown eyes went child-like wide, and full of thrill. "Are you the fucking Seeker?"

So maybe the guy wasn't a complete asshole, Ford decided. "Yeah, that's right."

"This is unreal. It's like *surreal*. Check this out." Standing, Steve yanked off his T-shirt, turned his back. There, among the other art decorating Steve's back, was a tattoo of the Seeker striding over the left shoulder blade.

"Well . . . wow." Ford's usually active mind switched off.

"Your dude is completely awesome. I mean, he totally rocks. He suffers, and I *feel* that." Steve punched a fist into his chest. "But he keeps going. Picks it up and goes, does what he has to do. And the bastard can walk through freaking walls! How do you come up with that shit?"

"Jesus, Steve, are you stripping again?" Cilla demanded as she came back out.

"You've got Ford Freaking Sawyer living across the street. Man, he's the Seeker."

Cilla studied the tattoo Steve tapped as he looked over his shoulder. "When are you going to stop that?"

"When my whole body tells a story. Still got you on my ass, doll."

"Do not pull down your pants," she said, knowing him. "Pizza will be here, thirty minutes or less."

"I'm going to grab a shower." Steve punched Ford's shoulder, gave the delighted Spock a quick scratch. "This is way, over-the-top cool."

As the screen door slammed behind Steve, Ford studied his beer. "That was just weird."

"That was just Steve."

"To whom you were married for five minutes."

"Technically, five months." She sat again, stretched out long legs. "You're looking for the story."

"I'd be a fool not to."

"There isn't that much of one. We met, we clicked. He wanted to be a rock star, and I was, at seventeen, an actor already trying for a comeback. Except, even then, I didn't really want one. And Steve was exactly the opposite image of what everyone expected from me. So he was perfect."

"Good girl meets bad boy."

"You could say. Still, I wasn't so good, and he wasn't so bad. We loved each other, made each other laugh and had really good sex. What else could you ask for? So the minute I turned eighteen, we ran off and got married. It took us about that five minutes to wonder, what the hell did we do this for?"

She tipped back her head and laughed. "We didn't want to be married, to each other or anyone else. We wanted to be friends, to hang out, and maybe have good sex now and then. So we fixed it, way before there was any ugliness or damage, and we still love each other. He's the best friend I ever had. And, tattoos aside, the most stable and solid."

"He didn't let you down."

Cilla looked over, nodded. "Not once. Not ever. I couldn't do what I'm doing here if it wasn't for Steve. He taught me. He's a fifth-generation contractor. Part of the rock star bit was a rebellion against that, you could say. Man, I'm banging a guitar, not a hammer. But he eventually figured out he was better, and let me say a hell of a lot better, with the hammer. I lent him some money for his first flip, this sad little dump in South L.A. He made it sweet, and paid me back, bought another. He asked me if I wanted in, and, well, one thing led to another. Now he owns his own company and has the TV gig. He still turns sad little dumps, and he turns million-dollar properties. He's launching a branch in New York, and there's talk about a spin-off for the show for the East Coast. He was up there, doing the business, so he swung by before he heads back to L.A."

"And he has you tattooed on his ass."

"For old time's sake. Got any?"

"Tattoos?" Oddly, he felt foolish. "No. You?"

She smiled, sipped her beer. "A lot happens in five minutes of marriage."

Ford ended up eating pizza, and wondering what sort of tattoo Cilla had chosen, and where she'd had it inked.

Because the idea wouldn't leave him alone, he decided Brid should probably have one. Researching symbols gave him something to do once he returned home other than obsess as to whether or not Cilla and Steve were talking rehab plans or having good sex.

By two A.M. both his eyes and his energy gave out. Still, curiosity had him wandering to one of his front windows to take a last look at the house across the road. A slow smile curved his lips when he spotted the beam of a flashlight cutting through the dark toward the barn.

If Steve was bunking in the barn, good sex wasn't on the night's agenda.

"Let's keep it that way," Ford muttered, stripped off his clothes and fell facedown on the bed.

"YOU HEAR THAT?" Steve poked Cilla awake, an easy job as they were sharing her sleeping bag.

"What? No. Shut up." Rolling over, Cilla vowed Steve would find other sleeping arrangements the next night.

"I heard something. Like a moan, like the way a door sounds when it opens in an abandoned house in a creepy movie. We ought to go check it out."

"Do you remember what I said when you proposed we have sex?"

"That was a no."

"Same answer for this. Go to sleep."

"I don't know how you can sleep with all this quiet." He rolled, rolled again until she snarled at him. "You need a white-noise machine."

"I need to get you your own sleeping bag."

"Harsh." He kissed the top of her head. "You'll be sorry when some wild-eyed mountain dude runs in here with a meat cleaver."

"When that happens, I promise to apologize. Now shut up or go away. Crew's coming at seven."

THE ELABORATE BRASS headboard banged rhythmically against the red wall, the sound punctuated by her cries of pleasure. A shaft of moonlight illuminated those blue crystal eyes, glazed now as he plunged into her. She called out his name, nearly sang it while her body surged under his.

Ford. Ford.

Yo, Ford.

He woke with a spectacular morning hard-on, the sun beaming into his eyes and a vague sense of embarrassment that it was Steve calling his name. But at least the realization was already doing the job of deflating the hard-on.

Ford stuck his head out the window, yelled, "Hold on." He dragged on the jeans he'd stripped off the night before, then stumbled his way downstairs.

"Got doughnuts," Steve said when Ford pulled open the door.

"Huh?"

"Hey, man, were you still in the sack?"

Ford stared at Steve's affable smile, at the box of Krispy Kremes. "Coffee."

"I hear that." When Ford turned and groped his

way to the kitchen, Steve followed. "Great house, man. Seriously. Use of space, choice of materials. Figured you were up since Cilla'd been over to use your gym. Thought I'd try trading doughnuts for some gym time."

"Okay." Ford set a mug in place, punched on the coffeemaker, then opened the box Steve set on the counter. The smell hit him like a lightning bolt.

"Caffeine and sugar." Steve grinned as Ford grabbed a jelly-filled. "Best way to start the day, after nooky anyway."

Ford grunted, got down a second mug.

"Things are hopping at Cill's this morning, so I cut out for the doughnuts. Guys in construction dig on the doughnuts. Hey, man, look at your dog."

Ford glanced toward the window, saw Spock running, leaping, nosing down to stalk. "Yeah, it's cats."

"What is?"

"He's hunting cats. Magic cats only he can see."

"Son of a bitch, that's just what he's doing." Steve grinned out the window, a ringed thumb hooked in his belt loop. "So it's cool if I catch a workout with Cill in the A.M., or hit it late in the day? Not cramping your style?"

"It's fine." The sugar rush got Ford's eyes open, and the first hit of coffee did the rest. "I figured you'd sleep in later today. Long day for you yesterday, and you probably didn't get the best night sleeping in the barn."

"I like long days." Steve took the coffee Ford gave him, then dumped in the milk Ford sat on the counter. "What barn? Cill's barn? Cill wouldn't make me bunk in the barn. I got a corner of her sleeping bag."

"Oh." Damn. "I was working late, saw you head out there. I just figured—"

"I didn't go out there. Man, it's *dark* out there. In-the-sticks dark. I'm a city boy." He cocked his head. "You saw somebody out there?"

"I saw a flashlight, the beam. I think. It was late, maybe I—"

"No freaking way!" He slammed a hand to Ford's arm hard enough to make Ford stumble back. "I told her I heard something, but she's all shut up and go to sleep. What time was this?"

"I don't know. Ah . . . little after two."

"That's *it*. Going for the barn? We gotta go check this out."

"Crap." Ford downed more coffee. "I guess we do. I need to get a shirt, shoes."

"Can I come up? I'm digging on the house."

"Whatever." It was annoying to feel himself tugged into friendship with the guy who was having sex with the woman *he* wanted to have sex with. But there didn't seem to be a way to dig in his heels and hold it off. "So . . . you didn't bring your own sleeping bag, I guess."

"Shit, man, I stay in hotels. Room service, bars, pillow-top mattresses. Cill's the one for roughing it. You don't have a spare, do you?"

"Actually—"

"Whoa! Holy shit! That's Cilla."

Before Ford could respond, Steve strode into his office and to the sketches pinned and hanging.

"Super Cilla. Dude." Steve tapped a finger to a corner of a sketch. "These are awesome. You're a genius. This isn't Seeker stuff."

"No. New character, new series. I'm just getting started."

"With Cill as the . . . what, like, model? Does she know?"

"Yeah. We worked it out."

Nodding, Steve continued to grin at the sketches. "I got the vibe when you came over there yesterday. But seeing this? I totally get why she turned down the on-site booty call last night."

"She—" Mentally, Ford pumped his fist. "So . . . the two of you aren't . . ."

"Road's clear there, man. I'm going to say, straight

out, doing her's one thing—if she's down with that. Messing with her? That's another. Do that, I'll rip your still-beating heart out. Otherwise? We're cool."

Ford studied Steve's face and decided every word spoken was the silver truth. "Got it. I'm going to get my shoes."

Steve poked his head in the bathroom, then into Ford's bedroom. "You've got good light in here. How come you're not tapping that yet?"

"What? Tapping the light?"

"Come on." Steve shook his head as Ford pulled on a T-shirt. "Cilla. How come you're not tapping that yet? I'd know if you were. And she's been over there about a month now."

"Listen, I don't see how that's your business. No offense."

"None taken. Except I see how it is, because there's nobody who matters more to me. I don't want to say she's like my sister, because that would just be sick, considering."

Ford sat on the side of the bed to pull on his shoes. "The lady seems to want to take it slow. So I'm taking it slow. That's it."

"That's solid. I like you, so I'm going to give you a tip. She's tough, and what you'd call resilient. She handles herself and what comes at her. But she's got depths, and in some of those deep places she hurts. So you've got to be careful there."

"She wouldn't be doing what she's doing over there if she didn't have depths, and if some of them didn't hurt."

"Okay. Let's go be men and check out the barn."

IN WHAT WOULD be her laundry/mudroom, Cilla straightened to stretch out her back. As she'd suspected, the old and yellowing linoleum covered a scarred but salvageable hardwood floor. She'd rather be upstairs having fun with power tools, but it made more sense for her to focus her sweat equity into ripping up the linoleum. Her carpenter didn't need her up there, especially with Steve on site, so . . .

Through the window she spotted Steve, who obviously wasn't upstairs, walking toward her barn with Ford. Setting aside her tools, she headed out to find out why Steve was out for a morning stroll instead of supervising the master suite rebuild.

The barn door stood open, and the two men were inside by the time she got there. They appeared to be debating which one of them should climb the ladder into the hayloft.

"What the hell are you doing?" she demanded.

"Checking it out," Steve told her. "Can you tell if anything's missing?"

"No, and why should it be?"

"Ford saw somebody skulking around out here last night."

"I didn't say 'skulking.' I said I saw someone out here with a flashlight last night."

"You're out on somebody else's property in the middle of the night, with a flashlight, that's skulking." Steve pointed at Cilla. "I told you I heard something."

Cilla shook her head at Steve, turned to Ford. "From all the way across the road, in the dead of night, you saw someone skulking around my barn?"

"While I have to agree with the definition of 'skulking,' what I said was I saw a light, the beam of it. The beam of a flashlight, moving toward the barn."

"It was probably a reflection. Moonlight or something."

"I know what a flashlight beam looks like."

"Plus," Steve interrupted, "when we opened the door, it groaned. *That's* the sound I heard last night. Somebody came in here. You've got a lot of shit in here, Cill."

"And it's pretty clear the lot of shit is still here."

"Maybe something, or some things, aren't," Ford

pointed out. "There's a lot of inventory here, and I'd say a valiant attempt to organize it, but I doubt you know everything that's here, or exactly where you put it the last time you worked in here."

"Okay, no, I don't." She set her hands on her hips to study the piles and stacks, the arrangement. Had she stacked those boxes that way? Had she turned that broken rocker to the left?

How the hell did she know?

"I've got a lot to go through, but I haven't found anything especially valuable yet. And okay," she continued before Steve could speak, "a teaspoon Janet Hardy dipped into a sugar bowl would be worth a spot of breaking and entering for a lot of people."

"Who knows you've got stuff in here?"

"Everyone." Ford answered Steve's question. "There's a bunch of people working in the house, and that bunch of people saw Cilla hauling this stuff out here—even helped. So anyone any of them talked to knows, and anyone the anyones talked to and so on."

"I'll get a padlock."

"Good idea. How about the letters?"

"What letters?" Steve wanted to know.

"Did you tell anyone besides me about the letters you found in the attic?"

"My father, but I hardly think—"

"You found letters in the attic?" Steve interrupted. "Like secret letters? Man, this is like one of those BBC mystery shows."

"You never watch BBC mysteries."

"I do if they have hot Brit chicks in them. What letters?"

"Letters written to my grandmother by the man she had an affair with in the year before she died. And yeah, secret letters. She had them hidden. I've only told Ford and my father—who probably told my stepmother. But it wouldn't go further than that." She hoped. "Except . . ." She blew out a breath. "I realized when I was telling my father we were standing right beside an open window so I pulled him away to finish. But if one of the men was anywhere near the window, they would have heard enough."

She rubbed her eyes. "Stupid. Plus, I pushed my mother yesterday morning about whether Janet had a lover—and one from out here—before she died. She'd blab, if the mood struck. Added to that, she's pissed at me."

Reaching over, Steve patted her shoulder. "Nothing new there, doll."

"I know. But in her current mood, she might have sent someone out here to poke around, looking for something of value."

"Give me the letters, and anything else you're worried about. No one's going to look at my place for them," Ford added when she frowned at him.

"Maybe. Let me think about it."

"Anyway," Steve said, "we can cross off the wild-eyed mountain man with a meat cleaver. Right? Or we can as soon as Ford climbs up there and makes sure there aren't any dead bodies or severed body parts."

"Oh, for Christ sake." Cilla turned toward the ladder.

Ford blocked her, nudged her back. "I'll do it."

He tested his weight on each rung on the climb, as he pictured himself crashing through and breaking any variety of bones on the concrete floor. As he reached the top, he cursed roundly.

"What is it?" Cilla called up.

"Nothing. Splinter. There's nothing up here. Not even the lonely severed head of an itinerant field-worker."

When he'd climbed down again, Cilla took his hand, winced at the chunk of ladder in the meat of his palm. "That's in there. Come on inside and I'll dig it out for you."

"I can just—"

"While you guys play doctor, I'll go strap on my tool belt and do a man's work."

Cilla glanced back at Steve. "About damn time."

"Had to make the doughnut run. Later," he said to Ford and strolled out.

"Did he bring you doughnuts?" Cilla asked.

"Yeah. A bribe for use of the gym."

"Mmm. Come on in, and bring the chunk of my ladder. I assume he also woke you up."

"You assume correctly." Ford shoved the barn door closed behind them. "And from a very interesting dream involving you, a red room and a brass headboard. But the jelly doughnuts almost made up for it."

"Steve believes in the power of the doughnut. So, just what was I doing in a red room with a brass headboard?"

"Hard to describe. But I think I could demonstrate."

She looked into his eyes, bold green against gold rims. "I don't have a red room. Neither do you."

"I'll go buy the paint."

Laughing, she reached for the mudroom door, and quickly found herself with her back to the wall of the house. It came as a constant surprise just how potent, how dangerous that mouth could be. The same mouth, she thought dimly as it assaulted hers, that smiled so charmingly, that spoke in such an easy drawl about everyday things. Then it closed over hers and spiked through her system like a fever.

He gave her bottom lip a light nip before he stepped back. "I thought it was Steve headed to the barn last night. To bunk down."

"Why would Steve sleep in the barn?" It took another minute for her brain to fire on all circuits again. "Oh. We're all grown-ups, Ford. I'm not asking Steve to sleep in the barn."

"Yeah, I got that. But he's going to borrow my old sleeping bag. I haven't used it for about fifteen years, or since sleeping in a bag on the ground lost its thrill for me. He'll like it. It's Spider-Man."

"You have a Spider-Man sleeping bag?"

"I got it for my eighth birthday. It was a highlight, and has never lost its luster." He leaned down, brushed her lips with his and opened the door behind her. "I'm more than happy to get it out of storage so Steve can use it while he's here."

"Neighborly of you."

"Not especially."

She opened the first aid kit, checked the contents. "I've got what I need here. Let's do this outside. In the light." When they stepped out onto the veranda, she gestured for him to sit. She doused a cotton ball with peroxide and cleaned the wound.

"It's not neighborly," Ford continued, "because

the motives are entirely self-serving. I don't want him sleeping with you."

She shifted her gaze up to his even as she began to clean a needle and tweezers with alcohol. "Is that so?"

"If you wanted to sleep with him, then I'd be out of luck."

"How do you know I don't? That I didn't?"

"Because you want to sleep with me. Ow!" He looked down at his hand and the hole she'd made at the top of the splinter with the needle. "Jesus."

"It's too deep to milk out, and needs a route. Suck it up. If I want to sleep with you, why haven't I?"

He eyed the needle in her hand warily. "Because you're not ready. I can wait until you are. But—and don't jab me with that again—I'm goddamned if I want you sleeping with someone else, old time's sake or not, while I'm waiting. I want my hands on you, all over you. And I want you thinking about that."

"So you'll lend Steve your treasured Spider-Man sleeping bag so I can think about it without caving in to my needs and sleeping with him because he's handy."

"Close enough."

"Look at that."

He turned his head to look in the direction she

indicated. The sharp, quick sting had him jolting. When he cursed, Cilla held the hefty splinter in the teeth of her tweezers. "Souvenir?"

"No, thanks."

"You're done." She packed up the kit, then grabbed him by the hair, crushed her mouth greedily to his. Just as quickly, she broke the kiss, rose. "And you can think about that while you're waiting."

With a cool smile, she walked back into the house, let the screen door slap shut behind her.

NINE

Cilla grew so accustomed to the cars that slowed or stopped at the end of her driveway she barely registered them. The lookie-loos, gawkers, even the ones she imagined took photos, didn't have to be a problem. Sooner or later, she thought, they'd grow accustomed to her, so the best solution to her way of thinking was to ignore them, or to toss out the occasional and casual wave.

To become part of the community, she determined, she had to demonstrate her intent and desire. So she shopped at the local supermarket, hired local labor, bought the majority of her materials from local sources. And chatted up the salesclerks, the subcontractors, and signed autographs for those who still thought of her as TV Katie.

She considered it symbolic, a statement of that intent, when she took Ford's advice and followed her first instincts and had the gates removed. To follow up, she planted weeping cherry trees to flank the drive. A statement, Cilla thought, as she stood on the shoulder of the road and studied the results. New life. And next spring, when they burst into bloom again, she'd be here to see it. From her vantage point, she looked down at the house. There would be gardens and young trees as well as the grand old magnolia. *Her* grand old magnolia, she thought, with its waxy white blooms sweetening the air. The paint on the house would be fresh and clean instead of dingy and peeling. Chairs on the veranda, and pots of mixed flowers. And when she could squeeze a little more out of the budget, pavers in earthy tones on the drive cutting through lush green lawns.

Eventually, when people slowed down to look, it would be because they admired a pretty house in a pretty setting, and not because they wondered what the hell the Hollywood woman was doing with the house where Janet Hardy had swallowed too many pills and chased them with vodka.

She stepped back toward the wall at the sound of an approaching car, then turned at the quick *beep-beep* as the little red Honda pulled to the shoulder.

It took her a moment—and brought on a twist

of guilt—to recognize the pretty blonde in cropped pants and a crocheted cami who hopped out of the car.

"Hi!" On a bubble of laughter, Angela McGowan, Cilla's half sister, rushed forward to catch Cilla in a squeeze.

"Angie." The fresh, sassy scent enveloped her as completely as the arms. "You cut your hair. Let me look at you. No! Don't hug me again. I'm filthy."

"You really are." On another bubble of laughter, Angie pulled back, met Cilla's eyes with her own enormous hazel ones. Their father's eyes, Cilla thought. Their father's daughter. "And you smell a little, too." Beaming, just beaming, Angie gripped Cilla's hands. "You shouldn't still be so beautiful, considering."

"You look amazing." Cilla brushed her fingertips over the very abbreviated ends of Angie's hair. "It's so short."

"Takes two seconds to deal with in the morning." Angie gave her head a quick shake so the sunny cap lifted, ruffled, settled. "I had to practically have a blindfold and a cigarette to get it done."

"It's fabulous. What are you doing here? I thought you were at college?"

"Semester's done for me, so I'm home for a while.

I can't believe you're *here*. And this." She gestured toward the house. "You're actually living here, and fixing it up and . . . all."

"There's a lot of *all*."

"These are so pretty. So much prettier than that old gate." Angie touched one of the curved branches with its blossoms of soft, spring pink. "Everyone's talking about what's going on here. I've only been home for a day, and already I've had my ears burned by all the talk."

"Good talk or bad talk?"

"Why wouldn't it be good?" Angie cocked her head. "This place was an eyesore. So yeah, it's not so pretty right now, either, but you're *doing* something. Nobody else has. Is it hard? I don't mean the work, because obviously . . . I mean is it hard being here, living here?"

"No." But Angie would ask, Cilla knew. Angie would care. "In fact, it's easy. It feels right, more than anything or anywhere else. It's strange."

"I don't think so. I think everyone's supposed to be somewhere, and the lucky ones find out where it is. So you're lucky."

"I guess I am." The bright side of optimism, Cilla remembered, was where Angie lived. Her father's daughter. *Their* father's daughter, Cilla corrected.

"Do you want to come in, take a look? It's in serious flux right now, but we're making progress."

"I would, and I will another time. I'm on my way to meet some friends, but I detoured, hoping to see you for a minute. Didn't expect to see you on the side of the road, so I guess I'm lucky, too. So if . . . uh-oh."

Cilla followed the direction of Angie's glance, noted the white van that slowed and pulled to the shoulder across the road.

"Do you know who that is?" Cilla asked. "I've seen that van pull up out here before, several times before."

"Yeah, that's Mr. Hennessy's van. His son was—"

"I know. One of the boys with Janet's son, in the accident. Okay. Stay here."

"Oh God, Cilla, don't go over there." Angie grabbed at Cilla's arm. "He's just awful. Mean son of a bitch. I mean, sure, what happened was terrible, but he hates us."

"Us?"

"All of us. It's a by-association kind of thing, Dad says. You should stay out of his way."

"He's in mine, Angie."

Cilla crossed over, met the bitter eyes in the thin, pinched-mouth face through the windshield as she crossed to the driver's-side door. A lift van, she saw now. One designed to handle his son's wheelchair.

The slope of the shoulder put her at a disadvantage—slightly off-balance and several inches lower than the man who glared out at her.

"Mr. Hennessy, I'm Cilla McGowan."

"I know who you are. Look just like her, don't you?"

"I was sorry to hear you lost your son last year."

"Lost him in 1972 when your worthless kin crushed his spine. Drunk and high and not giving a damn about anything but himself, because that's how he was raised. Not to give a damn."

"That may be. I know those three boys paid a terrible price that night. I can't—"

"You're no better than she was, thinking you're better'n anybody else 'cause you've got money to spend, and expecting people to kowtow."

The well of Cilla's sympathy began to dry up. "You don't know me."

"Hell I don't. I know you, your kind, your blood. You think you can come here where that woman whored around, let her kids run like wolves, where she cost my boy his arms and legs, his life?" His anger slapped out, bony fingers, in short, brittle blows. "You think you can buy some wood, some paint and use it to cover up the stink of that place?

Shoulda burned it down years back. Burned it to the godforsaken ground."

"It's a house, Mr. Hennessy. It's wood and glass." And you, she thought with no sympathy at all, are a lunatic.

"It's as cursed as she was. As you are." He spat out the window, barely missed the toe of Cilla's boot. "Go back where you came from. We don't want you or your kind here."

He pulled out so fast, fishtailing, that Cilla had to scramble back. She slid on the slope, lost her balance and went down on her knees as Angie ran across the road.

"Are you okay? Jesus, Jesus, he didn't hit you, did he?"

"No. No." But her eyes were narrowed, iced blue, on the speeding van. "I'm fine."

"I'm calling the police." Quivering with indignation, Angie pulled a hot pink cell phone out of her pocket. "He *spat* at you! I saw him, and he nearly ran you over, and—"

"Don't." Cilla put a hand to the phone as Angie flipped it open. "Let it go." She sighed, rubbed at her knee. "Just let it go."

"Are you hurt? You went down hard. We need to look at your knee."

"It's okay, Mom."

"Seriously. I'll drive you down to the house, and we'll see if you need to have it checked out. That old bastard."

"The knee's fine. I'm not hurt, I'm pissed off."

As if to stabilize, Angie took a couple of whooshing breaths while she studied Cilla. "You don't look pissed off."

"Believe me. Whoring around, wolves, cursed, your *kin*. Asshole."

Angie laughed. "That's more like it. I'm driving you down to the house, now don't argue."

"Fine. Thanks. Does he act that way to you?" Cilla asked as they crossed to Angie's Honda.

"He snarls and sends what you could call burning stares, mutters. No spitting. I know he's gone off on Dad. And I mean, *God*, do you know anybody with more compassion than Dad? Just because he was friends with Mr. Hennessy's son, and the rest of them, doesn't make him responsible for what happened. He wasn't even *there* that night. And clue in, you weren't even born."

"He's got the sins-of-the-father thing going, I'd say. If he wants to drive by, stop and glower and think bad thoughts, let him."

At the end of the drive, Cilla opened the car door. She took a breath herself now, and realized she felt better, more *level*, she supposed, with Angie there. "Thanks, Angie."

"I want to look at your knee before I go."

"The knee's fine." To prove it, and to change the mood, Cilla swung into a quick tap routine on the patchy lawn, and ended with a flourish while Angie giggled.

"Wow. I guess it is fine."

"Nice stems, doll." Steve stepped onto the veranda, tattoos and tool belt. "And who's your friend?"

"We're not friends," Angie said, "we're sisters."

"Angela McGowan, Steve Chensky. Steve's a friend from L.A. He's giving me a hand for a few days."

"Maybe longer." Steve smiled, big and bold.

"Angie's just home from college, and heading out to meet some friends."

"I am. I'm late. You tell him about Mr. Hennessy," Angie ordered, climbing back into her car.

"Mr. who?"

"I will. Have fun."

"That's the plan. I'll be back. Nice meeting you, Steve." With a wave out the window, she did a neat three-quarter turn and drove out.

"Your sister's hot."

"And barely legal, so hands off."

"'Barely' would be the key word. You gotta love that McGowan DNA."

"No. No, you don't. How's it coming in the attic?"

"It's fucking hot. They need to finish getting the AC up and running. But it's coming along. Get your tools, doll. Daylight's wasting."

"I'm right behind you."

HE'D BEEN RIGHT about the heat. Cilla calculated she'd dropped a couple of pounds in sweat alone by the time she unhooked her tool belt for the day. She treated herself to a long, cool shower in her one nearly completed bathroom. Paint and light fixtures yet to go. And thought about fixing herself an enormous sandwich.

She ate it in solitary, pig-out splendor on her back veranda, and imagined the blooming shrubs, ornamental trees, the colorful plants in place of the hacked overgrowth. She imagined a rugged stone bench under the spread of the big sycamore and pictured the new slates and bricks on the patios and paths. The drip of willows at the pond, the shade of red maples, the glossy beauty of magnolias.

Not cursed, she thought, rubbing lightly at the

knee that was a little stiff and sore. Ignored, neglected for too long, but not cursed, despite the accusations of a bitter old man.

She'd put up a martin house, and hummingbird feeders. And the birds would come. She'd plant a cutting garden with her own hands—after she researched what should be planted—and draw more birds and butterflies that would wing about as she harvested blooms for vases.

She'd buy a dog, one who'd chase sticks and squirrels and rabbits, and she'd have to chase *him* when he dug in the gardens. Maybe she'd even see if she could hunt up an appealingly ugly one, like Spock.

She'd have parties with colored lights and music with people wandering through the house, over the lawn, filling it, filling it with sound and movement. Pulses and heartbeats and voices.

And she'd wake up every morning inside a home. Her home.

She looked down at the paper plate in her lap, watched the tear plop. "Oh God, what's this?" She rubbed her hands over her wet cheeks, pressed them to the tightness in her chest. "What's this, what's this?"

On the sagging veranda facing the ruined gardens,

she sat alone while the sun slid toward the mountains. And gave in to the sobs. Meltdown, part of her brain thought. Had to happen.

Dogs, people, colored lights? Failure was a lot more likely. No, the house wasn't cursed. It had good bones, good muscle. But wasn't she cursed? What had she ever done that mattered? What had she ever finished? She'd fail here, too. Failure was what she did best.

"Stop it. Stop this *crap*."

She choked back the next sob as she pushed to her feet. Grabbing the plate and the half-eaten sandwich, she marched inside, tossed them away. Breathing slowly, she splashed cold water on her face until it was drown or suck it up. Steadier, she went upstairs, deliberately applied makeup to conceal her pity bout, then picked up the copy of *Gatsby*.

She carried it across the road and knocked on Ford's door.

"This is handy," he said when he came to the door. Spock stopped his aliens-at-the-door trembling and raced forward to press his body to Cilla's legs. "I was just going over a short list of excuses, deciding which one to pick that covered going over to your place. I was sitting out back so I wouldn't appear to be obviously casing your house."

She stepped in, handed him the book. "You said I could keep this here."

"Sure. The letters?"

"Yeah." Because the dog looked up at her with love shining in his protruding eyes, she crouched for a moment to scratch and rub him into ecstasy. "I'm in a mood. I don't want them in the house right now."

"Okay."

"Would you read them sometime, when you get a chance? I think I'd like someone else's take."

"That's a relief. Now I don't have to fight a daily war between curiosity and integrity. I'll put them in my office. Do you want to come up a minute? I've got some sketches I think you'll like."

"Yeah." Restless, she thought. She felt restless, itchy, a little headachy. Better to keep moving, keep doing. "Yeah, why not?"

"Want a beer, some wine?"

"No, no. Nothing." Alcohol wasn't the best idea after a meltdown.

"Where's Steve? I thought I heard his bike a while back."

"He went out. He said he wanted some action, maybe he'd play a little pool with some of the guys on the crew. I think he's hoping to get lucky with one of the landscapers. Her name's Shanna."

"Shanna and I go back. Not that way," he said quickly. "Been friends since we were kids. Me, her, Bri, Matt."

"Nice. Nice to have friends you go back with. Oh. Wow."

He had two boards loaded with sketches. Action poses, she thought. Mid-leap, mid-stride, mid-spin. In all she looked—there was no mistaking her face—she looked strong, fierce, bold and brilliant.

Everything, she realized, everything she didn't *feel* at that moment.

"I'm thinking tattoo. I got hung up on that. Now I'm figuring out what and where." He tucked his hands in his back pockets as he gave the sketches a critical study. "Small of the back, shoulder blade, biceps. I'm thinking small and symbolic, and some-where people wouldn't notice it on Cass. Or better, it's not *on* Cass, but forms when she changes to Brid. That way, it's not just a symbol but part of the power source."

He narrowed his eyes as he scanned the sketches. "I need to figure it out before I start on the panels. The story's outlined, and I like it. It holds up, but . . ."

Because Spock had begun to whine, Ford glanced over. And his trend of thought snapped into tiny pieces. Tears streamed down Cilla's face.

"Oh man. Crap. What? Why?"

"Sorry. Sorry. I thought it was finished. I thought I was done." Backing up, she swiped at her cheeks. "I have to go."

"No. Uh-uh." There might have been a hole spreading in the pit of his stomach, but he took her arm, and his grip was firm. "What's the matter? What did I do?"

"Everything. Nothing."

"Which?"

"Everything's the matter. You did nothing. It's not you. It's me. It's me, me, me. That's not me." She gestured wildly toward the sketches. The tone, the gesture had Spock slinking over to his bed. "I'm nothing like that. I can't even gear myself up to have sex with you. Do you want to know why?"

"I'm pretty interested."

"Because I'll end up messing it up, ruining it, then I won't have anyone to talk to. I don't make things work. I screw up everything, fail at everything."

"Not from where I'm standing." Baffled, he shook his head. "Where's this coming from?"

"From reality. From *history*. You don't know anything about it."

"So tell me."

"For God's sake, I was washed up at *twelve*. I had the tools, I had the platform, and I screwed it up. I failed."

"That's bullshit." His tone was matter-of-fact, and so much more comforting than soft sympathy. "You're too smart to believe that."

"It doesn't matter that I *know* it's not true— exactly. But when you're told you're a failure over and over, you start believing it. That goddamn show was my family, then bam! Gone. I couldn't get it back, not the family, not the work. Then it's do concerts, live shows, and I *can't*. Stage fright, panic attacks. I wasn't going to take pills."

"What pills?"

"God." She pressed her fingers to her eyes, grateful the tears had stopped. Spock slunk back over, dropped a half-chewed stuffed bear at her feet. "My manager, my mother, people. You just need something to smooth the edges, to get you out there. So you can keep bringing in the money, keep your name in the public consciousness. But I wouldn't, I didn't, and that was that. So there's bad movies, horrible press—then worse from some viewpoints, no press. And Steve."

Wound up, she tossed out her arms, paced the room. "I jumped into marriage two seconds after I turned eighteen because finally, finally, here was someone who loved me, who cared, who understood. But I couldn't make that work.

"I tried college, and I hated it. I was miserable and

I felt stupid. I wasn't prepared, and I didn't expect so many people to actually want me to fail. So I did. I matched their low expectations of me. One semester and I was out. Then there were voice-overs and humiliating bit parts. I'd write a screenplay, no, couldn't do that, either. Photography, maybe? No, I sucked. I had income, thanks to Katie—and the fact, which I found out years later, that my father went to the wall to make sure my income was legally protected until I was of age.

"I was in therapy when I was fourteen. I thought about suicide at sixteen. Hot bath, pink candles, music, razor blade. Except after I got in the tub, I thought, this is just *stupid*. I don't want to die. So I just took a bath. I tried things. Maybe I could manage someone else, or do choreography. Name it. Tried it. Bombed. I don't get things done. I don't stick."

"Take a breather," Ford ordered, in such stern, authoritative tones she could only blink at him. "You were a cute kid, a cute, talented kid on TV."

"Oh hell."

"Just shut up a minute. I don't know how these things work, exactly, but I'd have to guess the show had run its course."

"And then some."

"But nobody took into account there was a kid

involved, one who'd grown up on that show and who had to feel as if she'd been ripped away from her family. Orphaned. Who might feel it was her fault."

"I did. I really did. I know better, but—"

"Anybody who offers much less pushes tranquilizers on a fourteen-year-old girl to get her to perform ought to be shot. There's no gray area there, not to me. You're not going to be able to claim those events as your failure. Sorry, they're off the list. Actually, it's a clean sweep," he continued as she stared at him. "College didn't work, writing, photography, whatever. It's not failing, Cilla, it's trying. It's exploring. You had a marriage that didn't work, and you've managed to remain friends—real friends—with the ex? That's a failure? See, that comes up strong in the plus column for me. And how about the houses back in California that you fixed up and sold? If you've hit a snag across the road, you'll just have to unsnag it."

"I haven't." She pushed at her hair, managed to take a clear, easy breath. "Things are actually going really well. I'm sorry. I'm sorry. I can't believe I dumped all this on you. I had a meltdown earlier, and I thought I'd finished it off. For some reason the sketches opened the floodgates again."

She bent down, stroked Spock as he continued to

look at her with great concern. She picked up the tattered little bear. "This is disgusting."

"Yeah. He's had it awhile. He only gives it to people he loves."

"Well." She leaned forward, kissed Spock on the nose. "Thanks, baby. Here, you better have it back."

His tail wagged as if to say, Crisis over, and he took the bear back to his bed.

"What brought on the meltdown in the first place?"

"Oh boy."

She walked away from Ford, from the sketches, to the window. The sun had dipped down behind the mountains so its light haloed their dignified peaks. The sight of them—distant, a bit aloof—was comforting.

"My half sister stopped by today. Angie, who I often think of internally as my father's daughter. I don't often think of myself that way, or didn't. It was easier not to. She's so *there*. Happy, smart, pretty. A nice girl, but not so nice you can't stand being around her. I haven't made any particular effort there, or with my stepmother. Cards and an appropriate gift at Christmas and on birthdays. I didn't recognize her for a minute, she's cut her hair, but that wasn't why. Not really. I just blanked at first. I felt stiff and awkward, and she didn't. So I have to feel guilty about that, which makes me feel more stiff, more awkward, and she's just bubbling over, happy to see me. No pretense, no agenda."

She sighed now, irritated with herself. Big whiny baby, she thought. Just can't stand that everything's going well. "I'd been congratulating myself on having the gates taken down—the symbol of it— and planting trees. Opening things up, putting in roots, looking to the future, and she made me realize I keep skimming over people and relationships, like a stone skipped over a river. Don't want to sink in."

"Maybe you're more treading water awhile now."

She glanced back. He looked so damn good, she thought, in the ancient sweatshirt, torn jeans, ragged hair. "Maybe I am. Anyway, while we're standing there talking, and I'm trying to figure it out, Mr. Hennessy pulls up across the road. I've seen his van out there before, just sitting there. Angie recognized it."

She turned around. "Did you know he's slapped out at my father and his family?"

"No. Maybe. He's a hard man, Cilla."

"So I found out when I went over to talk to him. He pretty much blames me and all my kin, as he put it, for what happened to his son. The house is cursed, I'm a whore like my grandmother, and so on. He actually spat at me."

"Bastard."

"I'll say. Then he pulls out so fast, I lost my balance, and Angie's all mother hen."

"You should call the cops. They'll talk to him."

"And tell him not to spit on my shoes? Better if I just make sure he doesn't have the chance to do it again. I'm done feeling sorry for what happened to him before I was born. I thought I was just pissed off, went back to work and sweated it out. But later, I guess it just all hit, resulting in the massive pity event I've just shared with you."

"I'd call it a more medium-sized event, and that it illustrates you're way too hard on yourself. I don't know anything about building houses, but I do know the person in charge of what's going on across the road. She's no screwup. She's smart and bold and she works for what she wants. She may not have the mystical powers of the goddess but . . ." He tapped one of the sketches. "That's her. That's you, Cilla. Just the way I see you." He took down one of Brid, gripping a two-headed hammer in both hands, her face alive with power and purpose.

"Take this one, put it up somewhere. You feel one of the events coming on again, take a look at it. It's who you are."

"I have to say, you're the first person to see me as a warrior goddess."

"That's not all she is."

Cilla looked from the sketch up into his eyes. There was tightness in her chest again, but not the sort that presaged tears. It was the flexing, she thought, of something starting to open again. "Thanks for this, and for the rest. As payback . . ."

She turned, had his pulse bounding when she lifted the back of her shirt, bent just a little at the waist so her jeans gapped at the spine. And there, at the base, in deep blue, the three lines of the triple spiral curved.

He felt the punch in his libido even as it hit the intellect. "Celtic symbol of female power. Maid, mother, crone."

She glanced over her shoulder, eyebrows cocked. "Aren't you smart?"

"I've been researching." He stepped closer to study the tattoo. "And that particular symbol was top of my list for Brid. That's freaking kismet."

"It should be on her biceps."

"What? Sorry. Very distracted."

"Biceps." Cilla turned, flexed hers. "It's stronger there. Not as sexy, maybe, but stronger, I think. And if you go with the idea of having it form when she transforms, it's a bigger statement."

"You were listening."

"So were you." She lifted a hand, touched his cheek. "You're good at it."

"Okay. We need to get out of the house now."

"We do?"

"Yeah. Because I could talk you into bed now, and I really want to. Then we'd both wonder if it was because you had a bad day and I was just here. Angst and awkwardness ensue. So . . . let's go get ice cream."

Another key word had Spock deserting bear and bed and leaping up.

Smiling, she stroked her fingers down to Ford's jawline. "I want you to talk me into bed now."

"Yeah. Shut up. Ice cream. Let's go."

He grabbed her hand, pulled her along. The dog passed them at a run in a race for the front door.

"You're a confusing man, Ford."

"Half the time I don't understand myself."

TEN

To Steve's mind very little topped the sensation of roaring along a country road, hugging the curves with the warm night wind streaming. Scoring with the hot brunette, Shanna the landscaper, would've edged that out, but he'd come close there.

And there was always next time.

He'd gotten a taste, anyway, and had the feeling the full dish would live up to the promise of the sample. Yeah. He grinned into the wind. Next time.

But for now, cruising along the deserted road after a little beer, a little pool, a few laughs and the prelude with Shanna hit all the chords. Swinging down, taking a couple of weeks to hook up with Cilla, yeah, that was working for him.

She'd taken on a big one, he mused. A big, complicated project, and a wicked personal one. But it was working for her, too. He could see it in the way she looked, the way she talked. And she'd make herself something—something big, complicated and personal. Just like she'd always needed to.

He could give her another week, maybe ten days on it. Because damn if the rehab didn't grab him, and tight enough he wanted to see it through a little longer. He wanted to hang with Cilla a little longer, too, watch her build the framework of her new life.

And hopefully close the deal with Shanna while he was at it.

A week ought to do it, he thought as he swung around the turn and onto Cilla's road. By then, the rural charm of the Shenandoah Valley would start to fade for him. He needed the action of the city, and though New York appealed to him for short stints, L.A.'s gloss and sparkle was home, sweet home.

Not for Cilla. Steve glanced idly at a car parked on the shoulder near a long, rising lane. No, for Cilla L.A. had always been just a place. Probably another reason getting married had been such a whacked idea. Even back then she'd been looking for a way out, and he'd been looking for a way in.

And somehow, they'd both found it.

He turned into her drive, smiling to himself when he noted she'd left a light on out front for him, and another inside that glowed against one of the windows. That was Cilla, he thought. She thought of the little things, remembered details.

And the light in the window reminded him it had to be after two in the morning. In the country quiet his Harley sounded like a tornado blowing out to Oz. She'd probably sleep through it—when Cilla went out, she went *out*—but he cut the engine halfway down the drive and coasted.

Singing under his breath, he hopped off the bike to guide it the rest of the way to the barn. He took off his helmet, strapped it onto the bike, then pulled open the creaking barn door. He left the headlight on to cut a swath through the dark and, with a belch that brought back the memory of Corona, slapped the kickstand down. When he angled the front wheel, the headlight cut across one of Cilla's storage boxes. It sat open, with its lid beside it, and scattered with photos and papers.

"Hey."

He took a step forward for a closer look. He heard nothing, saw nothing, and felt only an instant of shattering pain before he pitched forward onto the concrete.

CILLA HAD the first of what she thought of as a heads-together with Matt just after seven A.M. She planned others with the electrician and the plumber, but she wanted Steve in on that. As long as he was here, she thought, she'd use him.

Plus, she wanted him to go with her on a buying trip. She needed to choose tile and hardware, fixtures, and order more lumber. By seven-thirty, the cacophony of saws, hammers and radios filled the house, and figuring Steve had had a late night, she took pity on him and carried a mug of coffee up to the bedroom where he slept in his borrowed Spider-Man sleeping bag.

When she saw Spidey was currently unoccupied, she blew out a breath. "Somebody got lucky," she muttered, and drank the coffee herself as she headed downstairs.

She grabbed her lists, her notebook, her purse. As she stepped outside, the landscape crew pulled in. Cilla's eyebrows quirked up when she spotted Shanna. Just who did Steve get lucky with? she wondered. Shanna lifted a hand in a wave, then, carrying a to-go cup of coffee, wandered over.

"Morning. Brian's got to site another job this morning, but he'll swing by in a couple hours."

"Fine. I'm heading in to pick up some materials. Do you need me for anything?"

"We're good. But you ought to come around when you get back. We'll be starting on hardscape—the patio and walkways today." Shanna glanced at the house. "So, is Steve among the living this morning?"

"Haven't seen him yet."

"I'm not surprised." Adjusting the cap over her dark braid, Shanna flashed a smile. "We about closed the place down last night. That Steve, he sure can dance."

"Yes, he can."

"He's a sweetie. Followed me home to make sure I got there safe, then didn't push—or not hard—to come in. He'd pushed a little harder, and who knows?" She hooted out a laugh.

"He didn't stay with you?"

"No." Shanna's smile faded. "Did he get home all right?"

"I don't know. I didn't see him inside, so I assumed . . ." With a shrug, Cilla jingled her keys. "I'll just go see if his bike's in the barn."

Shanna fell into step beside her. "He was fine when he left, I mean he hadn't been drinking much. A couple of beers all night. I only live about twenty minutes from here."

"I probably just missed him in the house." But her stomach started to jump as Cilla reached the barn door. "Maybe he went up while I went down."

Sunlight splashed into the barn and erupted with dust motes. Cilla blinked to adjust her eyes and felt a fresh wave of anxiety when she didn't immediately spot the Harley.

Stepping in, she noted some of her storage boxes were tipped over, the contents spilled. An old chair lay broken on its side. She saw the Harley then, on the floor, handlebars up as if its rider had wiped out. Steve, arms and legs splayed, sprawled under the weighty bulk of it.

"Oh God." She sprang forward, Shanna beside her, to lift the bike off Steve. Blood matted his hair, and more stained his raw and bruised face. Afraid to move him, Cilla pressed her fingers to his throat. And nearly shook as she felt his pulse beat.

"He's alive. He's got a pulse. Call—"

"I am." Crouching, Shanna punched nine-one-one on her cell phone. "Should we get a blanket? Should we—"

"Tell them to hurry. Don't move him." Cilla leaped up and ran for the house.

HE COULD USUALLY sleep through anything. But the shouting scraped along Ford's consciousness, then the sirens drove straight in. Too bleary to put them together, he rolled out of bed, stumbled out onto the veranda. Yawning, he scanned across the road, wished he could conjure a cup of coffee with the power of his mind. The sight of the ambulance outside Cilla's barn had him snapping awake. When he didn't see her in his quick, panicked search, he rushed back inside to drag on clothes.

He streaked across the road, up Cilla's drive, keeping his mind blank. If one image, even one image, formed, a dozen horrible others would follow. He pushed through the crowd of workers, said her name once, like a personal prayer.

When he saw her standing behind the portable gurney, his heart started beating again. Then it slammed into his belly when he realized Steve lay on the gurney.

"I'm going with him. I'm going." Her voice teetered on the thin edge between control and hysteria. "He's not going alone." She gripped the edge of the gurney, stuck like glue as they transported it to the ambulance.

The fear in her eyes chilled Ford to the bone. "Cilla. I'm going to follow you in. I'm going to be there."

"He won't wake up. They can't wake him up." Before anyone could deny her, Cilla climbed into the back of the ambulance.

He took her purse because Shanna had retrieved it and pushed it into his hands. Shanna, Ford thought, who'd had tears streaking down her face.

"He was in the barn," Shanna choked out, and slid into Ford's arms for comfort. "Lying on the floor, under the bike. The blood."

"Okay, Shan. Okay, honey. I'm going to go. I'm going to find out how he is."

"Call me, please. Call me."

"First thing."

After a wild drive to the hospital, Ford carried Cilla's purse into the ER, too worried to feel even marginally foolish.

He found her standing outside a pair of double doors, looking helpless.

"I gave them his medical history, the stuff I could remember. Who remembers all of that kind of thing?" She pawed at the neck of her shirt, as if looking for something, anything, to hold on to. "But I gave them his blood type. I remembered his blood type. A-negative. I remembered."

"Okay. Let's go sit down."

"They won't let me in. They won't let me stay with him. He won't wake up."

Ford put an arm around her shoulders and firmly steered her away from the doors and to a chair. Instead of sitting, he crouched in front of her so her eyes were on his face. "They're going to fix him now. That's what they're doing. Okay?"

"He was bleeding. His head. His face. Lying there bleeding. I don't know how long."

"Tell me what happened."

"I don't *know!*" She pressed both hands to her mouth, and began to rock. "I don't know. He wasn't in his room, and I figured, I thought, well, I figured, he shoots, he scores. That's all. I almost left. God, God, I almost left without even looking, even checking. It would've been hours more."

"Breathe." He spoke sharply, took her hands and squeezed. "Look at me and breathe."

"Okay." She breathed, and she trembled, but Ford saw a hint of color come back into her face. "I thought he'd stayed at Shanna's, so I was going to go buy materials, but he didn't. I mean, she got there and said he didn't. I worried that he might've gotten lost or something. I don't even know. But I went to see if his bike was there. And we found him."

"In the barn."

"He was lying under his bike. I don't know what could've happened. His head, his face." Now she rubbed a hand between her breasts. Ford could almost hear the slam of her heart against the pressure. "I heard them say he's probably got a couple of broken ribs, from the bike falling on him. But how did the bike fall on him? And . . . and the head injuries. His pupils. They said something about a blown pupil. I know that's not good. I had a guest spot on *ER* once."

She hitched in three raw breaths, then let them out in a gush. And the tears came with it. "Who the hell has a motorcycle accident in a barn? It's so goddamn stupid."

Taking the tears, and the hint of anger, as good signs, Ford sat beside her and held her hand.

When the door flew open, they lurched to their feet together. "What is it? Where are you taking him? Steve."

"Miss." One of the ER nurses put herself in Cilla's path. "They're taking your friend up to surgery."

"Surgery for what? For what?"

"He has bleeding in his brain from the head injury. They need to operate. I'm going to take you up to the surgical waiting area. One of the doctors can explain the procedure to you."

"How bad? You can tell me that. How bad?"

"We're doing everything we can. We have a good surgical team prepping for the procedure." She gestured them to an elevator. "Do you know if Mr. Chensky was in some sort of fight?"

"No. Why?"

"The injury to the back of his head. It looks as though he's been struck. It's just not consistent with a fall. Of course, if he was driving without his helmet . . ."

"It didn't happen when he was driving. It didn't happen on the road."

"So you said."

"Cilla." Ford laid a hand on hers before she could get into the elevator. "We need to call the cops."

HOW WAS SHE supposed to think? How could she sit in this room while somewhere *else* strangers operated on Steve? An operating room. Operating theater. They called it a theater sometimes, didn't they? Would the patient and doctor be costars? Who got top billing?

"Miss McGowan?"

"What?" She stared into the blank eyes of the cop. What was his name? She'd already forgotten it. "I'm sorry." She groped through the chaos of her mind for the question he'd asked. "I'm not sure what time he got back. I went to bed about midnight, and he wasn't back. Shanna said he left her before two. Just before two, she said."

"Do you have Shanna's full name?"

"Shanna Stiles," Ford supplied. "She works for Brian Morrow. Morrow Landscape and Design."

"You found Mr. Chensky at approximately seven-thirty this morning?"

"I said that. Didn't I say that?" Cilla pushed at her hair. "He wasn't in the house, so I checked the barn for his bike. And I found him."

"You and Mr. Chensky live together?"

"He's visiting. He's helping me out for a few weeks."

"Visiting from?"

"Los Angeles. New York. I mean, he was in New York, and he's going back to L.A." Whatever churned in her belly wanted to rise up to her throat. "What difference does it make?"

"Officer Taney." Ford put a hand over Cilla's, squeezed. "Here's the thing. A few nights ago, I saw someone walking around, going into Cilla's barn. It was late. I was working late, and I looked out the window on the way to bed and saw someone, saw a flashlight. I thought it was Steve, and didn't think anything of it."

"But it wasn't." Remembering, Cilla shut her eyes. "I was supposed to buy a padlock, but I didn't. I forgot about it, didn't think about it, and now—"

"What do you keep in the barn?" Taney asked her.

"I cleaned out the attic and stored things there. A lot of things I have to sort through. And there's other stuff. Old tack, tools, equipment."

"Valuables?"

"For some, anything connected to my grandmother is valuable. Stupid, stupid to think I could turn it all around, make it new." Make it mine, she thought. Stupid.

"Was anything taken?"

"I don't know. I just don't know."

"Mr. Chensky went out at approximately eight last evening, to a bar. You don't have the name of the bar—"

"No, I don't have the name of the bar. You can ask Shanna Stiles. And if you're thinking he was drunk and somehow bashed himself on the back of the head, smashed his face into the concrete and knocked his bike on top of him, you're wrong. Steve wouldn't get on his bike drunk. You can ask Shanna or anyone else who was in the bar last night about that."

"I'm going to do that, Miss McGowan, and if it's all right with you, I'll go over and have a look at your barn."

"Yes, go ahead."

"I hope your friend comes through okay. I'll be in touch," he added as he rose.

Ford watched him cross to the nurses' station, take out a card.

"He thinks it was drunken clumsiness, or that Steve was stoned and stupid."

"Maybe he does." Ford turned back to Cilla. "Maybe. But he's still going to look at things, talk to people. And Steve can fill in the blanks when he's able."

"He could die. They don't have to tell me that for me to know it. He might never wake up." Her lips trembled before she managed to firm them. "And I keep seeing him in there, in this scene out of *Grey's Anatomy*, with the interns up there in that glass-walled balcony looking down at Steve. And everybody's thinking more about sex than they are about Steve."

Ford took her face in his hands. "People do their jobs while they think about sex. All the time. Otherwise nothing would ever get done." When she let out a weak laugh, he kissed her forehead. "Let's take a walk, get some air."

"I shouldn't leave. I need to be here."

"It's going to be a while. Let's clear the head, hunt up some decent coffee."

"Okay. A few minutes. You don't have to stay." She looked down at her hand as they walked to the elevator, saw it was caught in his again. "I wasn't thinking. You don't have to stay. You barely know Steve."

"Don't be stupid. I do know him, and I like him. Anyway, I won't leave you alone."

She said nothing, couldn't, as they rode down. Her eyes stung, wanted to flood. Her body ached to turn into his, press against the solidity of him, be enfolded. Safe. She could hold on there, she thought. Be allowed to hold on.

"You want food?" he asked as they stepped out at the lobby level.

"No, I couldn't."

"Probably still sucks anyway."

"Still?"

"My dad was in for a couple days a few years ago, so I choked down the cafeteria fare a time or two. It hadn't improved since I was a kid and did my own time."

"What were you in for?"

"Overnight observation—concussion, broken arm. I, uh, got the idea to put these Velcro strips on my snow gloves and socks. Thought I'd be able to climb up and down buildings like Spider-Man. Fortunately my bedroom window wasn't that high up."

"Maybe you should've tried climbing up before climbing down."

"Hindsight."

"You're taking my mind off Steve, and I appreciate it. But—"

"Five minutes," Ford said as he drew her outside. "Fresh air."

"Ford?"

Cilla looked over as he did toward the pretty woman wearing a suit of powerful red. A laugh played over lips painted the same bold color, while she drew off sunglasses to reveal eyes of deep, dark brown.

Her arms opened wide, then closed around Ford in a hard, proprietary hug. She added sound effects, Cilla noted, a low mmmmmMM! before she broke off, shook back the short swing of glossy brown hair. "It's been ages!"

"A while," Ford agreed. "You look seriously great."

"I do my best." She turned those eyes, those smiling lips on Cilla. "Hi there."

"Cilla, this is Brian's mom, Cathy Morrow. Bri's doing a job for Cilla."

"Of course," Cathy said. "Janet Hardy's granddaughter. I knew her a little. You certainly have the look of her. And you're fixing up the old farm."

"Yes." It was surreal, the conversation. Cilla thought of it as lines from a play. "Brian's a big help. He's talented."

"That's my boy. What are y'all doing here?"

"Cilla's friend's in surgery. There was an accident."

"Oh God, I'm so sorry." The bright, flirtatious smile transformed into a look of concern. "Is there anything I can do?" Cathy's arm went around Cilla in a gesture so genuine, Cilla leaned into it instinctively.

"We're just . . . waiting."

"The worst. The waiting. Listen, I volunteer here a couple of days a week, and I head a couple of the fund-raising committees. I know a lot of the staff. Who's his surgeon?"

"I don't know. It happened so fast."

"Why don't I find out, see if I can get you some information? I don't know why they don't understand we do better if we know things."

The offer was like water on a burning throat. "Could you?"

"I can sure try. Come on, honey. You want some coffee, some water? No, I'll tell you what. Ford, run on down and get Cilla a ginger ale."

"Okay. I'll meet you back upstairs. You're in good hands."

It felt like it. For the first time in too long to remember, Cilla felt as if it was okay to just let go and allow somebody else to take charge.

"What happened to your friend?"

"We don't know, exactly. That's part of the problem."

"Well, we'll find out what we can." Cathy gave Cilla a comforting squeeze as they crowded onto an elevator with visitors and flowers and Mylar balloons. "What's his name?"

"Steve. Steven Chensky."

Cathy took out a red leather notebook and a silver pen to note it down. "How long's he been in?"

"I'm not sure. I've lost track. We got here about eight, I think, into the ER, and he was there for a little while before they brought him up. Maybe an hour ago?"

"I know that seems long, but it's not, really. Here now." Cathy patted Cilla on the back when the elevator doors opened. "You go on and sit, and I'll see what I can find out."

"Thank you. Thank you so much."

"Don't you give it a thought."

Cilla walked back to the waiting room but didn't sit. She didn't want to sit with the others who were waiting for word on a friend, on a loved one. On life and death. She wished for a window. Whose idea had it been to design an interior waiting room with no windows? Didn't they understand people needed to stare out? To will their minds outside the room?

"Hey." Ford stepped up beside her with a large go-cup.

"Thanks."

"Cathy's talking to people."

"It's very kind of her. She's very fond of you. When she first came up, I thought she was an old girl-friend."

"Man." Mortification flashed. "She's a mom. She's Brian's mom."

"A lot of men go for older women, sport. And she looks really good."

"Mom," Ford repeated. "Brian's mom."

Cilla started to smile, then tensed when Cathy stepped in.

"First, Dr. North is operating," Cathy began in brisk, practical tones that were enormously comforting. "He's one of the best. You're very, very lucky there."

"Okay." Cilla's breath eased out. "All right."

"Next, do you want all the medical terms, the jargon?" Cathy held up her notebook.

"I . . . No. No, I want, just, to know."

"He's holding his own. He's stable. It's going to be another couple of hours, at least. And there are other injuries that need to be addressed." She flipped the book open now. "Two broken ribs. His nose and left cheekbone were broken, and his kidney's bruised.

His head injuries are the most serious, and Dr. North's working on him. He's young, fit, healthy, and those factors are in his favor."

"Okay." Cilla nodded. "Thank you."

"Why don't I check back in a little while?" Cathy took Cilla's hand.

"I appreciate it, Mrs. Morrow, very much."

"Cathy. And it's nothing. Take care of her," she said to Ford, and left them alone.

"I'm going to go out, call the house. Let everyone know what's going on."

"I did that," Ford told her, "when I got your drink. But we can do an update."

They walked. They sat. They stared at the waiting room TV someone had tuned to CNN. As the projected couple of hours became a few, Cathy came back in.

"He's out of surgery. Dr. North will come in to talk to you."

"He's—"

"They won't tell me much right now, except that he made it through. That's a good thing. Ford, you make sure Cilla has my number. You call me if you need anything. All right?"

"Yes." Cilla's fingers tightened like wires on Ford's when the man in green scrubs paused in the doorway. His gaze scanned the room, paused on Cathy with a flicker of acknowledgment. And Cathy's hand rested briefly on Cilla's shoulder.

"You call," she repeated, and moved away as the doctor crossed the room.

"Miss McGowan?"

"Yes. Yes. Steve?"

North sat. His face looked quiet, Cilla thought. Almost serene, and smooth, smooth as brown velvet. And he angled his body toward hers, kept his dark eyes on her face as he spoke.

"Steve suffered two skull fractures. A linear fracture here," he said, running his finger along the top of his forehead. "That's a break in the bone that doesn't cause the bone to shift. Those usually heal on their own. But the second was a break here." Now he held his hand to the base of his skull. "A basilar fracture. And this more severe break caused bruising of his brain, and bleeding."

"You fixed him."

"He came through the surgery. He's going to need further tests. We'll monitor the pressure inside his skull in the ICU with a device I inserted during surgery. When the swelling goes down, we'll remove it. He has a good chance."

"A good chance," she repeated.

"There could be brain damage, temporary or permanent. It's too soon to tell. Right now, we wait and we monitor. He's in a coma. His heart is very strong."

"Yes, it is."

"He has a good chance," North repeated. "Does he have family?"

"Not here. Just me. Can I see him?"

"Someone will come in to take you up to ICU shortly."

When they did, she stared down at him. His face under the clouds and streams of bruises was deathly pale. It wasn't right, was all she could think. None of this was right. He didn't even look like Steve with those blackened, sunken eyes, and his nose all swollen, and the white bandages around his head.

They'd taken his earring off. Why did they do that?

He didn't look like Steve.

She took the small silver hoop out of her ear and, bending over him, fixed it to his. And brushed his bruised cheek with a kiss.

"That's better now," she whispered. "That's better. I'm going to be here, okay?" Lifting his hand, she kissed his fingers. "Even when I'm not here, I'll be here. You don't get to leave. That's the rule. You don't get to leave me."

She stayed, holding his hand, until the nurse shooed her out.

Part Two

REHAB

Change your opinions,
keep to your principles;
Change your leaves,
keep intact your roots.

—VICTOR HUGO

ELEVEN

"We can take shifts." Ford glanced over at Cilla as he drove. She hadn't objected when he insisted she needed to go home, get some rest, have a meal. And that worried him. "They're pretty strict in ICU anyway, and don't let you hang out very long, so we'll take shifts. Between you and me, Shanna and some of the guys, we'll cover it."

"They don't know how long he'll be in a coma. It could be hours, or days, and that's if—"

"When. We're going with *when*."

"I've never had a very optimistic nature."

"That's okay." He tried to find a tone between firm and sympathetic. "I've got one and you can borrow a piece."

"It looked like he'd been beaten. Just beaten."

"It's the skull fracture. I talked to one of the nurses when you were in with him. It's part of it." Knowing it, even knowing it, he thought, hadn't dulled the shock when he'd been allowed a minute with Steve. "So's the coma. The coma's not a bad thing, Cilla. It's giving his body a chance to heal. It's focusing."

"You do have plenty of optimistic pieces. But this isn't a comic book where the good guy pulls it out every time. Even if—or we can go with your rainbow *when*—he comes out of it, there could be brain damage."

He'd gotten that, too, but saw no point in pushing through to worst-case scenario. "In my rainbow world, and in your darker version, the brain relearns. It's a clever bastard."

"I didn't get the goddamn padlock."

"If somebody got in the barn and went at Steve, why do you think a padlock would've kept them out?"

She curled her fingers into her palms as they approached her drive. "I took down the gates. And planted fucking trees."

"Yeah, I figure the trees are what did it. Makes it all your fault." He waited for her to take a shot at him—better, to his mind, than wallowing. But she said nothing. "Okay, again, if someone wanted in, how would a couple of wrought-iron panels stop them? What happened to pessimism?"

She only shook her head and stared at the house. "I don't know what I'm doing here. That crazy old man was probably right. The place is cursed. My uncle died, my grandmother, and now Steve may die. For what? So I can buff and polish, paint and trim this place? Looking for that link, that click, that connection with my grandmother because I've got none with my own mother? What's the point? She's dead, so what's the *point?*"

"Identity." Ford gripped her arm before she could push the car door open. "How can we know who we really are until we know where we came from, and overcome it, build on it or accept it?"

"I know who I am." She wrenched free, shoved the door open. Slammed it behind her.

"No, you really don't," Ford responded.

She strode around the side of the house. Work, she thought, a couple hours of sweaty work, then she'd clean up and go back to the hospital. The patio had been repaired, the new slate laid, with the walkways roped and dug except for the one she'd added to the plans. The one leading to the barn. Yellow crime-scene tape crossed over her barn door like ugly ribbon over a nasty gift. She stared at it as Shanna dropped her shovel and raced over the lawn.

Cilla willed her compassion back into place. She

wasn't the only one worried and distressed. "There's no change." She gripped Shanna's extended hand.

The rest of the landscape crew stopped working, and some of the men from inside the house stepped out. "No change," she repeated, lifting her voice. "They've got him in ICU, monitoring him, and they'll be doing tests. All we can do is wait."

"Are you going back?" Shanna asked her.

"Yeah, in a little while."

"Brian?"

Brian gave Shanna a quick nod. "Go ahead."

Yanking her phone out of her pocket, Shanna strode toward the front of the house.

"Her sister can pick her up," Brian explained. He pulled his cap off his short brown hair, raked grimy fingers through it. "She wanted to knock off when you got here, go by and see Steve herself."

"Good. That's good."

"The rest of us, and Matt and Dobby and such, we'll go by, too. Don't know as they'll let us in to see him, but we'll go by. Shanna had a jag earlier. She's blaming herself."

"Why?"

"If she'd let him stay the night, and so on." Sighing, he replaced his cap. After one glance at Ford, he got the picture. Taking off his sunglasses, he focused his summer blue eyes on Cilla. "I told her there's no ifs, and no blame except for whoever did that to Steve. Start hauling out the ifs and the blame, you could just as soon say if Steve hadn't gone out to play pool, if he hadn't gone in the barn. And that's crap. Best thing is to hold good thoughts. Anyway."

He took a bandanna out of his pocket to wipe the sweat from his face. "The cops were here, as I guess you can see. Asking questions. I can't say what they're thinking about this."

"I hope they've stopped thinking he was drunk and did that to himself."

"Shanna set them straight on the drunk part."

"Good." It loosened one of the multitude of knots in her belly. "I met your mother."

"Did you?"

"At the hospital. She was a lot of help. Well." Tears continued to burn the back of her eyes as she stared into the sunlight. "The patio looks good."

"Helps to have work."

"Yeah. So give me some, will you?"

"That I can do." He shot a smile at Ford. "How about you? Want a shovel?"

"I like to watch," Ford said easily. "And I've got to check on Spock."

"Just as well. Give this guy a shovel or a pick?" he said to Cilla. "And if there's a pipe or a cable in the ground, he'll hit it, first cut."

"That only happened once. Maybe twice," Ford qualified.

WHEN THE CREW KNOCKED OFF, she knocked off with them and hit the shower. She wanted to say she felt human again, but was still well shy of the mark. Like an automaton, she pulled on fresh clothes. She decided she'd buy some magazines, something to occupy her mind at the hospital, and maybe snag a sandwich from a vending machine.

When she jogged downstairs, Ford stood in her unfinished living room.

"I'd say you're making progress, but I don't know that much about it, and it doesn't look like it to me."

"We're making progress."

"Good. I've got dinner out on the veranda. Spock sends his regards as he's dining at home this evening."

"Dinner? Listen, I—"

"You have to eat. So do I." He grabbed her hand, pulled her out. "We've got my secondary specialty."

She stared at the paper plates and cups, the bottle of wine and the can of Coke. And in the center of the folding table sat a dish of macaroni and cheese.

"You made mac and cheese?"

"Yeah, I did. That is, I put the package in the microwave and programmed according to directions. It's mac and cheese if you aren't too fussy." He poured some wine in a paper cup. "And the wine'll help it along."

"You're not having wine."

"That's 'cause I like the nuked version just fine, and I'm driving you to the hospital."

A hot meal, companionship. Help. All offered, she thought, without a need for asking. "You don't have to do that, do this."

He pulled her chair out, nudged her into it. "It's more satisfying to do something you don't have to do."

"Why are you?" She looked up, into his eyes. "Why are you doing this for me?"

"You know what, Cilla, I'm not entirely sure. But . . ." He pressed his lips to her forehead before he sat. "I believe you matter."

She clutched her hands in her lap as he scooped out two heaping spoons of the macaroni and cheese onto her plate. Then, to clear her throat, she took a sip of wine. "That's the second thing you've said to me today no one else ever has."

Those eyes of his lifted, zeroed in on hers. "No one ever told you you mattered?"

"Maybe Steve. In different words, in different ways. But no, not just that way."

"You do. Go on and eat. That stuff gets cold, it turns to cement."

"The second thing—or the first, actually, that you said to me today was you wouldn't leave me alone."

He only looked at her, and she couldn't tell if it was pity or understanding, or simply patience, on his face. Whatever it was, she knew it was exactly what she needed. And so much what she'd never expected to find.

"I guess you meant it, because here you are." She stabbed up a forkful, slid it into her mouth and smiled around it. "It's terrible. Thanks," she said and stabbed another bite.

"You're welcome."

THERE WAS NO CHANGE when they arrived at the hospital, and no change when they left hours later. Cilla slept with the phone clutched in her hand, willing it to ring, willing the on-duty nurse to call to tell her Steve was awake and lucid.

But no call came. The dreams did.

SHENANDOAH VALLEY
1960

"This is how it looked, the first time I saw it. My little farm."

In red capri pants, a white shirt tied at the midriff and white Keds, Janet strolled arm in arm with Cilla. Janet's sunshine hair bounced in a jaunty ponytail.

"Of course, that's not true—exactly—as when I first came here there were the trailers, the lights, the cables, the trucks. The city we make on locations. You know."

"Yes, I know."

"But we're looking through that now. As I did then. What do you see?"

"A pretty house, with simple lines. A family home with wide, welcoming porches with old rocking chairs where you can sit and do absolutely nothing. Sweet little gardens and big shade trees."

"Keep going."

"The big red barn, and oh! Horses in the paddock!" Cilla rushed over to the paddock fence, thrilled with the breeze that fluttered through her hair and rippled the manes on the mare and her foal. "They're so beautiful."

"Did you always want a pony?"

"Of course." Laughing, Cilla turned her head to smile at Janet. "Every little girl wants a pony. And a puppy, a kitten."

"But you never got them."

"No, I had call sheets and script changes. You know."

"Yes, I know."

"A chicken house! Just listen to them cluck." The sound made her laugh again. "And pigs rooting in their pen. Look at the fields. Is that corn? And there's a kitchen garden. I can see the tomatoes from here. I could grow tomatoes."

Janet's smile was both indulgent and amused. "And have a pony, a puppy and a kitten."

"Is that what I want? I'm not ten anymore. Is that what I want? I can't seem to figure it out. Is it what you wanted?"

"I wanted everything I didn't have, and if I got it, it was never exactly what I wanted after all. Or in the long run. Even this place." She swept out an arm, a graceful dancer's gesture, to encompass the farm. "I fell in love, but then I fell easy and often, as everyone knows, and out again. And I thought, I have to have it."

Lifting both her arms, Janet turned, circle after circle. "The family home with the wide, welcoming porches, the big red barn, tomatoes on the vine. That's what I've never had. But I can buy it, I can own it." She stopped spinning. "Then, of course, I had to change it. The gardens had to be lusher, the colors bolder, the lights brighter. I needed bright, bright lights. And even though I made it bolder, brighter, even though I brought the stars here to stroll like Gatsby's ghosts across the lawn, it never really changed. It never lost its welcome. And I never fell out of love."

"You came here to die."

"Did I?" Janet cocked her head, looked up under her lashes, suddenly sly. "You wonder, don't you? It's one of the reasons you're here. Secrets—we all have them. Yours are here, too. It's why you came. You told yourself you'd put it back, as it was, and somehow put me back. But like me, you'll make changes. You already have. It's not me you're look-ing for. It's you."

In the dream she felt a quick shiver, a chill from truth. "There is no me without you. I see you when

I look in the mirror. I hear you when I speak. There's a filter over it all, just enough to dim the brilliance, but you're under there."

"Did you want the pony or the call sheets, Cilla?"

"For a while, I wanted both. But I'd have been happier with the pony." Cilla nodded, looked back toward the house. "Yes, and the family home. You're right. That's why I'm here. But it's not enough. The secrets, the shadows of them. They're still here. People get hurt in the dark. Steve got hurt in the dark."

"Then turn on the lights."

"How?"

"I'm just a dream." Janet smiled, shrugged. "I don't have any answers."

WHEN SHE WOKE, Cilla grabbed the phone she'd dropped in her sleep and speed-dialed the hospital. No change.

She lay in the dim light of predawn, the phone pressed between her breasts, wondering if she should feel fear or relief. He hadn't died in the night, hadn't slipped away from her while she slept. But he still lay trapped in that between world, that place between life and death.

So she'd go talk to him, nag him, browbeat him into waking up. She climbed out of bed, cleaned herself up. She'd make coffee, she thought, make lists for any of the subs she might miss while she was at the hospital.

As she passed the next bedroom she stopped, and studied Ford. He slept half in, half out of the sleeping bag. And what was out, she had to admit, was very nice.

The dog curled at the foot of the bag, snoring like a chain saw in mid-massacre. Ford hadn't wanted Spock to spend the night alone, she remembered, and went to get him when they returned from the hospital. Went to get his dog, she thought, after he told her he'd be sleeping in the spare room.

He wouldn't leave her alone.

She went down, made the coffee, drinking hers on the back veranda. There had been no patio in the dream, but her subconscious had known Janet had added that, and the walkways. The crops in the field, another given. The kitchen garden? She couldn't remember if that had been original, or one of Janet's additions. Either way, it was something she herself wanted.

And the barn? It was no longer red. That bright color had weathered away long ago. The coffee turned bitter in her throat as she stared at the yellow tape crossing the door. If Steve died, she'd tear the bastard down. Tear it down, burn it, and everything inside it.

Squeezing her eyes shut, she battled back the anger that wanted to scream out of her. If he lived, she told herself, if he came back whole, she'd paint it that bright, happy red again. Red with white trim.

"Please, God."

Why God gave a damn if she burned the barn to the ground or painted it red with yellow smiley faces she couldn't say. But it was the best she had.

She went back inside, poured another mug and carried it upstairs to Ford.

She sat cross-legged beside him and, sipping her own second cup of coffee, gave him a good study. Unlike his dog, he didn't snore, which added points in his favor, but the way he sprawled indicated bed hog. Points deducted. He had a good growth of stubble going, considering he hadn't shaved the day before, but she had to admit it added a sexy edge to the package.

He wasn't what she'd call buff or ripped, but reasonably toned over a build that leaned toward skinny. Just a touch of gawkiness, she mused. Add a few cute points for that.

He had good arms. Strong, lean rather than bulky. Best, she thought, they knew how to hold on.

Major points, she decided. He just kept racking them up.

And the lips—top score. Leaning over, she rubbed hers to his. He made a humming sound in his throat, reached out. When she eased back, his eyes blinked open.

"Hey."

"Hey yourself."

"Did you have a bad dream?"

"No. A strange one, but I'm prone to them. It's morning."

"Uh-uh." He shifted enough to turn his wrist, blink at his watch. At the foot of the bag, Spock yawned, a high-pitched whine, then went back to snoring. "Nope. Six-forty isn't morning. Crawl in here with me. I'll prove it."

"Tempting." More so when he tugged her head down again and improved, considerably, on her casual wake-up kiss. "Very tempting," she said. "But some of the crew should be pulling up in about twenty minutes."

"I can get it done in twenty minutes." He winced. "That probably didn't translate to my advantage."

"Have coffee." She held out the mug, waved it slowly under his nose.

"You brought me coffee?" He sat up, took the first sip. "Now you have to marry me."

"Really?"

"Yeah, and bear me eight young, dance naked for my pleasure every Tuesday and wake me with coffee—that's after the sex—every morning. It's the law of Kroblat."

"Who's Kroblat?"

"Not who. The planet Kroblat. It's a very spiritual place," he decided on the spot. "I try to live my life by its laws. So, we'll have to get married and all the rest."

"We'll get on that, first chance." She brushed her hand over his hair. "Thanks for staying."

"Hey, I got coffee, a wife and eight kids out of it. You checked on Steve?"

"No change. I'm going to go see him. Maybe I can bitch-talk him awake, you know?"

"Maybe. Give me ten minutes, I'll drive you."

"No. No, I'm fine. I'm going to sit with him awhile, nag him awhile. Then I'm going to pick up some supplies and materials, drop them back here. I'll be back and forth a lot today. Let me ask you something. If I made a bargain with myself—or with God, fate. Whatever. And it was that I'd paint the barn red, red with white trim if Steve comes out of this okay, would I be jinxing it if I bought the paint before . . . before he comes out of it?"

"No. In fact, it shows faith."

She shook her head. "I knew you'd say that. I'm just the opposite. Too scared to buy the damn paint." She pushed to her feet. "I'll see you later."

"I'll be by the hospital."

She stopped at the door, hesitated, then turned back to look at him. "I can pick up dinner for tonight, if you want."

"That'd be great."

"I really want to sleep with you." She smiled when he nearly bobbled the coffee and when Spock's tiny ears perked. What a pair they were. "I really want to know what it's like, to just let go. But I guess it's like buying the paint, for now."

He kept his gaze on hers, and smiled. Slowly. "I've got time. For later."

Ford sat where he was, drinking coffee and making a mental note to write down that stuff about Kroblat. It could come in useful sometime, somewhere.

He felt pretty damn good for a man who'd slept on the floor, he decided. And one who'd had some trouble not thinking about the woman sleeping on the floor in the next room.

Now, since he was up at this ungodly hour, he'd drag his ass across the road, get in a workout, check on Steve, get a couple solid hours in on the novel, then drop by the hospital.

"You get your lazy ass up, too," he said to Spock, and juggled the dog fully awake with his foot. He heard the first truck pull up as he pulled on his pants. By the time he was dressed and pouring a second cup of coffee, with Spock doing what Spock had to do in the backyard, the noise and activity level hit the red zone. Deciding he'd just borrow the mug and bring it back later, Ford headed outside with the coffee.

He saw Brian directing one of his men toward the back of the house with what looked like a load of sand. Ford shot up a wave. "Hey, Bri."

"Well, hey." With his thumbs in his front pockets, Brian strolled over and shot a meaningful look toward the house. "And hey."

"Nah. Separate rooms. I didn't want her to be alone."

"How's she doing?"

"Seems steadier this morning. She's already on her way to see Steve."

"Shanna called the hospital. No change yet. It's the damnedest thing. Hell of a nice guy."

"Yeah." Ford looked over at the barn. "How much paint do you figure it'd take to do that barn?"

"Hell if I know. Ask a painter."

"Right." He glanced over as another car pulled

up. "This place is a madhouse half the time. I'm going home."

"Cops." Brian jerked his chin. "Cops're back. I hope to hell they don't want to talk to Shanna again. It gets her going."

"I'll see if I can take it."

Neither of the men who stepped out of the Crown Vic were the cop—Taney, Ford remembered—they'd talked to the day before. Neither of them wore a uniform, and instead sported suits and ties. Detectives, he assumed.

"Hey, how's it going?"

The taller of the two, with snow-salted gray hair and prominent jowls, gave Ford a curt nod. The second, small, lean and black, eyed him coolly.

And both, he noted, stared down at the dog that stared up at them.

"Cilla—Miss McGowan's—not home," Ford began. "She left for the hospital about fifteen, twenty minutes ago."

Tall White Guy studied him. "And you'd be?"

"Sawyer. Ford Sawyer. I live across the road. I spoke with Officer Taney yesterday."

"You live across the road, but you stayed here last night. With Miss McGowan."

Ford sipped his coffee, met Short Black Guy's eyes

while Spock grumbled. "Is that a statement or a question?"

"Your hair's still wet from the shower."

"So it is." Ford offered an easy smile, then sipped his coffee.

Tall White Guy took out a notebook, flipped pages. "Can you tell us where you were night before last, between two and five A.M.?"

"Sure. Would you mind doing the ID thing? It's not just for TV."

"Detective Urick, and my partner, Detective Wilson," Tall White Guy said as they both produced their badges.

"Okay. I was in bed—over there—from about one A.M. until I heard the sirens yesterday morning."

"Have company?"

"Yeah, Spock." He gestured at the dog. "You could take a statement from him, but I'd have to translate so it probably wouldn't work. Look, I get you have to check out everything and everyone, but the fact is somebody was out here a few nights before. I saw somebody skulking around with a flashlight."

"We got that." Urick nodded. "You're the only one who claims to have seen anything. What's your relationship with Miss McGowan?"

Ford beamed an exaggerated country-rube grin. "Friends and neighbors."

"We have the impression, from other sources, that your relationship is more than friendly."

"Not yet."

"But you'd like it to be."

As Ford blew out a breath, Spock began to circle the cops. He wouldn't bite, but Ford knew if irritated enough, Spock would sure as hell lift his leg and express his opinion.

Bad idea—probably.

"Spock, say hello. Sorry, he's feeling a little irritated and ignored. If you'd take a minute and shake, he'll settle."

Wilson crouched, took the paw. "How's it going? Damnedest-looking dog I ever saw."

"Got some bull terrier in there," Urick commented, and leaned down to shake.

"Yeah, at least that's what I've been told. Okay, back to would I like it to be more than friends and neighbors. Have you seen Cilla? Met her? If so, you'd know I'd have to be stupid not to like it to be. What does that have to do with Steve?"

Urick gave Spock an absent scratch before straightening. "Miss McGowan's ex-husband, staying with her. Three's a crowd."

"Again, only if you're stupid. But you've made it clear that none of what happened was an accident." Ford turned, studied the barn. "Somebody was in there, and whoever it was fractured Steve's skull and left him there. Just left him there."

The thought of that, just the thought of that stirred the rage he'd managed to hold still and quiet. "Son of a bitch. What the hell were they looking for?"

"Why do you think someone was looking for anything?" Urick demanded.

Ford's eyes were cold green ice when he turned back. "Give me a fucking break. Not some scavenger, either, not some asshole poking around trying to score a pair of Janet Hardy's shoes to sell on eBay. That doesn't follow."

"You've given this some thought."

"I think a lot. Listen, look at me as long as you want, as hard as you want. If you've got more questions, I'll be around."

"We'll find you, if and when," Wilson called out.

No doubt about it, Ford thought as he headed for home with his dog.

TWELVE

He wanted to get into the barn, and Ford figured if he tried it, it would add a few more layers to the suspect cake the cops were baking for him.

He was a suspect. It was actually kind of cool.

God, once a nerd always a nerd, he thought as he went through a series of lats and flys.

Once he'd worked up a sweat and an appetite, he checked in with the hospital, downed some cereal. Showered, shaved, dressed, he stepped into his office, up to his workstation.

He closed his eyes, held up his hands and said, "Draco braz minto."

The childhood ritual put everything outside the work, and Ford into it. He sat, picked up his tools and began to draw the first panel for Brid.

CILLA HAD her chair angled toward the bed so she could look directly into Steve's face as she spoke.

And she spoke, keeping up a constant one-sided conversation, as if any appreciable stretch of silence could be deadly.

"So it's moving. Clicking along better than I anticipated, even with the changes and additions I made to the original plans. The attic space shows real promise. Later on, I'm going to go pick out the flooring for up there, and the fixtures and tiles for that bath, and the master. We'll be able to have a beer out on the patio, soon as you're ready. What I need is pots. A couple of big-ass pots. Monsters. Oh, and I'm going to plant tomatoes. I think it's about the right time to do that. And, like, peppers, maybe carrots and beans. I should wait until next year when the house is done, but I think I could scratch out a square for a little garden now. Then—"

"Miss McGowan."

Cilla took a breath. When it hurt her chest to draw it in, it told her she'd been pushing too hard. "Yes." What was the nurse's name, the nurse with the curly blond hair and warm brown eyes? "Dee. It's Cilla."

"Cilla. The police are out there. A couple of detectives. They asked to speak to you."

"Oh. Sure. Just a sec. I've got to do this thing," she told Steve. "I'll be back."

Spotting the cops was the easiest thing she'd done all day, Cilla thought. She stepped up to them. "I'm Cilla McGowan."

"Detective Wilson. My partner, Detective Urick. Is there somewhere we could talk?"

"There's a little waiting room down here. They've got something they call coffee. You're looking into what happened to Steve now," she said as she led the way.

"Yes, ma'am."

"Then you know he didn't trip over his own feet, bash himself in the head and fall under his own bike." She hit the coffeepot, added powdered creamer. "Do you know what did happen?"

"We're looking into it," Urick said. "Do you know anyone who'd wish Mr. Chensky harm?"

"No. He's only been here a few days. Steve makes friends, not enemies."

"You were married."

"That's right."

"No hard feelings?" Wilson prompted.

"None. We were friends before we got married. We've stayed friends."

"He's living with you."

"No, he's visiting me, and giving me a hand for a couple of weeks on the house. I'm rehabbing the house. He's in the business."

"*Rock the House*," Urick commented. "I've caught the show."

"Best there is. You want to know if we're sleeping together. No. We have, but we're not."

Wilson pursed his lips, nodded. "Your neighbor, Mr. Sawyer, states that he saw a prowler on your property a few nights ago."

"Yeah, the night Steve got in. Steve heard something outside."

"You didn't."

"No, I sleep like a rock. But Steve woke me up, said he heard something. I brushed it off." The guilt wormed its way back. "Then Ford mentioned the flashlight he'd seen. I was supposed to get a padlock for the barn, and I let it slip by."

"We noticed you seem to be using the barn to store things. Boxes, furniture . . ."

"Junk," Cilla finished, and nodded at Urick. "I brought it down from the attic. I'm having the attic finished off and needed to clear it out. I've been sorting, but it's a big job. I thought I'd separated what struck me as potentially valuable, but it's hard to tell on a couple of passes."

"You didn't notice anything missing?"

"Not at this point."

"Some of the boxes were crushed, the furniture knocked over." Wilson gestured. "It looked, possibly, as if Mr. Chensky drove his bike into the barn, lost control, went down."

"That's not what happened. You know he wasn't drunk or stoned."

"His alcohol level was well under the legal limit," Urick agreed. "There were no drugs in his system."

Inside her chest, her heart began a tripping beat. "A sober man, and one who's straddled a Harley for about a dozen years, doesn't get off the bike, open the door, get back on the bike and *yee-haw* drive in over a bunch of boxes and furniture."

"The X-rays indicate Mr. Chensky was struck at the base of the skull. Probably a crowbar or tire iron."

Cilla pressed her hand to her heart as it tightened to a fist. "Oh, God."

"The force of the blow pitched him forward, dropped him so that he hit the concrete floor, which caused the second fracture. Our reconstruction indicates the Harley was rolled to where Mr. Chensky lay, then pushed over on top of him, breaking two of his ribs and bruising his kidney."

Urick waited, watched as Cilla set her coffee down, as her hand trembled. Her color went from pale to ghostly. "Now, let me ask you again. Do you know anyone who'd wish Mr. Chensky harm?"

"No. No, I don't know anyone who'd want to hurt him. Who'd do something like that to him."

"How did Sawyer get along with him?"

"Ford?" For a moment she went blank. "Fine. They hit it off. Big-time. Steve's a fan. He's even got . . . Oh, for God's sake."

Understanding, Cilla pressed her fingers to her eyes, then dragged them back through her hair. "Okay, follow the dots, please. I am not and was not sleeping with Steve. I am not and was not sleeping with Ford, though that is on the table. Ford did not attack Steve in a jealous rage as I don't think he has a lot of rage in the first place and, more importantly, he knew there was nothing to be jealous about. I was up front with him regarding my relationship with Steve, and in fact was out with Ford the night Steve got hurt. The night both myself *and* Ford knew Steve had gone out to sniff around Shanna Stiles. There's no romantic or sexual triangle here. This isn't about sex."

"Miss McGowan, it looks as though someone was in your barn, and may have been lying in wait. You and Sawyer knew Mr. Chensky had gone out for the evening, and that he stored his motorcycle in the barn."

"That's right, that's absolutely right, Detective Wilson. Just like we both knew he'd gone out to try to score with a very attractive brunette. Neither of us could know if he'd get lucky or bomb out. So you're suggesting that after spending the evening with me, Ford snuck back, hid out in my barn, just in case Steve came back. It doesn't make any sense."

Shock, anger, guilt, annoyance all drained into sheer misery. "None of this makes any sense."

"We'd like you to go through the items you have stored in the barn, see if anything's been disturbed or taken."

"All right."

"Your grandmother left a deep mark," Wilson continued. "I'd guess most people figured anything of hers in that house was taken away a long time ago. Word gets out, as word will, there's still some things around, someone might be interested enough to break into a barn."

"And fracture a man's skull. Yeah. The thing is? Most of what's in the barn is from the McGowans. The ordinary side of the family."

She went back to Steve, but this time sat in silence.

When she left, walked to the elevator, she saw her father get off the car. "Dad."

"Cilla." He strode quickly toward her, took her shoulders. "How is he?"

"The same, I guess. He's critical. He came through the surgery, and that's a plus, but . . . A lot of buts and ifs and maybes."

"I'm so sorry." He pulled her tight for a moment. "I know I only met him a couple of times, but I liked him. What can I do?"

"I just don't know."

"Let me take you downstairs, get some food in you."

"No, actually, I'm just leaving for a while. I have some errands." To get out, to do, to stop thinking for just a couple of hours. "Maybe . . . Do you think you could go in and sit with him for a little bit? Talk to him? He liked you, too."

"Sure, I will."

"And when you leave? Remind him that I'll be back later. I'll be back."

"All right."

Nodding, she pressed for the elevator, hitched her bag on her shoulder. "I appreciate . . . I really appreciate you coming. You barely know him. Hell, you barely know me."

"Cilla—"

"But you came." She stepped into the elevator, turned, met her father's eyes. "You came. It means a lot," she said as the doors closed between them.

WORK. WORK GOT HER THROUGH the day. And the next day. She was better at work, she thought, than at sentiment, at expressing emotions—unless they were scripted. She made her schedule, and stuck to it. So many hours on the house, on the landscaping, so many at the hospital, so many in the barn.

That left her so many hours to fall on her air mattress and clock out.

So far, she thought, so good.

Except Steve's mother had jumped down off her broomstick and thrown the schedule into the Dumpster. So, more time for work, Cilla told herself. More time to get things done.

She picked up a pole lamp, scowled at the six funnel-shaped shades running down the spotted brass rod. "What were they smoking when they bought this?"

On impulse, she took a few running steps and launched it at the open barn doors like a javelin. Then yipped when Ford stepped into view. He jumped back so the lamp whizzed by his face with a few layers of dust to spare.

"Jesus *Christ!*"

"I'm sorry, I'm sorry. I didn't see you."

"Shouldn't you yell 'fore,' or something?" he demanded. "How the hell would I have explained that one? Yes, Doctor, I've been impaled through the brain by perhaps the ugliest pole lamp in the history of pole lamps."

"I don't think it would've impaled. More dented. Anyway, it offended my eye."

"Yeah, mine too. Almost literally. What are you doing back here? It's early for you," he added when she frowned at him. "I saw your car. I thought maybe . . ."

"No. Nothing new. Except Steve's mother's there."

"Yeah. I ran into her this morning for a minute." He dipped his hands into his pockets, hunched a little. "She's scary."

"She hates me. For marrying Steve, for divorcing him. She doesn't actually like Steve all that much, but me? She hates. So I cleared the field. Deserted, actually. I don't do well with mothers."

"You do okay with your stepmom. She sent over that nice casserole last night."

"Tuna noodle. I'm not sure that's a sign of affection."

"It is, take my word." He stepped through and around some of the mess to get to her, to touch her cheek. "You're working too hard, beautiful blond girl."

"I'm not." She pulled away, kicked at one of the boxes. "The cops want me to go through this stuff, to see if anything's missing."

"Yeah. I think I've been bumped down the suspect

list, which is oddly disappointing. Tall White Guy asked me to sign a copy of *The Seeker: Indestructible* for his grandson."

"Tall . . . oh, Urick. I told them it wasn't about you or Steve or me. But what the hell is here? What's here somebody would want so damn bad? It's junk. It's trash. It should be tossed, all of it. I'm tossing it," she decided in an instant. "Help me toss it."

He grabbed her, pulled her back up as she started to drag up a box. "No. You don't toss when you're churned up. And you know that what someone might have wanted isn't here. Because you already found it and put it somewhere else."

"The letters."

"That's right. Did you tell the cops about the letters?"

"No."

"Why not?"

"I don't know, exactly. Partly because all I could really think about at first was Steve. And what would they do with the letters? Thirty-five-year-old letters, unsigned, no return address."

"Fingerprints, DNA. Don't you watch *CSI*?"

"Fact, fantasy. And it'll leak. It always leaks, that *is* a fact. Letters from a lover, days before her death. Was it suicide? Was it murder? Was she carrying a love child? All the speculation, the print, the airtime, the reporters, the obsessed fans, it all pumps up. Any chance I had here, at peace, at a life, pretty much goes up in flames."

"Why?"

"I don't want to live like that, in the crosshairs of the camera lens. I want this to be my home." She heard the edge of desperation in her own voice but couldn't dull it. "I wanted to bring something back from her, and for her. But I wanted it to be mine at the end of the day."

"You don't want to know who wrote those letters?"

"Yes, I do. I do. But I don't want to ruin his life, Ford, or his children's lives because he had an affair, because he broke off the affair. Even if he was cruel about it. There has to be a statute of limitations. Thirty years should cover it."

"Agreed."

He said nothing more, just watched her, looked into her eyes until she closed them.

"How could anyone prove it?" she demanded. "If, if, if she didn't kill herself. If, if, if some of the conspiracy theories have been close to true and someone—this someone—made her take the pills, or slipped them to her. How could we prove it?"

"I don't know, but the first step would be asking the right people the right questions."

"I don't know the people or the questions, and I can't think about this. Not now. I need to get through today, then get through tomorrow. I need—"

She threw herself against him, locking her arms around his neck while her mouth latched on to his. He wasn't prepared for the eruption, the bursts of desperation and appetite. Who could have been? With quick, catchy gasps, low, sexy moans, she devoured. She hooked one of those long, long legs around him, sank her teeth into his bottom lip, tugged. And he went instantly, helplessly, hard as stone.

She rubbed her body against his until he could literally feel the blood draining out of his head and heading south. "Lock the door." Her lips moved to his ear, parted on a breathless whisper. "Lock the door."

He quivered, felt the shock of need ram into him—head, belly, loins—like fists. "Wait." Even as he said it his mouth collided with hers again for one more greedy gulp. But he managed to order himself to pull back, to get his hands on her shoulders to peel her away, a couple of inches.

"Wait," he repeated, and momentarily forgot his train of thought as those brilliant blue eyes burned into his.

"No. Now."

"Cilla. Whoa. Jeez. I can pretty much feel myself growing breasts as I say this."

She took his hands, pulled them down, pressed. "Those are mine."

"Yeah." Soft, firm. "They are." And with considerable regret, and what he considered heroic restraint, he put his hands back on her shoulders. "Where was I? I meant to say, even at the risk of sounding like a girl, this isn't right."

She slid her hand over his crotch. "Then what's this?"

"The penis has a mind of its own. And boy, oh boy," he managed as he took her wandering hand and yanked it up. "I should get an award for this. A monument. Let's just step back."

"Step *back*?" Shock and insult leaped out with the words. "Why? What the hell is wrong with you?"

"The penis is asking those exact questions. But the thing is . . . wait," he ordered, taking a firm hold of her arms when she started to jerk away. "The thing is, Cilla, you don't toss stuff out when you're churned up. Just like when you're churned up, you don't . . . lock the barn door."

"It's just sex."

"Maybe. Maybe. But when it happens? It's going to be just you and me. Just you." He tested his willpower by leaning down and taking her mouth in a slow, soft kiss. "Just me. No Steve or Steve's mom, no Janet Hardy, no letters. Just us, Cilla. I want lots of alone with you."

She let out a sigh, gave one of the boxes a half-hearted kick. "How am I supposed to feel pissed off and rejected after that?" Hooking her thumbs in her pockets, she lowered her gaze deliberately to his crotch. "Looks like that's still doing a lot of thinking. What are you going to do about it?"

"I just need to get a picture of Maylene Gunner in my head."

"Maylene Gunner."

"Maylene was mean as a snake, big as a battleship and ugly as homemade sin. She beat the living snot out of me when I was eight."

No, she couldn't possibly stay pissed off. "Why would Maylene do that?"

"Because I had drawn a very unflattering portrait of her. I didn't possess the talent to draw a flattering one. Da Vinci didn't possess that much talent. I drew her as a kind of Goodyear Blimp, soaring and farting. Very colorful. Little people on the ground clutching themselves or lying sprawled and unconscious, running for cover."

"Cruel," Cilla said as her lips twitched.

"I was eight. In any case, she got wind—so to speak—and ambushed me and proceeded to pound me to dust. So when I need to, I just picture that Jupiter-sized face, and . . ." He glanced down, smiled. "There we go. Retired from the field."

Cilla studied him a moment. "You're a very strange man, Ford. Yet oddly appealing. Like your dog."

"Don't get me started again. Even Maylene Gunner has only so much power. Why don't I give you a hand here, then we'll go see Steve together. Between the two of us, we can take his mama."

Yes, she thought, a very strange and appealing man. "Okay. You can start by taking what's left of that pole lamp out there to the Dumpster."

SHE GOT THROUGH THE DAY, got through the night. And Cilla geared herself up for her second visit of the day, and second confrontation with Steve's mother. Pacing in front of the hospital entrance, she gave herself a pep talk.

It wasn't about her, wasn't about old business, grudges, one-upmanship. It wasn't about tossing a bucket of water on the Wicked Witch of the West.

It was about Steve.

She bounced her shoulders to loosen them like a boxer before a bout, and stepped toward the doors as someone called her name.

Relief at the temporary interruption might have

been cowardly, but she'd take what she could get. Turning, she smiled at Cathy and Tom Morrow.

Cathy reached out to rub a hand along Cilla's arm. "How's your friend?"

"The same. Pretty much the same. I want to thank you again for your help when Steve was in surgery."

"It was nothing."

"It was a lot to me. Are you volunteering today?"

"Actually, we're here to see our goddaughter. She had a baby."

"That's nice. Well . . ." Cilla looked back toward the doors.

"Would you like me to go up with you first?" Cathy offered.

"No, no, I'm fine. It's just . . . Steve's mother's probably up there. She harbors extreme dislike for me. It makes it pretty tight in that room with both of us in there."

"I can fix that." Cathy held up a finger. "Why don't I go up, lure her away for fifteen or twenty minutes."

"How?"

"Volunteer mode. I'll buy her a cup of coffee, lend a shoulder. It'll give her a break and give you a few minutes alone with your friend."

"She can do it," Tom said with a shake of his head. "Nobody resists Cathy."

"I'd be so grateful."

"Nothing to it. Tom, keep Cilla company for a few minutes. Five should do it." With a cheery wave, Cathy strode into the hospital.

"She's great."

"Best there is," Tom agreed. "Let's sit down over here, give her that head start. I was sorry to hear about your friend."

"Thank you." Three days, she thought. Three days in a coma.

"Do the police have any idea how it happened?"

"Not really. I guess we're all hoping Steve can tell us if . . . when," she corrected, "he wakes up."

She caught a glimpse of a white van crossing the parking lot and, with a shudder, looked away.

"I hope that's soon." Tom gave her hand an encouraging pat. "How's Brian doing on your place?"

"It's shaping up. He does good work. You must be proud of him."

"Every day. It's an ambitious project you've taken on. The grounds, the house. A lot of time, money and sweat. Word gets around," he added.

"It'll be worth it. You should drop by sometime, look at the progress."

"I was hoping you'd ask." He winked at her.

"Anytime, Mr. Morrow."

"Tom."

"Anytime," Cilla repeated, and pushed to her feet. "I'm going to sneak up, see if Cathy had any success."

"You can take it to the bank. I'll say a prayer for your friend."

"Thanks."

And this, Cilla thought as she crossed the lobby to the elevators, was the reason to make this home. People like the Morrows, and like Dee and Vicki and Mike, the ICU nurses she saw every day. People who cared, who took time.

People like Ford.

Hell, even people like cranky, dyspeptic Buddy.

She stepped off the elevator and spotted Mike at the nurses' station. "How's he doing?"

"Holding steady. Kidney functions are normal. That's an improvement."

"Yeah, it is. Is anyone with him?"

Mike wiggled his eyebrows. "Mrs. Morrow breezed in and took Mrs. Chensky down for coffee. You got a clear road."

"Hallelujah."

Bruises still covered his face, but they were turning yellow at the edges. Thick stubble masked his jawline and pricked her when she leaned over to kiss him. "I'm back. It's hot out this afternoon. Strip-it-off weather."

She tuned out the machines, started to turn to the window to describe the view for him before she relayed construction progress. And she saw the sketch taped to the glass wall.

"What have we got here? Con the Immortal?" She glanced back at Steve. "Did you see this? Striking resemblance."

Ford had drawn it. Cilla didn't need to see the signature looped in the bottom corner to know it. Steve stood, wearing what she supposed was a loincloth, with thick black straps crossing over his chest, and knee boots. His hair flew out as if in a strong wind, and his face was set in a fierce, fuck-you grin. His hands rested on the hilt of a sword, with its point planted between his spread feet.

"Big sword, obvious symbolism. You'd love that. And the biceps bulging over the armbands, the tats, the necklace of fangs. Con the Immortal. He's got you pegged, doesn't he?"

Tears rose hot in her throat, were ruthlessly swallowed down. "You've really got to see this, okay?" She crossed back to take Steve's hand. "You've got to wake up and see this. It's been long enough now, Steve, I mean it. Goddamn it. This bullshit's gone on long enough, so stop screwing around and . . . oh God."

Had his hand moved? Had it moved in hers or had she imagined it? She let her breath out slowly, stared down at the fingers she held in hers. "Don't make me yell at you again. You know if I cut loose I can out-bitch your mother. Who's going to come back here pretty soon, so . . ."

The fingers twitched, curled. The lightest of pressure on hers.

"Okay, okay, stay there, don't go anywhere." She reached for the call button, held her finger down on it. "Steve, come on, Steve, do it again." She lifted his hand, pressed her lips to it. Then, narrowing her eyes, bit. And laughed when his fingers twitched and curled again.

"He squeezed my hand," she called out as Mike came in. "He squeezed it twice. Is he waking up? Is he?"

"Talk to him." Mike moved to the side of the bed, lifted one of Mike's eyelids. "Let him hear your voice."

"Come on, Steve. It's Cill. Wake up, you lazy bastard. I've got better things to do than stand around here and watch you sleep."

On the other side of the bed, Mike checked pulse, pupils, BP. Then pinched Steve hard on the forearm. The arm jerked.

"He felt that. He moved. Steve, you're killing me. Open your eyes." Cilla grabbed his face, put her nose nearly to his. "Open your eyes."

They fluttered, and she felt another flutter on her chin. More than his breath, she realized. A word.

"What? What? Say it again."

She leaned down, her ear at his lips. She caught his slow, indrawn breath, and heard the hoarse, raw whisper of a single word. He said, "Shit."

Cilla let out a sob that choked into a laugh. "Shit. He said shit!"

"Can't blame him." Quickly, Mike strode to the door to signal another nurse. "Page Dr. North. His patient's waking up."

"Can you see me?" Cilla demanded when his eyes opened. "Steve? Can you see me?"

He let out a weary sigh. "Hi, doll."

SHE SPOKE to the doctor, even managed to smile genuinely at Steve's mother before she locked herself in a bathroom stall for a jag of weeping relief. After she'd washed her face, slapped on makeup and sunglasses to hide the damage, she went back to the nurses' station.

"He's sleeping," Mike told her. "Natural sleep. He's weak, and he's still got a lot of healing to do.

You should go home, Cilla. Get a good night's sleep yourself."

"I will. If he asks for me—"

"We'll call you."

For the first time Cilla stepped into the elevator with an easy heart. As she crossed the lobby, she pulled out her phone and called Ford.

"Hey, beautiful blond girl."

"He woke up." She moved down the sidewalk toward the parking lot with a bounce in every step. "He woke up, Ford. He talked to me."

"What'd he say?"

" 'Shit' came first."

"As it should."

"He knew me, his name and all that. His left side's a little weaker than his right, just now. But the doctor says he's looking good. They have to do tests, and—"

"Looking good works. Do you want me to come by, bring you some dinner?"

"No, I'm heading home now. He's sleeping. Just sleeping. I wanted to tell you. I just wanted to say that I saw your sketch, and I was teasing him about it right before . . . I think it might have done the trick."

"Nothing stops Con the Immortal for long."

"You are so— Oh God! Son of a bitch!"

"What? What was that?"

She stared down at the door of her truck. "I'll be home in a few minutes. I'll come by."

She clicked off before Ford could respond. And read what someone had written on the driver's-side door in black marker.

WHORES BEGET WHORES!

THIRTEEN

Ford watched Cilla take digitals of the pickup's door. His rage wanted to bubble up, but he couldn't figure out what he'd do with it if he spewed.

Kick the tires? Punch a couple of trees? Stalk around and froth at the mouth? None of the options seemed particularly helpful or satisfying. Instead he stood with his hands jammed in his pockets, and the rage at a low, simmering boil.

"The cops'll take pictures," he pointed out.

"I want my own. Besides, I don't think Wilson and Urick are going to make this a priority."

"It could be connected. They'll be here in the morning."

She shrugged, then turned the camera off, stuck it in her pocket. "That's not coming off. The sun baked that marker on so it might as well be paint. I'll have to have the whole damn door done. I haven't had this truck three months."

While he watched, she kicked a tire. He decided he'd been right. She didn't look satisfied. "You can use my car until it's fixed."

"I'll drive this." Both the defiance and the temper glared out of her eyes. "I know I'm not a whore. I saw Hennessy's van in the parking lot before I went in to visit Steve. He could've done this. He could've hurt Steve. He's capable."

"Did Steve say anything about it?"

"We didn't ask him. He was still so weak and dis-oriented. Probably tomorrow, the doctor said. He'd be up to talking to the police tomorrow. Damn it!"

She stalked for a few minutes but, he noted, didn't froth at the mouth or punch a tree. Then she stopped, heaved out a breath. "Okay. Okay. I'm not going to let some asshole spoil this really excellent day. Does the liquor store in town have any cham-pagne in stock?"

"Couldn't say. But I do."

"How come you have everything?"

"I was a Boy Scout. Seriously," he said when she laughed. "I have the merit badges to prove it." She was right, he decided, no asshole should be allowed to spoil an excellent day. "How about we heat up a frozen pizza and pop the cork?"

From his perch on the veranda, Spock leaped up and danced.

"Sounds good to me, too." As she moved in to kiss him, a horn beeped cheerfully.

"Well," Ford said when a Mustang convertible in fire-engine red pulled in behind Cilla's car, and Spock tore down the steps to spin in delirious circles, "it had to happen sometime."

The vivid color of the car had nothing on the windswept red mop of the woman who waved from the passenger seat, who tipped down her big, Jackie O sunglasses to peer at Cilla over the top as she stepped out onto peep-toe wedges to greet the bouncing, spinning dog.

The driver unfolded himself. It was the height and the build that alerted Cilla, even before she got a good look at the shape of the jaw.

Her palms automatically went damp. This was definitely meet-the-parents. An audition she invariably failed.

"Hello, my cutie-pie!" Penny Sawyer clamped her hands on Ford's cheeks once he'd walked down the slope to her. She kissed him noisily. Her laugh was like gravel soaked in whiskey.

"Hey, Mama. Daddy." He got a one-armed bear hug from the man with hair of Cary Grant silver. "What are y'all doing?"

"Heading out to Susie and Bill's. Texas Hold 'Em tournament." Penny poked Ford in the chest while

Ford's father squatted to shake hands with Spock. "We had to drive right by, so we stopped in case you wanted in."

"I always lose at poker."

"You don't have gambling blood." Penny turned her avid eyes on Cilla. "But you do have company. You don't have to tell me who this is. You look just like your grandmama." Penny moved forward, hands outstretched. "The most beautiful woman I ever saw."

"Thank you." Left with no choice, Cilla wiped her hands hurriedly on her pants before taking Penny's. "It's nice to meet you."

"Cilla McGowan, my parents, Penny and Rod Sawyer."

"I know your daddy very well." Penny shot a sly glance at her husband.

"Now you cut that out," Rod told her. "Always trying to make me jealous. Heard a lot of good things about you," he said to Cilla.

"Heard hardly a syllable out of this one." Penny poked Ford again.

"I am the soul of discretion."

Penny let out her quick, rumbling laugh again, then dug into her purse. She pulled out an enormous Milk Bone that sent Spock into a medley of happy growls, grunts and groans while his body quivered and his bulging eyes shone.

"Be a man," she said to the dog, and Spock rose up on his hind legs to dance in place. "That's my sweetheart," she crooned and held the biscuit out. Spock nipped it and, with a full-body wag, ran off to chomp and chew. "I have to spoil him," she said to Cilla. "He's the closest thing resembling a grandchild I've gotten out of this one."

"You have two of the human variety from Alice," Ford reminded her.

"And they get cookies when they visit." She gestured to the house across the road. "It's a good thing you're doing, bringing that place back to life. It deserves it. Your grandfather's going to be at the game tonight, Ford. My daddy was madly in love with your grandmother."

Cilla blinked. "Is that so?"

"Head over. He has scores of pictures she let him take over the years. He wouldn't sell them for any price, even when I had a notion to frame a few and display them at the bookstore."

"Mama owns Book Ends in the Village," Ford told Cilla.

"Really? I've been there. I bought some landscaping and design books from you. It's a nice store."

"Our little hole in the wall," Penny said. "Oh now, look, we're going to be late. Why do you let me talk so much, Rod?"

"I have no idea."

"Y'all change your mind about the game, we'll make sure you get a seat at a table. Cilla, they'd just love to have you, too," Penny called out as Rod pulled her down to the car. "I'm going to have Daddy bring those pictures over for you to look at."

"Thank you. Nice to meet you."

"Ford! You bring Cilla over for dinner sometime."

"In the car, Penny."

"I'm getting, I'm getting. You hear?"

"Yes, ma'am," Ford called back. "Win a bundle."

"I'm feeling *lucky*!" Penny shouted as Rod zipped into reverse, then zoomed on down the road.

Cilla said, "Wow."

"I know. It's like being lightly brushed by the edge of a hurricane. Leaves you a little surprised and dazed, and sure that much more and you'd be flat on your ass."

"You look a lot like your father, who is very handsome, by the way. But your mother? She's dazzling."

"She is, as her own father likes to say, a corker."

"Corker." Cilla laughed as they walked into the house. With a polite burp, Spock trotted in with them. "Well, I like her, and I tend to eye mothers suspiciously. Speaking of corks. Where's the champagne?"

"Spare fridge, mudroom."

"I'll get that, you get the pizza."

Moments later, she came back into the kitchen with a bottle of Veuve Clicquot and a puzzled frown. "Ford, what are you doing with all that paint?"

"The what?" He looked over from setting the oven. "Oh that. There's a zillion gallons of primer, a zillion of exterior red, and a slightly lesser amount of exterior white, for trim."

As her heart did a slow somersault, she set the bottle on the counter. "You bought the barn paint."

"I don't believe in jinxes. I do believe in positive thinking, which is just really hope anyway."

Everything inside her shifted, settled. Opened. She stepped to him, laid a hand on his cheek, laid her lips on his. Warm as velvet, tender as a wish, the kiss flowed. Even when he shifted so she pressed back against the counter, it stayed slow and silky, deep and dreamy.

When their lips parted, she sighed, then rested her cheek against his in a gesture of simple affection she gave to very few. "Ford." She drew back, sighed again. "My head's too full of Steve to meet your requirements for sex tonight."

"Ah. Well." He trailed a fingertip up her arm. "Realistically, they're more loose guidelines than strict requirements."

She laughed, caressed his cheek once more. "They're good requirements. I'd like to stick to them."

"Got no one to blame but myself." He stepped around her to slide the pizza into the oven.

"So we'll eat bad pizza, get a little buzzed on champagne and not have sex."

Ford shook his head as he removed the foil and the cage on the bottle. "Almost my favorite thing to do with a beautiful woman."

"I don't fall for guys. It's a policy," she said when he paused and glanced over at her. "Considering the influence of inherited traits—and the track record of my grandmother and mother in that area—I've taken a pass. Steve was an exception, and that just showed how it can go. So I don't fall for guys. But I seem to be falling for you."

The cork exploded out of the bottle as he stared at her. "Does that scare you?"

"No." He cleared his throat. "A little. A moderate amount."

"I thought it might because it's got me jumpy. So I figured heads-up."

"I appreciate it. Do you have, like, a definition for the term 'fall for'?"

God, she thought as she looked at him. Oh my God, she was a goner. "Why don't you get the glasses? I think we could both use a drink."

SHE HIRED PAINTERS, and had some of the crew haul the paint to the barn. She talked to the cops, and made a deal with a local body shop to paint the door of her truck. Whenever she caught sight of the white van, she had no qualms about shooting up her middle finger.

No evidence, the cops said. Nothing to place Hennessy at the scene on the night Steve was attacked. No way to prove he decorated her truck with hate.

So she'd wait him out, Cilla decided. And if he made another move, she'd be ready.

Meanwhile, Steve had been bumped down to a regular room, and his mother had hopped back on her broomstick to head west.

Dripping sweat from working in the attic, Cilla stood studying the skeleton of the master bath. "It's looking good, Buddy. It's looking good for tomorrow's inspection."

"I don't know why in God's world anybody needs all these showerheads."

"Body jets. It's not just a shower, it's an experience. Did you see the fixtures? They came in this
morning."

"I saw. They're good-looking," he said, grudgingly
enough to make her smile.

"How are you coming with Mister Steam?"

"I'll get it, I'll get it. Don't breathe down my
neck."

She made faces at his back. "Well, speaking of
showers, I need one before I go in to see Steve."

"Water's turned off. You want this done, water's
got to stay off."

"Right. Shit. I'll grab one over at Ford's."

She didn't miss the smirk he shot her, but opted
to ignore it. She grabbed clean clothes, stuffed them
in her purse. Downstairs, she had a few words with
Dobby, answered a hail from the kitchen area, then
spent another ten minutes outside discussing foundation plantings.

She dashed across the road before someone could
catch her again, and decided to slip into the shower
off the gym rather than disturb Ford.

It wasn't until she was clean, dry and wrapped in
a big white towel that she realized she'd left her
purse—and the clothes in it—sitting on her front
veranda.

"Oh, crap."

She looked down at the sweaty, grungy clothes she'd stripped off and dragged a hand through her clean hair. "No, I am *not* crawling back into them."

She'd have to disturb Ford after all. Bundling her underwear and baggy work shorts in her T-shirt, she tied it off and carried the bundle with her.

She opened the door to the kitchen, to a very surprised Ford.

"Oh, hi. Listen—"

"Ford, you didn't tell us you had company."

"I didn't know I did. Hey, Cilla."

Her expression went from slightly harried to mildly ill as she looked over and saw Ford's mother sitting at the kitchen bar with an older man.

While she stood frozen, Spock dashed over to rub against her bare legs. "Oh God. Oh God. Just . . . God. I'm sorry. Excuse me."

Ford grabbed her arm. "Back up like that, you'll pitch right down the steps. You've met my mother. This is my grandfather, Charlie Quint."

"Oh, well, hello. I apologize. I'm, well, what can I say? Ford, I didn't want to interrupt you. I thought you'd be working. They had to turn the water off at my place for a while, so I ran over to use your shower downstairs—thanks for that. And then realized that when I was being distracted by varieties of spirea, I left my bag and my clothes sitting on the veranda. I came up to ask if you wouldn't mind running over there and, you know, getting them. My clothes."

"Sure." He sniffed at her. "My soap smells better on you than on me."

"Hah."

"Cilla, I bet you'd like a nice glass of iced tea." Penny rose to get a glass.

"Oh, don't bother, I—"

"No bother. Ford, go on now, get this girl her clothes."

"All right. But it's kind of a shame. Isn't it, Granddad?"

"Pretty legs on a pretty woman are easy on the eyes. Even old eyes. You look more like her in person than you do in pictures I've seen of you."

How much more awkward could it be? Cilla wondered when Ford winked and slipped out. "You knew my grandmother."

"I did. I fell in love with her the first time I saw her on the movie screen. She was just a little girl, and I was just a boy, and that was the sweetest kind of puppy love. You never forget your first."

"No, I guess you don't."

"Here you go, honey. Why don't you sit down?"

"I'm fine. Thanks." She stared at the glass Penny offered and wondered how to take it as she had one hand holding the bundle of filthy clothes, and the other clutched on the towel.

"Oh, are those your dirty clothes? Just give those to me. I'll toss them in Ford's machine for you."

"Oh, no, don't—"

"It's no trouble." Penny pulled them away, pushed the cold glass into Cilla's hand. "Daddy, why don't you show Cilla the pictures? We were going to drop by to do just that," Penny continued from the mudroom. "Just stopped to say hi to Ford first. My goodness! You must've worked up a storm today."

Casting her eyes to the ceiling, Cilla moved closer to the counter as Charlie opened the photo album.

"These are wonderful!"

At the first look, she forgot she was wearing only a towel and edged closer. "I haven't seen these before."

"My personal collection," he told her with a wistful smile. "This one here?" He tapped a finger under a picture. "That's the first one I ever took of her."

Janet sat on the steps of the veranda, leaning back, relaxed and smiling in rolled-up dungarees and a plaid shirt.

"She looks so happy. At home."

"She'd been working with the gardeners—walking around with them, showing them where she wanted her roses and such. She got word I took pictures and asked if I'd come over, take some of the house and grounds as things were going on. And she let me take some of her. Here she is with the kids. That'd be your mother."

"Yes." Looking bright and happy, Cilla thought, alongside her doomed brother. "They're all so beautiful, aren't they? It almost hurts the eyes."

"She shone. Yes, she did."

Cilla paged through. Janet, looking golden and glorious astride a palomino, tumbling on the ground with her children, laughing and kicking her feet in the pond. Janet alone, Janet with others. At parties at the farm. With the famous, and the everyday.

"You never sold any of these?"

"That's just money." Charlie shrugged. "If I sold them, they wouldn't be mine anymore. I gave her copies of ones she wanted, especially."

"I think I might have seen a couple of these. My mother has boxes and boxes of photos. I'm not sure

I've seen all of them. The camera loved her. Oh, this! It's my favorite so far."

Janet leaned in the open doorway of the farmhouse, head cocked, arms folded. She wore simple dark trousers and a white shirt. Her feet were bare, her hair loose. Flowers spilled out of pots on the veranda, and a puppy curled sleeping at the top of the steps.

"She bought the puppy from the Clintons." Penny stepped beside her father, rested a hand on his shoulder. "Your stepmama's people."

"Yes, she told me."

"Janet loved that dog," Charlie murmured.

"You need to make copies for Cilla, Daddy. Family pictures are important."

"I guess I could."

"Granddad's going to make copies for Cilla," Penny announced as Ford walked in with Cilla's bag. "He has the negatives."

"I could scan them. If you'd trust me with them. Here you go." Ford passed the bag to Cilla.

"Thanks." Sensing Charlie's hesitation, Cilla eased back. "They're wonderful photographs. I'd love to look through the rest, but I have to get to the hospital. I'm just going to . . ." She held up the bag. "Downstairs."

"You look more like her than your mother," Charlie said when Cilla reached the door. "It's in the eyes."

And in his lived such sadness. Cilla said nothing, only slipped quickly downstairs.

CILLA DID a mental happy dance as the first tiles were laid in the new master bath. She glugged down water and executed imaginary high kicks through the first run of subway tiles in what would be her most fabulous steam shower.

The black-and-white design, retro cool Deco, added just the right zing.

Stan, the tile guy, glanced over his shoulder. "Cilla, you *gotta* get the AC up."

"We're working on it. By the end of the week, I promise."

It had to be running by week's end, she thought. Just as the bed she'd ordered had to be delivered. Steve couldn't recuperate in a steamy house, in a sleeping bag.

She went back to framing in the closet in the master bedroom. In a couple of weeks, she thought, if everything stayed on schedule, she'd have two completed baths, the third, fourth and the powder room on the way. She'd be ready for Sheetrock up in her attic office suite, the replastering should be about wrapped. Then Dobby could start work on the ceiling medallions. Well, he could start once she'd settled on a design.

She ran through projections while she checked her level, adjusted, shot in nails.

And in a few weeks, she'd take the contractor's exam. But she didn't want to think about it. Didn't want to think if she didn't make it, she'd have to ask one of her own subs for a job by the end of the year. If she didn't make it, she couldn't afford to buy that sweet little property down the road in the Village that she *knew* would make an excellent and profitable flip.

If she didn't make it, it would be another failure. She really thought she was at her quota already.

Positive thinking, she reminded herself. That's what Ford would say. No harm in trying.

"Gonna make it," she stated aloud and stepped back from the framing with a nod of approval. "Gonna kick exam *ass*. Cilla McGowan, Licensed Contractor."

Gathering her tools, she started out to check on the progress of her exterior office stairs with a quick peek at the tile work on the way. She joined the carpenter crew as the painters, working on her new scaffolding, added the first strokes of red to the barn.

The air smelled of the mulch freshly laid around new plantings, and salvaged ones. Roses, hydrangeas, spirea and old-fashioned weigela, and beds of hopeful new perennials, eager annuals already blooming insanely.

More to come, she thought, more to do. But here was progress. Tear-out time was done. Renewal time was here.

She thought of Charlie's photo album. And breaking off from the work, ran in to get her camera to document.

Shirtless men slick with sweat and sunscreen high on scaffolding. Shanna in shorts and a bright pink T-shirt and ball cap working with Brian on a low, dry stone garden wall. The bones of her stairs, the half-finished back veranda. And around front, the completed one.

For a moment, in her mind's eye, she saw Janet, leaning on the jamb of the open front door, smiling out.

"It's coming back," Cilla said softly.

Turning, she saw Ford and Spock walking down the drive.

The dog trotted up to her, leaned on her legs,

then sat back to look up at her, all love and cheer. She rubbed, petted, kissed his nose.

"Brought you a present." Ford handed her one of the two Cokes he carried. "I swung in to see Steve. He tells me they're going to spring him in a couple days."

"He's coming back strong." Like the farm, she thought. "I'm pushing to get the AC up, and I've got a bed coming."

"You want him to recoup from having his skull fractured in a construction zone. Do you hear that?" Ford asked, tapping his ear.

Cilla shrugged off the buzzing, the banging, the whirl of drills. "To people like me and Steve, that's chamber music."

"I'll have to take your word for it. But he could bunk at my place. I've got the bed, the AC. And digital cable."

She took a long drink, watching him. "You really mean that."

"Damn right. I pity anyone without digital cable."

"I bet. But you're not going to take on my ex-husband. He'll need to be . . . Who's this?" she wondered as a black Lexus turned cautiously into her drive.

"City car," Ford commented. "Big city."

"I don't know who . . . Crap."

Ford lifted his brows as men exited from both sides of the car. "Friends of yours?"

"No. But the driver's my mother's Number Five."

"Cilla!" Mario, handsome as sin, Italian style, in Prada loafers and Armani jeans, threw out his arms and a wide, wide smile. His graceful forward motion was spoiled when he stopped, then sidestepped around the sniffing Spock.

The sunglasses hid his eyes, but she suspected they were dark and sparkling. Tanned, panther lean, dark hair flowing, he crossed to her, caught her in an enthusiastic embrace and kissed her cheeks. "Look at you! So fit, so competent."

"I am. What are you doing here, Mario?"

"A little surprise. Cilla, this is Ken Corbert, one of our producers. Ken, Cilla McGowan, my step-daughter."

"It's a real pleasure." Ken, small and wiry, silver-winged black hair, pumped Cilla's hand. "Big fan. So . . ." He scanned the farm. "This is the place."

"It's my place," she said coolly. "Ford, Mario and Ken. I'm sorry, I can't ask you in. We're a work in progress."

"So I see." Mario's smile never dimmed. "And hear."

"Spock, say hello," Ford ordered—after his dog had finished with the tires. "He wants to shake," Ford explained, "to make sure you're friendly."

"Ah." Mario studied the dog dubiously as he put the tips of his thumb and forefinger on the offered paw.

Spock didn't appear to be impressed.

Ken gave Spock's paw the same salesman pump he'd given Cilla's.

"Lovely country," Mario continued. "Just lovely. We drove down from New York. We had some meetings. Such scenery! Your mother sends her love," he added. "She would have come, but you know how difficult it is for her. The memories here."

"She's in New York?"

"A quick trip. We barely have time to catch our breath. Fittings, rehearsals, meetings, media. But Ken and I must steal you away, a late lunch, an early drink. Where can we take you?"

"Nowhere, but thanks. I'm working."

"Didn't I tell you?" Mario let out a hearty laugh while Spock squatted on his haunches and stared at him with suspicious eyes. "Cilla is the most amazing woman. So many talents. You can spare an hour, *cara.*"

"I really can't. Especially if this is about performing in Mom's show. I told her I wasn't interested."

"We're here to persuade you that you are. Perhaps you'd excuse us," Mario said to Ford.

"No, he won't." Cilla pointed at Ford. "You won't."

"I guess I won't."

Irritation tightened Mario's mouth briefly. The grumbling growl from Spock had him eyeing the dog with some trepidation. "You have a chance to make history, Cilla. Three generations performing together. You saw Céline perform with Elvis? We have that technology. We can bring Janet onstage with you and Bedelia. One extraordinary performance, live."

"Mario—"

"I understand you're reluctant to commit to doing the full set of duets with your mother, though I can tell you—as will Ken—what that would mean to the show, and to you. Your career."

"The advertising and promotion we've got lined up," Ken began. "We can all but guarantee sellouts in every venue. Then the cable special, the CD, the DVD. The foreign markets are already buzzing. We may be able to work a deal to attach a second CD, a special package, for you, solo. In fact, Mario and I were kicking around ideas for videos there. And you're right, Mario, shooting here would add punch."

"You've been busy, haven't you?" Cilla's voice was as soft, and as meaningful, as Spock's growl. "And you've been wasting your time. No. I'm sorry, Ken, I don't believe Mario made it clear. I'm not looking to be persuaded or revived or promoted. You have no business talking to producers, promoters, advertisers about me," she said to Mario. "You're not my agent or my manager. I don't have an agent or a manager. I run the show now. And this is what I do. Houses. I do houses. Enjoy the scenery on the way back."

She knew Mario would come after her. Even as she turned on her heel to stride away, she heard him call her name. And she heard Ford speak to Ken, caught the extra yokel he put in his voice.

"Spock, stay. So y'all drove down from New York City?"

"Cilla. *Cara*. Let me—"

"Touch me, Mario, and I swear I'll deck you."

"Why are you angry?" There was puzzled sorrow in his voice. "This is an insanely rich opportunity. I'm only looking out for your interests."

She stopped, struggled with temper ripe to bursting. "You may actually believe that on some level. I can look after my own interests, and have been for a long time."

"Darling, you were mismanaged. Otherwise you'd be a major star today."

"I might be a major star today if I'd had the talent and the aptitude. Listen to what I'm saying to you: I don't want to be a major star. I don't want to perform. I don't want that kind of work. I don't want that kind of life. I'm happy here, Mario, if that matters to you. I'm happy with what I have, and I'm getting happy with who I am."

"Cilla, your mother needs you."

"And here it comes." She turned away in disgust.

"She has her heart set. And the backers will do so much more with this addition. She's so—"

"I can't do it, Mario. And I won't. I'm not just being a hard-ass. I can't. It's not in me. You should have talked to me before you came here, and brought him. And you should *listen* to me when I say no. I'm not Dilly. I don't bullshit, I don't play. And she's already used up all her guilt points with me. I'm not doing this for her."

His face, his voice, held nothing but sadness now. "You're very hard, Cilla."

"Okay."

"She's your mother."

"That's right. Which makes me, let's see. Her daughter. Maybe, this time—this one time—she could think about what I need, about what I want." She held up a hand. "Believe me, if you say anything else, you'll only make it worse. Cut your losses here. You're smart enough. Tell her I said knock them dead, break a leg. And I mean it. But that's all I've got."

He shook his head as a man might over a sulking child. He walked away in his excellent shoes, and got into the big city car with Ken to drive away.

Ford wandered over, stared off at the barn while Spock rubbed himself against Cilla's legs. "That red's going to look good."

"Yeah. You're not going to ask what that was about?"

"I got the gist. They want, you don't. They pushed, you didn't budge. They pissed you off, which is fine. But in the end it made you sad. And that's not. So I don't care about them or what they want. I say fuck 'em, and that red looks good going on that barn."

It made her smile. "You're good to have around, Ford." She leaned down, ruffled Spock. "Both of you. Back in L.A., I'd have paid several hundred dollars for this kind of therapy."

"We'll bill you. Meanwhile, why don't you show me what's going on around here today?"

"Let's go bug the tile guy. It's my favorite so far." She took Ford's hand and walked into the house.

FOURTEEN

When Cilla showed Dobby the design she wanted for the medallions, he scratched his chin. And she saw his lips twitching at the corners.

"Shamrocks," she said.

"I've had me a few beers on Saint Patrick's Day in my time. I know they're shamrocks."

"I played around with other symbols. More formal, or more subtle, more elaborate. But I thought, screw that, I like shamrocks. They're simple and they're lucky. I think Janet would've gotten a kick out of them."

"I expect she would. She seemed to like the simple when she was around here."

"Can you do it?"

"I expect I can."

"I'll want three." The idea made her giddy as a girl. "Three's lucky, too. One for the dining room, one for the master bedroom, and one in here, in the living room. Three circles of shamrocks for each. I'm not looking for uniformity but more symmetry. I'll leave it to you," she said when he nodded.

"It's good working on this place. Takes me back."

They sat at a makeshift table, plywood over a pair of sawhorses. She'd brought him a glass of tea, and they drank together while Jack finished up the last of the plaster repairs.

"You'd see her around, when she came out to stay here?"

"Now and again. She always had a word. Give you that smile and a hello, how are you."

"Dobby, in that last couple of years, when she came out, was there any talk about her being . . . friendly with a local man?"

"You mean being sweet on one?"

Sweet on, Cilla thought. What a pretty way to put it. "Yes, that's what I mean."

The lines and folds on his face deepened with thought. "Can't say so. After she died, and all those reporters came around, some of them liked to say so. But they said all kinds of things, and most weren't in the same neighborhood as the truth."

"Well, I have some information that makes me think she was sweet on someone. Very sweet. Can you think of anyone she spent time with in that last year, year and a half? She came out fairly often during that period."

"She did," he agreed. "Talk was, after her boy died, the talk was she was going to sell the place. Didn't want to come here no more. But she didn't sell. Didn't have the parties or the people, either. Never brought the girl out again—that'd be your mother—that I saw or heard about. The best I can recall, she came alone. If anybody had wind of her seeing a man from around here, their jaws would've been working."

"Weren't so many people around to jaw back then," Jack commented as he set his trowel. "I mean to say there weren't so many houses around the farm here. Isn't that right, Grandpa?"

"That'd be true. Weren't houses on the fields across the road back then. Started planting them back twenty-five years on to thirty years back, I guess it was, when the Buckners sold their farm off."

"So there weren't any close neighbors."

"Buckners would've been closest, I expect. About a quarter mile down."

And that was interesting, Cilla decided. How hard could it be to have a secret affair when there were no nosy neighbors peeking out the window? The media would have been an extra challenge, but reporters hadn't been camped on the shoulder of the road seven days a week when Janet had traveled to the farm.

According to what she'd read or been told, Janet had been an expert at keeping certain areas of her private life private. After her death, facts, fallacies, rumors, secrets and innuendos abounded.

And still, Cilla mused, the identity of Janet's last lover remained blank. Just how badly, she wondered, did she want to fill in that blank in her grandmother's life?

Badly enough, she admitted. The answer to that single question could finally give clarity to the bigger question.

Why did Janet Hardy die at thirty-nine?

CILLA FOUND BRINGING Steve home both thrilling and terrifying. He was alive, and considered well enough to leave the hospital. Two weeks before, she'd sat beside his bed, trying to will him out of a coma. Now she stood with him as he studied the farmhouse. He leaned on a cane, a ball cap on his head, dark glasses over his eyes, and his clothes bagging a bit from the weight he'd lost in the hospital.

She wanted to bundle him inside, into bed. And feed him soup.

The terror came from wondering if she was competent enough to tend to him.

"Stop staring at me, Cill."

"You should probably get inside, out of the sun."

"I've been inside, out of the sun. Feels good out here. I like the barn. Barns should always be red. Where the hell is everybody? Middle of the day, no trucks, no noise."

"I told all the subs to take me off today's schedule. I thought you'd need a little peace and quiet."

"Jesus, Cilla, when did I ever want peace and quiet? You're the one."

"Fine, I wanted peace and quiet. We're going in. You look shaky."

"Goes with the territory these days. I've got it," he snapped at her when she started to take his free arm. He managed the stairs, crossed the veranda.

The scowl smoothed away when he stepped inside the house, took his first look around.

"The plastering looks good. Getting rid of that door over there, widening the opening, that works for you. Better flow."

"I'm thinking of using that area as a kind of morning room. It gets nice light. Then later on, if I'm still inclined, I could add on a sunroom, put in a hot tub, a couple of machines, some nice plants. Down the road."

"Be sweet."

And because she heard the strain in his voice, she nearly fussed about taking him up to bed. Instead she tried a different tack. The first step would be to get him upstairs.

"We've done a lot on the second floor. The master suite's really coming along. You've got to see it."

These steps were longer. She all but felt his weaker left side begin to tremble on the journey up. "We should've taken Ford up on his offer. You'd be more comfortable at his place."

"I can walk up a damn flight of steps. Got a headache, that's all. Goes with the territory now, too."

"If you want to lie down . . . I've got your pills right here."

"I don't want to lie down. Yet." He pushed her offered hand aside. Again, some of the strain eased on his face when he studied the new bedroom space. "You always had an eye. Good lines, good light. Nice closet, doll."

"A girl's best friend. I built the organizer yesterday." She opened the door, gave a Vanna White flourish.

"Cedar paneling. Good work."

"I learned from the best."

He turned away to limp toward the bath, but she'd seen the look in his eyes. "What is it? What's wrong?"

"Nothing. Sexy, classy," he said of the bathroom. "Deco deal. Glass block for the shower wall? When did you decide on that?"

"Last-minute change. I liked the effect, and the way it looks with the black-and-white tiles." She gave up, just leaned her forehead on his shoulder. "Please tell me what's wrong."

"What if I can't do this anymore? If I can't handle the tools? It takes me longer to think, and these headaches about drop me."

She wanted to hold him, hug him, nuzzle him into comfort. And instead flicked at him with mild annoyance. "Steve, it's your first day out of the hospital. What did you think, you'd walk out swinging a hammer?"

"Something like that."

"You're on your feet. You're talking to me. The doctor said it's going to take time. Just as he said you've already made an amazing recovery, and there's every reason to believe you'll get it all back."

"Could take months. Even years. And I can't remember." A trace of fear eked through frustration. "Goddamn it, I can't remember anything that happened that night after I left here. Can't remember going to the bar, or hanging out, trailing Shanna home like she says I did. It's blank. I can remember getting on the bike. I can remember thinking I might just score with Shanna of the big brown eyes and amazing rack. Next thing I remember is you yelling at me, and your face leaning down over mine. Everything between is gone. Just gone."

She shrugged, as if it was no big deal. "If you're going to forget something, that would be the night."

He smiled a little. "Fricking ray of sunshine, aren't you? I'm going to crash awhile, take some drugs and crash."

"Good idea."

He let her take his weight to lead him to the guest room. Then stopped at the doorway. The walls were painted a soft and restful blue, as was the bead-board wainscoting. The original walnut trim, stripped and restored by her own hands, framed the windows. The floor gleamed, deep, rich and glossy. The iron headboard and footboard in dignified pewter suited the simple white and blue quilt, the star-patterned rug with its blue border. White daisies sprang up out of a cobalt vase on a table in front of the window.

"What the hell's this?"

"Surprise. I think it's marginally more appealing than a hospital room."

"It's a great room." Even as he jabbed a finger at her, pleasure shone on his face. "What are you thinking, getting the floors refinished in one room?"

"I'm thinking it's nice to see one room finished— or nearly. Need some art for the walls, and I have to finish the rest of the trim, but otherwise. And check it out." She opened an old wardrobe, revealed a flat-screen TV. "Got cable." She grinned at him. "Digital, at Ford's insistence. The bath's finished, too. And looks great if I say so myself."

Steve sat on the side of the bed. "Going at rehab this way screws up the schedule."

"I'm not in a hurry." She poured a glass from the pitcher she'd placed on the nightstand, then got out the pill bottle. "Bottoms up, then we'll get you undressed and into bed."

The faintest twinkle winked in his eyes. "Time was you'd've gotten in with me, doll."

"Time was." She crouched down to take off his shoes.

"I want those subs back here tomorrow."

"Who made you job manager?" Rising, she gestured so he lifted his arms. But she smiled as she drew off his shirt. "They'll be back. They wanted to have a welcome-back party. Beer and subs. I scotched that. I guess I shouldn't have."

"I don't think I'm ready to party." He lay back so she could take off his jeans. "The day I can have a woman strip me down and not want to return the favor's not a day for partying."

"I give you a week." Now, no longer able to resist, she stroked his cheek. "I heard how you hit on all the nurses."

"It's expected. I skipped Mike." He gave her a wan smile. "Not that there's anything wrong with that."

She turned down the bed, eased him into it, slipped off his shades, took the cap off his shaved head. The smooth dome marred by the line of stitches hurt her in every cell of her body. "I'm going to be downstairs doing some paperwork. You need anything, just call. If you want the TV, there's the remote. If you want anything, Steve, I'm right here."

"Just a few z's for right now."

"Okay." She kissed his forehead, then slipped out.

Alone, he stared up at the ceiling. And, sighing, closed his eyes.

Cilla took her laptop outside to work. Though she snuck up to check on Steve twice in the first hour, she made headway with bills and cost projections.

When she heard the crunch of feet on gravel, she glanced up to see Ford and Spock.

"Hi, neighbor," he called out. "I figured if you were out here, the returning hero's doing all right."

"Sleeping." She looked at her watch. "God, how did it get to be five o'clock?"

"The earth orbits around the sun as it turns on its axis, thereby—"

"Smart-ass."

"Present. And speaking of." He shook the bag in his hand. "I've got something for Steve. Some DVDs, since you've got the set up in his room."

Cilla cocked her head. "DVDs? Porn?"

Ford's eyebrows drew together. "Porn's such a hard word. Just hear how it comes out of the mouth. That short, hard syllable. *Spider-Man*, the three-movie box set. It seemed appropriate. And a couple of others that involve naked women and motorcycles, which I'd call adult entertainment. Spock picked those out."

She slid her glance down to the dog, who cocked his head and looked innocent. "I'm sure Steve will appreciate them."

"Spock believes *Sleazy Rider* was very underrated."

"I'll take his word." She heard the footsteps first, sprang to her feet. She pulled open the screen door as Steve reached for it from the inside. "You're up.

Why didn't you call me? You shouldn't take the steps by yourself."

"I'm fine. I'm good. Ford."

"Good to see you out."

"Good to be. Hey, Spock. Hey, boy." He sat on one of the white plastic chairs, stroking the dog, who laid his front legs on Steve's knee.

"You look better," Cilla decided.

"Magic pills and sleep. I nap like a three-year-old these days, but it does the job."

"You're probably hungry. Why don't I fix you some food? Something to drink? Get you—"

"Cill." He started to tell her not to bother, changed his mind. "Yeah, I could use a sandwich or something. Not hospital food or smuggled-in goods. Maybe you could throw something together for all of us."

"Sure. Give me a few minutes."

When she dashed inside, Steve shook his head. "She's hovering, man."

"I talked her out of the little bedside john."

"I owe you. What's in the bag?"

Ford passed it over, and after a quick look, Steve broke out in a grin. "Now we're talking. Thanks. Listen, I need to get the exercise in. You spot me on a walk around?"

"Okay."

Ford waited until Steve handled the stairs, then walked with him away from the house. "Something on your mind?"

"Lots of shit, man. It still gets a little bogged coming through the channels. Cops don't have dick, right?"

"That'd be about it."

"It looks like a one-time thing. Just bad luck. I mean, nothing's happened since."

"No."

Steve stared at Ford's profile. "You'd tell me straight?"

Ford thought of Cilla's car door, but set it aside. "Nobody's broken into the barn, bothered the house."

"You were bunking here while I was in the hospital. I got word on that."

"Hey. My sleeping bag."

"So you and Cilla aren't in the sack?"

"Not quite yet."

"But you're into her. Look, that's your business, her business and all that bullcrap, but I'm asking because I need to know if you're going to look out for her when I'm gone."

Ford paused as Steve did. "Going somewhere?"

"I haven't said anything to her yet. I was going to when we got back, but Jesus, she fixed up the room for me. Down to flowers, you know. Oh, and thanks for the push on the cable."

"It's only right."

With a nod, Steve began to walk again. "The thing is, I should've headed back last week, latest. Plans changed on account of brain surgery. I'd stay if I thought she needed me to watch out for her, or I could help out. She can take care of herself, that's Christ's truth, but . . . Hell, maybe it's the near-death experience. Whatever. I want to get home. I want to sit on the beach, soak up the rays. But I need to know somebody's got her back."

"I've got her back, Steve."

Steve stopped to stare at the barn. "She said you bought the paint. While I was still out of it." He nodded, as if satisfied. "You're all right, Ford. Totally not the type she usually lets get a taste. It's about time. She digs on candles. When you're making it," Steve added. "She digs on lots of candles around. Doesn't mind music, either. Doesn't need it, like some do, but she's good with it. Lights on, lights off; she's okay either way. But she does dig on the candle thing."

Ford cleared his throat. "Appreciate the tips. How are you getting back to L.A.?"

"The doc wants to see me Friday, so I'm going to stick till Saturday. I've got a friend in New Jersey who's coming down in an RV. We'll load me and the bike up, head west. Don't say anything to her, okay? I want to tell her myself."

Cilla whistled from the veranda. "You guys want to eat?"

Spock's answer was to run toward her as if hellhounds were on his heels.

"The mountains are cool," Steve commented as they turned back. "That's part of what pulled her out east. She told me how the mountains seem like home. Me? I miss the ocean." He nudged Ford with his elbow. "And the women in very small bikinis."

SHE SLEPT POORLY, with one ear cocked for Steve, and her mind niggling over the fact he planned on leaving in a matter of days.

How could she take care of him if he was three thousand miles away?

One day out of the hospital, and he was planning cross-country trips. In an RV? It was so *like* him, she thought as she tossed over onto her back. Always had to move, never stay in one place too long. That's where the whole flipping houses came from, she reminded herself. You didn't have to settle on one if you kept turning them.

But he wouldn't listen to reason on this. And the

fact that he *was* just out of the damn hospital made it impossible to kick his ass. Who'd check on him two or three times a night as she'd done? So he'd been fine when she had. What if he hadn't been?

She rolled over again, punched her pillow. And gave up.

Dawn was about to break anyway. She'd go check on him again, then go down and make some coffee. She'd have her quiet time outside before the crew started piling in.

As she heard Steve snoring before she reached his doorway, she headed straight for coffee. In another few months, she thought, she'd have an actual kitchen. Refitted antique appliances, countertops, cabinets. Actual dishes. And damn if she wasn't treating herself to a fancy espresso maker.

Maybe she'd actually learn how to cook. She'd bet Patty could teach her some good basics. Nothing fancy and gourmet. She'd tried that route and failed spectacularly. But your basic red sauce, or meat and potatoes. Surely she could learn how to cook a chicken breast.

Once the house was finished, she promised herself. Once she had her license, geared up for business, found a routine. She'd learn how to cook for herself instead of living on sandwiches, canned soup and takeout.

She carried the coffee outside, drawing in its scent as the first sleepy light played over her new gardens, over earth still turned and waiting. She sipped while the mists rose off the pond she still had to clean.

Every day, she thought. She wanted to do this every day. To step out of her home in the soft, sleepy light and see what she could do, what she had done. What had been given to her.

Whatever she'd paid her mother for this place, this life, didn't count. In that soft and sleepy light, she knew everything she could see and smell and touch had been a gift from the grandmother she'd never met.

She would've taken coffee on a morning walk, Cilla thought as she stepped off the veranda to wander. Accounts spoke of her as an early riser, used to the demands of filming. Often up at dawn.

Often up *till* dawn, too, Cilla admitted. But that was another side of the woman. The party girl, the Hollywood queen, the star who drank too much and leaned too heavily on pills.

In the quiet morning, Cilla wanted the company of the Janet Hardy who fell in love with this little slice of Virginia. Who brought home a mongrel pup and had roses planted under the window.

The big red barn made her smile as she strolled around the house. The police tape was gone, the padlock firmly in place. And Steve, she thought, was snoring in the pretty iron bed in the pretty room upstairs.

That nightmare was done. A scavenger looking for scraps who'd panicked. The police believed that to be the case, so who was she to argue? If she wanted to solve a personal mystery, it would be the author of the letters inside *Gatsby*. And in that way, she'd put another piece of Janet's together, for her own knowledge. Her own history.

The light grew as she neared the front of the house. Birdsong sweetened the air as did the scent of roses and turned earth. Dew tickled coolly on her bare feet. It pleased her more than she could say to know she walked on her own land, over dewed grass, wearing a tank and cotton pajama pants.

And no one cared.

She finished the coffee on the front veranda, gazing out over the lawn.

Her smile faded slowly, changing into a puzzled frown as her eyes scanned the front wall.

Where were her trees? She should be able to see the bowing tops of her weeping cherries from the veranda. As the frown deepened, she set her mug on the rail, stepped down to walk along the lawn beside the gravel drive.

Then she began to run.

"No. Goddamn it, no!"

Her young weepers lay on the narrow swatch of green between her wall and the shoulder of the road. Their slender trunks bore the hack marks of an ax. It wouldn't have taken much, she thought as she crouched down to brush her fingers over the leaves. Three or four swings at most.

Not to steal. Digging them up would have taken a bit more time, a bit more trouble. To destroy. To kill.

The sheer meanness of the act twisted in her belly in a combination of sorrow and fury. Not a scavenger, she thought. Not kids. Kids bashed mailboxes along the road, so she'd been warned. Kids didn't take the time to hack down a couple of ornamental trees.

She straightened to take a steadying breath, and looked over at the broken stump of one of her dying trees. That breath caught. Her body trembled, that same combination of sorrow and fury. Black paint defiled the old stone wall with its ugly message.

GO BACK TO HOLLYWOOD BITCH!
LIVE LIKE A WHORE DIE LIKE A WHORE

"Fuck you," she said under her breath. "Goddamn it, Hennessy, fuck you."

Riding on pure fury now, she stormed back to the house to call the police.

WITH BLOOD IN HER EYE, Cilla warned every one of the crew that anyone who mentioned the trees or the wall to Steve would be fired on the spot. No exceptions, no excuses.

She ordered Brian back to the nursery. She wanted two new trees planted, and she wanted them planted that very day.

By ten, when the cops had come and gone, secure that her threat would hold and that the crew would keep Steve busy inside, she went out to work with the mason on cleaning the stone.

Ford saw her, scrubbing at the stone, when he stepped out with his first cup of coffee. And he saw the message sprayed over the wall. As she had done earlier, he left his coffee on the rail and jogged down to her in bare feet.

"Cilla."

"Don't tell Steve. That's the first thing. I don't want you to say a word about this to Steve."

"Did you call the cops?"

"They've been here. For whatever good it does. It has to be Hennessy, it has to be that son of a bitch. But unless he's got black paint and wood chips under his goddamn fingernails, what are they going to do about it?"

"Wood . . ." He saw the stumps then, swore. "Wait a minute. Let me think."

"I don't have time. I have to get this *off*. Can't risk sandblasting this stone. It's too harsh. It'd damage the stone, the mortar, do as much harm, potentially, as the stupid paint. This chemical's the best alternative. Probably have to have the wall repointed, but it's all I can do."

"Scrub at the stone with a brush?"

"That's right." She attacked the C in BITCH like she would a sworn enemy. "He's not going to get away with this. He's not going to soil or damage what's mine. I wasn't driving the goddamn car. I wasn't even born, for Christ's sake."

"And he's eighty if he's a day. I have a hard time seeing him chopping down a couple of trees and tagging a stone wall in the middle of the night."

"Who else?" She rounded on Ford. "Who else hates me or this place the way he does?"

"I don't know. But we'd better work on finding out."

"It's my problem."

"Don't be an ass."

"It's my problem, my wall, my trees. I'm the bitch."

He met her hot glare with a cool stare. "I wouldn't argue with the last part right at the moment, but as for the rest? Bullshit. You don't want to tell Steve, fine. I get it. But I'm not leaving. I'm not heading back to L.A. or anywhere else."

He grabbed her arm, pulled her back around to face him. "I'm staying right here. Deal with it."

"I'm trying to deal with this, and with having my best friend leave when he can hardly walk more than five yards at a time. I'm trying to deal with making a life I didn't even realize I wanted until a few months ago. I don't know how much more I can deal with."

"You'll have to make room." He cupped her face, kissed her hard. "Got another brush?"

FIFTEEN

Cilla sweated over the long, tedious process most of the day, with breaks to handle scheduled work. She concentrated on the obscenities first as people slowed on the drive by, or stopped altogether to comment or question.

Sometime during the process, the burning edge of her rage banked down to simple frustration. Why had the asshole written so damn much?

She picked up the task again the next morning, before the mason or any of the crew arrived. Two new trees flanked her entrance. She thought of them as defiant now rather than sweet. And that pumped up her energy.

"Hey."

She glanced around to see Ford, ratty sweatpants and T-shirt, standing on the opposite shoulder of the road with a red bandanna-sporting Spock quivering, but sitting obediently at his feet. "Early for you," she responded.

"I set the alarm. It must be love. Come over here a minute."

"Busy."

"When aren't you? Honey, you can wear me out just watching. Come on, take a minute. I got coffee." He held up one of the oversized mugs he carried.

He'd set the alarm, and though she didn't know quite what to think about that, she owed him for it. And for the time he'd put in the day before, even after she'd been rude and snarly. She set the bristle brush down, crossed the road.

He handed her the coffee, gestured to the wall as she greeted Spock. "Read it from here. Out loud."

She shrugged, turned, and even as she took a gulp of the coffee felt a little bubble of amusement rise in her throat. "Go to Hollywood, live like an ore ike."

"Ore-ike," he mused. "I can use that. Seems to me he tried to hurt and intimidate you, and you've made him a joke. Nicely done."

"Unexpectedly ridiculous. I guess that's a plus. I've nearly run out of mad. You don't have to get into this again today, Ford. How are you going to make me a warrior goddess if you're scrubbing off graffiti?"

"That's cruising along pretty well. I can give you a couple of hours before I get back to it. Spock's looking forward to being what Brian and Matt call a job dog today. He's just going to go over and hang out with the guys. Hence the bandanna."

"You know, I'm probably going to have sex with you, without the offer of manual labor."

"I'm hoping." He gave her an easy, uncomplicated smile. "You know I'd offer the labor even if you weren't going to have sex with me."

She took a contemplative sip of coffee. "I guess that evens it out. I do better on even ground. Well." She started back across the street, and he and Spock fell into step beside her. "My father heard about this, called me last night. What could he do? How could he help? Why didn't I come stay there for a while, until the police figured it out? Which is looking like, hmm, never. Then my stepmother got on the phone. She wants to take me shopping."

"For a new wall? This one's cleaning up okay."

"No, not a new wall." She gave him a light punch, then handed him protective gloves. "Patty, Angie and Cilla do the outlets. Like trolling for bargains would solve my problem."

"I take it you're not going?"

"I don't have the time or the inclination to search out peek-toe pumps or a flirty summer dress."

"Red shoes, white dress. Sorry," he added at her quiet stare. "I think in visuals."

"Uh-huh. The point, I guess, is that I'm not used to people offering—time or company or help—without any number of strings attached."

"That's a shame, or perhaps living like an ore-ike."

She laughed, began to scrub.

"Go play," he told Spock, who trotted off toward the house in his red bandanna.

"I'm trying to learn to accept the offers without the lingering haze of cynicism. It's going to take a little while."

He worked for a few moments in silence. "You know what I see when I look over here?"

"Trucks, big-ass Dumpster, a house in desperate need of paint?"

"Sleeping Beauty's castle."

"How? Where? Why?"

"First, I risk impinging my manhood by admitting I dug on those kind of stories as a kid, as much as I did the Dark Knight, X-Men, and so on. And consider Disney's version solid, with Maleficent one of the top villains of all time. Anyway."

He shrugged as she continued to stare at him. "You know how the evil Maleficent cast the spell, and surrounded the castle with giant briar, those big, wicked thorns. Closed it in to a dark, forbidding place that held sorrow and, well, trapped beauty."

"Okay."

"The hero had to fight his way through the blocks, the thorns, the traps. A lot of risk, a lot of work, but when he reached the goal, the castle came back to life. And, you know, peace reigned across the land."

She worked her wire brush against the wall. "I have to kiss the princess?"

"Okay, new visual. Interesting. There are some flaws in the metaphor, but basically, the trapped, sleeping castle needs a hero to wake it up. Some people like having a part in that. And some . . ." He tapped his brush on a large black *E*. "They like to fuck it up."

"I find myself fascinated by a man who admits to enjoying fairy tales and uses the word 'impinge'— and barely misses a beat while indulging in a brief girl-on-girl fantasy. You're a man of layers, Ford."

"Me and Shrek, we're onions."

Oh yeah, she thought. Falling for him, and falling fast.

She stopped as Buddy's truck pulled up beside them. The plumber leaned out the window, scowled. "What the hell is that supposed to mean?"

"According to Ford, it means some people like to mess things up."

"Damn kids. No respect."

"I don't want Steve to hear about this. He's got enough on his mind. I need to talk to you about the venting for the steam shower. I took another look last night, and . . . I really need to go over this with Buddy on site," she said to Ford.

"Go ahead. I've got this for a while."

"Thanks. Give me a lift, Buddy." She hopped into the cab of the truck, and as Buddy turned in the drive, tried to imagine the house as Sleeping Beauty's castle, with about half of the briars hacked away.

FORD GOT IN a solid day before stepping back from the work to take a long look at the panels and the pencils. The story had turned on him a bit, but he considered that a good thing. He'd edit the script later that evening to suit the new images and action that had come to mind.

To do that, he needed to let it stew. To stop pushing while it cooked on one of the back burners of the brain. Which meant, for his process, it was probably time for a beer and a little PlayStation.

Downstairs, he opened the front door to take a quick look at what he thought of as Cilla World before wandering back to the kitchen. He saw Steve picking his way up the walk, the cane in one hand, a six-pack in the other.

"This is what I call superior timing."

Beside Ford, Spock all but jumped up and applauded.

"I escaped. The warden had to make a supply run, so I stole her beer and booked."

"Who could blame you?" Ford took the beer, flicked a thumb at a chair.

"Doc cleared me. I'm heading out tomorrow." He sat, with an audible whoosh of breath, then scrubbed his hand over Spock's head.

"You'll be missed." Ford popped the tops on two beers, passed one over.

"I'm going to try to come back out in the fall, if I can manage it. The way she's going, she'll be down to punch-out work."

Ford glanced dubiously across the road. "If you say so."

"I'm mostly in her way now."

"She doesn't see it that way."

Steve took a long pull on the beer. "She reamed my ass for going up in the attic to hang out with the guys. Wanted to set me out in a rocker like her grandfather, and give me a paint fan to play with. Jesus, next thing it'll be crossword puzzles or some such shit."

"Could be worse. Could be knitting."

With a grunt, Steve frowned at the stone wall across the road. "What's your take on what went down on that?"

"Sorry?"

"Don't bullshit. My brain's not that damaged. Guys on construction crews gossip like girls. I heard some asshole tagged the wall. Got about six different versions of what it said, but all the same basic idea."

"My take is some asshole tagged the wall, and he's got a mean streak. It might be the same one that went after you, or it might not. She thinks it's old man Hennessy."

"And you don't."

"Old man's the defining term. Then again, I can't think of anybody who has anything against her except him. And he's tough. Stringy, but tough."

"If I was a hundred percent—or closer to it—I'd stay. But I wouldn't be much help to her right now."

He tipped his beer at Ford. "Up to you, Sparky, and your little dog, too."

"We've got it."

"Yeah." Steve took another sip of beer. "I think you do."

SHE DIDN'T CRY when Steve climbed into the passenger seat of the RV on the cool and wet Saturday. She censored herself from making any suggestion he wait until the weather cleared to begin the long trip cross-country. Instead, she kissed him goodbye and stood in the rain to wave him off.

And felt horribly, painfully alone.

So alone, she closed herself in the house. The rain took planting or painting off the slate. She considered moving her things into the guest room Steve had vacated, but that struck her as too much *housekeeping*. She wanted work, not chores.

She switched on the radio, turned up the volume to fill the house with sound. And got down to the business of building the shelving and framing out the storage closet for the utility room off the kitchen. The task wasn't on the agenda for weeks yet, but it was exactly the kind of job that smoothed out nerves, soothed the mind.

She measured, marked, sawed, lost herself in the

rhythm of carpentry. Content again, she sang along with the radio as her cordless screwdriver spun a wood screw home.

She nearly dropped the drill on her foot when she turned and caught a movement out of the corner of her eye.

"I'm sorry! I'm sorry!" Patty threw up her hands, as if the tool were a loaded gun. "I didn't mean to scare you. We knocked, but . . . It's so loud in here."

Cilla walked over to shut off the radio. "I need it loud to hear it over the tools."

"I got worried when you didn't answer the door, and there was all the noise, and your car out front. So we just came in."

"It's all right. You just startled me. We?"

"Angie and Cathy. We tried to get Penny, but she's covering the store. It's such a poopy day we decided we'd brave the mall, then catch a movie and round it out with dinner. We came to kidnap you."

"Oh, that sounds like fun." Like torture, she thought. "I appreciate it, but I'm in the middle of this."

"You deserve a day off. My treat."

"Patty—"

"I can hardly believe . . ." Cathy stepped in, trailed

off with a wide-eyed stare at Cilla. "We've invaded. Gosh, you look so HGTV. I'm nervous about banging a nail into the wall to hang a picture, and look at you."

"My sister, the handyman." Perky in a pink hoodie, Angie beamed at her. "Can we look around? Is it all right? The buzz is the action's on the second floor."

"Sure. Um, it's got a ways to go. Actually, it all has a ways."

"I confess, I've been dying to get a look inside this place for years." Cathy glanced around at the bare walls, the bare floors, the stacks and piles of lumber and supplies. "How do you manage without a kitchen?"

"I'm not much of a cook anyway. I'm having the stove and refrigerator that were in here retrofitted—they're fairly fabulous. It takes time, so the kitchen's way down on the list. Ah, the dining area's over there, so it makes it an open floor plan. It's good light, nice views."

"The back gardens look so pretty!" Patty stepped closer to the French doors. "Was this patio here?"

"It needed work, and we redesigned it. The gardens have been a job. Your son does good work," she said to Cathy. "And he's got a real talent for landscape design."

"Thank you. We certainly think so."

"The dining room opens to the patio, and from the interior flows into this area I'm going to use as a sort of sitting/TV room off the living area. Powder room there's getting new tiles, new fixtures. Coat closet here off the entryway. It's a lot of space. It's good space."

"I love that you can step outside from every room." Angie turned a circle.

Cilla led them upstairs where the three unexpected guests cooed over the tiles and fixtures of the completed bath, chattered over the projected master.

"I don't know what I'd do with a steam shower, but I would *love* heated tile floors in my bathroom." Patty beamed at Cilla. "I don't know how you know all of this, and figure it out, but the two finished rooms are just beautiful. Like something out of a magazine."

"The resale value's going to skyrocket," Cathy commented.

"I think it would, if I were planning on selling."

"Sorry, my husband's influence." Cathy chuckled. "And I know without asking him he'd want first crack if you ever change your mind about selling. What wonderful views. It seems so solitary, even with the other houses around. I admit I like the convenience and the security of living closer to town, but if I had more country girl in me, this would be the spot."

"Do you ever feel her around? Janet?"

"Angie."

At her mother's frown, Angie blinked. "I'm sorry. Is that the wrong thing to ask?"

"It's all right," Cilla told her. "I do sometimes. I like to think she'd approve of what I'm doing, even the changes I'm making. It matters to me."

"There's such history in this house," Cathy added. "All the people who came here, the parties, the music. The tragedy, too. It makes it more than a house. It's a legend, isn't it? I remember when it happened. I was pregnant with my middle child— just a couple months along, and had such morning sickness. I'd just had a bout, and Tom was trying to feed Marianna—our oldest—breakfast. She wasn't quite two, and there was oatmeal everywhere. My next-door neighbor—Abby Fox, you remember her, Patty?"

"I do. If there was a drop of gossip, she squeezed out more."

"Knew everything first, and this was no exception. She came over and told us. I burst right into tears. Hormones, I guess. I got sick again, and I remember how Tom was at his wit's end trying to figure out how to deal with me and the baby. It was an awful day. I'm sorry." She shook herself. "I don't know why I started on that."

"The house stirs it up," Patty decided. "Go on, Cilla, get cleaned up and come with us. This rain and gloom's going to make us sad. We're just not taking no for an answer."

She supposed she went along as it was three against one, and because Cathy's memory had made her sad. It surprised her that she enjoyed herself, poking around a mall, sitting through a weepy chick flick, drinking margaritas and eating grilled chicken Caesar salad.

In the restaurant ladies' room, Angie joined her to fuss with her hair and lip gloss. "It's no Rodeo Drive, premiere and dinner at the latest hot spot, but it was a pretty good day, huh?"

"I had fun. And Rodeo Drive wasn't my usual stomping grounds."

"It would be mine, if I lived out there. Even if I could only window-shop and fantasize. You really don't miss it?"

"I really don't miss it. I— Sorry," she said when her phone rang. Drawing it out, Cilla saw her mother's number on the readout, put it away without answering.

7

"You can take it. I'll step out."

"No. It's the kind of call that's guaranteed to spoil my nice, subtle margarita buzz. Do you do this a lot? Hang out with your mother on a rainy Saturday?"

"I guess. She's fun to be around. We always tried to have a day together, and since I went to college, we try harder when I'm home on break. Sometimes we have friends along, sometimes just the two of us."

"You're lucky."

Angie laid a hand on Cilla's arm. "I know she's not your mother, but I know, too, she'd really like to be your friend."

"She is my friend. We just don't know each other very well."

"Yet?"

"Yet," Cilla agreed, and made Angie smile.

WHEN SHE GOT HOME, Cilla checked her voice mail. Two from Ford, she noted—probably when she'd turned off her phone in the movie—and one from her mother.

She got her mother's over with. It ran long, as expected, covering the gamut from cold disdain to angry resentment, with a short stint of teary tremor between.

Cilla deleted it, played Ford's first.

"Hey. My mother decided to cook up spaghetti and meatballs, and told me to come over to pig out and bring a friend. You didn't answer the door, and you're not answering this. So now I'm wondering if I should worry, mind my own business or be insanely jealous because you ran off with some piece of beefcake named Antonio. Anyway, give me a call so I know."

She played the second. "Ignore that message. My father ran into your father, so have fun with the girls. Ah, that was your father's term. The girls. You're going to miss some seriously awesome meatballs."

"God, you're so cute," Cilla murmured. "And if I wasn't so tired, I'd walk right over there and jump your bones."

Yawning, she climbed the steps with two shopping bags. A real bed waited upstairs, she remembered. She could curl up on an actual mattress with actual sheets. Snuggle right in, sleep as late as she liked. The idea shimmered like heaven in her mind as she turned into the guest bath.

It was like being struck in the heart. The lovely floor lay broken—tiles chipped, shattered, heaved up from long cracks. The bowl of the new sink lay scattered over it in pieces. Shocked, she staggered back, the bags dropping out of her hands. The contents spilled out as she turned, with a fist twisting in her belly, to run to the newly tiled master.

The same senseless destruction met her.

A sledgehammer, she thought, maybe a pick. Someone had pounded, chipped, gashed the tiles, the glass block, the walls. Hours and hours of work, destroyed.

With ice coating that fist in her belly, she walked downstairs and outside into the rain to make the now familiar call to the police.

"CAME IN THROUGH the back door," Wilson told her. "Broke the glass, reached in, turned the lock. It appears he used your tools—that short-handled sledgehammer, the pickax—to do the damage. Who knew you'd be out for the evening?"

"Nobody. *I* didn't know I'd be out. It was spur of the moment."

"And your car remained here, in full view from the road?"

"Yes. I left the veranda light on, and two lights on inside—one up, one down."

"And you left here about two in the afternoon, you said?"

"Yes, about then. We went to the mall, to the movies, to dinner. I got back about ten-thirty."

"The three women you were with knew your house would be vacant?"

"That's right. My neighbor knew, as he called me while I was out. My father knew, and my neighbor's parents. I suppose Mrs. Morrow's husband knew, or could have. Basically, Detective, pretty much anyone who had any interest in my whereabouts could have known or found out."

"Miss McGowan, I'm going to suggest you get yourself a security system."

"Is that what you'd suggest?"

"This area is lightly developed, it's part of its charm. You're relatively remote here, and your property has been a repeated target of vandalism. We're doing what we can. But if I were you, I'd take steps to protect my property."

"You can believe I will."

Cilla pushed to her feet when she heard Ford's voice, raised in obvious frustration as he argued with one of the cops currently prowling her house and grounds. "That's my neighbor. I'd like him to come in."

Wilson signaled. A moment later Ford rushed in.

"Are you hurt? Are you all right?" He took her face in his hands. "What happened now?"

"Someone broke in while I was out. They did a number on two of the second-floor bathrooms."

"Mr. Sawyer, where were you this afternoon and evening, between two and eleven?"

"Detective Wilson—"

"It's okay." Ford took Cilla's hand, squeezed it. "I was home working until about four. I went out to buy some wine and some flowers for my mother. I had dinner at my parents', got there about five. Got home, I don't know, about nine, maybe nine-thirty. I watched some TV, fell asleep on the couch. When I surfaced, I started upstairs. I looked out the front door—it's a habit now—and I saw the cops."

"Ms. McGowan stated you knew she wasn't home."

"Yeah, I called her to invite her to dinner at my parents'. No, walked over first to invite her. She didn't answer, and I got a little worried with every-thing that's been going on. Then I called. And a little while later, I talked to my father; my mother wanted me to stop and pick up some milk. I told him I was trying to reach Cilla to ask her over, and he said he'd run into her dad, and that she was out with girlfriends."

"What time did you come over here?"

"Ah, about three, some after, I guess. I walked to the barn when you didn't answer, but the lock was on, and I walked around the house. I was worried, a little. Everything looked okay. Where did they break in?"

"Back door," she told him.

"The back door was fine when I did the walk-around. How bad is it?"

"Way bad enough."

"You can fix it." He reached for her hand. "You know how."

She shook her head, walked over to sit on the steps. "I'm tired." After scrubbing her hands over her face, she dropped them into her lap. "I'm tired of it all."

"Why don't you go over to my place, get some sleep? I'll bunk here so somebody's in the house."

"If I leave, I'm not going to come back. I need to think about that. I need to see if staying here matters anymore. Because right now? I just don't know."

"I'll stay with you. I'll take the sleeping bag. Are you going to leave any cops here?" Ford demanded of Wilson.

Wilson nodded. "We'll leave a radio car and two officers outside. Ms. McGowan? I don't know if it makes any difference to the way you're feeling, but this is starting to piss me off."

She offered Wilson a sigh. "Get in line."

WHILE FORD WENT over to get the dog, she fixed plywood over the broken glass herself—a kind of symbol. At that moment, Cilla wasn't sure if it was a symbol of defense or defeat. When she set down the hammer, all she felt was brutal fatigue.

"You don't have to take the sleeping bag. It's a big bed, and you're too decent a guy to try anything under the circumstances. And the fact is, I don't want to sleep alone."

"Okay. Come on. We'll figure everything out to-morrow."

"He used my own tools to ruin things." She let Ford lead her through the house, up the stairs. "It makes it worse somehow."

In the bedroom, she toed off her shoes. Then pulled off her shirt. And had just enough left in her to be touched and amused when Ford cleared his throat, turned his back.

Spock, on the other hand, cocked his head and—if it was possible—ogled.

"He didn't bust up the johns," she said as she

changed into a tank and cotton pants. "I don't know if he ran out of steam, or if he knew the tiles, the sinks, the block were all more expensive and would take more time and trouble to replace. He'd be right about that. But you don't have to go outside if you have to pee."

"I'm good, thanks."

"You can turn around now."

She crawled onto the bed, didn't bother to turn it down. "You don't have to sleep in your clothes. I don't know if I'm as decent as you, but I'm too damn tired to start up anything."

Taking her at her word, he stripped down to his boxers, then stretched out on the bed, leaving plenty of space between them.

She reached out, turned off the light. "I'm not going to cry," she said after a few moments of silence. "But if you wouldn't mind, I'd like you to hold on to me for a while."

He shifted to her, turned, then, draping an arm around her, drew her back against his body. "Better?"

"Yeah." She closed her eyes. "I don't know what to do. What I want, what I need, what I should, what I shouldn't. I just don't know."

He kissed the back of her head, and the quiet gesture pushed tears into her throat. "Whatever it is, you'll figure it out. Listen, it's starting to rain again. It's a nice sound, this time of night. It's like music. You can just lie here and listen to the music."

She listened to the music, how it played on and around the house she'd come to love. And, with his arm curled around her, slipped into exhausted sleep.

SIXTEEN

There was music when she woke. The same steady drum and plink of rain that had lulled her to sleep greeted her when she stirred. He'd held on to her, she thought—a little dreamily—when she'd asked. Just held on to her while the rain played and sleep took her under.

Though she had a dim memory of just dropping down on top of the bed, she found herself cozily tucked in.

And alone.

The part of her that didn't want to face it, didn't want those memories to clear, urged her to sink down again, to just let the rain and the watery gloom stroke her back to sleep.

Come too far for that, Cilla, she reminded herself. You've come too far for the slide and stroke. Pull it up, face the facts. Decide. Then deal.

As she pushed herself up to sit, she thought that nagging, practical voice in her head a coldhearted bitch.

Then she saw the coffee.

Her insulated travel mug sat on the nightstand. Propped against it, one of her notepads sported a mercilessly accurate and wincingly unflattering sketch depicting exactly how she imagined she looked at that precise moment. Tousled, heavy-eyed, rumpled and scowling. Beneath, in bold block letters, the caption read:

I AM COFFEE!!
DRINK ME!
(THEN TURN THE PAGE)

"Funny guy," she grumbled. She picked up the pad, tossed it on the bed before lifting the mug. The coffee it held was only a few degrees above lukewarm, but it was strong and sweet. And just what the doctor ordered. She indulged, sitting, sipping, letting the coffee give her system that first kick start.

And idly, turned the page in the notebook.

She hadn't expected to laugh, wouldn't have believed anything could cut through the fog of depression to pull a quick, surprised chuckle out of her.

He'd drawn her vivid, wide-eyed, exaggerated breasts and biceps bulging out of her sleep tank, hair streaming in an unseen wind, smile full and fierce. The travel mug, a hint of steam puffing out of the drink hole, gripped in her hand.

"Yeah, you're a funny guy."

Laying the notepad back down, she went to find him.

She heard the clattering sound when she opened the bedroom door. Glass—no, broken tiles, she decided—against plastic. She wended her way to the master bedroom, pushed open that door, then crossed to the doorway of the bath.

He'd dug up work gloves, she noted, and a small spade, several empty drywall compound buckets. Two of them were filled with tile shards. It struck her almost harder than it had the night before, to stand there and see the methodical clearing of destruction.

"You're losing your status as a morning slug."

He dumped another handful of shards, straightened. He scanned her face. "You may have ruined me for life. How's the coffee?"

"Welcome. Thanks. You don't have to do this, Ford."

"I don't know anything about building, but I know a lot about cleaning up."

"We're going to need a lot more than a couple of buckets and a spade."

"Yeah, I figured. But I also figured I might as well get started because lying in bed with you on a rainy Sunday morning had me . . . energized."

"Is that what you call it?"

His face remained very solemn. "In polite company."

She nodded, stepped over to stare at the cracks and breaks in her glass-block wall. She'd loved the look of that, the patterns in the glass, the way the light stole through. She'd imagined painting the walls a sheer, subtly metallic silver to pick up the glints of chrome. Her classy oasis, and yes, maybe a personal salute to old Hollywood.

The roots of her roots.

"I don't know what I'm going to do yet. I honestly don't know if I want to put this back together. If I've got it in me to fight this war someone's declared on me. I didn't come here to fight wars. I wanted to build something for myself, and for her. Maybe to build something for myself from her. But you know, when the foundation's cracked, things keep falling down."

"It didn't fall down, Cilla, it was knocked down. That's a different thing." He tipped his head to one side, then the other, making a deliberate study of

her face. So she saw he understood she meant herself as much as—maybe more than—the room. "I
don't see any cracks."

"She was a junkie, a drunk. Maybe she was made
into one, exploited, used. Pampered and abused. I
know what that's like. Not on her level, but enough
to have a glimmer of what it was for her. I could
have tried to build anywhere, but I made a deliberate choice to come here. She's part of the reason.
This place is part of the reason. My own wounded
psyche and need to prove my own worth on my
own terms. All part of the reason."

"Those are good reasons." He shrugged in that
easy way of his. "So you stay, you clean it up. And
you build it. On your terms."

She shook her head. "You have no idea how
screwed up I am."

"I've got a few clues. How about you? Any idea
how strong you are?"

How could she argue against that straight-line,
stubborn conviction? "It vacillates. I'm on a low ebb
right now."

"Maybe you just need a boost."

"More coffee?"

"A hearty Sunday breakfast." He pulled off the
work gloves, tossed them on the lid of the john.
"You don't have to decide the rest of your life this

minute, or today, or tomorrow. Why don't you give yourself a break? Take a little time. Let's blow off the day. We'll get Spock from outside where he'd be chasing his cats about now. Gorge ourselves at The Pancake House, go . . . to the zoo."

"It's raining."

"It can't rain forever."

She stared at him a moment, at that relaxed smile, the warm, patient eyes. He'd held on to her, she thought. He'd left her coffee, and made her laugh before she was fully awake. He was cleaning up her mess, and demanding absolutely nothing.

He believed in her, in a way, on a level no one, not even she, had believed in before.

"No, it really can't, can it? It really can't rain forever."

"So, get dressed and we'll go overload on carbs, then go check out the monkeys."

"Actually, the pancakes sound pretty good. After."

"After what?"

She laughed, and this time the sound didn't seem so surprising. She took hold of the front of his shirt, watched the awareness come into his eyes. "Come back to bed, Ford."

"Oh."

She backed up, tugging him with her. "It's just us.

Right this minute, I've got nothing else on my mind.
And I really could use that boost."

"Okay." He scooped her up, closed his mouth
over hers.

When her head stopped spinning, she smiled.
"Really nice start."

"I've been planning it out. Change in venue and
basic approach," he said as he carried her to the
bedroom. "But I'm flexible."

Her smile was slow, like a long, low purr. "So
am I."

"Oh, boy."

She was laughing as she hooked her arms around
his neck, caught his mouth with hers. Just them, she
thought as they tumbled onto the bed. Everything
else was later. Just them, and the music of the rain.
In the soft and lazy light, on the rumpled bed, she
let herself sink into the here and now. She drew his
shirt up, away, hooked her legs around him and
said, "Mmmm."

He could have lingered on her mouth, the taste,
the shape, the movement of it, endlessly. That wonderful deep dip in her top lip held a world of fasci-
nation for him. The sexy, seeking slide of her tongue
against his could have held him enthralled for
hours.

But there was so much more. The graceful stem of her neck allured him, the curve of her cheek, the smooth skin just under her jaw offered him countless pleasures as he roamed, as he sampled before finding her lips again.

The flavors there had become familiar over the weeks since they'd begun this dance, and only the more desirable to him. Now, finally, there would be more.

He could glide his lips down her, learn the tastes and textures, madden himself with the subtle swell above simple cotton. He teased and tormented them both, lingering there even as she arched up in invitation. He found warmth and silk and secrets while her heart beat strong against his lips. And when his tongue slid under the cotton, when she moaned in approval, he found more.

He eased the tank up, inch by torturous inch, fingers gliding light as moth wings as he lifted his head to look into her eyes.

Her heart stuttered. Her body simply sighed.

"You're really good at this."

"If something's worth doing . . . I've looked at you a lot. In an artistic capacity." His gaze shifted down as his fingers brushed over her breasts. "I've thought about you a lot."

Thumbs, fingertips sent shivers through her.

"I've imagined touching you. Watching you while I did. Feeling you tremble under my hands. You've been worth waiting for."

He lowered his mouth to hers again, taking the kiss deep. Lowered his body to hers. Heat spread where flesh met flesh, sent her pulse to pound. Now her body quivered as he journeyed down it, slow and easy, hands and lips.

She thought she'd let go when they tumbled onto the bed. But she'd been wrong. That had been acquiescence. This, what he seduced from here, was surrender.

He touched with a care, a curiosity, as if she were the first woman he'd touched. And made her feel as if she'd never been touched before. Sensations swam and coiled inside her, shimmered over her skin until pleasure coated her like light. And the light bloomed with such intensity she gripped the tangled sheets to anchor herself in the glow.

He guided her up, up where the light flashed, where in the quick, stunning blindness pleasure turned on its edge and shot through her.

He steeped himself in the shape of her, even as she quaked under him. The slender line of her torso that curved into her waist enchanted him. The feel of her hips, rising up as she peaked, thrilled. Long, lovely thighs led him to gorgeous calves that flexed at the light nip of his teeth.

She moaned, and the sound of it seeped into him when he roamed up again to explore that warm, wet, welcoming center. She said his name when she came, a quick, breathless gasp. Her fingers raked through his hair, then down his back on the coil and release. Damp flesh slid over damp flesh until he looked back down into her eyes.

She touched his face, held the look, trembling, trembling as he slipped into her. And as those icy blue eyes glazed, he took her with long, slow thrusts.

She ached, every part of her. She rose to him, helplessly caught. Swamped in needs he met, stirred and met once more. When they built again, impossibly, she held on.

And she let go.

Limp, loose, languid, she lay under him. The world eked back so she heard the drumming rain again, felt the hot twisted sheet under her back. When the mists cleared from her brain enough to allow random thoughts to wind through, she wondered if the fact that she'd just had the best sex of her life meant it was all downhill from here.

Then he turned his head, rubbed his lips against her shoulder, and she *swore* she felt her skin glow.

He lifted his head, brushed her hair away from her cheek as he smiled sleepily down at her. "Okay?"

"Okay?" She let out a mystified laugh. "Ford, you seriously deserve a medal, or at least a certificate of excellence. I feel like every inch of me has been . . . tended," she decided.

"I'd say my job is done, but I really like the work." He dipped his head, and the kiss sent sparkles dancing in her brain to go with the glow. "Probably need, ah, a coffee break though."

Deciding she'd never been more relaxed or content in her life, she hooked her arms around his neck. "Understandable. When my bones resolidify, I could use a shower. And it just occurs to me we can't shower here."

He saw the worry come back into her eyes and, rolling away, pulled her up to sitting. "We'll go over to my place." Where what had happened wouldn't keep slapping her in the face, he thought. "Toss something on, grab what you want. It turns out I've also imagined you wet and slippery. Now I'll find out how close I was to right."

"All right. There was a mention of pancakes, too, as I recall."

"Stacks of them. We're going to need fuel to get through the rest of the day."

THEY DIDN'T MAKE it to The Pancake House. After a long, steamy, energetic shower, the idea struck to stay in and make pancakes. The result was messy but reasonably edible.

"They just need a lot of syrup." Sitting at the kitchen counter in Ford's T-shirt, Cilla drowned the oddly shaped stack on her plate.

If the sounds from the mudroom were an indication, Spock had no trouble with his share.

"They're not so bad." Ford forked a dripping pile. "And more fun than Eggos. I had this other idea. Instead of going out to see monkeys, we stay in and have monkey sex."

"So far your ideas are working out pretty well. Who am I to argue? What do you usually do on rainy Sundays?"

"You mean when I'm not eating pancakes with gorgeous blondes?" He shrugged. "I might work some, depending on how that's going, or fat-ass around and read. Maybe hang out with Brian or Matt, or both. If I had absolutely no choice, I'd do laundry. How about you?"

"Back in L.A.? If I had a project going, I'd tackle

some interior work, or paperwork, or research. If I didn't have a project, I'd scour the Internet and real estate ads looking for one. That'd pretty much sum up my life for the past few years. That's pitiful."

"It's not. It's what you wanted. A lot of people thought it was pitiful I'd rather hole up scribbling and sketching than, say, play basketball. Being tall, you know. I sucked at basketball. Never got it. On the other hand, I was good, and got better, at the scribbling and sketching."

"You're frighteningly well adjusted. Or maybe just compared to me."

"You seem pretty steady from where I sit."

"I have abandonment issues." She gestured with a dripping forkful of pancakes. "I have a drug phobia due to a family history of drug abuse that has me sweating taking an aspirin. I suffer from acute stage fright that escalated in my teens to the point that I could barely cope with being in the same room with three people at a time. The only way I can cope with my mother, sanely, is to stay away from her, and I spent the majority of my life alternately blaming myself or my father for the fact that we didn't— don't, really—know each other."

He made a *pfft* sound. "Is that all?"

"Want more?" She ate pancakes, stabbed more. "I

got more. I have dreams where I engage in detailed conversations with my dead grandmother, whom I never met, and to whom I feel closer than I do to any living member of my family. My best friend is my ex-husband. I've had four stepfathers, and countless 'uncles,' and being not stupid, understand that is part of the reason that I've never had a long-term, healthy relationship with a man other than Steve. I expect to be exploited and used, or I expect the attempt, and, as a result, have successfully sabotaged any potentially long-term, healthy relationship I might have had. Fair warning."

He forked more pancakes, ate them. "Is that the best you can do?"

With a laugh, she shoved her plate away, picked up her coffee. "That's probably enough over breakfast." She rose, held out a hand. "Let's take a walk in the rain. Then we can come back and dive in your Jacuzzi."

They left the mess, took a long walk with the dog. Was there anything more romantic than being kissed in the rain? Cilla wondered. Anything more lovely than the mountains, shrouded in clouds and mist? Anything more liberating than strolling hand in hand through the summer rain while all the world huddled inside, behind closed doors and windows?

Drenched, they raced back to the house to strip off dripping clothes. In the hot, bubbling water, they took each other slowly.

Drained, they went upstairs to curl together like puppies to sleep on Ford's bed.

She woke him with love, the sleepy joy of it, the warm tangle of limbs and soft press of lips. When they dozed again, the rain slowed to a quiet patter.

Later, Cilla slipped out of bed. Tiptoeing to Ford's closet, she found a shirt. Pulling it on, she eased out of the room. She intended to go down to search out a bottle of water—preferably ice cold—but detoured to his studio. Thirst could wait for curiosity.

When she switched on the light, the drawings pinned to his display board pulled her forward. So odd to see her face, she thought, on the warrior's body. Well, her body, she admitted.

He'd added her tattoo, but as she'd once suggested, it rode on Brid's biceps.

Wandering over to his workstation, she frowned at the papers on his drawing board. Small sketches covered them—sparse sketches, she mused, all in separate boxes, and each with a dotted vertical line running top to bottom. Some of them had what she thought she recognized as speech balloons, with numbers inside. She spread them out for a better look.

It was like a storyboard, she realized. The characters, the action, some staging. Blocking. And if she wasn't mistaken, the sizes and shapes of the boxes had been calculated mathematically as well as artistically. Balance, she mused, and impact.

Who knew so much went into a comic?

On the other side of the board, a larger sheet lay on the counter. More squares and rectangles, she noted, holding detailed drawings, shaded and . . . inked. Yes, that was the word. Though no dialogue had been added, the setup, the art, drew the eye across, just as words in a book would do.

In the center, Dr. Cass Murphy stood in what Cilla thought of as her professor suit. Conservative, acceptable. Bland. The clothes, the dark-framed glasses and the posture defined personality in one shot. That was a kind of brilliance, wasn't it? she thought. To capture and depict in one single image the character. The person.

Without thinking, she picked up the panel, took it to the display board to hold it against the sketch of Brid.

The same woman, yes, of course the same woman. And yet the change was both remarkable and complete. Repression to liberation, hesitation to purpose. Shadow to light.

When she started to walk back to replace the

panel, she saw another stack of pages. Typewritten pages. She scanned the first few lines.

FORD WOKE HUNGRY, and deeply disappointed Cilla wasn't beside him to slake one area of appetite. Apparently, he decided, he couldn't get enough of her.

She was all beautiful and sexy and wounded and smart. She knew how to use power tools, and had a laugh that made his mouth water. He'd watched her hang tough, and fall to pieces. He'd witnessed her absolute devotion to a friend, watched her handle acute embarrassment and lash out with temper.

She knew how to work, and oh boy, she knew how to play.

She might be, he mused, pretty damn close to perfect.

So where the hell was she?

He rolled out of bed, snagged a pair of pants and stepped into them on his way to hunt her down.

He was just about to call her name when he spotted her. She sat at his work counter, legs tucked up and crossed, shoulders hunched, one elbow propped. He had the quick and fleeting thought that if he sat like that for more than ten minutes, his neck and shoulders would lock up for days.

Walking over, he set his hands on her shoulders to rub what he imagined would be knotted muscles. And she jumped as if he'd swung an ax at her head.

She pitched forward, caught herself, reared back as her legs scissored out. Then, spinning around in his chair, she clutched her hands at her chest as her laughter bubbled out.

"God! You *scared* me!"

"Yeah, I picked that up when you nearly bashed your head on my drawing board. What're you up to?"

"I was . . . Oh God. Oh shit!" She shoved the chair back, dropped her hands into her lap. "I'm sorry. I completely breached your privacy. I was looking at the sketches you had sitting out, and I saw the book. I just meant to skim the first page. I got caught up. I shouldn't have—"

"Whoa, whoa, save the self-flagellation. I told you before you could read it sometime. I just hadn't written it yet. If you got caught up, that's a plus."

"I moved things around." She picked up the panel, held it out. "I hate when people move my things around."

"I know where it goes. Obviously, you're lucky I'm not as temperamental and touchy as you are." He lay the panel back in its place. "So, what do you think?"

"I think the story is fun, exciting and entertaining, with a sharp thread of humor, and with strong underpinnings of feminism."

He lifted his brows. "All that?"

"You know damn well. The character of Cass behaves in certain ways, and expects certain behavior and attitudes toward her because she was raised by a domineering, unsympathetic father. She's sexually repressed and emotionally clogged, has been reared to accept the superiority of men and accept a certain lack of respect in her male-dominated field. You see a great deal of that in the single portrait. The one you just put back.

"She's betrayed, and left for dead, *because* she's so indoctrinated to taking orders from male authority figures. To subverting her own intellect and desires. And by facing death, by fighting against it, she becomes a leader. Everything that's been trapped inside her, and more, is released in the form of Brid. A warrior. Empowerment, through power."

Fascinating, he thought, and flattering, to listen to her synopsize his story, and his character. "I'm going to interpret that as you like it."

"I really do, and not just due to the recent sexual haze. It's like a screenplay, a very strong screenplay. You even have camera angles and direction."

"It helps remind me how I saw it when I wrote it, even if that changes."

"And you add in these little boxes like the ones on the art."

"Helps with the layout. That may change, too. Just like the story line took some turns on me."

"You added Steve. You added the Immortal. He's going to be so . . . well, insane over that."

"She needed the bridge, the link between Cass and Brid. A character who can straddle her worlds, and help the two sides of our heroine understand each other."

Not unlike, Ford thought now, how Steve helped Cilla. "Adding him changed a lot of the angles, added a lot of work, but it's stronger for it. And something I should've thought of in the first place. Anyway, it's still evolving. The story's down, and now I have to tell it with art. Sometimes, for me anyway, the art can shift the story. We'll have to see."

"I especially like the one up there, of Brid in what's almost a fouetté turn, as I assume she's about to kick out her leg against a foe."

"Fouetté turn?"

"A ballet move." Cilla crossed over to tap the sketch she spoke of. "This is very close, even the arms are in position. To be precise, the supporting foot should be turned out slightly more, but—"

"You know ballet? Can you do that?"

"A fouetté? Please. Eight years of ballet." She executed a quick turn. "Of tap." And a fast-time step. "Jazz."

"Cool. Hold on." He opened a drawer, pulled out a camera. "Do the ballet thing again."

"I'm mostly naked."

"Yeah, which is why I'll be posting these on the Internet shortly. I just want the feet business you were talking about."

He had no idea what an enormous leap of faith it took for her to do the turn as he snapped the camera.

"One more, okay? Good. Great. Thanks. A fouetté turn. Ballet." He set the camera back down. "I must've seen it somewhere, sometime or other. Eight years? I guess that explains how you did those high leaps in *Wasteland Three*, when you were running through the woods, trying to escape the reanimated psycho killer."

"Grand jetés." She laughed. "So to speak."

"I thought you were going to make it, the way you were flying. I mean you got all the way back to the cabin, avoiding the death trap *and* the flying hatchet, only to pull open the door—"

"To find the reanimated psycho killer had taken a convenient shortcut to beat me there. Sobbing relief," she said, miming the action, "shock, scream. Slice."

"It was a hell of a scream. They use voice doubles for that stuff, right? And enhance."

"Sometimes. However . . ." She sucked in her breath and let out a bloodcurdling, glass-shattering scream that had Ford staggering back two full steps. "I did my own work," she finished.

"Wow. You've got some lungs there. How about we go down, have some wine, while we see if my eardrums regenerate."

"Love to."

SEVENTEEN

She didn't think about the vandalism. Or when thoughts of what waited for her across the road crept into her mind, Cilla firmly slammed the door. No point in it, she told herself. There was nothing she could do because she didn't know what she wanted to do.

There was no harm in a day out of time. A fantasy day, really, filled with sex and sleep inside the bubble of rain-slicked windows. She couldn't remember the last time she'd been content to spend the day in a man's company, unless it had been work-related.

Even the idea of wine and video games held an appeal. Until Ford severely trounced her for the third time in a row.

"She—what's her name?—Halle Berry."

"Storm," Ford provided. "Halle Berry's the actress, and really hot. Storm is a key member of the X-Men. Also really hot."

"Well, she just *stood* there." Cilla scowled down at the controls. "How am I supposed to know what to push and what to toggle, and whatever?"

"Practice. And like I said, you need to form your team more strategically. You formed your all-girl alliance. You should've mixed it up."

"My strategy was gender solidarity." Under the coffee table, Spock snorted. "That's enough out of you," she muttered. "Besides, I think this controller's defective because I have excellent hand-eye coordination."

"Want to switch and go another round?"

She eyed him narrowly. "How often do you play this?"

"Off and on. Throughout my entire life," he added with a grin. "I'm currently undefeated on this version of Ultimate Alliance."

"Geek."

"Loser."

She handed him her controller. "Put your toys away."

Look at that, she thought when he rose to do just that. Tidy hot guy. Tidy straight hot guy. How many of *them* were there in the world?

"Saving the world worked up my appetite. How about you?"

"I didn't save the world," she pointed out.

"You tried."

"That was smug. I see the smug all over you."

"Then I'd better wash up. I got leftover spaghetti and meatballs, courtesy of Penny Sawyer."

"You've got a nice setup here, Ford. Work you love, and a great house to do it in. Your ridiculously appealing dog. The tight circle of friends going back to childhood. Family you get along with, close enough you can cop leftovers. It's a great platform."

"No complaints. Cilla—"

"No, not yet." She could see in his eyes the offer of sympathy and support. "I'm not ready to think about it yet. Spaghetti and meatballs sounds like just the thing."

"Cold or warmed up?"

"It has to be exceptional spaghetti and meatballs to warrant cold."

He crossed back, took her hand. "Come with me," he said and led her around to the kitchen. "Have a seat." He took the bowl out of the fridge, peeled off the lid, got a fork. "You'll get yours," he told Spock as the dog danced and gurgled. Turning back, he set the bowl on the bar, then wound some pasta on a fork. "Sample."

She opened her mouth, let him feed her. "Oh. Okay, that's really good. Really. Give me the fork."

With a laugh, he passed it to her. After adding some to Spock's dish, he topped off both glasses of wine. They sat at the counter, eating cold pasta straight from the bowl.

"We had this cook when I was a kid. Annamaria from Sicily. I swear her pasta wasn't as good as this. What?" she said when he shook his head.

"Just strikes me weird that I know somebody who can say, 'We had a cook when I was a kid.'"

She grinned around more pasta. "We had a butler."

"Get out."

She raised her brows, inclined her head and stabbed at a meatball. "Two maids, chauffeur, gardener, under-gardener, my mother's personal assistant, pool boy. And once, when my mother discovered the pool boy, whom she was banging, was also banging one of the maids, she fired them both. With much drama. She had to go to Palm Springs for a week to recover, where she met Number Three—ironically, by the pool. I'm pretty sure, at some point, *he* also banged the pool boy. The new pool boy, whose name was Raoul."

He gestured at her with his fork until he swallowed. "You grew up in an eighties soap opera."

She thought it over. "Close enough. But, in any case, Annamaria had nothing on your mother."

"She'll get a kick out of hearing that. What was it like, seriously? Growing up with maids and butlers?"

"Crowded. And not all it's cracked up to be. That sounds snotty," she decided. "And I imagine some woman with a house and family to run, a full-time job and the need to get dinner on the table would be tempted to bitch-slap me for it. But." She shrugged. "There's always somebody there, so genuine privacy is an illusion. No sneaking a cookie out of the jar before dinnertime. Actually no cookies for the most part as the camera adds pounds. If you have a fight with your mother, the entire household knows the details. More, the odds are that those details will be recounted sometime down the road in a tabloid interview or a disgruntled former employee's tell-all book.

"All in all," she concluded, "I'd rather eat leftover spaghetti."

"But, if I remember right, you don't cook."

"Yeah, that's a problem." She reached for her wine. "I've thought about maybe asking Patty for pointers in that area. I like to chop." She hacked down a few times with the flat of her hand to demonstrate. "You know, vegetables, salads. I'm a hell of a chopper."

"That's a start."

"Self-sufficiency, that's the key. You manage."

"True, but I've been butler-free all my life. I do have a biweekly cleaning service, and am well acquainted with the primary and alternate routes to all takeout facilities. Plus, I have a direct line to Brian and Matt and Shanna, who will handle small household emergencies for beer."

"It's a system."

"Well oiled." He tucked her hair behind her ear.

"If and when I learn to cook something other than a grilled cheese sandwich and canned soup, I'll have reached another lofty personal goal."

"What are some of the others?"

"Lofty personal goals? Rehabbing a house and selling it at a profit. I hit that one. Having my own business and having said business generate an actual income. Which first requires reaching the goal of getting my contractor's license, which in turn requires passing the test for same. In a couple weeks, actually, if I—"

"You've got to take a test? I love tests." His eyes actually lit up. "Do you need a study buddy? And yes, I capitalize the *N* in nerd."

She paused with what she swore would be her last bite of pasta halfway to her mouth. "You love tests?"

"Well, yeah. There are questions and answers. True or false, multiple choice, essay. What's not to love? I kill on tests. It's a gift. Do you want any help?"

"Actually, I think I'm good. I've been prepping for it for a while now. I think I met your kind during my brief and unfortunate college experience. You're the one who screwed the curve for me, every time. You are, therefore, one of the primary reasons I'm a one-semester college dropout."

"You should've asked my kind to be your study buddy. Besides, you should thank my kind for putting you exactly where you want to be right now."

"Hmm." She deliberately nudged the bowl toward him and away from herself. "That's very slick and clever. Previous humiliation and failure lead to current spaghetti-and-meatball-induced contentment."

"Or, condensing, sometimes shit happens for the best."

"There's a bumper sticker. I have to move." She pressed a hand on her stomach, slid off the stool. "And I'll demonstrate my self-sufficiency and gratitude for current contentment by doing the dishes, which includes everything back to breakfast, apparently."

"We were busy with other things."

"I guess we were."

For a moment, he indulged himself with wine and

watching her. But watching wasn't enough. He stood and crossed to her, turned her to face him. She had a wooden spoon in her hand and an easy smile curving her lips. He wrapped her hair around his hand—and saw her eyes widen in surprise, heard the spoon clatter to the floor—as he used it like a rope to tug her head back.

And ravished her mouth.

A new and rampant hunger surged through him, a whip of need and now. He released her hair to drag off her shirt. Even as his mouth crushed back down to hers, he yanked her pants down her hips.

It was a tornado of demand and speed. It seemed she was naked before she could catch the first breath. Plucked up off the ground while her head spun and her heart lurched. He dropped her down on the counter, shoved her legs apart.

And ravished her.

Her hand flailed out for purchase. Something shattered; she wondered if it was her mind. His fingers dug into her hips as he pounded into her, pounded greed and scorching pleasure. Mad for more, she locked her legs around his waist.

His blood pounded under his skin, a thousand brutal drumbeats. The hunger that had leaped into him seemed to snap its teeth and bite even as he drove himself into her to slake it. Its dark excitement pushed him to take, to fill her with the same wild desperation that burned in him.

When it broke, it was like shooting out of the black, into the blind.

Her head dropped limply onto his shoulder while her breath came in short, raw gasps. She felt him tremble, found herself pleased she wasn't the only one.

"Oh," she managed, "*God.*"

"Give me a minute. I'll help you down."

"Take your time. I'm fine where I am. Where am I?"

His laugh muffled against the side of her neck. "Maybe it was something in the spaghetti sauce."

"Then we need the recipe."

Steadier, he leaned back, took a good look at her. "Now I really want my camera. You're the first naked woman to sit on my kitchen counter, which I now plan to have sealed in Lucite. I'd like to document the moment."

"Not a chance. My contract specifies no nude scenes."

"That's a damn shame." He stroked her hair back. "I guess the least I can do after playing Viking and maiden is help you with the dishes."

"The least. Hand me my shirt, will you?"

"See, I've confiscated your clothes. You'll have to do the dishes naked."

Her head cocked, her eyebrows lifted. On a sigh, Ford scooped up her shirt. "It was worth a shot."

HE WOKE in the dark to a quiet house and an empty bed. Groggy and baffled, he rose to look for her. One part of his brain reserved the right to be pissed if she'd gone back across the road without waking him.

He found his front door open, and saw the silhouette of her sitting in one of the chairs on his veranda with Spock stretched at her feet. He smelled coffee as he pushed open the screen.

She glanced over. "Morning."

"As long as it's still dark, it's not morning." He sat beside her. "Give me a hit of that."

"You should go back to bed."

"Are you going to give me a hit of that coffee or make me go get my own?"

She passed him the cup. "I have to decide what to do."

"At . . ." He took her wrist, turned it up and squinted at her watch. "Five-oh-six in the morning?"

"I didn't deal with it yesterday, didn't think about

it. Or not much. I even left my phone over there so the police couldn't contact me. So no one could. I ducked and covered."

"You took a break. There's no reason you can't take a couple more days before you try to figure it all out."

"Actually, there are real and practical reasons I can't take more time. I have subs coming in about two hours, unless I call them off. If I take them off for a couple of days, it's more than screwing up my schedule, which is, of course, already screwed. It messes up theirs, and their employees'. And subs are always juggling jobs, so I could lose key people for more than a couple of days if I hold them off. If that decision is to walk away, I have to tell them that."

"The circumstances aren't of your making, and no one's going to blame you."

"No, I don't think anyone would. But it still creates a domino effect. I also have to consider my budget, which is also screwed. I have insurance, but insurance has a deductible that has to be factored into the whole. I'm already over the high end of my projections, but that was my choice, with the changes and additions I made."

"If you need—"

"Don't," she said, anticipating him. "I'm okay financially, and if I can't make it on my own, I can't make it. If I really needed extra, I could make a few calls, grab a couple voice-over jobs. Bottom line is I can't leave the place the way it is, half done. I've got custom cabinets I ordered back in March, and the balance due when I take delivery. The kitchen appliances will be back in another couple months. Other details, small and large. It has to be finished, that's not really a question. The questions are do I want to finish it, and do I want to stay? Can I? Should I?"

He took another hit of her coffee. Serious conversations, he thought, required serious attention. "Tell me what you'd do if you decided to turn it over to someone else to finish. If you left."

"There are a lot of places I could slip into without the baggage I have here. Stick a pin in a map, I guess, and pick one. Take some of those voice-overs to thicken the bankroll, if I need to. Find a place with potential to flip. I can get a mortgage. Regular and very nice residuals from *Our Family* look good on an application. Or if I don't want the stress of that, I could get a job with a crew. Hell, I could work for Steve's new New York branch."

"You'd be giving up your lofty personal goals."

"Maybe I'd just postpone reaching them. The problem is . . ." She paused, sipped the coffee he'd handed back to her. "The problem is," she repeated,

"I love that house. I love what it was, what I know I can make it. I love this place, and how I feel here. I love what I see when I look out my windows or step out my door. And I'm pissed off that someone's meanness makes me consider giving that up."

Something that had tightened inside him relaxed. "I like it better when you're pissed off."

"I do, too, but it's hard to hold up the level. The part of me that isn't pissed off or discouraged is scared."

"That's because you're not stupid. Someone's set out to deliberately hurt you. You're going to be scared, Cilla, until you know who and why, and make it stop."

"I don't know where to start."

"Do you still think it's old man Hennessy?"

"He's the only one I've met or had contact with around here who's made it clear he hates me. Which, if this were a screenplay, means he couldn't be behind all this because he's the only one who hates me. But—"

"We'll go talk to him, face-to-face."

"And say what?"

"It'll come to us, but basically you're sticking, you're making your home here, and neither you nor a house is responsible for something that happened over thirty years ago. And words to that effect. I'm also going to make copies of those letters you found. I'm going to read them more carefully and so are you. You need to think about passing them to the cops. Because if it's not Hennessy, the next best possibility is it's someone connected to those letters who got wind they still exist and you have them. Janet Hardy's married secret lover revealed? That'd be news. Big, juicy, scandalous news."

She'd thought of that. Of course she'd thought of that. But . . . "They aren't signed."

"Might be clues in there about the identity. Might not be, but we're talking thirty-five years ago. Do you remember everything you wrote thirty-five years ago?"

"I'm twenty-eight, but I get what you're saying." In the still, softening dark, she stared at him. "You've given this a lot of thought."

"Yeah. The first, the prowler in your barn. That could've been somebody hoping to pick up a few Janet Hardy souvenirs. I've got to weigh in the place has been empty for years now, and sure I've seen some people poking around now and then. Against that, I've got to factor most people didn't know there was anything left inside, and any who did probably thought it was worthless junk left by tenants, not the woman herself. But then you come along."

"I clear it out, store it in the barn, and it's clear

and obvious that I'm sorting through it, culling out anything that belonged to my grandmother."

"Somebody gets curious, a little greedy. Possibility. The second, the attack on Steve, could come from the same root. Poking around, somebody's coming. Panic. But that takes it way over harmless if annoying trespass. Also above, if the letters are the goal, trespass to preserve reputation. It's up to assault, arguably attempted murder."

She shivered. "Of discouraged, pissed and scared, scared just leaped way into the lead."

"Good, because then you'll be more careful. Next, your truck door. That one's personal and direct to you. So was the message on the stone wall. Maybe there are two separate people involved."

"Oh, that really helps. Two people who hate me."

"It's another possible. Last, the destruction inside the house. It's more personal, more direct, and it's ballsier. So today, you're going shopping for a security system."

"Is that what I'm going to do?"

The cold bite in her tone didn't break his skin. "One of us is. Since it's your place, I assume you'd rather do it yourself. But if you don't, today, I will. I'm now authorized as I've had you naked on my kitchen counter. No point in whining to me if you didn't bother to read the fine print."

She said nothing for a moment, struggling against the urge to stew. "I intended to arrange that anyway—stay or go."

"Good. And you don't care for ultimatums. Neither do I, but in this particular case, I'm making an exception. I can sleep over there with you. Happy to. But sleep is a foregone conclusion at some point, just as the house being empty at some time or other for some period of time is inevitable. You need to be safe, and to feel safe. You need to protect your property.

"And Cilla, there's no 'go.' You've already decided to stay."

She really did want to stew, she thought, and he was making it damn hard to indulge. "How come you're all macho and pushy with your ultimatum, but you're not all macho and pushy telling me to flee to safety while you slay the dragon?"

"My shining armor's in the shop. And maybe I just like the sex, which would be hard to come by with all the fleeing. Or it could be I don't want to see you give up something you love."

Yeah, he made it damn hard. "When I came out here to sit, I told myself it was just a house. I've put a lot of myself into other houses—it's what makes the rehab worthwhile—and I've let them go. It's just a house, wood and glass and pipes and wire, on a piece of ground."

She looked down when he laid his hand over hers, when the gesture told her he understood. "Of course it's not just a house, not to me. I don't want to let it go, Ford. I'd never get it back, never get back what I've found if I let it go."

She turned her hand over, laced her fingers with his. "Plus, I like the sex."

"It can't be overstated."

"Okay then." She took a deep breath. "I've got to get back. Get ready. Get started."

"Let me get some shoes on. I'll walk you home."

MATT STOOD in the center of the master bath, hands on his hips, face grim. "I'm awful damn sorry about this, Cilla. I don't know what gets into people, I swear I don't. We're going to fix that wall for you, don't worry. And Stan'll come back and do the tile. I can get one of my men to chip out what's damaged in place, but it'd be better to leave the glass block for Stan. I'll give him a call for you."

"I'd appreciate that. I need to go pick up the replacement tile and block, some supplies. Arrange for a security system."

"I hear that. People didn't lock their doors half the time around here when I was a kid. Times change. Another damn shame when it comes to things like this. You said they busted out a pane in the back door? I'll get somebody to replace that for you."

"I'm going to order a new door, and a lock set for that and the front. The plywood's okay for now. You'll need to take down that drywall rather than try to repair it. There's enough on site."

"Sure there is. Anything else I can do, Cilla, you just let me know. Got the other bathroom up here, too?"

"Yeah. Got it good."

"I guess we'd better take a look."

They assessed damage, talked repairs. As she gathered her lists and checked on other areas of the project, crew offered sympathy, asked questions, expressed outrage and disgust. By the time she left, her ears were ringing from it, and with the more comforting sound of whirling drills and buzzing saws.

INEVITABLY, SHE HAD to explain to her usual consultant at the flooring center why she needed to buy considerable square footage of tile she'd already bought, as well as grout. It slowed the process, but Cilla supposed that, too, was inevitable. Even in L.A. she'd formed relationships with specific tile guys, lumber guys, appliance guys. It went with the trade, and good relationships paid off the time spent.

She ran into the same situation at the home supply store when she stopped in to buy the replacement sink and other items on her list. While she waited for the clerk to check stock, she cruised the faucets. Chrome, nickel, brass, copper. Brushed, satin, antiqued. Single handles, vessel style. Matching towel bars, robe hooks.

All the shapes, the textures, the tones, gave her the same rush of pleasure others might find browsing the glittery offerings in Tiffany's.

Copper. Maybe she'd go with copper on her office bath. With a stone vessel-style sink and—

"Cilla?"

She broke off from her visualization to see Tom Morrow and Buddy coming down the aisle. "I thought that was you," Tom said. "Buying or deciding?"

"Both, actually."

"Same for me. I'm outfitting a spec out. Usually my bath and kitchen designer takes care of this, but she's out on maternity leave. Plus, I like to get my hand in occasionally. You know how it is."

"Yes, I do."

"Got my consultant here," he said with a wink. "Buddy'll make sure I don't go buying a center set when I need a wide, or vice versa."

"You've done it before," Buddy pointed out.

"And you never let me forget. I heard you ladies had a fine time on Saturday."

"We did."

"Cathy always says shopping's her hobby. I've got golf, she's got the mall and the outlets."

"Don't see the point in either." Buddy shook his head. "Fishing's got a point."

"Excuse me." The clerk strode up. "Everything's in stock, Ms. McGowan. You got the last we have of the wall-hung sink."

"What wall-hung?" Buddy wanted to know. "I'm plumbing for a pedestal in the third bath."

"It's a replacement. The sink you installed in the second-floor guest bath was damaged."

If he'd been a rooster, Cilla thought, Buddy's cockscomb would have quivered.

"How the hell did that happen? Nothing wrong with it when I put it in."

Okay, Cilla thought, one more time. "I had a break-in Saturday. Some vandalism."

"My God! Were you hurt?" Tom demanded.

"No, I wasn't home. I was out with your wife and Patty and Angie."

"They busted up a sink?" Buddy pulled off his cap to scratch his head. "What the hell for?"

"I couldn't say. But both second-floor baths we'd

finished took a hit. They used my sledge and pickax from the look of it, smashed a lot of tile, one of the walls, the sink, some glass block."

"This is terrible. It's not the sort of thing that happens around here. The police—"

"Are doing what they can," she said to Tom. "So they tell me, anyway." Since she wanted the word spread, she kept going. "I'll be installing a security system."

"Can't blame you. I'm so sorry to hear this, Cilla."

"Wouldn't want my daughter living out that far on her own." Buddy shrugged. "Just saying. Especially after what happened to Steve."

"Bad things happen everywhere. I've got to get my supplies and finish my run. Good luck with the spec."

"Cilla, if there's anything we can do, Cathy or I, you just give a call. We're a growing area, but that doesn't mean we don't take care of our own."

"Thank you."

It warmed her, and stayed warm inside her, even as her supplies were loaded, even as she drove away.

Our own.

EIGHTEEN

Cilla gave herself the pleasure of removing the old, battered doors with their worn or missing weather stripping, and installing their replacements. She salvaged the old, stored them in the barn.

You just never knew, to her mind, when you might need an old door.

She'd opted for mahogany—damn the budget—in an elegantly simple Craftman style. The three-over-three seeded glass panes on the entrance door would let in the light, and still afford some privacy.

Sucker fit, she thought with pleasure after one of the laborers helped her haul it into position. Fit like a fricking dream. She waited until she was alone to stroke her hands over the wood and purr, "Hello, gorgeous. You're all mine now." Humming under her breath, she went to work on the lock set.

She'd gone with the oil-rubbed bronze she'd chosen for other areas of the house and, as she began the install on the lock set, decided she'd made the perfect choice. The dark tones of the bronze showed off well against the subtle red hues in the mahogany.

"That's a nice-looking door."

She looked over her shoulder to see her father stepping out of his car. Cilla was so used to seeing him in what she thought of as his teacher clothes, it took her a minute to adjust her brain to the jeans, T-shirt and ball cap he wore.

"Curb appeal," she called back.

"You're certainly getting that." He paused to look over the front lawns. The grass had been neatly mowed, with its bare patches resowed and the tender new shoots protected by a thin layer of straw. The plantings had begun there, too, with young azaleas and rhododendrons, a clutch of hydrangeas already heading up, a slim red maple with its leaves glowing in the sunlight.

"Still got some work, and I won't put in the flower beds until next spring, unless I manage to put in some fall stuff. But it's coming along."

"You've done an amazing job so far." He joined her on the veranda, close enough she caught a whiff of what she thought might be Irish Spring. He studied the door, the lock set. "That looks sturdy. I'm glad to see it. What about the security system? Word gets around," he added when she raised her eyebrows.

"I was hoping that word would. It might be as much of a deterrent as the system itself. Which went in yesterday."

His hazel eyes tracked to hers, solemnly. "I wish you'd called me, Cilla, about the vandalism."

"Nothing you could've done about it. Give me a second here, I'm nearly done." She whirled the last screws in place, then set aside the cordless screwdriver before admiring the result. "Yeah, it looks good. I almost went with a plate style, but thought it would look too heavy. This is better." She opened and closed the door a couple of times. "Good. I'm using the same style on the back entry, but decided to go with an atrium on . . . sorry. You couldn't possibly be interested."

"I am. I'm interested in what you're doing."

A little surprised by the hurt in his tone, she turned to give him her full attention. "I just meant the odd details—knob or lever style, sliding, swinging, luminary. Do you want to come in?" She opened the door again. "It's noisy, but it's cooler."

"Cilla, what can I do?"

"I . . . Look, I'm sorry." God, she was lousy at this father-daughter thing. How could she be otherwise?

"I didn't mean to imply you don't care what I'm doing."

"Cilla." Gavin closed the door again to block off the noise from inside. "What can I do to help you?"

She felt guilty, and a little panicked, as her mind went blank. "Help me with what?"

He let out a sigh, shoved his hands into his pockets. "I'm not a do-it-yourselfer, but I can hammer a nail or put in a screw. I can fetch and carry. I can make iced tea or go pick up sandwiches. I can use a broom."

"You . . . want to work on the house?"

"School's out for the summer, and I didn't take on any summer classes. I have some time to help, and I'd like to help."

"Well . . . why?"

"I'm aware you have plenty of people, people who know what they're doing, that you're paying to do it. But, I've never done anything for you. I sent child support. I was legally obligated to. I hope you know, or can believe, I'd have sent it without that obligation. I didn't teach you to ride a bike, or to drive a car. I never put toys together for you on Christmas Eve or your birthday—or the few times I did you were too young to possibly remember. I never helped you with your homework or lay in bed waiting for you to come home from a date so I could sleep. I never did any of those things for you, or hundreds more. So I'd like to do something for you now. Something tangible. If you'll let me."

Her heart fluttered, the oddest combination of pleasure and distress. It seemed vital she think of something, the right something, and her mind went on a desperate scavenger hunt. "Ah. Ever done any painting?"

She watched the tension in his face melt into a delighted smile. "As a matter of fact, I'm an excellent painter. Do you want references?"

She smiled back at him. "I'll give you a trial run. Follow me."

She led him in and through to the living room. She hadn't scheduled painting this area quite yet, but there was no reason against it. "The plasterwork's done, and I've removed the trim. Had to. Some of it needed to be stripped, and that's done. I'm still working on making what I need to replicate and replace damaged areas, then I'll stain and seal. Anyway, you won't have to tape or cut in around trim. Oh, and don't worry about the brick on the fireplace, either. I'm going to cover that with granite. Or marble. There's no work going on in this area right now, so you won't be in anyone's way, and they shouldn't be in yours. We can drop-cloth the floors and the supplies stored here."

She set her fists on her hips. "Got your stepladder, your pans, rollers, brushes right over there. Primer's in those ten-gallon cans, and marked. Finish paint's labeled with the L.R. for living room. I hit a sale on Duron, so I bought it in advance. You won't get past starting the primer anyway."

She ran through her mental checklist. "So . . . do you want me to help you set up?"

"I can handle it."

"Okay. Listen, it's a big job, so knock off anytime you get tired of it. I'm going to be working on the back door if you need anything meanwhile."

"Go ahead. I'll be fine."

"Okay. Ah . . . I'll check in after I'm done with the kitchen door."

She pulled away twice during the process of replacing the door—once for the sheer pleasure of walking up and down her newly completed outside stairs. They required staining, sealing, and the doorway cut into what would be her office suite would be blocked with plywood until she installed *that* door. But the stairs themselves delighted her so much she executed an impromptu dance number on the way down, to the applause and whistles of the crew.

Her father and the painting slipped her mind for

over three hours. With twin pangs of guilt and concern, she hurried into the living room, fully expecting to see a weekend DIYer's amateurish mess. Instead, she saw a competently dropped area, a primed ceiling and two primed walls.

And her father, whistling a cheery tune, as he rolled primer on the next wall.

"You're hired," she said from behind him.

He lowered the roller, chuckled, turned. "Will work for lemonade." He picked up a tall glass. "I got some out of the kitchen. And caught your act."

"Sorry?"

"Your Ginger Rogers down the stairs. Outside. You looked so happy."

"I am. The pitch, the landings, the switchbacks. An engineering feat, brought to you by Cilla McGowan and Matt Brewster."

"I forgot you could dance like that. I haven't seen you dance since . . . You were still a teenager when I came to your concert in D.C. I remember coming backstage before curtain. You were white as a sheet."

"Stage fright. I hated that concert series. I hated performing."

"You just did."

"Perform? No, there's performing and there's playing around. That was playing around. Which you're obviously not, here. This is a really good job. And you?" She walked over for a closer inspection—and damn if she couldn't still smell the soap on him. "You barely have a dot of paint on you."

"Years of experience, between painting sets at school and Patty's redecorating habit. It looks so different in here," he added. "With the doorway there widened, the way it changes the shape of the room and opens it."

"Too different?"

"No, honey. Homes are meant to change, to reflect the people who live in them. And I think you'll understand what I mean when I say she's still here. Janet's still here." He touched her shoulder, then just left his hand there, connecting them. "So are my grandparents, my father. Even me, a little. What I see here is a revival."

"Want to see where the stairs lead? My garret?"

"I'd like that."

She got a kick out of showing him around, seeing his interest in her design and plans for her office. It surprised her to realize his approval brought her such satisfaction. In the way, she supposed, it was satisfying to show off to someone ready to be impressed.

"So you'll keep working on houses," he said as they started down the unfinished attic steps.

"That's the plan. Rehabbing either for myself to flip, or for clients. Remodeling. Possibly doing some consulting. It hinges on getting my contractor's license. I can do a lot without it, but with it, I can do more."

"How do you go about getting a license?"

"I take the test for it tomorrow." She held up both hands, fingers crossed.

"Tomorrow? Why aren't you studying? says the teacher."

"Believe me, I have. Studied my brains out, took the sample test online. Twice." She paused by the guest bath. "This room's finished—for the second time."

"This is one that was vandalized?"

"Yeah. You'd never know it," she said, crouching down to run her fingers over the newly laid tile. "I guess that's what counts."

"What counts is you weren't hurt. When I think about what happened to Steve . . ."

"He's doing good. I talked to him yesterday. His physical therapy's going well, which may in part be due to the fact that the therapist is a babe. Do you think Hennessy could have done it?" she asked on impulse. "Is he capable, physically, character-wise?"

"I don't like to think so, when it comes to his character. But the fact is, he's never stopped hating."

After a pause, Gavin let out a sigh. "I'd have to say he hates more now than he did when it happened. Physically? Well, he's a tough old bird."

"I want to talk to him, get a sense. I just haven't decided how to approach it. On the other hand, if it was him, I'm not sure that wouldn't get him even more riled up. I haven't had any problems for nearly two weeks now. I'd like to keep it that way."

"He's been out of town for a few days. He and his wife are visiting her sister. Up in Vermont, I think it is. My neighbor's boy mows their lawn," Gavin explained.

Convenient, she thought as her father went back to painting.

And since the living area was getting painted, she decided to set up her tools outside and get to work on the trim.

IN THE MORNING, Cilla decided she'd been foolish and shortsighted to bar Ford from the house the night before. She hadn't wanted any distractions while she reviewed her test manual, and had planned on an early night and a solid eight hours' sleep.

Instead she'd obsessed about the test, pacing the house, second-guessing herself. When she slept, she tossed and turned with anxiety dreams.

As a result she woke tense, edgy and half sick with nerves. She forced herself to eat half a bagel, then wished she hadn't as even that churned uneasily in her stomach.

She checked the contents of her bag three times to make absolutely certain it held everything she could possibly need, then left the house a full thirty minutes early, just in case she ran into traffic or got lost. Couldn't find a parking place, she added as she locked the front door. Was abducted by aliens.

"Knock it off, knock it off," she mumbled as she strode to her pickup. It wasn't as if the fate of the damn world rested on her test score.

Just hers, she thought. Just her entire future.

She could wait. She could take the test down the road, wait just a little longer. After she'd finished the house. After she'd settled in. After . . .

Stage fright, she thought with a sigh. Performance anxiety and fear of failure all wrapped up in a slippery ribbon. With her stomach knotted, she opened the truck door.

She made a sound that was part laugh, part *awww.*

The sketch lay on the seat, where, she supposed, Ford had put it sometime the night before.

She stood in work boots, a tool belt slung from her hips like a holster. As if she'd drawn them from it, she held a nail gun in one hand, a measuring tape in the other. Around her were stacks of lumber, coils of wire, piles of brick. Safety goggles dangled from a strap around her neck, and work gloves peeked out of the pocket of her carpenter pants. Her face carried a determined, almost arrogant expression.

Below her feet, the caption read:

THE AMAZING, THE INCREDIBLE
CONTRACTOR GIRL

"You don't miss a trick, do you?" she said aloud.

She looked across the road, blew a kiss to where she imagined he lay sleeping. When she climbed into the truck and turned on the engine, all the knots had unraveled.

With the sketch riding on the seat beside her, Cilla turned on the music and drove toward her future, singing.

FORD SETTLED ON his front veranda with his laptop, his sketchbook, a pitcher of iced tea and a bag of Doritos to share with Spock. He couldn't be sure when Cilla might make it back. The drive to and from Richmond was a bitch even without rush hour factored in. Added to it, he couldn't be sure how long the exam ran, or what she might do after to wind down.

So around two in the afternoon, he stationed himself where he couldn't miss her return and kept himself busy. He sent and answered e-mail, checked in with the blogs and boards he usually frequented. He did a little updating on his own website.

He'd neglected his Internet community for the last week or two, being preoccupied with a certain lanky blonde. Hooking back in entertained him for a solid two hours before he noticed at least some of the crew across the road were knocking off for the day.

Matt pulled out, swung to Ford's side of the road, then leaned out the window. "Checking the porn sites?"

"Day and night. How's it going over there?"

"It's going. Finished insulating the attic today. Fucking miserable job. Yeah, hey, Spock, how's it going," he added when the dog gave a single, deep-throated, how-about-me bark. "I'm going home and diving into a cold beer. You coming by for burgers and dogs on the Fourth?"

"Wouldn't miss it. I'll be bringing your boss."

"I thought that's how it was. Nice work, dog. Not you," he added, pointing at Spock. "Don't know what she sees in you, but I guess she settled since she knows I'm married."

"Yeah, that was it. She had to channel her sexual frustration somewhere."

"You can thank me later." With a grin and a toot of the horn, Matt pulled out.

Ford poured another glass of tea and traded his laptop for his sketch pad. He wasn't yet satisfied with his image of his villain. He'd based Devon/Devino predominantly on his tenth-grade algebra teacher, but turns in his original story line made him think he wanted something slightly more . . . elegant. Cold, dignified evil played better. He played around with various face types hoping one jumped out and said: Pick me!

When none did, he considered a cold beer. Then forgot the work and the beer when Cilla's truck pulled into his drive.

He knew before she got out of the truck. It didn't matter that her eyes were shielded by sunglasses. The grin said it all. He headed down, several paces behind a happy Spock, as she got out of the truck, then braced himself as she took a running leap into his arms.

"I'm going to take a wild guess. You passed."

"I *killed!*" Laughing, she bowed back recklessly so he had to shift, brace his legs, or drop her on her head. "For the first time in my life, I kicked exam ass. I kicked its ass down the street, across county lines and out of the goddamn state. Woo!"

She threw her arms into the air, then around his neck. "I am Contractor Girl! Thank you." She kissed him hard enough to vibrate his teeth. "Thank you. Thank you. I was a nervous, quivering mess until I saw that sketch. It just gave me such a high. It really did." She kissed him again. "I'm going to have it framed. It's the first thing I'm going to hang in my office. My licensed-contractor's office."

"Congratulations." He thought he'd known just how much the license meant to her. And realized he hadn't even been close. "We have to celebrate."

"I've got that covered. I bought stuff." She jumped down, then scooped a thrilled Spock into her arms and covered his big head with kisses. Setting him down, she ran back to her truck. "French bread, caviar, a roasted chicken with trimmings, stuff, stuff, stuff, complete with little strawberry shortcakes and champagne. It's all on ice."

She started to muscle out a cooler, before he nudged her aside.

"God, the traffic was a bitch. I thought I'd never get here. Let's have a picnic. Let's have a celebration picnic out back and dance naked on the grass."

The *stuff* she'd bought had to weigh a good fifty

pounds, he thought, but looking at the way she just shone made it seem weightless. "It's like you read my mind."

HE DUG UP a blanket and lit a trio of bamboo torchères to add atmosphere, and discourage bugs. By the time Cilla spread out the feast, half the blanket was covered.

Spock and his bear contented themselves with a ratty towel and a bowl of dog food.

"Caviar, goat cheese, champagne." Ford sat on the blanket. "My usual picnic involves a bucket of chicken, a tub of potato salad and beer."

"You can take the girl out of Hollywood." She began to gather a selection for a plate.

"What is that?"

"It's a blini, for the caviar. A dollop of crème fraîche, a layer of beluga, and . . . You've never had this before?" she said when she read his expression.

"Can't say I have."

"You fear it."

"Fear is a strong word. I have concerns. Doesn't caviar come from—"

"Don't think about it, just eat." She held the loaded blini to his lips. "Open up, you coward."

He winced a little but bit in. The combination of flavors—salty, smooth, mildly sweet—hit his taste buds. "Okay, better than I expected. Where's yours?"

She laughed and fixed another.

"How do you plan to set up?" he asked as they ate. "Your business."

"Mmm." She washed down caviar with champagne. "The Little Farm's a springboard. It gets attention, just because of what it is. The better job I do there, the more chance people see I know what I'm doing. And the subs I've hired talk about it, and about me. I need to build on word of mouth. I'll have to advertise, make it known I'm *in* business. Use connections. Brian to Brian's father, for instance. God, this chicken is great. There are two houses within twelve miles up for sale. Serious fixer-uppers that I think are a little overpriced for the area and their conditions. I'm keeping my eye on them. I may make a lowball offer on one of them, see where it goes."

"Before you finish here?"

"Yeah. Figure, even if I came to terms with the seller straight off, there'd be thirty to ninety days for settlement. I'd push for the ninety. That'd put me into the fall before I have to start outlaying any cash. And that's seven, eight months into the Little Farm.

I juggle the jobs, and the subs, work out a realistic time frame and budget. Flip the house in, we'll say, twelve weeks, keeping the price realistic."

She loaded another blini for both of them. "Greed and not knowing your market's what can kill a flip just as quick as finding out too late the foundation's cracked or the house is sitting in a sinkhole."

"How much would you look to make?"

"On the house I'm looking at? With the price I'd be willing to pay, the budget I'd project, the resale projection in this market?" She bit into the blini while she calculated. "After expenses, I'd look for about forty thousand."

His eyebrows shot up. "Forty thousand, in three months?"

"I'd hope for forty-five, but thirty-five would do it."

"Nice." She was right about the chicken, too. "What if I bought the other one? Hired you?"

"Well, Jesus, Ford, you haven't even seen it."

"You have. And you know what you're doing— about houses and picnics. I could use an investment, and this has the advantage of a fun factor. Plus, I could be your first client."

"You need to at least look at the property, calculate how much you're willing to invest, how long you can let that investment ride." She lifted her champagne glass, gestured with it like a warning. "And how much you can afford to lose, because real estate and flipping are risks."

"So's the stock market. Can you handle both houses?"

She took a drink. "Yeah, I could, but—"

"Let's try this. Figure out a time when you can go through it with me, and we'll talk about the potential, the possibilities, your fee and other practical matters."

"Okay. Okay. As long as we both understand that once you've seen the property and we've gone over those projections, and you tell me you'd rather buy a fistful of lottery tickets than that dump, no harm, no foul."

"Understood and agreed. Now, with the business portion of tonight's program out of the way." He leaned over to kiss her. "Do you have any plans for the Fourth?"

"The fourth what? Blini?"

"No, Cilla. Of July. You know, hot dogs, apple pie, fireworks."

"Oh. No." My God, she thought. It was nearly July. "Where do people go to watch fireworks around here?"

"There are a few options. But this is the great state of Virginia. We set off our own."

"Yeah, I've seen the signs. You all are crazy."

"Be that as it may, Matt's having a cookout. It's a short walk from his place to the park where the Roritan band plays Sousa marches, there's the world-famous pie-eating contest, won four years running by Big John Porter, and other various slices of Americana before the fireworks display. Wanna be my date?"

"Yes, I would." She leaned over the picnic debris, linked her arms around his neck. "Ford?"

"Yeah."

"If I eat another bite of anything, I'm going to be sick. So . . ." She leaped up, grabbed his hands. "Let's dance."

"About that. My plans were to lie here like a dissipated Roman soldier and watch you dance."

"No, you don't. Up, up, up!"

"There's just one problem. I don't dance."

"Everybody dances. Even Spock."

"Not really. Well, yes, he does," Ford admitted as Spock got up to demonstrate. "I don't. Did you ever catch *Seinfeld*? The TV deal."

"Of course."

"Did you see the one where Elaine's at this office party, and to get people up to dance, she starts it off?"

"Oh yeah." The scene popped straight into her mind, made her laugh. "That was bad."

"I make Elaine look like Jennifer Lopez."

"You can't be that bad. I refuse to believe it. Come on, show me."

Those gold-rimmed eyes showed actual pain. "If I show you, you'll never have sex with me again."

"Absolutely false. Show me your moves, Sawyer."

"I have no moves in this arena." But with a heavy sigh, he rose.

"Just a little boogie," she suggested. She moved her hips, her shoulders, her feet. Obviously, to Ford's mind, to some well-oiled internal engine. Clutching the bear between his paws, Spock gurgled his approval.

"You asked for it," he muttered.

He moved, and could swear he heard rusty gears with mismatched teeth grind and shriek. He looked like the Tin Man of Oz, before the oil can.

"Well, that's not . . . Okay, that's really bad." She struggled to swallow a snort of laughter, but didn't quite succeed. The disgusted look he shot her had her holding up her hands and stepping quickly to him. "Wait, wait. Sorry. I can teach you."

This time, Spock snorted.

"Others have tried; all have failed. I have no

rhythm. I am rhythmically impaired. I've learned to live with it."

"Bull. Anyone who has your kind of moves horizontally can have them vertically. Here." She took his hands, set them on her hips, then put hers on his. "It starts here. This isn't a structured sort of thing, like a waltz or quickstep. It's just moving. A little hip action. No, unlock your knees, it's not a goose step, either. Just left, right, left. Shift your weight to the left, not just your hip."

"I look and feel like a spastic robot."

"You don't." She shot Spock a warning glance, and the dog turned his head away. "Relax. Now, keep the hips going, but put your hands on my shoulders. That's it. Feel my shoulders, just a little up and down. Feel that, let that go up your arms, into your shoulders. Just up and down. Don't stiffen up, keep those knees loose. There you go, there you are. You're dancing."

"This isn't dancing."

"It is." She put her hands on his shoulders, then slid them down his arms until they held hands. "And now you're dancing with me."

"I'm standing like an idiot in one spot."

"We'll worry about the feet later. We're starting slow, and smooth. It would even be sexy if you took that pained expression off your face. Don't stop!"

She did a quick inward spin so her back pressed into him, and lifted an arm to stroke it down his cheek.

"Oh, well, if *this* is dancing."

Laughing, she spun back again so they were front to front. "Sway. A little more." She wrapped her arms around his neck, lifted her lips to a breath from his. "Nice."

He closed the distance, sliding slowly into the kiss while his hands ran down her back to her hips.

"Feels like dancing to me," she whispered.

He surfaced to see he was facing in the opposite direction, and several feet away from where they'd started. "How'd that happen?"

"You let it happen. You stopped thinking about it."

"So, I can dance, as long as it's with you."

"Just one more thing." She danced back with a provocative rock of hips, and began unbuttoning her shirt.

"Whoa."

"I believe the celebration called for naked dancing."

He glanced in the direction of his closest neighbors. Dusk had fallen, but torches tossed out light. He glanced down at his dog, who sat, head cocked, obviously fascinated.

"Maybe we should move that event inside."

She shook her head, and her blouse slid down with the movement of her shoulders. "In the grass."

"Ah, Mrs. Berkowitz—"

"Shouldn't spy on her neighbor, even if she could see through that big black walnut tree." Cilla unhooked her pants, kicked off her shoes, which Spock retrieved and carried territorially to his ratty towel. "And when we've finished dancing naked, there's something else I'm going to do on the grass."

"What?"

"I'm going to give you the ride of your life." She stepped out of her pants, continued to sway, turn as she ran her hands over her own body, marginally covered now in two tiny white swatches.

Ford forgot the dog, the shoes, the neighbors. He watched, all of the blood draining out of his head as she flicked open the front hook, opened her bra inch by delicious inch. The torchlight glimmered gold over her skin, danced in her eyes like sun on a pure blue sea.

When the bra floated to the ground, she ran a fingertip under, just under the low-riding waist of her panties. "You're still dressed. Don't you want to dance with me?"

"Yeah. Oh yeah. Can I just say something first?"

She trailed her fingers down her breasts, smiled at him. "Go ahead."

"Two things, actually. Oh Christ," he managed when she lifted her hair, let it fall over those glowing shoulders. "You're the most beautiful thing I've ever seen. And at this moment? I'm the luckiest man in the known universe."

"You're about to get luckier." Tossing her hair back, she started toward him. She pressed her naked body to his. "Now, dance with me."

NINETEEN

On the morning of the Fourth, Ford rolled out of Cilla's bed. It didn't surprise him she was already up, even on a holiday. He considered it his duty as an American to sleep in, but apparently she didn't share his staunch sense of patriotism. He groped his way downstairs, and followed the now familiar sound of *whoosh-bang!* to the living room.

She stood on a ladder shooting nails into window trim.

"You're working." It was an accusation.

She glanced back. "A little. I wanted to see how this trim looks against the paint since my father finished it. I still can't believe he painted all this, and so well. If he didn't have a job, I'd hire him."

"Is there coffee?"

"Yes, there is. Spock's out back. He fears the nail gun."

"Minute."

He heard more *whoosh-bang*ing behind him as he

dragged himself into the kitchen. The coffeemaker stood on a small square of counter as yet un-demoed. Shielding his eyes from the sunlight blasting through the windows, he found a mug, poured. After the first couple sips, the light seemed more pleasant, and less like an alien weapon designed to blind all humankind.

He drank half the mug standing where he was, and after topping it off felt mostly awake. Carrying it with him, he walked back to the living room and watched her work for a few minutes while the caffeine wove its magic.

She stood on the floor now, fitting the diagonal edges of the bottom piece to the sides she'd already nailed up. In what struck him as wizard-fast time, the dark, wide trim framed the window.

She set the gun down, took several steps back. He heard her whisper, "Yes, exactly."

"It looks good. What did you do with what was there before?"

"This is what was there before, or mostly. I had to build the sill to match because it was damaged."

"I thought it was white."

"Because some idiot along the way slapped white paint on this gorgeous walnut. I stripped it. A little planing, a little stain and a couple coats of poly, and it's back to its original state."

"Huh. Well, it looks good. I didn't get the paint

color until now. Thought it looked a little dull. But it looks warmer against the wood. Like, ah, a forest in the fog."

"It's called Shenandoah. It just seemed right. When you look out the windows in this room, it's the mountains, the sky, the trees. It's just right." She walked back, picked up another piece of trim.

"You're still working."

"We don't have to leave for . . ." She looked at her watch, calculated. "About ninety minutes. I can get some of this trim run before I have to get ready."

"Okay. I'm taking the coffee and my dog and heading across the road. I'll pick you up in an hour and a half."

"Great. But you might want to put some pants on first."

He glanced down at his boxers. "Right. I'm going to put on pants, possibly shoes, take the coffee and so on."

"I'll be ready."

HE DIDN'T EXPECT her to be ready. Not because she was female, but because he knew what often happened when he himself got lost in the work. If he didn't set an alarm, being late, or in fact missing an appointment or event altogether, was the norm.

So it surprised him when she came out of the house even as he stopped in front of it. And her appearance left him momentarily speechless.

She'd left her hair down, as she rarely did, so it spilled dark, aged gold, down her back. She wore a dress of bright red swirled against white, with a kind of thin and floaty skirt and thin straps that set off those strong shoulders.

With his paws planted on the window, Spock leaned out. Ford translated the series of sounds the dog made as the canine version of a wolf whistle.

He got out of the car—he just had to—and said, "Wow."

"You like? Check this." She did a turn, giving him a chance to admire the low dip of the back with the flirt of crisscrossing ties.

"And again, wow. I've never seen you in a dress before, and this one pulls out some stops."

Instant distress ran across her face. "It's too much, too fussy for a backyard cookout. I can change in five minutes."

"First, over my dead body. Second, 'fussy' is the last word I'd use. It's great. You look all summery sexy, ice-cream-sundae cool. Only now I wish I'd thought to take you out where you'd wear dresses. I feel a fancy dinner coming on."

"I prefer backyard picnics."

"They are permanently top of my list."

SHE'D EXPECTED IT to be awkward initially, the introductions, the mixing. But she knew so many of the people there that it was as easy and pleasant as Matt's backyard with its generous deck and smoking grill.

Josie, Matt's pretty and very pregnant wife, snatched Cilla away from Ford almost immediately. "Here." Josie handed Ford a beer. "Go away. Wine, beer, soft?" she asked Cilla.

"Ah, I'll start with soft."

"Try the lemonade, it's great. Then I'm going to steal you for ten minutes over there in the shade. I'd say walk this way, but waddling's unattractive unless you're eight months pregnant. I've been dying to meet you."

"You're welcome to come by the house, anytime."

"I nearly have a couple times, but with this." She patted her belly as they walked. "And that." And pointed toward a pack of kids on a swing set. "The little guy in the blue shorts and red shirt squeezing Spock in mutual adoration is mine. So between this and that, and a part-time job, I haven't made it by. Either to welcome you to the area, or to poke my nose in to see what's going on. Which Matt claims is pretty great."

"He's terrific to work with. He's very talented."

"I know. I met him when my family moved here. I was seventeen and very resentful that my father's work dragged me away from Charlotte and my friends. My life was over, of course. Until the following summer when my parents hired a local contractor to put an addition on the house, and there was a young, handsome carpenter on the crew. It took me four years," she said with a wink, "but I landed him."

She sat with a long, heartfelt sigh.

"I'll get this out of the way. I adored Katie. I had a Katie doll. In fact, I still do. It's stored away for this one." She ran a gentle circle over her belly. "We're having a girl this time. I've seen most if not all of your grandmother's movies and have *Barn Dance* on DVD. I hope we come to like each other because you're seeing Ford and I love him. In fact, Matt knows if I ever get tired of him and decide to ditch him, I'm going after Ford."

Cilla sipped her lemonade. "I think I already like you."

IN THE HEAVY, drowsing heat, people sought out the shade of deck umbrellas or gathered at tables under the spread of trees. Seemingly unaffected by spiraling temperatures and thickening humidity, kids clambered over the swing set or raced around the yard like puppies with inexhaustible energy. Cilla calculated that Matt's big yard, sturdy deck and pretty two-story Colonial held nearly a hundred people spanning about five generations.

She sat with Ford, Brian and a clutch of others at one of the picnic tables, plates loaded with burgers, hot dogs, a wide variety of summer salads. From where she sat, she could see her father, Patty and Ford's parents talking and eating together on the deck. As she watched, Patty laughed, laid a hand on Gavin's cheek and rubbed. He took his wife's hand, kissed her knuckles lightly as the conversation continued.

It struck, a dull blade of envy and its keener edge of understanding. They loved each other. She'd known it, of course, on some level. But she saw it now, in the absent gestures she imagined neither of them would remember, the steady and simple love. Not just habit or contentment or duty, not even the bonds of—how long had they been together? she wondered. Twenty-three, twenty-four years? No, not even the bonds of half a lifetime.

They'd beaten the odds, won the prize.

Angie walked by—so young, fresh, pretty—with

the gangly guy in baggy shorts she'd introduced to Cilla as Zach. Angie stopped, and for a moment Cilla was stunned to realize how much she wished she was close enough to hear the quick, animated conversation. Then with her hand resting on her mother's shoulder, Angie leaned down to kiss her father's head before moving on.

That said it all, Cilla decided. They were a unit. Angie would go back to college in the fall. She might move a thousand miles away at any point in her life. And still, they would always be a unit.

Deliberately, she looked away.

"I think I'll get a beer," she said to Ford. "Do you want one?"

"No, I'm good. I'll get it for you."

She nudged him back as he started to rise. "I can get it."

She wandered off to the huge galvanized bucket filled with ice and bottles and cans. She didn't particularly want a beer, but figured she was stuck now. She fished one out and, thinking of it as a prop, crossed over to where Matt manned the grill.

"Do you ever get a break?" she asked him.

"Had a couple. People come and go all day, that's how it is at these things. Gotta keep it smoking."

His little boy raced up, wrapped his arms around Matt's leg, chattering in a toddlerese Cilla was incapable of interpreting. Matt, however, appeared to be fluent. "Let's see the proof."

Eyes wide, the boy pulled up his shirt to expose his belly. Matt poked at it, nodding. "Okay then, go tell Grandma."

When the boy raced off again, Matt caught Cilla's puzzled expression. "He said he finished his hot dog and could he have a big, giant piece of Grandma's cake."

"I didn't realize you were bilingual."

"I have many skills." As if to prove it, he flipped a trio of burgers expertly. "Speaking of skills, Ford told me you ran some of the living room trim this morning."

"Yeah. It looks, if I must say—and I do—freaking awesome. Is that your shop?" She gestured with the beer to the cedar building at the rear of the property.

"Yeah. Want to see?"

"You know I do, but we'll take the tour another time."

"Where are you going to put yours?"

"Can't decide. I'm debating between putting up something from scratch or refitting part of the existing barn. The barn option's more practical."

"But it sure is fun to build from the ground up."

"I never have, so it's tempting. How many square

feet do you figure?" she continued, and fell into the comfortable, familiar rhythm of shoptalk.

As evening drifted in, people began the short pilgrimage to the park. They crowded the quiet side street, carting lawn chairs, coolers, blankets, babies and toddlers. As they approached, the bright, brassy sound of horns welcomed them.

"Sousa marches," Ford said, "as advertised." He shifted the pair of folding chairs he had under his arm while Cilla led Spock on a leash. "You having fun?"

"Yes. Matt and Josie put on quite a cookout."

"You looked a little lost back there, just for a couple minutes."

"Did I?"

"When we were chowing down. Before you got up to get a beer, and I lost you to Matt and Tool Time Talk."

"Probably too much pasta salad. I'm having a really good time. It's my first annual Shenandoah Valley backyard July Fourth extravaganza. So far, it's great."

The park spread beneath the mountains, and the mountains were hazed with heat so the air seemed to ripple over them like water. Hundreds of people scattered through the park, sprawling over its greens. Concession stands did a bustling business under the shade of their awnings, in offerings of country ham sandwiches, sloppy joes, funnel cakes, soft drinks. Cilla caught the scents of grease and sugar, grass and sunscreen.

Over loudspeakers came a whine of static, then the echoey announcement that the pie-eating contest would begin in thirty minutes in front of the north pavilion.

"I mentioned the pie-eating contest, right?"

"Yes, and four-time champ Big John Porter."

"Disgusting. We don't want to miss it. Let's grab a square of grass, stake our claim." Stopping, Ford began to scan. "We need to spread out some, save room for Matt and Josie and Sam. Oh hey, Brian's already homesteaded. The girl he's with is Missy."

"Yes, I met her."

"You met half the county this afternoon." He slanted Cilla a look. "Nobody expects you to remember names."

"Missy Burke, insurance adjuster, divorced, no kids. Right now she's talking to Tom and Dana Anderson, who own a small art gallery in the Village. And Shanna's strolling over with Bill—nobody mentioned his last name—a photographer."

"I stand corrected."

"Schmoozing used to be a way of life."

They'd barely set up, exchanged more than a few

words with their companions, before Ford dragged her off to the pie-eating contest.

A field of twenty-five contestants sat at the ready, white plastic bibs tied around their necks. They ranged from kids to grandpas, with the smart money on Big—an easy two-fifty big—John Porter.

At the signal, twenty-five faces dropped forward into crust and blueberry filling. A laugh burst straight out of her, drowned away in the shouts and cheers.

"Well, God! That *is* disgusting."

"Yet entertaining. Man, he's going to do it again! Big John!" Ford shouted, and began to chant it. The crowd picked up the rhythm, erupting with applause as Big John lifted his wide, purple-smeared face.

"Undefeated," Ford said when Porter was pronounced the winner. "The guy can't be beat. He's the Superman of pie-eaters. Okay, there's the raffle in the south pavilion. Let's go buy some chances on the ugliest, most useless prize."

They settled, after considerable debate, on a plastic rooster wall clock in vibrant red. Target selected, Ford moved to ticket sales. "Hi, Mrs. Morrow. Raking it in?"

"We're doing well this year. I smell record breaker. Hello, Cilla. Don't you look gorgeous? Enjoying yourself?"

"Very much."

"I'm glad to hear it. I imagine it's a little tame and countrified compared to the way you usually spend your holiday, but I think we put on a nice event. Now, how much can I squeeze you for? I mean . . ." Cathy gave an exaggerated flutter of lashes. "How many tickets would you like?"

"Going for twenty."

"Each," Cilla said and pulled out a bill of her own.

"That's what I like to hear!" Cathy counted them off, tore off their stubs. "Good luck. And just in time. We'll start announcing prizewinners over the loudspeaker starting in about twenty minutes. Ford, if you see your mama, tell her to hunt me up. I want to talk to her about . . ."

Cilla tuned out the conversation when she saw Hennessy staring at her from the other side of the pavilion. The bitter points of his hate scraped over her skin. Beside him stood a small woman, with tired eyes in a tired face. She tugged at his arm, but he remained rigid.

The heat went out of the day, the light, the color. Hate, Cilla thought, strips away joy. But she wouldn't turn away from it, refused to allow herself to turn away.

So it was he who turned, who finally bent to his wife's pleas to stride away from the pavilion across the summer green grass.

She said nothing to Ford. The day would not be spoiled. She soothed the throat the silent encounter had dried to burning with lemonade, wandered through the crowd as the sun began to dip toward the western peaks.

She talked, laughed. She won the rooster wall clock. And the tension drained away. As the sky darkened, Sam climbed up into Ford's lap to hold a strange, excited conversation.

"How do you know what he's saying?" Cilla demanded.

"It's similar to Klingon."

They announced "The Star-Spangled Banner," and the crowd rose. Beside her, Ford hitched the boy on his hip. Around her, under an indigo sky, with the flicker of glow tubes and fireflies in the dark, mixed voices swelled. On impulse, out of sudden need, she took Ford's hand, holding on until the last note died away.

Moments after they took their seats again, the first boom exploded. On the sound Sam leaped out of Ford's lap and into his father's. And Spock leaped off the ground and into Ford's.

Safe, Cilla thought, while lights shattered indigo. Where they knew they'd always be safe.

"GOOD?" Ford asked as they drove down the quiet roads toward home.

"Very good." Amazingly good, she realized. "Beginning, middle and end."

"What are you going to do with that thing?" He glanced down at the clock.

"Thing?" Cilla cradled the rooster in her arms. "Is that any way to speak about our child?" She patted it gently. "I'm thinking the barn. I could use a clock out there, and this is pretty appropriate. And I like having a memento from my first annual Fourth. It'll be way too late in the year for a cookout when my place is done. But after today, I think I'm going to plan a party. A big, sprawling, open-house-type thing. Fire in the hearth, platters of food, flowers and candles. I'd like to see what it's like to have the house filled with people who aren't working on it."

She stretched out her legs. "But tonight, I'm partied and festived out. It'll be nice to get home to the quiet."

"Almost there."

"Want to share the quiet with me?"

"I had that in mind."

They glanced at each other as he turned into her drive. When he looked back, the headlights flashed over the red maple. "What's that hanging—"

"My truck!" She reared forward, gripping the dash. "Oh, goddamn it, son of a bitch. Stop! Stop!"

She was already yanking off her seat belt, shoving at the door before he'd come to a complete stop behind her truck.

Loose clumps of broken safety glass hung in the back window. More sparkled in the gravel, crunching under her feet as she ran.

Ford had his phone out, punching in nine-one-one. "Wait. Cilla, just wait."

"Every window. He smashed every window."

Cannonball holes gaped in the windshield, erupted into mad spiderwebs of shattered glass. As the cold rage choked her, she saw her headlights had been smashed, her grille battered.

"A lot of good the alarm did me." She could have wept. She could have screamed. "A lot of damn good."

"We're going to go in, check the alarm. I'm going to check the house, then you're going to stay inside."

"It's too much, Ford. It's just too damn much. Vicious, vindictive, *insane*. The crazy old bastard needs to be locked up."

"Hennessy? He's out of town."

"He's not. I saw him tonight, at the park. He's back. And I swear to God if he could've used the bat or pipe or whatever he used here on me then and there, he would have."

She whirled around, riding on the fury. And saw in the car's headlights what Ford had seen hanging from a branch of her pretty red maple.

Ford grabbed her arm when she started forward. "Let's go in. We'll wait for the cops."

"No." She shook off his hand, crossed from gravel to grass.

She'd been six, Cilla recalled, when they marketed that particular doll. She wore her hair—a sunny blond that hadn't yet darkened—in a pair of pony-tails tied with pink ribbons above her ears. The rib-bon sashing the pink-and-white gingham dress matched. Lace frothed at the white anklets above the glossy patent leather of her Mary Janes.

Her smile was as sunny as her hair, as sweet as the pink ribbons.

He'd fashioned the noose out of clothesline, she noted. A careful and precise job, so that the doll hung in horrible effigy. Just above the ribbon sash, the cardboard placard read: WHORE.

"Optional accessories—sold separately—for this one included a scale model tea set. It was one of my favorites." She turned away, picked up a whining, quivering Spock to hug. "You're right. We should go inside, check the house just in case."

"Give me the keys. I want you to wait on the veranda. Please."

A polite word, Cilla thought. How odd to hear the absolute authority under the courtesy. "We know he's not in there."

"Then it's no problem for you to wait out on the veranda." To close the issue, he simply opened her purse, pulled out the keys.

"Ford—"

"Wait out here."

The fact that he left the door open told Cilla he had no doubt she'd do what he ordered. With a shrug, she stepped over to the rail, nuzzling Spock before she set him down. No one had been in the house, so there was no harm in waiting. And no point in arguing about it.

Besides, from here she could stare at her truck, brood over the state of it. Wallow in the brooding. She'd felt so damn *good* the day she bought that truck, so full of anticipation when she loaded it up for her trip east.

The first steps toward her dream.

"Everything's okay," Ford said from behind her.

"It's really not, is it?" Some part of her, some

bitchy, miserable part of her, wanted to shrug off the comforting hands he laid on her shoulders. But she stopped herself.

"Do you know how it felt to me today? Like I was in a movie. I don't mean that in a bad way, just the opposite. Little slices and scenes of a movie I actually wanted to be part of. Not quite there yet, still pretty new on the set. But starting to feel . . . really feel comfortable in my skin."

She drew in a long breath, let it out slowly. "And now, this is reality. Broken glass. But the odd thing, the really odd thing. That was me today. It was me. And this? Whatever this is directed at? That's the image, that's the mirage. The smoke and mirrors."

FOREST LAWN CEMETERY 1972

The air sat hot and still while the smog lay over it like a smudge from a sweaty finger. Graves, housing stars and mortals alike, spread, cold slices in the green. And all the flowers, blooming tears shed by the living for the dead.

Janet wore black, the frame within the dress shrunk from grief. A willow stem gone brittle. A wide black hat and dark glasses shaded her face, but that grief poured through the shields.

"They can't put the stone up yet. The ground settles first. But you can see it, can't you? His name carved into white marble, the short years I had him. I tried to think of a poem, a few lines to have carved, but how could I think? How could I? So I had them carve 'Angels Wept.' Just that. They must have, I think. They must have wept for my Johnnie. Do you see the angels that look down on him, weeping?"

"Yes. I've come here before."

"So you know how it will look. How it will always look. He was the love of my life. All the men, husbands, lovers, they came and went. But he? Johnnie. He came *from* me." Every word she spoke was saturated with grief. "I should have . . . so many things. Can you imagine what it is for a mother to stand over the grave of her child and think, 'I should have'?"

"No. I'm sorry."

"So many are. They pour out their sorry to me, and it touches nothing. Later, it helps a little. But these first days, first weeks, nothing touches it. I'll be there." She gestured to the ground beside the grave. "I know that even now because I've arranged it. Me and Johnnie."

"And your daughter. My mother."

"On the other side of me, if she wants it. But she's young, and she'll go her own way. She wants . . . everything. You know that, and I have nothing for her now, not in these first days, first weeks. Nothing to give. But I'll be there soon enough, in the ground with Johnnie. I don't know when yet, I don't know how soon it comes. But I think of making it now. I think of it every day. How can I live when my baby can't? I think about how. Pills? A razor? Walking into the sea? I can never decide. Grief blurs the mind."

"What about love?"

"It opens, when it's real. That's why it can hurt so much. You wonder if I could have stopped this. If I hadn't let him run wild. People said I did."

"I don't know. Another boy died that night, and the third was paralyzed."

"Was that my fault?" Janet demanded as bitterness coated the grief. "Was it Johnnie's? They all got into the car that night, didn't they? Drunk, stoned. Any one of them could've gotten behind the wheel, and it wouldn't have changed. Yes, yes, I indulged him, and I thank God for it now. Thank God I gave him all I could in the short time he lived. I would do it all again." She covered her face with her hands, shoulders shaking. "All again."

"I don't blame you. How can I? I don't know. Hennessy blames you."

"What more does he *want*? Blood?" She dropped her hands, threw out her arms. And the tears slid down the pale cheeks. "At least he has his son. I have a name carved into white marble." She dropped to her knees on the ground.

"I think he does want blood. I think he wants mine."

"He can't have any more. Tell him that." Janet lay down beside the grave, ran her hands over it. "There's been enough blood."

TWENTY

Cilla told no one. As far as anyone knew, she'd taken the loaner her insurance company arranged to do a supply run.

She pulled up in front of the Hennessy house, on a shady street in Front Royal. The white van sat in the drive, beside a ramp that ran to the front door of the single-story ranch house.

Her heart knocked. She didn't question if it was nerves or anger. It didn't matter. She'd do what she needed to do, say what she needed to say.

The door opened before Cilla reached it, and the woman she'd seen the night before came out. Cilla saw her hand tremble on the knob she clutched at her back. "What do you want here?"

"I want to speak to your husband."

"He's not home."

Cilla turned her head to stare deliberately at the van, then looked back into Mrs. Hennessy's eyes.

"He took my car into the shop. It needed work. Do you think I'm a liar?"

"I don't know you. You don't know me. I don't know your husband any more than he knows me."

"But you keep sending the police here, to our home. Again this morning, with their questions and suspicions, with *your* accusations." Mrs. Hennessy drew in a ragged breath. "I want you to go away. Go away and leave us alone."

"I'd be happy to. I'd be thrilled to. You tell me what it's going to take to make him stop."

"Stop *what?* He's got nothing to do with your troubles. Don't we have enough of our own? Don't we have enough without you pointing your finger at us?"

She would not back down, Cilla told herself. She would not feel guilty for pushing at this small, frightened woman. "He drives by *my* home almost every day. And almost every day he parks on the shoulder, sometimes for as long as an hour."

Mrs. Hennessy gnawed her lips, twisted her fingers together. "It's not against the law."

"Trespassing is against the law, cracking a man's skull open is against the law. Breaking in and destroying private property is against the law."

"He did none of those things." The fear remained,

but a whip of anger lashed through it. "And you're a liar if you say different."

"I'm not a liar, Mrs. Hennessy, and I'm not a whore."

"I don't know what you are."

"You know, unless you're as crazy as he is, that I'm not responsible for what happened to your son."

"Don't talk about my boy. You don't know my boy. You don't know anything about it."

"That's absolutely right. I don't. Why would you blame me?"

"I don't blame you." Weariness simply covered her. "Why would I blame you for what happened all those terrible years ago? There's nobody to blame for that. I blame you for bringing the police down on my husband when we did nothing to you."

"When I went over to his van to introduce myself, to express my sympathy, he called me a bitch and a whore, and he spat at me."

A flush of shame stained Mrs. Hennessy's cheeks. Her lips trembled as her eyes shifted away. "That's what you say."

"My half sister was right there. Is she a liar, too?"

"Even if it is so, it's a far cry from everything you're laying at our door."

"You saw the way he looked at me last night, in

the park. You know how much he hates me. I'm appealing to you, Mrs. Hennessy. Keep him away from me and my home."

Cilla turned away. She'd only gotten halfway down the ramp when she heard the door shut, and the lock shoot home.

Oddly, the conversation, however tense and difficult, made her feel better. She'd done something besides calling the police and sitting back, waiting for the next assault.

Pushing forward, as that was the direction she was determined to go, she swung by the real estate office to make an offer on the first house she'd selected. She went in low, a fair chunk lower than she felt the house was worth in the current market. To Cilla, the negotiations, the offers, the counters, were all part of the fun.

Back in the loaner, she contacted the agent in charge of the second listing to make an appointment for a viewing. No point, she decided, in letting the moss grow. She drove back to Morrow Village, completed another handful of errands, including a quick grocery run, before heading back toward home.

She spotted the white van before Hennessy spotted her. Since he came from the direction of the Little Farm, she assumed he'd had time to go home, talk to his wife and drive out while she'd been running around Front Royal and the Village.

He caught sight of her as their vehicles passed, and the flare of recognition burned over his face.

"Yeah, that's right," she muttered as she rounded a curve, "not my truck, since you beat the hell out of it last night." She shook off the annoyance, took the next turn. Her gaze flicked up to the rearview mirror to see the van coming up behind her.

So you want to have this out? she wondered. Have what Ford called a face-to-face? That's fine. Great. He could just follow her home where they'd have a—

The wheel jerked in her hands when the van rammed her from behind. The sheer shock didn't allow room for anger, even for fear, as she tightened her grip.

He rammed her again—a smash of metal, a squeal of tires. The truck seemed to leap under her and buck to the right. She wrenched the wheel, fighting it back. Before she could punch the gas, he rammed her a third time. Her tires skidded off the asphalt and onto the shoulder while her body jerked forward, slammed back. Her fender kissed the guardrail, and her temple slapped smartly against the side window.

Small bright dots danced in front of her eyes as

she gritted her teeth, prayed and steered into the skid. The truck swerved, and for one hideous moment she feared it would flip. She landed with a bone-jarring thud, nose-down, in the runoff gully on the opposite shoulder as her air bag burst open.

Later, she would think it was sheer adrenaline, sheer piss-in-your-face mad that had her leaping out of the truck, slamming the door. A woman ran across the lawn of a house set back across the road. "I saw what he did! I saw it! I called the police!"

Neither Cilla nor Hennessy paid any attention. He shoved out of the van, fists balled at his sides as they came at each other.

"You don't come to my house! You don't talk to my wife!"

"Fuck you! *Fuck* you! You're crazy. You could've killed me."

"Then you'd be in hell with the rest of them." Eyes wheeling, teeth bared, he knocked her back with a vicious shove.

"Don't you put your hands on me again, old man."

He shoved her again, sending her feet skidding until she slammed into the back of the truck. "I see you in there. I see you in there, you bitch."

This time he raised his fist. Cilla kicked him in the groin, and dropped him.

"Oh God. Oh my God!"

Dazed, adrenaline seeping out like water through cracks in a dam, Cilla saw the Good Samaritan racing down the road toward her. The woman had a phone in one hand, a garden stake in the other.

"Are you all right? Honey, are you all right?"

"Yes, I think. I . . . I feel a little sick. I need to—" Cilla sat, dropped her head between her updrawn knees. She couldn't get her breath, couldn't feel her fingers. "Can you call someone for me?"

"Of course I can. Don't you think about getting up, mister. I'll hit you upside the head with this, I swear I will. Who do you want me to call, honey?"

Cilla kept her head down, waiting for the dizziness to pass, and gave her new best friend Ford's number.

He got there before the police, all but flew out of his car. She'd yet to try to stand, and would forever be grateful that Lori Miller stood like a prison guard over Hennessy.

Hennessy sat, sweat drying on his bone-white face.

"Where are you hurt? You're bleeding."

"It's okay. I just hit my head. I think I'm okay."

"I wanted to call for an ambulance, but she said no. I'm Lori." The woman gestured in the direction of her house.

"Yeah. Thanks. Thanks. Cilla—"

"I'm just a little shaky. I thought I was going to be sick, but it passed. Help me up, will you?"

"Look at me first." He cupped her chin, studied her eyes. Apparently what he saw satisfied him enough for him to lift her to her feet.

"Knees are wobbly," she told him. "This hurts." She laid her fingers under the knot on her temple. "But I think that's the worst of it. I don't know how to thank you," she said to Lori.

"I didn't do anything, really. You sure know how to take care of yourself. Here they come." Lori pointed to the police car. "Now *my* knees are wobbly," she said with a breathless laugh. "I guess that's what happens after the worst is over."

SHE TOLD the story to one of the county deputies as, she imagined, Lori gave her witness statement to the other across the road. She imagined the skid marks told their own tale. Hennessy, as far as she could tell, refused to speak at all. She watched the deputy load him into the back of the cruiser.

"I've got stuff in the truck. I need to get it out before they tow it."

"I'll send someone back for it. Come on."

"I was nearly home," she said as Ford helped her

into his car. "Another half mile, I'd have been home."

"We need to put some ice on that bump, and you need to tell me the truth if you hurt anywhere. You need to tell me, Cilla."

"I can't tell yet. I feel sort of numb, and exhausted." She let out a long sigh when he stopped in front of his house. "I think if I could just sit down for a while, in the cool, until I, I guess the phrase is collect myself. You'll call over, ask a couple of the guys to get the stuff out of the truck?"

"Yeah, don't worry about it."

He put his arm around her waist to lead her into the house. "Bed or sofa?"

"I was thinking chair."

"Bed or sofa," he repeated.

"Sofa."

He walked her into the lounge so he could keep an eye on her while he got a bag of frozen peas for her temple. Spock tiptoed to her to rub his head up and down her arm. "It's okay," she told him. "I'm okay." So he planted his front paws on the side of the couch, sniffed at her face, licked her cheek.

"Down," Ford ordered when he came in.

"No, he's fine. In fact . . . maybe I could have him up here for a while."

Ford patted the couch. On cue, Spock jumped

up, bellied in beside Cilla and laid his heavy, comforting head below her breasts.

Ford eased pillows behind her head. He brought her a cold drink, brushed his lips lightly over her forehead, then laid the cold bag at her temple.

"I'll make the calls. You need anything else?"

"No, I've got it all. Better already."

He smiled. "It's the magic peas."

When he turned away, stepped out onto the back veranda to make the calls, the smile had turned to a look of smoldering fury. His fist pounded rhythmically against the post as he punched numbers.

"Can't go into it now," he said when Matt answered. "Cilla's here. She's all right."

"What do you mean she's—"

"Can't go into it now."

"Okay."

"Her truck's about a half mile down, headed toward town. I need you to send somebody down to get whatever she picked up today out of it. Hennessy was at her, and now the cops have him."

"Holy sh—"

"I'll call you back later when I can talk about it."

He clicked off, glanced at his hand and saw he'd pounded it often and hard enough to draw some blood. Oddly, it helped.

Deciding he was calm enough, Ford stepped back

inside. Because she lay quiet, eyes closed, one arm over the dog, he opened the window seat to take out one of the throws stored inside. Her eyes opened when he draped it over her.

"I'm not asleep. I was trying to remember how to meditate."

"Meditate?"

"California, remember? Anyone living in California over a year must meet minimum meditation requirements. Unfortunately, I always sucked at it. Empty your mind? If I empty part of mine, something jumps right in to fill the void. And I know I'm babbling."

"It's okay." He sat on the edge of the couch, turned the bag of peas over to lay the colder side on her temple.

"Ford, he really wanted to kill me." Her eyes clung to his, and he saw the shadow of pain in them as she pushed herself up to sit. "It's not like doing grand jetés through the woods while the reanimated psycho killer chases you. I've had people dislike me. My own mother from time to time. I've even had people try to hurt me. I dated this guy once who slapped me around good one night. One night," she repeated. "He never got the chance to do it again. But even he didn't hate me. He didn't want me dead.

"I don't know how to resolve that someone does.

I don't know how to fit that into my life and deal with it."

"You don't resolve it. You don't resolve something that has no sanity or logic. And, Cilla, you are dealing with it. You did. You stopped him."

"A really lucky kick into seventy-, maybe eighty-year-old balls. I was so *pissed*, Ford, that I didn't think. Do I stay in the truck, lock the doors, call nine-one-one, or you, or the half a dozen guys a half mile away like a rational person? No, I jump out and confront this . . . this lunatic who's just tried to run me off the road, like he's going to fear the sharp lash of my tongue. And I'm *still* so pissed when he starts shoving me, I don't take off. Like I couldn't outrun a man old enough to be my grandfather?"

"You're not a runner." He laid his finger over her lips when she started to speak. "You're not. Do I wish it had occurred to you to lock yourself in the truck and call me? Maybe. Because then I could've come speeding to the rescue. I could've kicked him in the balls. But the fact is, I feel some better knowing that when somebody tries to hurt you, you know how to take care of yourself."

"I could go a long time without having to take care of myself like that again."

"Me too." He stroked her hair when she laid her head on his shoulder. "Me too."

And maybe he could've gone a little while longer without realizing he was in love with her. He could've strolled into that, the way he strolled across the road to her house. Casual and easy. Instead, he'd had it slammed into him, clutched in the meaty fist of fear and rage, in one hard and painful punch when he'd seen her sitting on the side of the road.

Nothing to do about it now, he told himself. Bad, bad timing. What she needed now was a shoulder to lean on, somebody to get her a bag of frozen peas and offer a quiet place to . . . collect herself.

"How's the head?"

"Strangely, it feels like I bashed it against a window."

"Will you take some aspirin?"

"Yeah. And maybe a session in your hot tub. I'm a little stiff and sore. I got jostled around pretty good."

He had to fight to keep his grip on her from tightening, to stop himself from squeezing her against him. "I'll set you up."

"Thanks." She turned her head to brush her lips against his throat. "Thanks especially for helping me stay calm. You too," she said, and kissed Spock.

"All part of our post-trauma service here at the House of Sawyer."

He helped her downstairs. He flipped back the lid of the hot tub, hit the jets, while she took off her shirt. "Want the iPod?"

"No, thanks. Maybe I'll give meditation another shot." She winced as she reached back for the hook of her bra. "Definitely stiff and sore."

"Let me. I have experience with these devices."

She smiled, let her arms drop as he moved behind her.

Fresh fury gushed into him, one hot blast of blind, mindless rage. Bruises purpled across her back, along her shoulder blades, in angry storm clouds. More bruising mottled the skin high on her left biceps, and a raw, red line like a burn rode over her shoulder.

"Having trouble with the mechanics?" Cilla asked him.

"No." Amazing, he thought, how calm his voice sounded. How matter-of-fact. "You've got some bruises back here."

"So that's what I feel. It must be from when he shoved me against the truck." She tipped her head to the side, down, then sucked in some air as she brushed her fingers over her shoulder and across her chest. "Seat belt burn, too. Shit. Well, better than the alternative."

"Fuck that." He said it softly, but still she shifted to look around at him.

"Ford."

"Fuck. That." He bit off the words now as that gush of fury spewed out, a raging, boiling geyser. "You'll have to get your calm and your Zen somewhere else, because I'm not up for it. Goddamn it. Goddamn it! The son of a bitch came *at* you. You're all bruised and bashed up. He did that to you. Did you see your truck? For Christ's sake, did you see what he did, what he tried to do? He hurt you."

She'd turned to face him, to stare at him. With hands stunningly gentle in contrast to his face, his voice, he unhooked her work pants, crouched to ease them down her legs.

"Your truck's in a fucking ditch, and the only reason you're not is because you took him out. There were skid marks on the road as far as I could see." He took off her shoes, her socks, lifted her foot, then the other to free them of the pants.

"Better than the alternative? Better comes when I kick that crazy, murderous bastard's teeth down his throat. That's when better comes." He turned her around, unhooked her bra.

He picked her up, eased her into the bubbling water where she just sat, staring at him.

"I'll get the aspirin and that robe you brought over."

After he strode away and up the stairs, Cilla let out a long breath. "Wow," was really all she could think of.

Meditation might not have worked very well for her, but Cilla found fifteen minutes in hot water with pulsing jets helped considerably. Especially with the image of Ford's anger playing behind her closed lids.

Steadier than she'd have believed possible, she carefully climbed out. As she wrapped herself in a towel, she heard him coming back down the stairs.

"I'll do that," he said when she started to flip the lid back over the tub. "Here."

He handed her pills, water, and when she'd taken them, helped her into the white terry robe she'd left at his place.

"Sorry about before. You don't need the ravings of another maniac."

"You're wrong. You helped me, you gave me exactly what I needed by staying calm when I was the shakiest. You stayed steady, and took me to the cool and the quiet. You gave me magic peas, and you let me lean on you. There have been a very limited number of people in my life that let me lean on them."

She laid her hands on his chest, on either side of

his heart. "And after I got through the worst of it, you gave me something else. The outrage, the anger, the blind thirst for revenge. It helps to know someone could feel that on my behalf. That while he was feeling all that, he could still take care. It's no wonder I fell for you."

"I'm so in love with you, Cilla."

"Oh." She felt a jolt, nearly as violent as she had while under attack. "Oh, Ford."

"Maybe it's lousy timing, but that doesn't change a thing. It's not what I was looking for. It's not simple and easy, just picking which bed we use and who walks home in the morning. That's how I figured it, and I was wrong."

"Ford—"

"I'm not finished yet. When that woman—Lori—called, she was careful to let me know right off you were okay. But all she had to do was say *accident*, and my heart stopped. I never really understood what it was to be afraid until that moment."

Everything he'd felt, and was feeling now, swirled in his eyes. So much, Cilla thought. So much in there.

"When I got there, and I saw you sitting on the side of the road. So pale. The relief came first, waves of it. Waves. There she is. I didn't lose her.

Waves of relief, Cilla, and this lightning strike at the same time. There she is. And I knew. I'm in love with you."

It had been a day for shocks and jolts, and huge moments, Cilla thought. "You're so steady, Ford, and I'm so disordered."

"That's just another way of saying, 'It's not you, it's me.'"

"It doesn't make it less true. I'm caught right now between the thrill, and the terror, of having someone like you tell me he loves me. And mean it. And that's complicated because I have such strong, real feelings for you. I think I'm in love with you, too. Wait."

She threw up a hand as he stepped toward her. "Just, wait. I probably have a mild concussion. I'm at a disadvantage. You're steady," she repeated. "And I bet you know exactly what you want out of being in love. I'm disordered, and I don't. What I do know, or at least what I'm pretty sure of, is you'll want, expect things to change."

"Yes. But they don't have to change today, or to-morrow. Part of being steady might be as basic as knowing how to appreciate what you've got, in the moment." He framed her face. "There she is," he murmured, and brushed his lips to hers.

Cilla closed her eyes. "Oh, God. I'm in such trouble."

"It's going to be fine. Now let's go up. You should get off your feet."

He lay her on the living room sofa this time, and as he'd expected, within twenty minutes the emotional and physical upheaval dropped her into sleep. He took his phone out onto the veranda, leaving the door open so he'd hear her if she stirred. Sitting where he could watch her through the window, he started his calls with her father.

When he spotted Matt heading up Cilla's drive toward his house, Ford figured his friend had been keeping an eye out for any sign. He finished up the call—this one to a friend, an RN, just to make sure he handled Cilla's injuries correctly.

He gestured Matt to a chair as he disconnected.

"What the hell, Ford?"

"Hennessy," he began, and ran through it.

"Jesus. Crazy bastard. Are you sure she's okay?"

"I just talked to Holly. Remember Holly?"

"Nurse Holly?"

"Yeah. She thinks it'd be better if I could talk Cilla into getting checked out. But in the meantime, heat, cold, rest, ibuprofen. Got that covered so far. You saw the truck."

"Yeah, did a number on it. His own van, too. She got him with a nut shot?"

"Apparently."

"Well, goddamn good for her," Matt said with both heat and admiration. "I'd like a shot at him myself."

"Take a number."

"Well, listen, you need anything, she needs anything, you know where I am. There are a lot of people across the road there who'd say the same."

"I know it."

"And tell her not to worry about the work. We've got it covered. You'll want to come over and set her alarm if she's staying here tonight."

"Yeah, I'll take care of it."

"Any questions, messages, whatever, I'll make sure I leave them in her famous notebook, and I'll pass the word to Brian. I'll check with you tomorrow."

At the two-hour mark, Ford debated rousing her just in case she actually did have a concussion. Before he could decide, he saw the unmarked car pull into her drive. So he waited, watched Wilson and Urick get out, go in. Come out, get back into the car and pull across into his driveway.

"Mr. Sawyer."

"Getting to be a habit, isn't it?"

"Miss McGowan's here?"

"Yeah. Banged up, worn out and sleeping. Where's Hennessy?"

"He's in a cell. Do you want a list of the charges against him?"

"No, as long as there's enough to keep him in a cell."

"We'd like to speak to Ms. McGowan, go over her statement."

"She's sleeping," Ford repeated, and rose. "And she's had more than enough for one day. More than enough period. If Hennessy had been in a cell where he belonged, he wouldn't have had a chance to try to kill her."

"If we'd had any evidence, we'd have put him in a cell before this."

"So what?" Ford shot back. "Better late than never?"

"Ford." Cilla pushed open the screen. "It's all right."

"Hell it is."

"Well, you're right. It's not. But I'll talk to the detectives. Let's get it done." She opened the door wider. "Would you wait in the living room a minute?" she asked Wilson and Urick.

After they passed, she let the screen door close behind her, and laid her hands on Ford's shoulders.

"No one's ever shielded me." She kissed him. "In my whole life, no one ever stood between me and something unpleasant. It's an amazing feeling. It's amazing to know I don't even have to ask if you'll stay with me while I do this. You can leave your silver armor in the shop. You don't need it."

She took his hand, and walked inside with him to get it done.

Part Three

FINISH TRIM

And though home is a name,
a word, it is a strong one;
stronger than magician ever
spoke, or spirit ever answered
to, in the strongest conjuration.
—CHARLES DICKENS

TWENTY-ONE

"How are you feeling?" Wilson asked when she sat on the sofa with Ford, with the dog between them.

"Oddly enough, lucky."

"Have you been checked out by a doctor?"

"No, it's bumps and bruises."

"It would be helpful to have a doctor's report, and photographs of your injuries."

"I don't have a local doctor yet. And I'm not—"

"I've got one," Ford interrupted. "I'll make a call."

"We interviewed Hennessy," Urick told them. "Took a first pass at him. He doesn't deny ramming your truck or forcing you off the road. He claims you were harassing his wife."

"I went to see her this morning. I forgot," she said to Ford. "It wasn't top of my mind after all this. I went to see him, actually, but she said he wasn't home. We had a conversation, out on her porch. Then I left. I didn't harass her, or anyone. And if he thinks having a conversation with his wife justifies running me into a ditch, he really is crazy."

"What time did you speak with Mrs. Hennessy?"

"I don't know. Around nine. I left and did a number of errands. Four or five stops, I guess, between Front Royal and Morrow Village. I saw his van coming from the direction of my farm as I was heading toward it. He saw me, and a minute later he was behind me, coming up fast. He rammed me. I don't know how many times now. Three or four, at least. I know I was all over the road. I went into a skid, thought I was going to flip. I went into the ditch. I guess the seat belt and air bag kept it from being any worse."

"You got out of the truck," Wilson prompted.

"That's right. Supremely pissed. I started yelling at him, he yelled at me. And he shoved me. He shoved me again, and knocked me back into the gate of the truck. He said, 'I see you in there.' And he raised his fist. That's when I kicked him."

"What do you think he meant by that? 'I see you in there'?"

"My grandmother. He meant he saw my grandmother. And I'd say if he had to hurt me to get to her, that's what he'd do. He attacked my friend, vandalized my property, and now he's attacked me."

"He hasn't copped to any of the incidents before this afternoon," Wilson told her. "He denies the rest."

"Do you believe him?"

"No, but it's hard to understand why a man who confesses to vehicular assault, reckless endangerment, assault with intent refuses to admit to trespass and vandalism. The fact is, Ms. McGowan, he seemed righteous about what happened today. Not remorseful or afraid of the consequences. If his wife hadn't gotten a lawyer in there when she did, we might've gotten more."

"What happens now?"

"Arraignment, bail hearing. Given his age, his length of time in the community, I'd expect his lawyer to request he be released on his own recognizance. And given the nature of the offense, his proximity to you, I expect the DA will ask for him to be held without bail. I can't say which way it'll go, or if it'll land somewhere between."

"His wife swears he didn't leave the house last night." Urick picked up the notebook in his lap. "That they left the park right after they saw you, and he stayed in all night. We did, however, pull out of her that he often spends time in their son's room, locks himself in, sleeps in there. So he could've left the house without her knowing about it. We'll push there, I promise you."

Cilla had barely settled herself down after the police left when her father arrived, with Patty and Angie. Even as the anger and emotion level rose toward what she thought might be the unbearable, Ford's mother sailed in carrying a large Tupperware container and a bouquet of flowers.

"Don't you get up, you poor thing. I brought you some of my chicken soup."

"Oh, Penny, that's so thoughtful!" Patty sprang up to take the flowers. "I never thought of food, or flowers. I never thought—"

"Of course you didn't. How could you, with so much on your mind? Cilla, I'm going to heat you up a bowl right now. My chicken soup's good for anything. Colds, flu, bumps, bruises, lovers' spats and rainy days. Ford, find Patty a vase for the flowers. Nothing cheers you up like a bunch of sunflowers."

Clutching them, Patty burst into tears.

"Oh now, now." Penny cradled the Tupperware in one arm, Patty in the other. "Come on with me, sweetie. You come on with me. We'll make ourselves useful, and you'll feel better."

"Did you see her poor face?" Patty sobbed as Penny led her away.

"She's just so upset." Angie sat beside Cilla, took her hand.

"I know. It's okay."

"It's not." Gavin turned from staring out the front windows. "None of it is. I should have confronted Hennessy years ago, had this out with him. Instead, I just stayed out of his way. I looked away from it because it was uncomfortable. It was unpleasant. And because he left Patty and Angie alone. He didn't leave you alone, and still, I stayed out of his way."

"Confronting him wouldn't have changed anything."

"It would make me feel like less of a failure as your father."

"You're not—"

"Angie," Gavin said, interrupting Cilla, "would you go help your mother and Mrs. Sawyer?"

"All right."

"Ford? Would you mind?"

With a nod, Ford slipped out behind Angie.

Cilla sat, her stomach twisting with a new kind of tension. "I know you're upset. We're all upset," she began.

"I let her have you. I let Dilly have you, and I walked away."

Cilla looked into his face and asked the single question she'd never dared ask him. "Why?"

"I told myself you were better off. I even believed it. I told myself you were where you belonged, and being there, being with your mother, allowed you to do what made you happy. Gave you advantages. I wasn't happy there, and whatever turned between your mother and me brought out the very worst in both of us when we dealt with each other. When we dealt with each other about you. I felt . . . free when I came back here."

"I was only about a year old when you moved out, and not even three when you went away."

"We couldn't speak two sentences to each other without it devolving. It was better, a little better, when we had a few thousand miles between us. I came out every month or two to see you for the first few . . . then less. You were already a working actor. It was easy to tell myself you had such a full life, to agree that it wasn't in your best interest to come here for part of your summer break when you could be making appearances."

"And you were building a life here."

"Yes, starting over, falling in love with Patty." He looked down at his hands, then dropped them to his sides. "You were barely real to me, this beautiful little girl I'd visit a few times a year. I could tell myself I did my duty—never failed to send the support check, or call on your birthday, Christmas, send gifts. Even if I knew it for a lie, I could tell myself. I had Angie. Right here, every step. She needed me, and you didn't."

"But I did." Cilla's eyes swam. "I did."

"I know. And I'll never be able to make it up to you, or to myself." His voice went thick. "I wanted a quiet life, Cilla. And I sacrificed you to get it. By the time I understood that, you were grown."

"Did you ever love me?"

He pressed his fingers to his eyes as if they burned, then, dropping his hands, walked over to sit beside her. "I was in the delivery room when you were born. They put you in my arms, and I loved you. But it was almost a kind of awe. Amazement and terror and thrill. I remember most, a few weeks after we brought you home. I had an early call, and I heard you crying. The nurse had fed you, but you were fussy. I took you, and sat with you in the rocking chair. You spit up all over my shirt. And then you looked at me. Looked right into my eyes. And I loved you. I shouldn't have let you go."

She took a breath as something opened in her chest. "You helped me pick out rosebushes, and a red maple. You painted my living room. And you're here now."

He put an arm around her, drew her against him. "I saw you," he whispered, "standing on a veranda you'd built with your own hands. And I loved you."

For the first time in her memory, for perhaps the first time in her life, she turned her face into his chest, and wept.

LATER, SHE ATE CHICKEN SOUP. It surprised her just how much better it made her feel. A tall green vase full of bright yellow sunflowers didn't hurt, either. Cilla decided she looked a great deal better when Ford didn't argue with the idea of her walking over to check on what work had been done that day.

"Walking around some'll help you not stiffen up too much, I imagine."

"It's cooled off some. It feels good to be outside. Smells like rain's coming."

"Aren't you turning into the country girl."

Smiling, she lifted her face to the sky. "That, and like any contractor, I checked the weather channel this morning. Evening thunderstorms, sixty percent chance. And speaking of weather, you weathered the emotional storm earlier very well."

"Barely, if you want to know the truth. My mother's giving Patty the there-theres, and Angie gets going, and that gets my mother started. So I've got three women crying in the kitchen while they're heating up soup and arranging flowers." Looking pained, he dragged a hand through his mass of disordered hair. "I nearly bolted. Spock slunk out through his dog door like a coward. I thought about doing the same."

"Sterner stuff is Ford made of."

"Maybe, but it was touch and go when I looked in the living room to see if that coast was clear and you're mopping at your eyes."

"Thanks for sticking it out."

"It's what we men in love do." He unlocked the door, pushed it open.

She paused in the doorway, as Spock made himself at home and walked straight in. "Were you ever, before?"

"Ever what?"

"In love?"

"I was in love with Ivy Lattimer when I was eight, but she treated me with derision and mockery. I was in love with Stephanie Provost at thirteen, who returned my affection for six glorious days before tossing me for Don Erbe and his in-ground swimming pool."

She pressed her finger into his chest. "I'm serious."

"Those were very serious love affairs to me, at the time. There were others, too. But if you mean has it ever been real, have I ever looked at a woman and known and felt and wanted and needed all at the same time? No. You're the first."

He lifted her hand, brushed his lips lightly over her knuckles and made her think of her father making the same gesture with Patty. "Looks the same in here to me. What do these guys do all day?"

She wandered into the living room. "Because you don't know where to look. Switch plates and outlet covers I special-ordered—hammered antique bronze—installed. That was a nice, unnecessary thing to do. Matt left the trim in here because he knows I have an emotional attachment to it and want to hang it myself."

She moved off, let out a happy sound at the doorway to the powder room. "Tile's laid." She crouched, studied. "Nice, very nice, the warm pallet in this mosaic ties in well with the color of the entrance foyer, the living area. I wonder if they got to the bathroom on the third floor, or finished the drywall?"

And she's up and running, Ford thought, following her through the house.

By the time she'd checked everything to her satisfaction, the first rumble of thunder sounded. Spock let out a pip of distress and clung to Ford's side like a burr.

She set the alarm, locked up.

"Wind's starting to kick. I love that. I really love when it waits to rain until night, and doesn't screw up time on the job. Brian's crew is scheduled for tomorrow, and we're finally going to work on the pond. Plus, we're . . . Oh damn, I completely forgot. I put an offer in on the house this morning. Just had the impulse hit, and hit strong enough, it said do it now. I should hear if they're going to counter tomorrow. Which is when I made an appointment for us to go through the other house. I figured if that didn't work for you, I'd just reschedule. And I forgot about it."

"Gee, wonder why? What time tomorrow?"

"Five. I've got a full slate, so five worked out."

"It's fine. We'll go right after your doctor's appointment. That's at four."

"But—"

"Four," he said in that tone she heard rarely. Which, she imagined, spoke to its success.

"Okay. All right."

"Now, what do you say we sit outside with some wine, and watch this storm roll in."

"I say that sounds like a nice way to end a seriously crappy day."

CILLA THOUGHT SHE was pulling it together pretty well. She'd gotten a decent night's sleep—maybe aided by two glasses of wine, two Motrin and another bowl of Penny's famous chicken soup. She'd managed to creak her way out of bed at seven without waking Ford. Another spin in the whirlpool, some very light and gentle yoga stretches followed by more Motrin and a breathlessly hot shower had her feeling almost normal.

Over a quiet cup of coffee she wondered why she needed a doctor's appointment. It didn't require a doctor to tell her she'd been banged around and would be a little stiff and sore, a little achy for a couple of days.

But she doubted Ford would see it that way.

And wasn't that nice, when you got right down to it? There was someone who cared enough to get pushy and bossy about her welfare. It didn't hurt to be flexible, to bend enough to accommodate.

Besides, the worst was over. Hennessy was in jail, and couldn't touch her or her property. She'd be able to live, and finish her rehab in peace. And move on to the next.

She'd be able to sit down and really think about what it meant to have a man like Ford in love with her. And, yes, to worry and obsess about what it meant for her to be in love—if she really understood the state of being—with a man like Ford.

They could take some time, couldn't they, to build on that? To restructure, to decide on tones and trim? They could take a good look at the foundation, evaluate. Because hers was so uneven. Lots of cracks there, she mused, but maybe they could be shored up, supported and repaired.

Since his were so solid, so sturdy, there had to be a chance to make the whole thing stand. To make it last.

She so badly wanted to make things last.

She wrote him a note to prop against the coffee-maker.

Feeling good. Gone to work.
Cilla

The truth would be closer to "less crappy," but "good" worked well enough.

She filled her insulated mug with coffee and headed for the door only two hours later than her usual start time.

She jolted back a step. Mrs. Hennessy stood on

the other side of the door, her hand lifted as if to knock.

"Mrs. Hennessy."

"Miss McGowan, I hoped you'd be here. I need to talk to you."

"I don't think that's a good idea, under the circumstances."

"Please. Please." Mrs. Hennessy opened the screen door herself, crowded in so that Cilla was forced to step back. "I know you must be upset. I know you have every reason to be, but—"

"Upset? Yeah, I'd say I have every reason. Your husband tried to kill me."

"No. No. He lost his temper, and that's partly my fault. He was wrong. He was wrong to do what he did, but you have to understand, he wasn't thinking straight."

"When wasn't he thinking? When he drove out here in the first place, or when he rammed into my truck, repeatedly, until he ran me off the road? Or would it be when he shoved me? Or when he raised his fist to me?"

Mrs. Hennessy's eyes shone—fear, distress, apology. "There's no excuse for what he did. I know that. I've come here to beg you to have some pity, some compassion. To open your heart and understand his pain."

"You suffered a tragedy, over thirty years ago. And he blames me. How can I understand?"

"Thirty years ago, thirty minutes ago. For him, there's no difference. Our son, our only child, lost his future that night. We could only have the one child. I had problems, and Jim, he said to me, it doesn't matter, Edie. We have everything. We have our Jimmy. He loved that boy more than anything in this world. Maybe he loved too much. Is that a sin? Is that wrong? Look, look."

She pulled a framed photo out of her handbag, pushed it at Cilla. "That's Jimmy. That's our boy. Look at him."

"Mrs. Hennessy—"

"The spitting image of his daddy," she said quickly, urgently. "Everyone said so, from the time he was born. He was such a good boy. So bright, so sweet, so funny. He was going to college, he was going on to college and to medical school. He was going to be a doctor. Jim and me, neither of us went to college. But we saved, we put money by so Jimmy could go. We were so proud."

"He was a handsome young man," Cilla managed, and handed the photo back. "I'm sorry about what happened. I'm sincerely sorry. But I'm not to blame."

"Of course you're not. Of course you're not." Tears

trembling on the brink, she pressed the photo to her heart. "I grieved, Miss McGowan, every day of my life, for what happened to my boy. Jimmy was never the same after that night. It was more than never walking again, or using his arms. He lost his light, his spark. He just never found himself again. I lost him, and I lost my husband that same night. He spent years tending to Jimmy. Most of the time he wouldn't let me do. It was for him to do. To feed him, to change him, to lift him. It took his heart. It just took his heart."

She drew herself back up. "When Jimmy died, I'm not ashamed to tell you I felt some relief. As if my boy was finally free again, to be again, and walk and laugh. But what was left in my Jim just shriveled. Jimmy was his reason for being, even if the being was bitter. He snapped, that's all. The weight of it all, it just broke him. I'm begging you, don't send him away to prison. He needs help. And time to heal. Don't take him, too. I don't know what I'll do."

She covered her face, her shoulders shaking with sobs. Out of the corner of her eye, Cilla saw a movement. As Ford came down the stairs, Cilla held up a hand to stop him.

"Mrs. Hennessy, do you know what he did yesterday? Do you understand what he's done?"

"I know what they're saying, and I know he hurt

you yesterday. I shouldn't have told him you came. I was upset, and I started on him, how he had to let it go, leave it, and you. How I couldn't take you coming to the house that way. And he went storming off. If I hadn't riled him up—"

"What about the other times?"

She shook her head. "I don't know about other times. Can't you see he needs help? Can't you see he's sick in his heart, his mind, in his soul? I love my husband. I want him back. If he goes to prison, he'll die. He'll die there. You're young. You have everything ahead of you. We've already lost the most important thing in our lives. Can't you find enough pity to let us try to find our peace?"

"What do you think I can do?"

"You could tell them you don't want him to go to jail." She reached out to grip Cilla's hands. "The lawyer says he could ask for a psychiatric evaluation and time in a hospital. That they could send Jim to a place where they'd help him. He'd have to go, isn't that punishment? He'd have to, but they'd help him."

"I don't—"

"And I'd sell the house." Her hands squeezed Cilla's harder, and her desperation passed from skin to skin. "I'd swear it to you, on the Bible. I'd sell the house and we'd move away from here. When he's well enough, we'd move to Florida. My sister and her husband, they're moving to Florida next fall. I'll find a place down there, and we'll move away. He'll never bother you again. You could tell them you want him to go to the psychiatric hospital until he's better. You're the one he hurt, so they'd listen to you.

"I knew your grandmother. I know she loved her boy, too. I know she grieved for him. I know that in my heart. It's that Jim never believed it, and he blamed her, blamed her every time he looked at our boy in that wheelchair. He couldn't forgive, and it made him sick. Can't you forgive? Can't you?"

How could she hold against such need? Cilla thought. Such terrible need. "I'll talk to the police. I can't promise anything. I'll talk to them. That's all I can do."

"God bless you. God bless you for that. I won't trouble you again. Jim won't, either. I swear it to you."

Cilla closed her eyes, then closed the door. With a tired sigh, she walked over to sit on Ford's steps. She leaned her head on his shoulder when he stepped down to sit beside her.

"There are all kinds of assaults," he said quietly. "On the body, the mind, and on the heart."

She only nodded. He understood she felt battered by the visit, by the pleas, by the tears.

"It's about redemption, isn't it?" she said. "Or some part of it. Me coming here, bringing her house back. Myself back. Looking for her in it, for the answers, the reasons. She never recovered from Johnnie's death. Was never the same. And most people say she took her life because of it. Couldn't you say Hennessy didn't have that luxury? His child was still alive, but so damaged, so broken, so needy. He couldn't turn away from it, and had to live with it every day. And that broke him."

"I'm not saying he doesn't need help," Ford said slowly. "That mandatory time in a psychiatric facility isn't the answer. But, Cilla, it's not him who's asking for pity or forgiveness. It's not Hennessy who's looking for redemption."

"No, it's not." And there, too, she knew he was right. "I'm not doing it for him. For whatever good it does, I'm doing it for that desperate and terrified woman. And more, I'm doing it for Janet."

IN CILLA'S EXPERIENCE working with a good crew in construction meant no coddling because you happened to be female. She got questions, concern, anger and disgust on her behalf, but no more than she'd have been afforded as a man.

And she got plenty of jokes and comments about being a ballbuster.

It helped put her back on track so she could spend the morning hanging trim.

"Hey, Cill." One of the laborers stuck his head in the living room as she stood on the stepladder nailing crown molding. "There's a lady out here, says she knows you. Name's Lori. Want me to send her in or what?"

"Yeah, tell her to come in." Cilla shot in the last nails, started down the ladder.

"If I'd been through what you went through yesterday, I'd be lying in bed, not climbing up ladders."

"It's just another kind of therapy." Cilla set the gun aside and turned to her Good Samaritan. "I was going to come by later today or tomorrow, thank you again."

"You thanked me yesterday."

"Not to diminish what you did, but I'm always going to have this image of you running down the road with a portable phone in one hand, and a garden stake in the other."

With a laugh, Lori shook her head. "My husband and I took this week off, short holiday week, to putter around the house and yard. He was off with our two boys buying peat moss and deer repellant while I restaked the tomatoes. I can tell you, if he'd been home, he'd likely've beat that idiot over the head with the stake, even as he went down."

With a sympathetic smile, she studied the bruise on Cilla's temple. "That looks painful yet. How are you doing?"

"Not too bad. I think it looks worse than it feels now."

"I hope so." She looked around the room. "I confess, while I did want to see you, I've always wanted a look inside this place."

"It's in major transition, but I'll give you a tour if you want."

"I'd love a rain check on that. This room's very nice. I love the color. Well, let me just wind my way around to the point. Of course I know who you are, and who your grandmother was. We moved here about twelve years ago, but Janet Hardy's legend looms large, so we knew this had been hers. It's good to see somebody finally tending to it, which is not the point I'm winding to."

"Is something wrong?"

"I don't know, because while I know who you are, and feel a particular interest in you now, I don't know you. I've had two reporters call me this morning, wanting quotes and information and my account of what happened yesterday."

"Oh. Of course."

"I told them I gave my account to the police. In both cases, they got pretty insistent, and that put my back up."

"I'm sorry you're being bothered by this."

Lori tossed up a hand, waved that aside. "I stopped by to let you know that someone's been talking to reporters. For all I know you might've talked to them yourself, though I can see now that's not the case."

"No, but I'll have to. I appreciate you letting me know."

"We're neighbors. I'm going to let you get back to work." She glanced around. "I think it's time to go nag my husband about painting the living room."

Cilla walked Lori to the door, then went back and sat on the stepladder. She considered the cleanest, most direct way to get out a statement. She still had contacts, and even if tapping any of them was dicey, the Hardy name would ring the bell. She needed something brief and concise, carefully written. She'd been taught not to duck a story but to confront it, spin it and ride it out with class.

She pulled her phone off her belt when it rang, then closed her eyes as she answered. "Hello, Mom."

"Cilla, for God's sake, what's going on out there?"

"I had some trouble. I'm handling it. Listen, could you contact your publicist? You're still using Kim Cohen?"

"Yes, but—"

"Please, contact her and give her this number. Ask her to call me as soon as she can."

"I don't see why I should do you any favors after the way you treated—"

"Mom. Please. I could use some help."

There was a beat of silence. "All right. I'll call her right now. Were you in an accident? Are you in the hospital? Are you hurt? I heard some crazy man thought you were Mama's ghost and tried to run you over with his car. I heard—"

"No, it's not like that. I'm not hurt. I need Kim to help me straighten it out, get out a statement."

"I don't want you to be hurt. I'm still mad at you," Dilly said with a sniff that made Cilla smile. "But I don't want you to be hurt."

"I know, and I'm not. Thanks for calling Kim."

"At least I know how to do a favor," Dilly said, and hung up.

Cilla couldn't deny it as the publicist called within twenty minutes. In another twenty, they'd refined a statement between them. By the time Cilla hung up, she knew she'd done the best she could.

"I'M NOT MAJOR JUICE," Cilla said to Ford as they drove from the doctor's office to the appointment with the realtor. "But there's always some ripples when there's any sort of violence or scandal. And the Hardy connection may give it a little more play. But the statement should cover most of it. There won't be much interest."

"There will be locally. It'll be big news around here, at least for a few days. And if it goes to trial. Did you get in touch with the cops?"

"Let's hope it doesn't—and yes. I know Wilson thought I was the crazy one for asking if they'd consider Hennessy's emotional and mental state."

"What did he say?"

"Psych evals are already in the works. One from the defense, one from the prosecution."

"Dueling shrinks."

"It sounds like it."

"I'd say it's going to be pretty clear to both that Hennessy downed a big bowl of crazy."

"Yeah. I guess the upshot depends on what the prosecution's guy has to say as to whether or not the DA holds on the charges, makes a deal or recommends a psychiatric facility and treatment. The house is coming up on the left. The little Cape Cod there."

"Huh?"

"Red compact out front. She's already here. Vicky Fowley. It's a rental—empty—the owner wants to unload. And Vicky's anxious to get it off her list."

Ford looked at the overgrown, weedy front yard and the small brown box of a house sitting on it. "I can't imagine why. Could it be the extreme uglies?"

"Perfect attitude. Keep that up, seriously." She gave his hand a bolstering pat. "And let me do the talking."

TWENTY-TWO

Ford knew he had a strong imagination. He considered himself to be a man of some vision. As far as Cilla's "little Cape Cod" went, he couldn't imagine how anyone could define it, however loosely, as a house, and could only visualize it being mercifully razed.

Stains of a suspicious and undoubtedly unpleasant nature stamped and streaked the carpet in the pint-sized living room. He could only be grateful he'd let Spock play job dog again, otherwise Spock would've been honor bound to re-mark all the previously marked areas.

Either an animal or an army of rodents had gnawed on the baseboard. The ceiling, also unpleasantly stained in one corner, was bumpy with what Cilla called popcorn.

The kitchen was a truly ugly hodgepodge of mismatched appliances, torn linoleum and a rusted sink. The stingy counters carried the round burn marks of pans carelessly set on blue-speckled white Formica. Grime, and God knew what else, lived in the corners.

In his mind's eye he imagined cockroaches flooding out of that rusted sink, armed with automatic weapons, driving tanks and armored vehicles to wage war against spiders in combat gear firing bazookas.

He found it easy to let Cilla do the talking. He was speechless.

The second floor consisted of two bedrooms scattered with the debris of former tenants and a bathroom he wouldn't have entered while wearing a hazmat suit.

"As you can see, there's work to be done!" Vicky showed white, white teeth in what could only be a pained, somewhat desperate smile. "But with some elbow grease and sweat equity, it could be a little dollhouse! Such a cute starter home for a young couple like yourselves."

"A couple of what?" Ford said and got the fish eye from Cilla.

"Vicky, would you mind if we just looked around on our own for a few minutes? Talked about it?"

"Of course not! Take all the time you want. I'll just step outside and make some calls. Don't rush on my account!"

"Why does she say everything in exclamation points?" Ford asked when Vicky was out of earshot. "Is it fear? Excitement? Does she have multiple, spontaneous orgasms?"

"Cute."

"Cilla, I think that pile of what may have once been clothing in that corner just moved. There may be a body in there. Possibly an army of cockroaches waiting to ambush. We should leave. And never come back."

"If there was a body, it would smell a lot worse than it does in here."

"How much worse?" he muttered. "And have you ever actually smelled a body?"

She gave him the fish eye again. "Cockroaches may be a factor, however. If the seller had any brains, he'd have cleaned this place out, ripped up this incredibly smelly carpet. But his loss could be our gain."

"You've got to be kidding. The only thing we could gain from this place is a rampant case of typhoid. Or bubonic plague." He kept a wary eye on the pile of rags. He wasn't entirely sure it *hadn't* moved. "Cilla, this place has no possible redeeming value."

"Because you don't know where to look. Deal was, you don't want to risk it, you don't. But let me give you the idea first. There's hardwood under this carpet. I checked when I went through before."

She walked over, crouched to pull up a loose corner. "Random-length oak, and in surprisingly good shape."

"Okay, it's got a floor."

"And a good foundation, a nice-sized lot."

"That looks like a minefield. Probably booby-trapped by the atomic spiders."

"New sod," she continued, undaunted, "some plantings, a pretty little deck on the back. Gut the bathroom."

"Wouldn't it be more humane to bomb it?"

"New tub, new sink, a nice ceramic tile. For a room that size, I could probably find enough of a discontinued style, neutral color. All the carpet goes. Replace the closet doors, add shelves. Redo the ceilings, paint. You've got a couple of nice kids' rooms."

"And where would the parents sleep?" He slid his hands into his pockets rather than risk accidentally touching something. "In a hotel if they have any sense."

She crooked her finger. "This wall moves out fifteen feet."

"It does?"

"It will and, running the width of the house, will hold the master suite, overlooking the backyard. Walk-in closet, attached bath with soaking tub and separate shower. Double sinks, granite countertop. Maybe slate tile. Have to price that out."

"What holds it up? Hopes and dreams?"

"The new kitchen/great room."

"Oh, that." But oddly enough, he began to see it as she did. Or as he thought she did.

"Horrible carpet treads out, oak treads in," she said as she started down the steps. "Replace skinny banister. Carpet goes, ceilings redone, new trim, some crown molding. New windows throughout. Gut kitchen."

"Thank the Lord."

"Half bath and laundry room here. Kitchen, dining area and family room, open floor plan, breakfast bar for the casual, family meal, all leading out through atrium doors to the nice little deck. Exterior paint in a cheerful color, replace the cracked concrete walkway with pavers, plug in some plants, a little dogwood tree. And that's about it."

"Oh, well, that's hardly anything."

She laughed. "It's a lot, but it'll be a lot. Poor, sad thing. Sixteen weeks. It could be done in twelve, but not with juggling, so I'd say sixteen. With the top offer I'd make and materials and labor, mortgage payments for, we'll say, five months, and the market value after improvements in this neighborhood, you could see between forty and forty-five K in profit."

"Seriously?"

"Oh yeah. Depending on the market when it's done, that could be closer to sixty thousand. The neighborhood's on an upswing." She began ticking items off on her fingers. "Younger couples, small families moving in, prettying things up. It's in a good school district, only about ten minutes from a shopping center. Master suites, kitchens and baths— that's where the sales are made and you get your biggest return on your investment."

"Okay."

"No, you have to be sure. Take a little time to think about it. I'll draw up some floor plans."

"No, I'm sold. Let's go make Vicky's day." And get the hell out while the cockroaches and spiders have their moratorium.

"Wait, wait. We need to let her suffer more. You're going to steal this place, Ford." He found the sly delight on her face infectious. "It deserves to be stolen because the seller couldn't even be bothered to make an attempt. We're going to tell her, very unconvincingly, that we'll think about it. Then we're going to walk away. In a week, ten days, I'll call her back."

"If somebody buys it in the meantime?"

"When it's been sitting here for over four months, even with two price reductions? I don't think so. We're going to go give Vicky the disappointment she's expecting. Then I want to go home, soak in your hot tub and relax."

RELAXING PROVED PROBLEMATIC because of the half-dozen reporters camped at her wall.

"Not much interest, you said?"

"This is nothing." And hardly more than she'd expected. "Just a spillover from the statement. They'll mostly be local, or out of D.C., maybe. We're close enough for that. You go inside. I'll handle it."

"You're going to give them interviews?"

"Not exactly. A few crumbs. They'll take the crumbs and fly away. There's no reason for you to be involved in this. And you'll just give them another angle."

But the minute they stepped out of the car, cameras lifted. Like one entity, reporters surged across the road, shouting Cilla's name, calling out questions. As it struck Ford as a kind of attack, he moved instinctively to Cilla's side.

"Georgia Vassar, WMWA-TV. Can you tell us your thoughts on the altercation yesterday with James Robert Hennessy?"

"How serious are your injuries?"

"Is it true Hennessy believes you're the reincarnation of Janet Hardy?"

"I've already issued a statement about the incident," Cilla said coolly. "I don't have any more to say."

"Isn't it true that Hennessy threatened you previously? And, in fact, assaulted Steve Chensky, your ex-husband, while Chensky lived with you? Was that assault the reason for your failed reconciliation?"

"To my knowledge, Mr. Hennessy hasn't been charged with the assault on Steve, who was visiting me for a short time this spring. We've been friends before, during and after our marriage. There was no reconciliation."

"Is that due to your relationship with Ford Sawyer? Mr. Sawyer, how do you feel about the attack on Ms. McGowan?"

"There's speculation that you and Steve fought over Cilla, and he was injured. How do you answer that?"

"No comment. Gosh, you guys seem to be on my property. We're pretty friendly around here, but you're going to want to step off."

"I won't be as friendly if any of you trespass on mine," Cilla warned.

"Is it true that you came here in an attempt to commune with the spirit of your grandmother?" someone shouted as she turned with Ford toward the house.

"Tabloid crap," Cilla stated. "I'm sorry. Most of that was tabloid crap."

"No problem." Ford shut the door behind them, locked it. "I've always wanted the opportunity to say 'No comment' in a stern voice."

"They'll give up. It won't play more than a day or two, and most of that'll be in the supermarket sheets alongside stories of alien babies being homeschooled in Utah."

"I knew it!" He shot a finger in the air. "I knew that was the reason for Utah. How about a glass of wine with that soak, while I figure out how to get my dog back?"

"Not a good idea. The wine, yeah, and Spock, but you've got a lot of glass in your gym." She offered an apologetic look, the best she could give him. "Glass, telephoto lenses. No point in handing it to them. They've got your name. You're going to find yourself alongside the alien babies, too."

"Finally, a lifelong dream fulfilled." He reached for glasses, glanced down at his answering machine. "Aren't I the popular guy today? Forty-eight messages." Even as he spoke, the phone rang.

"You should screen, Ford. I really thought by issuing a short, clear statement I'd head this off. Kim, the publicist, agreed with me. But for whatever reason, some of the media wants to run with it, and turn down cockeyed angles."

"Let's do this." He lifted the phone, switched off the ringer. "I'll do the same with the others. My family, my friends have my cell number if they need to reach me. I'll call Brian, see if he'll take Spock home with him tonight. We'll take some wine, cook up a frozen pizza and camp upstairs in the bedroom behind the curtains. At last, the opportunity to expose you to a marathon running of *Battlestar Galactica*."

She leaned back on the counter as the tension in her shoulders dissolved. Not angry, she realized. Not upset. Not even especially irked. How had she ever managed to connect with someone so blessedly *stable*?

"You really know how to keep it simple."

"Unless the Cylons are bent on destroying your entire species, it usually is simple. You get the pizza, I'll get the wine."

CILLA WOKE at five A.M. to the beep of the internal clock she'd set in the middle of the night after the alarms had sounded at the Little Farm. Something else she should have expected, she thought as she went to shower. There were some members of some media who routinely ignored the law in pursuit of a story. So she'd spent an hour with the police and Ford across the road.

And she had a lock set on her back door bearing the scratches of a botched jimmy attempt.

She dressed, left a note for Ford. The radio car remained in her drive, where it had been posted after the attempted break-in. Birds chirped, and she caught sight of a trio of deer at her pond. But no reporters camped outside her walls.

Maybe she'd gotten lucky, she thought, and that was that. Using Ford's car, she drove into town. She was back by six-thirty, and carried a box of doughnuts and two large coffees down her drive.

The cop behind the wheel rolled down his window.

"I know it's a cliché," she said, "but."

"Hey. That was nice of you, Miss McGowan. It's been quiet."

"And a long night for both of you. It looks like the invaders have retired the field. I'm going to start work. Some of the crew will be coming along by seven."

"It's a nice spot you've got here." The second cop pulled a glazed with sprinkles out of the box. "Heck of a bathroom up there on the second floor. My wife's been wanting to update ours."

"If you decide to, give me a call. Free consult."

"Might do that. We'll be going off shift pretty soon. Do you want us to call in and request another car?"

"I think we'll be fine now. Thanks for looking out for me."

Inside, she set up to finish her run of baseboard. By eight, the hive of activity buzzed. Grouting, drywall mudding, consults on driveway pavers and pond work. Turning her attention to the third bedroom, Cilla checked her closet measurements. As she removed the door, Matt stepped in.

"Cilla, I think you'd better take a look outside."

"What? Is there a problem?"

"I guess you need to look, decide that for yourself."

She propped the door against the wall, hustled

after him. One look out the front window of the master bedroom had her gasping.

Six reporters had been a nuisance, and not unexpected. Sixty was a disaster.

"They just started showing up, kind of all at once," Matt told her. "Kinda like there was a signal. Brian called me out, said some of them are yelling questions at his crew. Jesus, there's TV cameras and everything."

"Okay, okay, I need to think." She had at least a dozen crew working between the house and the grounds. A dozen people she couldn't possibly censor or control.

"There shouldn't be this kind of interest in me being in a wreck, even with the circumstances. A few blips on the entertainment news maybe, reports locally. I need to make a call. Matt, if you could try to keep the men from talking to them, at least for now. I need a few minutes to . . ." She trailed off as the gleaming black limo streamed through her entrance.

"Man, look at that."

"Yes, look at that," Cilla echoed. She didn't have to see Mario climb out of the back to know who'd arrived. Or why.

By the time Cilla reached the veranda, Bedelia Hardy stood under the supportive protection of her husband's arm. She tilted her face out at the perfect angle, Cilla thought with burning resentment, so those long lenses could capture her poignant expression. She wore her hair loose so it shone in the sun over the linen jacket the same color as her eyes.

As Cilla let the screen door slam behind her, Dilly threw open her arms, keeping her body angled for the profile shots. "Baby!"

She came forward in rather spectacular Jimmy Choo sandals with three-inch heels. Trapped, Cilla walked down the steps in her work boots and into the maternal arms and clouds of Soir de Paris. Janet's signature scent that had become her daughter's.

"My baby, my baby."

"You did this," Cilla whispered in Dilly's ear. "You leaked to the press you were coming."

"Of course I did. All press is good press." She leaned back, and through the amber lenses of Dilly's sunglasses, Cilla saw the calculatedly misted eyes widen in genuine concern. "Oh, Cilla, your face. You said you weren't hurt. Oh, *Cilla*."

It was that, that moment of sincere shock and worry, Cilla supposed, that dulled the sharpest edge of resentment. "I got some bumps, that's all."

"What did the doctor say? Oh, that horrible man, that Hennessy. I remember him. Pinched-faced bastard. My God, Cilla, you're *hurt*."

"I'm fine."

"Well, why don't you at least put on some makeup? No time for that now, and it's probably better this way. Let's go. I've worked it all out. You'll just follow my lead."

"You sicced them on me, Mom. You know this is exactly what I didn't want."

"It's not all about you, and what you want." Dilly looked past Cilla to the house, then turned away. And again, Cilla saw genuine feeling. Pain. "It never has been. I need the column inches, the airtime. I need the exposure, and I'm going to take it. What happened, happened. Now you can let them keep pushing on that, on you, or you can help spin some of it, maybe most of it, around to me.

"Jesus! What is that?"

Cilla glanced down and saw Spock sitting patiently, paw out, big, bulbous eyes latched onto Dilly.

"That's my neighbor's dog. He wants you to shake."

"He wants . . . Does it bite?"

"No. Just shake his paw, Mom. He's decided you're friendly because you hugged me."

"All right." She leaned over carefully and, to her credit, in Cilla's mind, gave Spock's paw a firm shake. Then smiled a little. "He's so ugly, but in a weirdly sweet way. Shoo now."

Dilly turned, her arm firm around Cilla's waist, and flung out a hand to her husband. "Mario!"

He trotted up, took her hand, kissed it.

"We're ready," she told him.

"You look beautiful. Only a few minutes this time, darling. You shouldn't be out in the sun too long."

"Stay close."

"Always."

Clutching Cilla, Dilly began to move toward the entrance, toward the cameras.

"Great shoes," Cilla complimented. "Poor choice for grass and gravel."

"I know what— Who's this? We can't have reporters breaking ranks."

"He's not a reporter." Cilla watched Ford shove through the lines. "Keep going," she told him when he reached them. "You don't want any part of this."

"This would be your mother? It's unexpected to meet you here, Miss Hardy."

"Where else would I be when my daughter's been hurt? The new love interest?" She scoped him head to toe. "I've heard a little about you. Not from you," she said with a glance at Cilla. "We'll have to talk. But now, just wait with Mario."

"No. He's no Mario, and he won't be hanging back at heel like a trained lapdog. Don't give them that, Ford."

"I'm going to go in and get some coffee," he decided. "Want me to call the cops while I'm at it?"

"No. But thanks."

"Isn't he all southern-fried and yummy," Dilly
commented as Ford continued toward the house.
"Your taste's improved."

"I'm so angry with you now." Indeed, the anger
vibrated and pulsed inside her chest. "Be careful,
very careful, what buttons you push."

"You think this is easy for me, coming to this
place? I'm doing what I need to do." Dilly lifted her
chin, the brave mother, supporting her injured child.
Questions hurled out, but Dilly walked through
them, a soldier stoically braving the front line.

"Please. Please." She held up a hand, lifting her
voice. "I understand your interest, and even on some
level appreciate it. I know your viewers and your
readers care, and that touches me. But you must
understand that our family is, once again, going
through a difficult time. And this is . . . painful. My
daughter has been through a terrible experience. I'm
here for her, as any mother would be."

"Dilly! Dilly! When did you hear about Cilla's
accident?"

"She called me as soon as she was able. No matter
how grown up, a child still wants her mother when

she's hurt. Even though she told me not to come, not to break off rehearsals for my cabaret act, not to expose myself to the grief and the memories this place holds for me, of course I came to her."

"You haven't been back, by your own statements, to this house since shortly after Janet Hardy's suicide. How does it feel, being here now?"

"I can't think of it. Not yet. My daughter is my only concern. Later, when we've had time to be together, in private, I'll explore those feelings. My mother . . ." Her voice cracked, on cue. "My mother would want me to give my daughter, her granddaughter, all my energies."

"Cilla, what are your plans? Will you open the house to the public? There's speculation you hope to house memorabilia here."

"No. I plan to live here. I am living here," she corrected, cold, clear-voiced, while the temper beat and beat. "The property has been in my family, on both the Hardy and the McGowan sides, for generations. I'm restoring and remodeling it, and it will be, as it's always been, a private home."

"Is it true that you've been plagued by break-ins, by vandalism during your restoration?"

"There have been incidents. I don't consider them a plague."

"What do you say to the claims that Janet Hardy's spirit haunts the house?"

"My mother's spirit is here," Dilly said before Cilla could answer. "She loved her little farm, and I believe her spirit, her voice, her beauty and her grace remain. We're proof of that." Dilly drew Cilla closer. "Her spirit's in us. In me, in my daughter. And now, in some way, three generations of Hardy women are here. Now please, I need to get my daughter inside, where she can rest. I ask you, as a mother, to respect our privacy. If you have any more questions, my husband will try to answer them."

Tipping her head close to Cilla's, Dilly turned and walked with her toward the house.

"A little heavy on the mother card," Cilla told her.

"I don't think so. What happened to the tree?"

"What tree?"

"That one, with the red leaves. It was bigger. A lot bigger."

"It was damaged, dead and dying. I replaced it."

"It looks different. There were more flowers." Dilly's voice shook, but Cilla knew it was uncalculated this time. "Mama loved flowers."

"There will be more when it's done." Cilla felt the

dynamic shift with every step until she supported Dilly. "You've trapped yourself. You have to go inside now."

"I know it. The porch was white. Why isn't it white?"

"I had to replace most of it. It's not painted yet."

"The door's not right." Her breath quickened, as if they were running instead of walking. "That's not her door. Why is everything changed?"

"There was damage, there was mold and dry rot. My God, Mom, there's only been the very minimum of maintenance in the last decade, and not much more than that for twenty years before. You can't neglect without incurring damage."

"I didn't neglect it. I wanted to forget it. Now I can't, can I?"

Cilla felt her mother quiver, and would have soothed, but Dilly nudged her away as they walked inside.

"This is wrong. It's all wrong. Where are the walls? The little parlor? The paint's the wrong color."

"I made changes."

Eyes hot and gleaming, she whirled toward Cilla on her fabulous shoes. "You said you were restoring it."

"I said I was rehabbing it, and I am. I'm making it mine, and respecting what it was."

"I'd never have sold it to you if I'd known you'd tear it apart."

"Yes, you would," Cilla said coolly. "You wanted the money, and I want to live here. If you'd wanted it caught in amber, Mom, you had decades to do it. You don't love this house, it's a jagged edge for you. But I do love it."

"You don't know what I feel! I had more of her here than anywhere else. Second to Johnnie, of course, always second to her beloved son." Tears ripped through the words. "But I had more of her when we were here than anywhere. And now it's all changed."

"No, not all. I had the plaster repaired, and the floor will be refinished. The floors she walked on. I'm having the stove and refrigerator she used retro-fitted, and I'll use them."

"That big old stove?"

"Yeah."

Dilly pressed her fingers to her lips. "She'd try to bake cookies sometimes. She was terrible at it. She'd always burn them, and laugh. We'd eat them anyway. Damn it, Cilla. Damn it. I loved her so much."

"I know you did."

"She was going to take me to Paris. Just the two of us. It was all planned. Then Johnnie died. He always did spoil everything for me."

"God, Mom."

"That's how I felt then. After the shock, and that first awful grief because I did love him. I did love him even when I wanted to hate him. But after that, and when she wouldn't go to Paris, I thought, he's spoiled that for me." Dilly took a slow, hitching breath. "She loved him more dead than she did me alive. No matter how hard I ran, I could never catch up."

I know how you feel, Cilla thought. Just exactly. In her way, Dilly loved her mother dead more than she could love her daughter alive.

Maybe this was about redemption, too. So Cilla took another step. "I think she loved you very, very much. I think things got horribly twisted and broken the summer he died. And she never fully mended. If she'd had more time—"

"Why didn't she take it, then? She took the pills instead. She left me. She left me. Accident or not— and I'll always, always believe it was an accident— she took the pills, when she could've taken me."

"Mom." Moving to her, Cilla touched Dilly's

cheek. "Why didn't you ever tell me that before? How you felt?"

"It's this house. It upsets me. It dredges everything up. I don't want it. I just don't want it." She opened her purse, took out a silver pill case. "Get me some water, Cilla. Bottled."

The irony, Cilla thought, would forever be lost on Dilly. The daughter who grieved because her mother chose pills over her, perpetuated the same behavior.

"All right."

In the kitchen, Cilla pulled a bottle of water out of her mini fridge. She got a glass, added ice. Dilly would have to live without her usual slice of lemon, she mused. Pouring the water, she glanced out.

Ford stood with Brian and her pond expert by the choked waters. He held a mug of coffee, and the thumb of his other hand was hooked through one of the belt loops of his jeans.

Long and lean, she thought, with just that hint of gawky. Messy brown hair with sun-kissed tips. So wonderfully, blessedly normal. It steadied her just to look at him, to know he'd stay—this man who created super-villains and heroes, who had every season of *Battlestar Galactica*—both series—on DVD. A man who, she was fairly certain, didn't know an Allen wrench from a Crescent, and trusted her to handle herself. Until he decided she couldn't.

"Thank God you're here," she murmured. "Wait for me."

She took the water back to her mother, so Dilly could wash down her tranquilizer du jour.

TWENTY-THREE

"So they're gone." Ford gestured toward the house with the Coke he'd copped from Cilla's kitchen.

"Yes. After a finale of motherly embraces in view of the cameras."

"Back to California?"

"No, they're staying over in D.C. for the night, at the Willard. In that way, she can stage another couple of press ambushes, and get in the plug for her show at the National Theater in September." Cilla held up her hands, shook her head. "It's not entirely that calculating. Only about eighty percent was calculated. The remaining twenty was actual concern for me, which she'd have expressed and assuaged on the phone if it hadn't been to her advantage to make the trip. It took a lot of need for her to come here, to this house. I didn't understand until today, or fully believe until today, how genuinely it upsets her. It makes it a little easier to forgive the neglect, and accept why she was so bitter when I made her an offer she couldn't refuse."

"And it doesn't enter into logical thinking that if she didn't want it, couldn't handle it, she could have given it to you?"

"Not in Dilly's world. It's tit for tat. I didn't know how much she felt unloved at the end, or how completely she felt pushed into second place to her brother in Janet's heart. I'm not sure she's wrong. And yes, I know she did something today she knew I didn't want, and can justify doing it not only because it was to her advantage, but by convincing herself it was what was best for me. It's a talent of hers."

"She'll be an interesting mother-in-law."

"Oh, really." Panic teeth clamped on her throat. "Don't go there."

"Already through that garden gate and meandering up the walk. 'Meander' being the key for now," he said, lifting his Coke for another sip. "No rush on it."

"Ford, you have to understand—"

"Cilla. Sorry," Matt added, stepping out. "Looks like the flooring for the third floor's coming in. Thought you'd want to take a look, check it out before we take it up."

"Yeah, yeah, I do. Be right there."

"Flooring already?" Ford asked her.

"It has to rest on site, a kind of acclimating, for a few days before installation. Since we're doing built-ins up there, the floor has to . . . Never mind."

"Okay. If my services are no longer needed here, I'm going to go try to salvage some of my workday."

"Good. Good," she repeated, struggling against nerves.

"Oh, I finished scanning those photos for you. Remind me to give them to you."

"God, I'd forgotten all about them. I'll have to thank your grandfather."

"I think he considers it thanks enough that he got to see you in a towel."

"And thanks for that reminder." They came around front where the delivery truck slowly backed down her drive. "Hot dog!"

"I'll leave you to the thrill of your wood planks." He caught her face in his hands, kissed her. "We'll be waiting for you."

They would, she thought. He and his strange little dog would do just that. It was both wonderful and terrifying.

FORD LOCKED HIMSELF in his box for four straight hours. It rolled, and it rocked along. Even with all the distractions—sexy neighbor, break-ins, a new friend in the hospital, worry about sexy neighbor and falling in love with her—he was making excellent progress.

It occurred to him that Brid might be finished just about the same time Cilla's house was. That was some superior synchronicity. But now, he deserved to shut it down and indulge in some serious sitting-on-the-veranda time. He unlocked the box, stepped back to take a long, critical look at the day's work.

"You're damn good, Sawyer. Don't let anybody tell you different."

With his back warm from the self-pat, he walked downstairs, stopping to look out the window. Not a reporter in sight, he noted, pleased for Cilla. No trucks in sight, either, which meant her day's work should be wrapped, too. He headed to the kitchen to get a cold one and to call Spock in from the back-yard for the veranda-sitting, wait-for-Cilla portion of their day.

He found a note inside the fridge, taped to a beer.

Finished? If so, drop over to Chez McGowan.
Come around back.

He grinned at the note. "Don't mind if I do."

She sat on the slate patio, at a teak table under a

bright blue umbrella. A trio of copper pots, filled to bursting with mixed plantings, cheered the three stairs of the veranda. With her ball cap on her head, her legs stretched out and crossed at the ankles of her work boots, and roses rioting behind her, he thought she looked both relaxed and extraordinary.

She smiled—relaxed and easy—when he sat across from her. "I'm basking," she told him, and gave Spock a rub.

"I noticed. When did you get this?" He flicked a finger up at the umbrella.

"It came in today, and I couldn't resist setting it up. After I did, Shanna hauled over the planters. I picked them up on one of my sorties, and figured I'd get around to doing something with them, eventually. But she saw the table here, and ran out to the nursery, picked up the plants and did the job, just because. I'll have to move them when we do the exterior staining and painting, but I really love looking at them now."

She shifted, reached down and pulled two beers out of the ice in a drywall compound bucket. "And now, even better, you can bask with me."

He twisted off the tops, then clinked his bottle to hers. "To the first of many basks under blue umbrellas. I take it you had a good day."

"Ups and downs. It couldn't get worse than it

started, though there were bumps. My excitement over the flooring was short-lived when I discovered they'd delivered the wrong hardwood. Then claimed I'd called in to change the order from walnut to oak, which is just so much bullshit, and will delay the third-floor work schedule a full week. I did finish the closet in the third bedroom, and got a start on the one in the fourth. The vendor messed up the cut on a panel of the steam shower doors, which means a delay there, but the soaking tub I've had my eye on for the third bath, second floor, just went on sale. The insurance company is balking at giving me another loaner after getting hit with two claims in two days, and will surely raise my rates. I decided to bask instead of being pissed."

"Good choice."

"Well, delays and glitches go with the territory. The roses are blooming, and I have a blue umbrella. So enough about me. How was your day?"

"Much better than average. I solved a major problem in the work, and it rolled from there. Then I found a very nice invitation in my refrigerator."

"I figured you'd see it first thing, after you surfaced. I actually came upstairs first, but if I've ever seen anyone in the zone, you were." Curious, interested, she cocked her head. "What was the problem solved?"

"The villain. Early version of him was Mr. Eckley, my tenth-grade algebra teacher. I'm telling you, the man was evil. But as the character developed, I knew I didn't have the right look—physically. I wanted leaner, a little meaner, yet handsome, maybe slightly aristocratic and dissipated. Everything I tried ended up looking like John Carradine or Basil Rathbone."

"Good looks, both. Hollowed cheeks, piercing eyes."

"And too obvious for the character. It kept bogging me down. Today I hit on it. I'm not looking for dissipation, cut cheekbones and intensity. I'm looking for a thin coat of polish and sophistication over a whole lotta smarm. Not the lean and bony Carradine, but something slighter, edging toward effete. The contrast between looks and intent," he explained. "Between image and purpose. It's a lot more evil when a guy coldly destroys while wearing an Armani suit."

"So you based him on a Hollywood agent?"

"Pretty much. He's Number Five."

She managed to swallow the beer, barely avoiding a spit take. "Mario? Are you serious?"

"Completely. One look at him out front today, and the scales fell from my eyes. He's got it all—the build, the posture, the five-hundred-dollar haircut and that sheer, shiny layer of oil. I don't know why I didn't see it when I met him before. Too locked into Mr. Eckley, I guess."

"Mario." She jumped up to grab Ford by the hair and crush her lips to his in a hard, smacking kiss that sent Spock into his happy dance. "This actually makes that clusterfuck this morning worthwhile. *Thank* you."

"I didn't actually do it for you. Any enjoyment you get from it's just a side benefit."

"I'll take it." She dropped back in her seat. "This has, indeed, turned out to be a better-than-average day."

CILLA TACKLED the next batch of trim in the shady shadow of the barn. She liked the work, and the quiet. There might have been miles of trim to strip, replicate, stain and seal through the farmhouse, but she wanted to keep the project her own. One day, she thought as she peeled away layers of white and, unfathomably, baby-blue paint from walnut, she'd walk through her house and admire every inch of restored trim. Best, she'd be able to say: I did that. Every inch.

She stripped down herself, to a tank and army-green cargo shorts as a concession to the heat that had snuck in, even in the shade. When she stopped to guzzle some water, she watched the pond crew removing and dividing water lilies, digging out over-propagated cattails.

Once it was done, she mused, ecologically balanced, she saw no reason she couldn't maintain the pond herself. She'd need some help with the grounds, she admitted, even once she bought a riding mower. She thought she'd enjoy puttering around, cutting the grass, pulling weeds, blowing and raking leaves in the fall, shoveling snow in the winter, planting new flowers in the spring.

But it wasn't realistic to believe she could handle it all—house, grounds, pond, gardens—and run a business.

Cleaning service, she thought, reholstering her water bottle and picking up her sandpaper block. That was a weekly definite. Maybe she'd talk to Brian about a once-a-month service, say March through October, at least until she got a better sense of what needed to be done, and just how much she could handle.

Plus, she needed advice on that kitchen garden she hoped to start, especially since she just hadn't been able to work it in this year as she'd hoped. And she needed to know if the fields should be plowed and planted—and with what. And who the hell would do that? More advice if she gave in to that nagging longing and got a horse. Which would require exercise, housing, feeding, grooming, and was probably a crazy idea.

But . . . wouldn't a couple of horses be gorgeous romping and grazing in one of the fields? Wouldn't they be worth the work, the time, the expense?

Next year, she told herself. Maybe.

She couldn't get cocky and complacent just because she'd had a couple of days of smooth sailing, because she was so damn happy. Reality included leaky faucets, and aphids and crabgrass, clogged gutters and fractious appliances. She'd be dealing with that, and a whole lot more, for the rest of her life.

And wasn't that just fabulous?

She sang as she sanded the old walnut trim.

"I'd forgotten how much you sound like her."

She looked up, squinted, then smiled as Gavin stepped from sun to shade. "Without her range, depth or natural vibrato."

"It sounded wonderful to me, and interesting that a girl of your age would sing 'Blue Skies.'"

"The place sort of calls for old standards. Or maybe she does. And, well"—she pointed up— "we've sure got them today."

"I came in through the front and saw the finished product." He tapped a finger on the trim. "That's another thing I'd forgotten, or never noticed when I came here all those years ago. It's beautiful. Truly beautiful."

"It makes me happy. Hence the singing. I was wondering when you might drop by again, so I could talk you into picking up another paintbrush."

"Show me the walls and the paint."

"I've got a bedroom just waiting for a couple coats of Spiced Cognac." She gestured to the newspapers he carried. "We provide drops. You don't have to bring your own." When he didn't smile, she felt a little warning dip in her belly. "Uh-oh."

"I heard about the media invasion, and your mother's visit the other day. There's been some coverage—TV, newspapers."

"Yeah, I've seen some of it. Look, I know they brought your name up, and—"

He cut her off with a wave of his hand. "That's not important. Cilla, I debated doing this, and decided someone would tell you or show you before much longer. It might be better if it was me. Patty was in the supermarket this morning. They'd just stocked these at checkout."

"The tabloids." She nodded, pulled off her work

gloves. "I knew they'd be hitting any day. Don't worry. I'm used to it." She held out a hand for the papers.

The headlines screamed. They always did in the tabs, she knew, but the screams seemed only more strident when her name was involved.

**JANET HARDY'S GHOST HAUNTS
HER GRANDDAUGHTER!
FORMER HOLLYWOOD PRINCESS IN
NEAR FATAL CRASH!
BEDELIA HARDY RUSHES TO HER
DAUGHTER'S SIDE AFTER
ATTACK BY MADMAN!
IS LITTLE KATIE THE REINCARNATION
OF JANET HARDY?**

The pictures were worse, grainy, exploitative. Splashed on one front page was a photo of Cilla, angled to spotlight her injured face, with Dilly holding her close, a single tear sliding down her cheek. Behind them floated the ghostly image of Janet with the caption: "'My mother's spirit remains trapped here,' Bedelia Hardy claims. Photographic PROOF corroborates her mournful statement."

An insert shot showed Cilla carrying the very trim

she now worked on out of the house. *Cilla struggles to exorcise Janet's ghost from her Virginia farm.*

Ford hadn't escaped, she noted. They'd slapped his photograph, his name, their ridiculous captions inside.

"Okay, worse. A lot worse than I expected it to be." She pushed the papers back at her father. "Front page, multiple stories in each. Mom will be thrilled. I don't *care* how that sounds," she snapped before her father could speak. "She amped it up. Everyone I work with, do business with, will see this crap. And Ford's sucked into the shit pile because he had the poor judgment to fall in love with me. Now he'll—"

"He's in love with you?" Gavin interrupted. Even as she started to shrug, Gavin set a hand on Cilla's shoulder. "He's in love with you? You're in love with him?"

"The *L* word's been spoken by both parties—or alluded to by me. Or, according to that rag there, spoken by Janet through me as they're speculating whether Cilla's outraged lover has been seduced by my grandmother's spirit. Don't *say* I shouldn't let it upset me. Don't say everyone knows this stuff is a load of crap. These papers sell because people love reading loads of crap."

"I was going to say I've always been fond of

Ford. If he makes you happy, I'm even more fond of him."

"He's not going to be happy with me when he sees all this, and has to explain to his family, his friends, his publisher, for God's sake, why his name and his face have been smeared all over the place." Helpless, she pressed a hand to her nervous belly. "I knew they'd pull him in, and I warned him, but I didn't know it would be this bad."

"You're either giving yourself too much credit or Ford not enough. Either way, you've got a right to be upset. To be thoroughly pissed. I don't have as much experience with celebrity as you do, but I know you have two choices."

He spoke calmly, his eyes solemn. "You go out, make a stink, demand corrections and retractions, threaten legal action, or you ignore it. Do the first, and you have a slim chance for some satisfaction, while the story gains legs and they sell more papers. Do the second and it burns in your guts, at least for a while."

"I have to ignore it, I know that. But it doesn't go away. They'll pull out those pictures, the worst of them, anytime they decide to run with another Janet Hardy story, or when Mom eventually divorces Number Five. I need a lot more thoroughly-pissed time before I can resign myself to it."

"I could buy you a puppy."

"A what?" Baffled, she pushed a hand at her hair. "Why?"

"Then you could spread these ridiculous papers on the floor for him to poop and pee on."

She smiled a little. "I always wanted a puppy, but I guess I should actually finish the house before I put on additions like pets."

"Then why don't I paint that bedroom for you instead? Spiced Cognac, right?"

"That's the one. I'll show you where it is."

FORD STEPPED OUT of the box for a bottle of water and to study the last pencils he'd completed. He liked the subtle changes in Cass, after she'd awakened and merged with Brid. The look in her eyes, the difference in posture when she was alone. She'd changed, and not just when she called out for power, and the symbol of her rank burned into her arm. The quiet, self-effacing academic would gradually come into her own, until that persona was more of a mask than her true self.

Then that loss would become an issue in future volumes.

To choose a path to destiny, as the Immortal told

her in panel three, page sixty-one, required sacrifice. She would never be exactly who or what she had been once that choice was made.

How would she deal? Ford wondered. How would she handle who she became, and who she left behind on that journey?

He thought it would be interesting to find out. He hoped the readers did, too.

It wouldn't hurt, he decided, to hit some blogs, give a few cryptic hints as to what was in store. He needed to check his e-mail anyway. And an hour break from the work would let the creative juices simmer.

He started to sit at his desktop when he heard a knock on his front door. Cautious since the Invasion of the Reporters, he checked out the window before he went down to answer.

"Hey, Mr. McGowan."

"Ford. I hope this isn't a bad time."

"No, actually, I was just taking a break. Come on in."

"There are a couple of things I'd like to talk with you about."

"Sure." Stupid to feel nervous, Ford told himself. It had been a long time since he'd had term papers and final exams on the line. "Ah, you want something cold?"

"That would be nice. I just finished doing some priming over at Cilla's."

"Is there a problem over there?" Ford asked as he led the way to the kitchen.

"Something about the hot water heater, a protracted debate over drawers versus doors on some sort of cabinetry and Buddy bitching about O rings. Otherwise, it looks to me as if the work over there is going very well."

"Cilla seems to be able to juggle all the balls. Have a seat. Tea work for you?"

"Perfect." Gavin waited while Ford poured the cold tea over ice in tall glasses. Then he set the tabloids on the counter.

Ford glanced down, turned the angle of the top paper for a better view. "Ouch. Has Cilla seen these?"

"Yes. I take it you haven't."

"No, I've been in Centuria most of the day. Working, I mean," he explained. "How'd she take it?"

"Not well."

"Jesus, could this be any cheesier?" Ford asked, tapping the photo with Janet's "ghost." "Any twelve-year-old can Photoshop better than that. But this insert of Cilla when she was a kid's pretty cute."

Saying nothing, Gavin opened the paper, watched as Ford skimmed down and saw his own face. "Man,

I need a haircut. I keep meaning to take care of that. Hmm, 'Cilla's Outraged Lover Rushes to Her Aid.' I don't appear especially outraged in this shot. Concerned would fit better. They ought to . . ."

The full phrase, and the fact that Cilla's father sat at his counter drinking iced tea, sank in, and had him clearing his throat. "Listen, Mr. McGowan, Cilla and I— That is, it's not . . . Well, it is, but—"

"Ford, I'm not shocked by the fact that you and Cilla are sleeping together, and I don't own a shotgun."

"Okay. Well." He took a deep gulp of tea. "Okay then."

"Is it?" Gavin opened another paper. "If you read this one, you'll see it's suggested you've been seduced by the lonely, trapped spirit of Janet Hardy—or you've seduced the granddaughter in an attempt to become Janet's lover."

Ford actually snorted. "Sorry, but it just strikes me funny. I don't know, if they had any real imagination, I'd be the reincarnation of somebody cool. Bogart or Gregory Peck, who's slaking his lust for the reincarnation of Janet Hardy by banging Cilla every chance he gets. And God, sorry about the banging comment. Really."

Gavin sat back, took a sip of his tea. "You were one of my best students. Bright, creative. A bit awkward and eccentric, but never dull. I always enjoyed what could be called your unique thought process. I told Cilla this morning I've always been fond of you."

"I'm really glad to hear that, considering."

"And considering, what are your intentions toward my daughter?"

"Oh boy. I just got this *thing* in my chest." Ford thumped on it. "Do you think extreme anxiety can cause a heart attack in somebody my age?"

"I doubt it, but I promise to call nine-one-one if necessary." Eyes direct, Gavin inclined his head. "After you answer the question."

"I want her to marry me. She's not there yet. Still got that thing," he added, rubbing now with the heel of his hand. "We've only been . . ." Probably not the way to go, Ford decided. "We've only known each other a few months, but I know how I feel. I love her. Am I supposed to tell you about my prospects and stuff? This is my first time."

"It's mine, too. I'd say between you and Cilla, your prospects are more than fine. I'd also say, in my opinion, you suit each other."

"There, it's going away." Ford took his first easy breath. "She needs me. She needs someone who understands and appreciates who she is, and who she's decided to be. And I need her, because who she is, and who she's decided to be are—big surprise to me—what I've been waiting for all my life."

"That's an excellent answer." Gavin rose. "I'm going to leave those here," he said, gesturing to the papers. "You handle that with Cilla however you think best. I'm going to go paint. I'll see myself out." At the edge of the kitchen, he turned back briefly. "Ford, I couldn't be more pleased."

Pretty damn pleased himself, Ford sat down at the bar and read through all the papers, all the stories. And knew just how he'd handle it.

It took considerable time, but the end result more than satisfied. He and Spock crossed the road, and finding the front door locked, Ford used the spare key she'd given him. He gave a shout and, when she didn't answer, started upstairs. The sound of the shower solved the mystery of where Cilla was. He thought briefly and intensely about joining her, but that would spoil the order of events.

Besides, surprising a woman in the shower in a locked house invited screams—and the woman could produce a serious scream. So he contented himself with sitting on the side of the guest room bed—as it remained the only bed in the house— to wait.

She didn't scream when she saw him, though from the amount of air she sucked in when she stumbled back, she'd have shattered every piece of glass for five miles if she'd cut loose.

"God, Ford. You scared the hell out of me!"

"Sorry. I figured I'd scare you more if I came in the bathroom while you were in the shower." He fisted his hand as if over the hilt of a knife, pumped it and did a fair imitation of the *Psycho* shower scene.

"It might've been worse. No Spock?"

"He wanted to go see if there were any invisible cats out back."

"I need to get dressed. Why don't you go sit out on the patio. I'll be out in a few minutes."

Unhappy, he thought. Irritated. And with a faint haze of discouragement. His idea would either help or make it worse. He might as well find out.

"I brought you something."

"What? Why don't you take it down, and I'll . . ." She trailed off when he took the thin package wrapped in tabloid paper from behind his back.

She hitched the towel a little more securely between her breasts. "So, you've seen them."

"Yeah. Oh, and two of your subs, my supposedly lifelong friends Matt and Brian, snuck off the job to come over and rag me about it. Punish them as you will. But meanwhile, open your present."

"I'm sorry. I'm really sorry. I completely underestimated the interest, the angles. And I walked straight into it by using my mother's publicist in the first place. Stupid, stupid, *stupid*."

"Okay, you can claim the stupid award. Open your present." He patted the bed beside him.

She sat, stared down at the package he put in her lap.

"I didn't use pages with any of the stories on them. We might want to make a scrapbook."

"It's not funny, Ford."

"Then you're really not going to like your present. I'll just take it back, bury it in the backyard. Where I may come across some worms we can both eat."

"Really not funny. You have absolutely no idea . . ." Temper had her ripping the paper. Then she could only stare down.

It was a slim volume, comic-book style, she supposed. The cover held a full-color drawing of her and Ford, locked in a passionate embrace. Over their heads, in what she could only call a lurid font, the title read:

THE AMOROUS ADVENTURES AND
MANY LIVES OF CILLA AND FORD

"You wrote a comic book?"

"It's really more a very short, illustrated story. Inspired by recent events. Come on, read it."

She couldn't think of anything to say, not initially. The five pages he'd done in black and white, complete with dialogue balloons, narrative captions and illustrations, ranged from the ludicrous, to pornographic to brutally funny.

She kept her face expressionless—she still had some acting chops—as she read it through.

"This." She tapped her finger on a panel depicting Ford, full monty, sweeping a naked Cilla into his arms while Spock covered his face with his paws. "I don't think this is to scale. A certain attribute is exaggerated."

"It's my attribute, and I'm the artist."

"And do you really think I'd ever say, 'Oh, Ford, Ford, hammer me home'?"

"Everyone's a critic."

"But I do like this part in the beginning, where the horny ghosts of Janet and Steve McQueen are floating over our sleeping bodies."

"It seemed appropriate as there's that legend of how they got it on in the pond. Plus, if I'm going to be possessed by the spirit of somebody, he'd be top of the cool scale."

"All-time champ," she agreed. "I also like how the paparazzo falls out of the tree while taking pictures through the bedroom window, and the little X's in his eyes in the next panel before Spock drags him off to bury him. But my favorite, possibly, is the last panel, where all four of us are in bed smoking cigarettes with expressions of sexual gratification on our faces."

"I like a happy ending."

She looked up from the book and into those green eyes. "And this is your way of telling me not to take all this so seriously."

"It's my way of giving you another way to take it, if you want."

She scooted back to prop herself at the head of the bed. "Let's have a table read. I'll be Cilla and Janet, you're Ford and Steve."

"Okay." He moved back to sit beside her.

"Then, we'll act it out."

He grinned over at her. "Even better."

TWENTY-FOUR

Every day brought visitors. Some she welcomed, and some she ignored. There was little she could do but ignore those who parked or stood on the shoulder of the road taking pictures of the house, the grounds, of her. She shrugged off the members of the crew who entertained themselves by posing. She couldn't blame them for getting a kick out of it, for grabbing a portion of that fifteen minutes of fame.

Sooner or later, she told herself, the interest would die down. When she caught sight of paparazzi stalking her while she shopped for hardware or lumber, she didn't acknowledge them. When she saw pictures of her home, of herself in the tabloids or gossip magazines, she turned her mind to other things. And when her mother's publicist called with requests for interviews and photo layouts, Cilla firmly hung up.

She went about her business, and prayed that one

of the current Hollywood crop of bad girls would do something outrageous enough to shift the attention. As July sweated its way toward August, she concentrated on the house. She had plenty to do.

"Why do you want a sink over here," Buddy demanded, "when you're putting a sink over there?"

"It's a prep sink, Buddy, and I don't honestly know why I want one. I just do. Sink here." She laid a fingertip on the revised, and absolutely final, drawing of her kitchen. "Dishwasher here. Refrigerator. And over here, the prep sink in the work island."

"It's your business." He said it in the way, as he often did, that told her she didn't know squat. "But I'm just saying, if you're putting this here island in, you're cutting into your counter space by putting a sink into it."

"It'll have a cutting-board top. On when I want to chop something, off when I want to wash something."

"What?"

"Jesus, Buddy. Um, vegetables."

He gave her his bulldog frown. "Then what're you going to wash in the other sink?"

"The blood off my hands after I stab you to death with my screwdriver."

His lips twitched. "You got some weird-ass ideas."

"Yeah? Wait for this one. I want a pot-filler faucet."

"You're going to have two damn sinks, *and* you want one of them gadgets that swings out on an arm from the wall over the stove to fill pans with water?"

"Yes, I do. Maybe I want to fill really big pots with water for pasta, or for washing my damn feet. Or for boiling the heads of cranky plumbers who argue with me. Maybe I've developed a faucet fetish. But I want it."

She walked over, tapped her fist on the wall where she'd drawn a circle with an X in it with a carpenter's pencil. "And I want it right here."

He cast his eyes to the ceiling, as if asking God what possessed her. "Gonna have to run pipes, so we're gonna have to cut that plaster to run 'em down, tie 'em in."

"I know that."

"It's your house."

"Yeah. It is."

"I heard you bought another one, that old place out on Bing."

"It looks that way." The little flutter in the belly signaled excitement and nerves. "We don't settle until October, but it looks that way."

"I guess you'll be wanting your fancy doodads in that one, too."

"You'll be pleased to know I plan to go more basic there." She had to fold her lips when she caught the disappointment on his face.

"You say that now. Well, I can start the rough-in on Thursday."

"That'd be great."

She left him to his scowling and calculations.

The kitchen cabinets should be done in a couple weeks, she estimated, and could be stored, if necessary, while the plumbing, the wiring were roughed, inspected, finished, inspected. The plaster repaired, the painting done, the floors laid. If her countertops came in on schedule, she might have a finished kitchen, excepting the refitted appliances, by Labor Day.

Maybe she'd have a party after all. And even thinking about planning a party probably jinxed the entire thing.

"Knock, knock!" Cathy Morrow poked her head in the front door. "Brian said you wouldn't mind if I came right in."

"I don't. How are you?"

"Just fine, except for dying of curiosity. Brian's been telling us how wonderful everything looks, so

Tom and I just had to come by and see for ourselves. Tom's out there in the back where you're having the stone wall built up. For shrubs, Brian said."

"It'll add height and depth to the yard and cut back on the mowing."

"I don't think Brian's ever done so much work for a private client—noncommercial, I mean. He's just . . . Oh, Cilla! This is just beautiful."

With a flush of pride, Cilla watched Cathy walk around the living room. "It's finished except for refinishing the floor, and we'll do all of them at the same time. And for furniture, and accessories, art, window treatments and a few minor details such as . . ."

"It's so open and warm. I love the light. Are those shamrocks on the collar, or whatever you call it?"

"Medallion, and yes. Dobby did an amazing job. And the fixture's true to the architecture of the house. I don't know what was there originally. I couldn't find any pictures showing it, and my father couldn't remember. But I think the straightforward Arts and Crafts lines and the design, with the diamond shapes of amber and deep blue, work."

"It's just lovely. But, oh my God, the fireplace."

"Focal point." Walking over, Cilla stroked her hand down the deep blue of the granite. "I wanted it to pop against the walls, the way the sky pops against the mountains. And a strong color like this needed a strong mantel."

"Wasn't it . . . Yes, it was brick before."

"Smoke-stained and pocked, and the hearth didn't meet code, which you can see by the burn marks from stray embers in the floor."

"It's funny, all I remember about this room, or the house, really, was so up-to-the-minute. The long sofa in lipstick pink with white satin pillows. I was so impressed. And the way Janet looked sitting on it in a blue dress. She was so beautiful. Well, everyone was," Cathy added with a laugh. "The celebrities, the rich and famous and important. I couldn't believe I was here. We were only invited because Tom's father was a very important local figure, but I didn't care why. We were invited here three times, and every time was almost painfully exciting.

"Lord, I was younger than you the last time I was here—in that era, I mean. So much time between," she said with a wistful sigh. "The last time was a Christmas party. All the decorations, the lights. Champagne, endless glasses of champagne, music. That amazing couch. People begged her to sing until she gave in. There was a white baby grand over by the window, and . . . Oh! Who was it, who was it everyone thought she was having a blistering affair with . . . the composer? And it turned out he was gay. He died of AIDS."

"Lenny Eisner."

"Yes, yes. God, gorgeous man. Anyway, he played, and she sang. Magic. It would've been the Christmas before your uncle was killed.

"I'm sorry," Cathy said suddenly. "I'm daydreaming out loud."

"No, I like hearing about the way it was. The way she was."

Cathy tucked back her swing of glossy hair. "I can tell you no one shone brighter than Janet. I think, yes, Marianna was just a few weeks old, and it was the first time we'd gotten a sitter. I was so nervous about leaving her, and so self-conscious because I still had all that baby weight on me. But Janet asked me about the baby, and told me how pretty I looked. It was kind of her, as I'd blown up like a whale with Marianna, and was barely down to hippo. And I remember because my mother-in-law nagged me about eating so many canapés. How would I lose the weight if I ate so much? Irritating woman. Oh, but Tom's father, I remember, too, how handsome he looked that night. So robust and dashing, and how Janet flirted with him, which irritated my mother-in-law and pleased me to no end."

She let out a laugh now, tickled by the memory. "We never did take, Tom's mother and I. Yes, he did look handsome that night. You'd never have believed cancer would take him so horribly just twelve years later. They stood right in here, Janet and Drew—Andrew, Tom's daddy. And then they were both gone.

"Now, I *am* sorry. How did I take such a morbid turn?"

"Old houses. They're full of life and death."

"I suppose you're right. It's about life now, isn't it, and what you're doing here. Oh, I completely forgot. I brought you two mimosas."

"You brought me drinks?"

Cathy laughed until she had to hold her stomach. "No. Trees. Well, they will be trees in a few years, if you want them. I started a couple dozen of them from seed, to give as gifts. I have a pair of lovely old mimosas. You may not want to bother with them, and I won't be offended if you don't. They're barely ten inches high at this point, and you won't see blooms for several years."

"I'd love to have them."

"They're out on your veranda in some old plastic pots. Why don't we take them around to Brian, see where he thinks they'd do best for you?"

"They're my first housewarming gift." Cilla led

the way out, and picked up one of the black plastic pots holding the delicate, fanning seedling. "I love the idea of planting them so young, and being able to watch them grow, year after year. It's funny, you coming by, talking about the parties. I was thinking about having one, maybe for Labor Day."

"Oh, you should! What fun."

"Problem being, the house won't be completely finished, and I won't have it furnished or decorated, or—"

"Who cares about that!" Obviously already in the swing, Cathy gave Cilla an elbow bump. "You can have another when you're all done. It'd be like . . . a prelude. I'd be happy to help, and you know Patty would. Ford's mother, too. In fact, we'd take over if you didn't whip us back."

"Maybe. Maybe. I'll think about it."

AFTER THE CREWS HAD GONE, and the house fell silent, after two fragile seedlings with their pink, powder-puff blossoms still years from bloom had been planted in a sunny spot bordering the yard and fallow field, Cilla sat on an overturned bucket in the living room of the house that had once been her grandmother's. The house now hers.

She imagined it crowded with people, beautifully dressed, beautifully coiffed. The colored lights of Christmas, the elegance of candle and firelight glowing, glittering, glimmering.

A lipstick-pink couch with white satin pillows.

And Janet, a light brighter than all the rest, gliding from guest to guest in elegant blue, a crystal glass bubbling with champagne in her hand.

The granddaughter sat on the overturned bucket, hearing the dream voices and drawing in the ghost scents of Christmas pine.

Ford found her, alone in the center of the room, in light going dim with the late summer evening.

Too alone, he thought. Not just solitary, not this time. Not quietly contemplative, and not basking, but absolutely alone, and very, very away.

Because he wanted her back, he walked over, crouched in front of her. Those spectacular eyes stared for another instant, two more, at what was away, then came back, came back to him.

"There was a Christmas party," she said. "It must have been the last Christmas party she gave, because it was the Christmas before Johnnie was killed. There were lights and music, crowds of people. Beautiful people. Canapés and champagne. She sang for them, with Lenny Eisner on the piano. She had a pink couch. A long, bright pink couch with white satin pillows. Cathy told me about it. It sounds so Doris Day, doesn't it? Bright pink, lipstick pink. It would never go in here now, that bright pink with these foggy green walls."

"It's just paint, Cilla; it's just fabric."

"It's statements. Fashions change, go in and out, but there are statements. I'd never be a pink couch with white satin pillows. I changed it, and I'm not sorry about that. It'll never be as elegant or bold and bright as it was, with her. I'm okay with that, too. But sometimes, when it's me in here, I need—and I know this sounds completely insane—but I need to ask her if she's okay with it, too."

"Is she?"

She smiled, laid her brow against his. "She's thinking about it." She sat back, sighed. "Well, since I'm making crazy statements, I might as well lead up to asking you a crazy question."

"Let's sit outside on the crazy-question section of the veranda. There's too damn much of me to squat down this way for long." He pulled her to her feet.

They sat on the veranda steps, legs stretched out, with Spock wandering the front yard. "You're sure this is the crazy-question section?"

"I have season tickets."

"Okay. Did you know Brian's grandfather? His father's father?"

"Barely. He died when we were just kids. I have more of an impression of him. Big, strapping guy. Powerful."

"He'd have been about, what, sixty that Christmas? That last Christmas party."

"I don't know. About, I guess. Why?"

"Not too old," Cilla considered. "Janet liked older men, and younger, and just about any age, race or creed."

"You're thinking Bri's grandfather and Janet Hardy?" His laugh was surprise and wonder. "That's just . . . weird."

"Why?"

"Okay, imagining grandparents having affairs, which means imagining grandparents having sex, is weird to begin with."

"Not so much when your grandmother is forever thirty-nine."

"Point."

"Besides, grandparents have sex. They're entitled to have sex."

"Yeah, but I don't want to fix the image in my head, or the next thing I'll be imagining *my* grandparents doing it, and see? See?" He gave her a mock punch on the arm. "There it is, in HDTV, in my head. Now I'm scarred for life. Thanks very much."

"Yes, definitely the crazy section of the veranda. Ford, he could've written the letters."

"My grandfather?"

"No. Well, yes, actually, now that you mention it. He had a crush on her, by his own admission. He took all those photographs of her."

Ford simply dropped his head in his hands. "It's a terrible, terrible series of images you're putting in my brain."

"Would he tell you if you asked?"

"I don't know, and I'm not going to ask. Not in any lifetime. And I'm moving out of the crazy section of the veranda."

"Wait, wait. We'll switch grandfathers. Brian's. It's hard to see yours holding so fondly on to all those photos if their affair ended so badly. But Brian's was the type, wasn't he? Powerful, important. Married. Married with a family, a successful—and public— career. He could've written those letters."

"Seeing as he's been dead for about a quarter century, it'd be hard to prove either way."

It was an obstacle, she thought, but didn't have to be insurmountable. "There are probably samples of his handwriting somewhere."

"Yeah." Ford let out a sigh. "Yeah."

"If I could get a sample, and compare it to the letters, then I'd know. They're both gone, and it could end there. There wouldn't be any point in letting it get out. But . . ."

"You'd know."

"I'd know, and I could put away that part of her life that I never expected to find."

"If they don't match?"

"I guess I'll keep hoping I'll ask the right question of the right person one day."

"I'll see what I can do."

IT TOOK FORD a couple of days to figure out an approach. He couldn't lie. Not that he was incapable of it; he was just so freaking bad at it. The only way he'd ever gotten away with a lie had been when the person being lied to felt pity for him and let it slide. He'd learned to sink or swim in the truth.

He watched Brian and Shanna turning a load of peat moss into the soil behind the completed stone wall.

"You could get a shovel," Brian told him.

"I could, but there is also value in the watching and admiring. Especially in the watching and admiring of Shanna's ass."

She wiggled it obligingly.

"We all know you're watching my ass," Brian shot back.

"It's true. Shanna is only the beard. To be more convincing, maybe she could bend over just a little more and . . . I'm sold," he said when she did so and laughed.

It came, Ford supposed, from being friends all their lives. Only one more reason a lie wasn't an option. But stalling was.

"What are y'all putting up there?"

Brian straightened, swiped a forearm over his sweaty forehead, then pointed to a group of shrubs in nursery pots. "Make yourself useful, since you don't seem to have anything better to do. Haul them up here so we can start setting them, see how they look."

"He's just bitchy because I'm taking ten days off. Going out to L.A. to visit Steve."

"Yeah?" Ford hefted an azalea. "So . . . ?"

"'The future has not been written.'"

You had to love a woman who quoted from *The Terminator*. "Tell him hey, and all that."

He waited while they arranged the plants he handed up, rearranged them, argued about the arrangement, and eventually jumped down to study and critique the arrangement.

"Okay, you're right," Shanna admitted. "We'll switch that rhodo and that andromeda."

"I'm always right." Smugly, Brian poked himself in the chest with his thumb. "That's why I'm the boss."

"As boss, can you take a minute?" Ford asked. "There's this thing."

"Sure," Brian replied as they walked away.

"Okay, this has to stay between you and me," Ford began. "Cilla found some letters written by a guy her grandmother had an affair with."

"So?"

"Big, secret affair, married guy, went sour right before she died."

"I repeat: So?"

"Well, they weren't signed, and Janet kept them and hid them away, so they became Mysterious Letters. In fact, we thought maybe, until Hennessy melted down, that the break-ins were an attempt by the mystery man to get the letters back."

"Wouldn't he be, like, a hundred years old?"

"Maybe, but not necessarily. And plenty of guys in their seventies once banged women not their wives."

"That's shocking," Brian said drily. "Hey, maybe it *was* Hennessy, and he had this wild fling with the beautiful, sexy movie star. Except I think he was born a dried-up asshole."

"It's not beyond the realm. But, ah, a little closer into the circle of logical possibility . . . See, she knew your grandfather, and he was an important man around here, and came to her parties."

Ford stood, scratching his head while Brian bent over double and laughed. "Jesus. Jesus!" Brian managed. "The late, great Andrew Morrow doing the nasty with Janet Hardy?"

"It's close to the circle of logical possibility," Ford insisted.

"Not in my world, Saw. I don't remember him all that well, but I remember he was a hard-ass, and self-righteous."

"In my world, the self-righteous are often the ones sneaking around getting blow jobs before they go home to the wives and kiddies."

Brian sobered, considered. "Yeah, you got a point. And God knows my grandmother must've been hard to live with. Water was never quite wet enough for her. God, she ragged on my mom all the damn time. Right up till she died. It'd be kind of cool," he decided, "if Big Drew Morrow had a few rounds with Janet Hardy."

It wasn't lying not to mention the claims of pregnancy, and the ugly tenor of the last letters. It was just . . . not mentioning. "Do you have anything he wrote? Birthday card, letter, anything?"

"No. My mother would, I guess. She keeps family papers and that kind of stuff."

"Can you get a sample of his handwriting without letting her know what it's for?"

"Probably. She's got a box of my stuff out in the garage. School papers, cards, that kind of shit. There might be something in there. She's been after me to take it to my place for years. I could get it out of her way, take a look through."

"Cool. Thanks."

"Hey!" Shanna shouted over. "Are you guys about finished or do I have to plant this whole terrace myself?"

"Nag, nag," Brian shouted back.

Ford studied her. Built, bawdy, beautiful. "How come you never went there?"

"Window of opportunity passed, and she became my sister." He shrugged. "But we've got a deal. If we're both single when we hit forty, we're going to Jamaica for a week and spend the whole time engaged in mad, jungle sex."

"Well. Good luck with that."

"Only nine years to go," Brian called out as he strode back toward Shanna.

For a moment, Ford was simply struck dumb. Nine years? Was that it? He didn't think about being forty. Forty was another decade. The grown-up decade.

How did it get to be only nine years off?

Jamming his hands in his pockets, he veered toward the house to find Cilla.

In the kitchen, where even the slices and chunks of counter had been torn out and hauled away, and odd-looking pipes poked out of a floor that might have been snacked on by drunken rodents, Buddy worked at a wide slice in the plaster wall.

He turned with some sort of large tool in his hand that made Ford think of a metal parrot head mated with a giraffe's neck.

"Who the hell puts a goddamn faucet over the goddamn stove?" Buddy demanded.

"I don't know. Ah, in case of fire?"

"That's a load of crap."

"It's the best I've got. Is Cilla around?"

"Woman's always around. Check up in the attic. Toilets in the attic," Buddy muttered as he went back to work. "Faucets over the stove. Want a tub in the bedroom next."

"Actually, I've seen . . . Nothing," Ford said when Buddy turned slitted eyes on him. "I see nothing."

He trooped his way through the house, noted that the trim was nearly finished in the hall, the entryway. On the second floor, he poked into rooms. He could still smell the paint in a room with walls of a subtle, smoky brown. In the master, he studied the three colors brushed on the wall. Apparently, she hadn't yet decided between a silvery gray, a gray-blue and a muted gold.

He wandered down the hall, then up the widened, finished stairs. She stood with Matt, each holding a sample of wood up to the light streaming through the window.

"Yeah, I like the contrast of the oak against the walnut." Matt nodded. "You know what we could do? We could trim it out in the walnut. You've got your . . . Hey, Ford."

"Hey."

"Summit meeting," Cilla told him. "Built-ins."

"Go right ahead."

"Okay, like this." With his pencil, Matt began to draw on the drywall, and Ford's attention shifted to the swaths of paint brushed on the opposite wall. She had the same silvery gray here, and a warm cheery yellow competing with what he'd call apricot.

He took a look in the bathroom, at the tiles and tones.

He tuned back in to hear Matt and Cilla come to an agreement on material and design.

"I'll get started on this in my shop," Matt told her.

"How's Josie feeling?"

"Hot and impatient, and wondering why the hell

she didn't do the math last winter and realize she'd be going through the summer pregnant."

"Flowers," Ford suggested. "Buy her flowers on the way home. She'll still be hot, but she'll be happy."

"Maybe I'll do that. I'll check, make sure the flooring's coming in on Tuesday. Barring another screwup, we'll start hammering it out up here. Roses always work, right?" he asked Ford.

"They're a classic for a reason."

"Okay. I'll let you know about the flooring, Cilla."

As Matt went down, Ford stepped over, tapped Cilla's chin up, kissed her. "The pale silver up here, the dull gold in the master."

She cocked her head. "Maybe. Why?"

"Streams better with the bathrooms than your other choices. And while they're both warm tones, the gray gives a sense of coolness. It's an attic, however jazzed up you make it. And in the bedroom, that color's restful but still strong. Now tell me why Buddy's putting a faucet over your stove."

"To fill pots."

"Okay. I talked to Brian."

"You often do."

"About the letters. His grandfather."

"You . . . you told him?" Her mouth dropped

open. "You just told him I think his grandfather might have broken commandments with my grandmother?"

"I don't think commandments were mentioned. You wanted a handwriting sample. Brian can probably get one."

"Yes, but . . . Couldn't you have been covert, a little sneaky? Couldn't you have lied?"

"I suck at sneak. And even if I gold-medaled in the sneak competition, I can't lie to a friend. He understands I told him in confidence, and he won't break a confidence to a friend."

She blew out a breath. "You people certainly grew up on a different planet than I did. Are you sure he won't say anything to his father? It's a stew pot of embarrassment."

"I'm sure. He did have an interesting comment though. What if Hennessy wrote the letters?"

Cilla went back to gape. "Kill-you-with-my-truck Hennessy?"

"Well, think about it. How crazy would you get if you'd been having an affair with a woman, then the son of that woman is responsible—in your eyes—for putting your son in a wheelchair? It's way-fetched, I agree. I'm going to reread the letters with this in mind. Just to see how it plays."

"You know what? If it turns in that direction,

within a mile of that direction, I don't think I want to know. Imagining my grandmother with Hennessy just gives me the serious eeuuwws."

She sighed, started downstairs with him. "I talked to the police today," she told Ford. "There won't be a trial. They did a deal, Hennessy took a plea, whatever. He'll do a minimum of two years in the state facility, psychiatric."

Ford reached for her hand. "How do you feel about that?"

"I don't honestly know. So I guess I'll put it aside, think about now."

She moved into the master, studied the paint samples. "Yeah, you're right about the color."

TWENTY-FIVE

Cilla used Sunday morning to pore through home and design magazines, scout the Internet for ideas and vendors and tear out or bookmark possibilities and potentials. She could hardly believe she'd reached the stage where she could begin considering furniture.

Weeks away, of course, and she needed to add in trolling antique stores, even flea markets—and possibly yard sales—but she was approaching the time when ordering sofas and chairs, tables and lamps, wouldn't be out of line.

Then there was bedding, she mused, a kitchen to outfit, an office, window treatments, rugs. All those fun, picky little details to fill in a house. To make a house a home. Her home.

Her first real home.

The closer it came to reality, the more she realized just how much she wanted home. All she had to do was step outside, look across the road and see it.

Sitting here now, at Ford's counter, with her laptop, her magazines, her notebooks, she thought of just how far she'd come since March. No, well before March, she corrected. She'd started this journey on that long-ago trek through the Blue Ridge, one she'd taken specifically, deliberately to see, firsthand, her grandmother's Little Farm, to see where her own father sprang from, and maybe to understand, a little, why he'd come back, and left her.

And she'd fallen in love, Cilla thought now, with the hills that bumped their way back to the mountains, the thick spread of trees, the little towns and the big ones, the houses and gardens, the winding roads and streams. Most of all, she'd fallen in love with the old farmhouse sagging behind a stone wall, closed in by its desolate, overgrown gardens.

Sleeping Beauty's castle, maybe, she mused, but she'd seen home, even then.

Now, what she'd dreamed of, yearned for, was very nearly hers.

She sat at the counter, sipping coffee, and imagined waking in a room with walls the color of a glowing and hopeful dawn, and of living a life she'd chosen rather than one chosen for her.

Ford gave a sleepy grunt as he walked in.

Look at him, she thought. Barely awake, that long, long, lean, edging-toward-gawky body dressed in navy boxers and a tattered Yoda T-shirt. All that sun-streaked brown hair rumpled and messy, and those green eyes groggy and just a little cranky.

Wasn't he just unbelievably adorable?

He dumped coffee into a mug, added sugar, milk. Said, "God, mornings suck through a straw," and drank as if his life balanced within the contents of the mug.

Then he turned, to prop his elbow on the counter. "How come you look so lucid?"

"Maybe because I've been up for three hours. It's after ten, Ford."

"You have no respect for the Sunday."

"It's true. I'm ashamed."

"No, you're not. But real estate agents also have no respect for the Sunday. Vicky just called my cell and woke me from a very hot dream involving you, me and finger paints. It was really getting interesting when I was so rudely and annoyingly interrupted. Anyway, the sellers came down another five thousand."

"Finger paints?"

"And as an artist I can say it was the beginning of a masterpiece. We're only ten thousand apart now, as Vicky the dream killer pointed out. So . . ."

"No."

"Damn it." He looked like a kid who'd just been told there were no cookies in the jar. "I knew you were going to say no, which you did not say when I was swirling cobalt blue around your belly button. Couldn't we just—"

"No. You'll thank me later when you have that ten k to put into improvements and repairs."

"But I really want that ugly dump now. I want it for my own. I love it, Cilla, like a fat kid loves cake." He tried a hopeful smile. "We could split the difference."

"No. We hold firm. No one else has made an offer on the property. The seller isn't interested in making any of those repairs and improvements. He'll cave."

"Maybe he won't." Those groggy eyes narrowed into a scowl. "Maybe he's just as pigheaded as you are."

"Okay, here's this." She leaned back, an expert at the negotiation table. "If he doesn't cave, if he doesn't accept your offer within two weeks, you can counter with the split. But you hold tight for fourteen more days."

"Okay. Two weeks." He tried the hopeful smile again. "Do you ever think about scrambling eggs?"

"Hardly ever. But I am thinking about something else. I'm thinking, looking at that big, soft sofa over there—as I've been in the sofa-hunting mode. And wondering, as I'm thinking, what would happen if I stretched out on that big, soft sofa."

She slid off the stool, aiming a smile over her shoulder as she strolled to the sofa. "And I'm wondering will I have to lie here all by myself, all alone with my unquenched desires and lascivious thoughts."

"Okay, lascivious did it."

He skirted the counter, crossed, then pounced. "Hi."

With a low laugh, she scissored her legs, reared and rolled until their positions reversed. "I think I'll be high this time." Dipping down, she caught his bottom lip between her teeth, chewed lightly.

"This is how I respect the Sunday."

"I was so wrong about you." He ran his hands down her, over the loose, white tank. "Cilla."

"You're all rumpled and sexy and . . ." She peeled Yoda off, tossed him away. "Mostly naked."

"All we're missing are the finger paints." He pushed up, locking his arms around her, fixing his mouth to hers. "I miss you. As soon as I'm awake and you're not there."

"I'm not far." She wrapped around him, only separating to let him strip the white tank away. And, oh, those hands, those slow, steady hands. "Here.

Here." She cupped his head, guided it down until his mouth closed over her breast.

Everything coiled and curled inside her, and opened again.

She wanted, wanted, with those hands pressing, that mouth feasting. Wanted him inside her, hot and hard. She wiggled out of her shorts, gasping as he touched and teased, moaning as she rose up, eased down, and filled herself with him.

"This is what I want, on Sunday morning."

She took him, riding up, riding down, her hands braced on the arm of the couch. Slim, hard muscles, burnt honey hair, iced blue eyes so clear they were a mirror into his heart.

No dream, no fantasy came close to the truth of her. No wish, no wonder compared.

"I love you, Cilla. I love you."

Her breath caught; her heart skipped beats. Her body bowed, and the arrow it shot struck home.

She slid down to him, snuggled right in. He loved the way they fit, line to line, the way her hair felt against his skin.

"So . . . where exactly do you buy finger paints?"

He grinned, lazily walked his fingers up and down her spine. "I'll find out, lay in a supply."

"I'll provide the drop cloth. Where did you get this couch?"

"I don't know. Somewhere where they sell furniture."

"It's a good size, shape, nice fabric. Comfortable. I need to start thinking furniture, and I have that great big living room to deal with. Conversation areas and lighting and art. I've never done all that before. It's a little intimidating."

He glanced over when Spock wandered in, took one look at them twined together naked on the couch and walked away. Just jealous, Ford thought. "Never bought furniture before?"

"Sure, you've got to sit on something. But I've never chosen things with the idea of keeping them any length of time. It's always been temporary." She brushed her lips over his collarbone, nuzzled at his shoulder. "And I've worked with stagers on flips. Staging a property can help it sell. So I know, or have opinions, about what works in a space. But this is different. Staging's like a set. Load it in, break it down."

"Didn't you have a house, an apartment, something in L.A.?"

"Steve had a place. After our five-minute marriage I lived at the BHH awhile."

"The BHH?"

"Beverly Hills Hotel. Then I traveled some, or stayed at Steve's when I picked up some work. There was my very brief college stint, and I had an apartment off campus. When Steve bought the property in Brentwood to flip, I camped there. I got in the habit of staying in the flip houses. It gave me a sense of them."

Place, house, property. Never home, he thought. She'd never had what he and everyone he knew took for granted. She'd never had home. He thought of how she'd sat in the big, empty living room with its beautiful walls and gorgeous trim, and imagined a long-ago holiday party.

She was reaching back to find her future.

"We can move the couch over there," he said, suddenly desperate to give her something. "You could see how it looks in place and have something to sit on besides the ever-versatile bucket."

"That's a very nice offer." She gave him an absent kiss before sitting up to hunt for her clothes. "But it's more practical to wait for furniture until after the floors are done. Of course, now that I've gotten trapped into giving a party, I'd better find some suitable outdoor furniture."

"Party?"

"Didn't I tell you?" She pulled on her tank. "I made the mistake of mentioning to Cathy Morrow that I'd like—maybe—to give a party around Labor

Day, but the house wouldn't be finished or furnished. She jumped right on the first part, completely ignored the second. Now I've got Patty calling me with menu ideas, and your mother offering to make her pork barbecue."

"It's great stuff."

"No doubt. The problem remains how I find time to squeeze in party planning while I'm installing kitchen cabinets, running trim, hanging doors, refinishing floors and hitting a very long punch-out list, not to mention exploring the world of sofas, couches, divans and settees."

"You buy a grill, a bunch of meat and a whole lot of alcoholic beverages."

She shook her head at him. "You're a man."

"I am. A fact which I've just proven beyond any reasonable doubt." And being Sunday, he should get a shot at proving it again. "A party's a good thing, Cilla. People come, people you know and like, enjoy being with. You show off what you've done. You share it. That's why you took down the gate."

"I . . ." He was right. "What kind of grill?"

He smiled at her. "We'll shop."

In an exaggerated gesture, she crossed her hands over her heart. "Words most women only dream about hearing from a man. I need to go get dressed.

I could pick up paint while we're out, and hardware, take another look at kitchen lighting."

"What have I wrought?"

She tossed a smile at him as she walked out of the room. "We'll take my truck."

He dragged on his boxers, but stayed where he was, thinking about her. She didn't realize how much she'd told him. She'd never once mentioned the house, or houses, where she'd grown up.

He, on the other hand, could describe in perfect detail the house of his childhood, the way the sun slanted or burst through the windows of his room at any given time of the day, the green sink in the bathroom, the chip in the kitchen tile where he'd dropped a gallon jug of apple juice.

He remembered the pang when his parents had sold it, even though he'd been in New York, even though he'd moved out. Even though they'd only moved a couple miles away. Years later, he could still drive by that old brick house and feel that pang.

Lovingly restored trim, letters hidden in a book, an old barn painted red again. All of that, every step and detail, were links she forged herself to make a chain of connection.

He'd do whatever he could do to help her forge it, even if it came down to shopping for a grill.

"Hey, Ford."

"Back here," Ford called out when he heard Brian's voice, and unfolded himself off the sofa as Brian walked in. "Weber or Viking?"

"Tough choice," Brian said without any need for explanation. "I went with the Weber, as you know, but a man can't go wrong with the Viking."

"How about a woman?"

"Women have no place behind a grill. That's my stand on it." He bent down, picked up Ford's discarded T-shirt. "This is a clue. It tells me that I've come too late to interrupt morning sex. Damn that second cup of coffee." He tossed the shirt at Ford's face, then leaned down to greet Spock.

"You're just jealous because you didn't have any morning sex."

"How do you know?"

"Because you're here. Why are you here?"

Brian gestured to the counter and Cilla's research pile as he crossed over to open Ford's refrigerator. "Where's Cilla?"

"Upstairs, getting dressed so we can go out and debate between Weber and Viking."

"You've got Diet Cokes in here," Brian observed as he pulled out a can of the real thing. "A sure sign a guy is hooked. I went by my mom's yesterday." Brian popped the top, took a swig. "Hauled off, to her surprised joy, not one but two boxes of junk she's saved for me. What am I supposed to do with a crayon drawing of a house, a big yellow sun and stick people?"

"I don't know, but you can't throw it out. According to my mother, dumping any childhood memorabilia they saved dares the gods." Ford got his own Coke. "I have three boxes."

"I won't forget it's your fault I took possession of that stuff." He pulled an envelope out of his pocket, tossed it on the counter. "However, as I didn't score female companionship last night, I went through some of it, came up with this. It's a card my grandfather gave my mother on the occasion of my birth. He wrote some stuff in it."

"Thanks. I owe you one."

"Damn right. I am now housing every report card I got from first grade through high school. You'll let me know if it matches. I'm kind of into it now."

"One way or the other." Ford picked up the card, studied the strong, bold lettering of Cathy's name.

"I gotta go, pick up Shanna. I'm driving her to the airport." He squatted down, rubbing Spock's head, the wiggling body. "Tell Cilla I'll have a couple guys there tomorrow to finish that mulching, and I should be able to swing by the new place she's buying, take a look at the yard."

"Okay. I'll get this back to you."

Brian smirked at the card. "Yeah, I'm worried about that."

Ford went upstairs, into the bedroom where Cilla was pulling her hair back into a tail. "I'm set," she told him. "I'm going to go over while you're getting dressed, take another look at a couple things before we go."

"Brian just came by."

"Oh, did he look at the new property already?"

"No, next week, he said. He brought this." Ford held up the card.

"Is that . . . Of course it is. I didn't expect him to find something so fast. Wow." She pressed a hand to her belly. "Big mystery could be solved. It makes me a little nervous."

"Do you want me to go check it out, then just tell you?"

She dropped her hand. "What am I? A weenie?"

"No, you're not."

"Then let's do it."

"They're in my office."

She went in with him, watched him take the book off the shelf, then set it on the counter for her to open.

"I keep thinking how she chose *Gatsby*. The rich, shining life, the glitter and then ennui, romance, betrayal, ultimate tragedy. She was so unhappy. I dreamed of her again not long ago. I didn't tell you. One of my Janet and Cilla dreams. Forest Lawn. They're both buried there. Her and Johnnie. I only went there once. Her grave was literally covered with flowers. It made me sad to look at it. All those flowers, brought by strangers, fading in the sun."

"You planted them for her here instead. And even when they fade, they come back new. Year after year."

"I like to think that would matter to her. My personal tribute." She opened the book, took the stack of letters out. "I'll open this," she said, choosing one. "You open that."

Ford took out the card. He'd expected a happy picture of a baby, or a sentimental one of a mother and child. Instead he found Andrew Morrow's initials on heavy, cream-colored stock. "Pretty formal," he commented, and opened the card.

Congratulations to my lovely daughter-in-law on the birth of her son. I hope these roses bring you pleasure. They're only a small token of my great pride. Another generation of Morrows is born with Brian Andrew.

Affectionately, Drew

Cilla laid the letter beside the card.

My Dear. My Darling.

There are no words to express my sorrow, my sympathy, my grief for you. I wish I could hold you, could comfort you now with more than words on a page. Know that I'm with you in my heart, that my thoughts are full of you. No mother should have to suffer the loss of her child, and then be forced to grieve in so public a manner.

I know you loved your Johnnie beyond measure. If there can be comfort now, take it in knowing he felt that love every day of his short life.

Only Yours

"Is that fitting, is that fate?" Cilla said quietly. "That I'd choose the loss of a son to compare to the birth of another? It's a kind letter," she continued. "They're both kind notes, and both strangely distant, so carefully worded, I think. When each occasion should have filled the page with emotions and intimacies. The tone, the structure. They could be from the same person."

"The writing's similar. Not . . . well, not exactly exact. See the S's in the card? When he starts a word—son, small—with an S, it's in curvy print. In the letter—sorry, sympathy—traditional lowercase cursive."

"But the uppercase T's are written the same way, and the Y's. The slant of the writing. It's very close. And they were written years apart."

"*My* and *my* in both really look like the same hand, and the uppercase I's, but the uppercase D's, not so much." Ford knew he looked with an artist's eye, and wasn't sure if that was a plus or a minus. "Then again, in the card, that's a signature. Some people write the first letter of their signature differently than they might a word. I don't know, Cilla."

"Results, inconclusive. I don't suppose you know any handwriting experts."

"We could find one." He looked up, into her eyes. "Do you want to go that route?"

"No. Maybe. I don't know. Damn it. No easy answers."

"Maybe we could get our hands on a sample closer to when the letters were written. I can ask Brian to try for that."

"Let's just put it away for now." She folded the letter, slipped it back into the envelope. "We know one thing after this. It wasn't Hennessy. I'd forgotten about the letter after Johnnie's death. No way, even if he was crazy in love, would he have written that after the accident. Not when he was with his own son in the hospital."

"You're right."

"So, if I had a list, I'd be able to cross a name off. That's something. I guess it's going to have to be enough for now. At least for now."

Ford closed the book, put it back on the shelf. He turned to her, took her hand. "What do you say we go buy a grill?"

"I'd say that's exactly what I want to do."

But he left the monogrammed note on his desk when he went to dress. He could find a grapholo-gist. Someone outside Virginia to whom the name Andrew Morrow meant nothing. And he could see where that led.

CILLA'S PLEASURE WHEN her walnut flooring finally arrived Tuesday morning hit a major road-block before noon when her tile layer stormed over to her work area beside the barn.

"Hi, Stan. You're not scheduled until Thursday. Are . . ."

She found herself backpedaling quickly as she caught the murderous look in his eye. "Hey, hey, what's the problem?"

"You think you can treat people that way? You think you can talk to people that way?"

"What? What?" He backed her right up into the side of the barn. Too shocked at seeing the usually

NORA ROBERTS

affable Stan with a vein throbbing in the center of his forehead, Cilla held up her hands as much in defense as a gesture of peace.

"You think 'cause you come from money and got yourself on TV you're better than the rest of us?"

"I don't know what you're talking about. Where—"

"You got some nerve, goddamn it, calling my wife, talking to her like that."

"I never—"

"You got a problem with my work, you talk to *me*. You got that? Don't you go calling my house and yelling at my wife."

"Stan, I've never spoken to your wife."

"You calling her a liar now?" He shoved his face into hers, so close she could taste his rage.

"I'm not calling her anything." Alarm lumped at the base of Cilla's throat, so she spaced her words carefully. "I don't know her, and I don't know what the hell you're talking about."

"I come home and she's so upset she can barely talk. Started crying. The only reason I didn't come straight over here last night is she begged me not to, and I didn't want to leave her when she was in that state. She's got hypertension, and you go setting her off 'cause you decide you don't like my work."

"And I'm telling you, I never called your house, I never spoke to your wife, and I'm not dissatisfied with your work. In fact, the opposite. Or why in God's name did I contract you to lay the floor in my kitchen?"

"You tell me, goddamn it."

"Well, I can't!" she shouted back at him. "What time was I supposed to have made this call?"

"About ten o'clock last night, you know damn well. I get home about ten-thirty, and she's lying down, flushed and shaking because you screamed at her like a crazy woman."

"Have you ever heard me scream like a crazy woman? I was at Ford's last night at ten o'clock. I nodded off in front of the TV. Ask him. Jesus, Stan, you've been working here off and on for months now. You should know I don't handle things that way."

"Said it was you. Cilla McGowan." But puzzlement began to show through the temper. "You told Kay she was a stupid hick, just like most of the people around here. How I couldn't lay tile for shit, and you were going to make sure word got out. When I lost work, I'd have nobody to blame but my own lazy ass. How maybe you'd sue me over the crap job I did for you."

"If your wife's a hick, I am, too. I *live* here now. I don't contract with subs who do crap work. In fact, I recommended you to my stepmother just last week, if she ever talks my father into updating their master bath." She realized she was breathless from reaction, but the alarm had dissolved. "Why the hell would I do that, Stan, if I thought your work was crap?"

"She didn't just make it up."

"Okay." She had to draw in air. "Okay. Is she sure whoever called gave my name?"

"Cilla McGowan, and then Kay said you . . . they," he corrected, obviously ready to give Cilla the benefit of the doubt, "said, 'Do you know who I am?' in that bitchy way people do when they think they're important. Then just laid into her. It took me almost an hour to calm her down when I got home from the summer league. I had to make her take a Tylenol P.M. to help her sleep. She was that upset."

"I'm sorry. I'm sorry somebody used my name to upset her. I don't know why . . ." Pressure lowered onto her chest, pushed and pushed. "The flooring supplier said I called in and changed my order. Walnut to oak. But I didn't. I thought there'd just been a mix-up. Maybe it wasn't. Maybe somebody's screwing with me."

Stan stood a moment, stuck his hands in his

pockets, pulled them out again. "You never made that call."

"No, I didn't. Stan, I'm trying to build a reputation, and a business here. I'm trying to build relationships with subs and service people. When someone broke in and went at the bathrooms, you juggled me in for the repair and re-lay, and I know you cut me a break on the labor."

"You had a problem. And the fact is, I was proud of that work and wanted to make it right."

"I don't know how to make this right with your wife. I could talk to her, try to explain."

"Better let me do that." He blew out a breath. "Sorry I came at you."

"I'd have done the same in your place."

"Who'd do something like this? Mess with you, get Kay all upset?"

"I don't know." Cilla thought of Mrs. Hennessy. Her husband was doing two years in a psych facility. "But I hope I can head it off before it happens again."

"I guess I'd better swing by home, straighten this out with Kay."

"Okay. You still on for Thursday?"

His smile was a little sheepish. "Yeah. Ah, you got any reason to call me at home, maybe you should come up with a code word or something."

"Maybe I should."

She stood in the shadow of her barn, with trim propped against the wall and laid out to dry, stretched across her sawhorses. And wondered how many times she'd have to pay for the crimes, sins, mistakes of others.

TWENTY-SIX

Cilla stood in her bedroom, staring at the freshly painted walls while her father tapped the lid back on the open can of paint. She watched the way the strong midday light flooded the room, and sent those walls to glowing.

"The trim's not even up, and the floors still have to be done, and still, standing here gives me an ecstatic tingle."

He straightened from his crouch, took a long look himself. "It's a damn fine job."

"You could make a living."

"It's always good to have a fallback."

"You've damn near painted the entire house." She turned to him then. She still couldn't quite think what to make of that, or what to say to him. "That's saved me weeks of time. Thanks doesn't cover it."

"It does the job. I've enjoyed it, on a lot of levels.

I've liked being part of this. This transformation. We missed a lot of summers, you and I. Spending some of this one with you, well, it's made me happy."

For a moment she could only stand, looking at him, her handsome father. Then she did something she'd never done before. She went to him first. She pressed a kiss to his cheek, then wrapped her arms around him. "Me too."

He held on, hard and tight. She felt his sigh against her. "Do you remember the day we first saw each other here? I came to the back door, and you shared your lunch with me on the sagging front veranda?"

"I remember."

"I didn't see how we'd ever get here. Too much neglect, too much time passed. For the house, and for us." He eased her back, and she saw with some surprise, some alarm, that his eyes were damp. "You gave it a chance. The house, and me. Now I'm standing here with my daughter. I'm so proud of you, Cilla."

When her own eyes flooded, she pressed her face to his shoulder. "You said that to me, that you were proud, after the concert in D.C., and once, earlier, when you came to the set of *Our Family* and watched me shoot a scene. But this is the first time I believe it."

She gave him a last squeeze, stepped back. "I guess we're getting to know each other, through interior latex, eggshell finish."

"Why stop there? How about we go take a look at the exterior."

"You can't paint the house. The rooms, that's one thing."

Lips pursed, he scanned the room. "I think I passed the audition."

"Interiors. It's a three-story building. A really big, three-story building. Painting it'll require standing on scaffolding and really tall ladders."

"I used to do my own stunts." He laughed as she rolled her eyes in a way he could only describe as daughterly. "Maybe I didn't, and maybe that was a long time ago, but I have excellent balance."

She tried stern. "Standing on scaffolding and really tall ladders in the dog-day heat of August."

"You don't scare me."

Then simple practicality. "It's not a one-man job."

"True. I'll definitely need some help. What color did you have in mind?"

And felt herself being gently steamrolled. "Listen, the old paint needs to be scraped where it's peeled, and—"

"Details, details. Let's take a look. Do you want it painted by Labor Day, or what?"

"Labor Day? It's not even on the schedule until mid-September. When it's, hopefully, a little cooler. The crew who painted the barn—"

"Happy to work with them."

Completely baffled, she set her hands on her hips. "I thought you were kind of—no offense—a pushover."

His expression placid, he patted her cheek. "No offense taken. What about the trim, the verandas?"

She puffed out her cheeks, blew the breath out. She saw it now. Pushover, her ass. He just ignored the arguments and kept going. "Okay, we'll take a look at the samples I'm thinking about. And once I decide, you can work on the verandas, the shutters. But you're not hanging off scaffolding or climbing up extension ladders."

He only smiled at her, then dropped his arm over her shoulders the way she'd seen him do with Angie, and walked her downstairs.

Though it wasn't on her list—and she *really* wanted to get up to her office and check on the progress of her floors, see if Stan had finished the tile, start running the bedroom trim—she opened the three pints of exterior paint. "Could go deep, with this blue. The gray in it settles it down a few notches, and white trim would set it off." She slapped some on the wood.

"Makes a statement."

"Yeah. Or I could go quiet and traditional with this buff, use a white trim again, or a cream. Cream might be better. Softer."

"Pretty and subdued."

"Or I could go with this more subtle blue, again gray undertones keeping it warm, and probably go with a soft white for the trim."

"Dignified but warm."

She stepped back, cocked her head to one side, then the other. "I thought about yellows, too. Something cheerful, but soft enough it doesn't pop out of the ground like a big daffodil. Maybe it should wait. Maybe it should just wait." She gnawed on her lip. "Until . . ."

"I've seen you make decisions, over everything that has to do with this house, with the grounds. Why are you having such a hard time with this?"

"It's what everyone will see. Every time they drive by on the road. A lot of them will slow down, point it out. 'That's Janet Hardy's house.'" Setting down the brush, Cilla wiped her hands on her work shorts. "It's just paint, it's just color, but it matters what people see when they drive by on the road, and think of her."

He laid a hand on her shoulder. "What do you want them to see when they drive by here?"

"That she was a real person, not just an image in an old movie, or a voice on a CD or old record. She was a real person, who felt and ate, who laughed and worked. Who lived a life. And she was happy here, at least for a while. Happy enough she didn't let it go. She held on, so I could come here, and have a life here."

She let out an embarrassed laugh. "And that's a hell of a lot to expect from a couple coats of paint. Jesus, I should probably go back into therapy."

"Stop." He gave her shoulder a quick shake. "Of course it matters. People obsess over something as mundane as paint for a lot less important reasons. This house, this place, was hers. More, it was something she chose for herself, and something she valued. Something she needed. It's been passed to you. It should matter."

"It was yours, too, in a way. I don't forget that. That matters more now than it did when I started. You pick."

He dropped his hand, actually stepped back. "Cilla."

"Please. I'd really like this to be your choice. The McGowan choice. People will think of her when they pass on the road. But when I walk the grounds or drive in after a long day, I'll think of her, and of you. I'll think of how you came here as a little boy, and chased chickens. You pick, Dad."

"The second blue. The warm and dignified blue."

She hooked her arm with his, studied the fresh color over the old, peeling paint. "I think it's going to be perfect."

WHEN FORD WALKED over late in the day, he saw Gavin on the veranda, scraping the paint on the front of the house.

"How're you doing, Mr. McGowan?"

"Slow but sure. Cilla's inside somewhere."

"I just bought a house."

"Is that so?" Gavin stopped, frowned. "You're moving?"

"No. No. I bought this, well, this toxic dump that Cilla says she can fix up. To flip. The seller just accepted my offer. I feel a little sick, and can't decide if it's because I'm excited, or because I can see this big, yawning money pit opening up under my feet. I'm going to have two mortgages. I think I should probably sit down."

"Pick up that scraper, give me a hand with this. It'll calm you down."

Ford eyed the scraper dubiously. "Tools and I have a long-standing agreement. We stay away from each other, for the good of mankind."

"It's a scraper, Ford, not a chain saw. You scrape ice off your windshield in the winter, don't you?"

"When I must. I prefer staying home until it thaws." But Ford picked up the spare scraper and tried to apply the process of scraping ice from glass to scraping peeling paint off the side of a house. "I'm going to have two mortgages, and I'm going to be forty."

"Did we just time-travel? You can't be more than thirty."

"Thirty-one. I have less than a decade until I'm forty, and five minutes ago I was studying for the SATs."

Gavin's lips twitched as he continued to scrape. "It gets worse. Every year goes faster."

"Thanks," Ford said bitterly. "That's just what I needed to hear. I was going to take my time, but how can you when there isn't as much as you think there is?" Turning, he waved the scraper, and nearly put it through the window. "But if you're ready, and she's not, what the hell are you supposed to do about that?"

"Keep scraping."

Ford scraped—the paint and his knuckles. "Crap. As a metaphor for life, that sucks."

Cilla came out in time to see Ford sucking his sore knuckles and scowling. "What are you doing?"

"I'm scraping paint and a few layers of skin, and your father's philosophizing."

"Let me see." She took Ford's hand, studied the knuckles. "You'll live."

"I have to. I'm about to have two mortgages. Ouch!" he said when Cilla gave his sore fingers a quick squeeze.

"Sorry. They accepted your offer?"

"Yeah. I have to go into the bank tomorrow and sign a bunch of papers. I'm going to hyperventilate," he decided. "I need a bag to breathe into."

"November settlement?"

"I followed the company line."

She gave him a poke. "Scared?"

His answering scowl was both sour and weak. "I'm about to go into debt. The kind that has many zeros. I'm having a few moments. Do you know that the olfactory sense is the strongest of the five senses? I keep having flashes of how that place smells."

"Put that down before you really hurt yourself." She took the scraper out of his hand, set it on the window ledge. "And come with me a minute." She gave her father a quick wink, then drew Ford into the house.

"Do you remember what the kitchen looked like in here when you first saw it?"

"Yeah."

"Ugly, dingy, damaged floors, cracked plaster, bare bulbs. Got that picture in your head?"

"I got it."

"Close your eyes."

"Cilla."

"Seriously, close them, and keep that picture in there."

He shook his head but obliged her, and let her lead him back. "Now I want you to tell me what you see when you open your eyes. No thinking it through, no qualifying. Just open your eyes and tell me what you see."

He obeyed. "A big room, empty. A lot of light. Walls the color of lightly toasted bread. And floors, big squares of tile—a lot of honey tones on cream with pipes poking up through them. Big, un-framed—untrimmed—windows that open it up to a patio with a blue umbrella, and gardens with roses blooming like maniacs, and green gone lush. And the mountains against the sky. I see Cilla's vision."

He started to step forward, but she tugged him

back. "No, don't walk on the tiles yet. Stan only finished the grout an hour ago."

"We can do this."

"We absolutely can. It takes planning, effort, a willingness to find a way around unexpected problems, and a real commitment to the end goal. We'll turn that place around, Ford, and when we do, we'll have something we can both be proud of."

He turned to her, kissed her forehead. "Okay. Okay. I've got some scraping to do."

She walked out with him, baffled when he signaled so long to her father and kept walking.

"Well, where's he going? He said he was going to do more scraping."

Gavin smiled to himself as Cilla shook her head and went back inside. It was good to know his daughter had found her place, her purpose, had found a man who loved her.

It was good to know she was out of reach of the man who'd wished her harm.

THE NEXT MORNING, Cilla walked over from Ford's to find her tires slashed. On the ground by the left front tire, another doll lay facedown, a short-handled paring knife stabbed into its back.

"You should've come back for me. Damn it, Cilla." Ford paced down the drive, then back to where she sat on the steps of the veranda. "What if he—she—whoever—had still been here?"

"They weren't. The cops were here within fifteen minutes. They're pretty used to the run by now. I didn't see the point in—"

"Because I can't run a skill saw or a damn drill I'm no use?"

"I didn't mean that, and you know I didn't mean that."

"Simmer down, Ford." Matt stepped between them.

"No way. It's the second time somebody killed one of those damn dolls to scare her, and she sits over here alone waiting for the cops and lets me sleep. It's goddamn stupid."

"You're right. Simmer down anyway. He's right," Matt said to Cilla. "It was goddamn stupid. You're a hell of a job boss, Cilla, and one of the best carpenters I've worked with, but the fact is someone's dogging you and threatening you, and standing around here alone after you come across something like this doesn't show much sense."

"It was a cowardly bully tactic, and nobody asked you to go running across the road dragging Ford out of bed so the pair of you can gang up on me.

I'm not stupid. If I was afraid, *I'd* have run across the road and dragged Ford out of bed. I was mad, damn it."

She shoved to her feet as sitting and looking up at two annoyed males made her feel weak and small. "I'm still mad. I'm pissed and I'm tired of being dogged and threatened, as you put it. Of being run off the road and having good work destroyed, and the whole rest of it. Believe me, if whoever did that had still been here, I'd have probably yanked that knife out of that idiot doll and stabbed him in the throat with it. And still been pissed."

"If you're so smart," Ford said, very coolly, "then you know it was stupid."

She opened her mouth, shut it and gave up. Then she sat back down. "I'll give you rash. I won't give you stupid."

"Hardheaded and rash," Ford countered. "That's my final offer."

"Have it your way. Now if you'd go back to bed, and you'd go get to work, I could sit here and wallow in my brood."

Saying nothing, Matt walked up, patted Cilla on the head and continued inside. Ford came over, sat beside her.

"Like I care if you can run a skill saw."

"Thank God you don't."

"I didn't think about coming to get you. I was too mad. I don't get it, I just don't get it." Shifting, she indulged herself—and him—by pressing her face to his shoulder a moment. "Hennessy's in psych. If his wife's doing this, why? I know he's doing two years, but how is that my fault? Maybe she's as crazy as he is."

"And maybe Hennessy didn't do it. Ran you off the road, no question. Is crazy, no argument. But maybe he didn't do any of the rest. He wouldn't admit to it."

"That would be just great, meaning I have at least two people out there who'd like to make my life hell." She leaned forward, propped her elbows on her thighs. "It could be about the letters. Someone else knows about them, knows I found them, that they still exist. If Andrew wrote them, someone might know about them, about the affair, the pregnancy . . . His name's still prominent around here. To protect his reputation . . ."

"Who, Brian's father? Brian? Besides, it doesn't look like Andrew Morrow wrote them. I sent copies to a graphologist."

"What?" She jerked straight again. "When?"

"A couple days after Brian brought the card over. Yes, taking that on myself without telling or consulting you was . . . rash. We'll call it even."

"God, Ford, if the press gets ahold of this—"

"They won't. Why would they? I found a guy in New York, one who doesn't know Andrew Morrow from Bruce Wayne. And the copy of the page of one of the letters I sent him had nothing in it that referred to Janet or the location, even the time frame. I was careful."

"Okay. Okay." He would have been, she admitted.

"The conclusion was, not the same hand. Guy wouldn't stake his reputation on it because they were copies, and because I told him they were written about four years apart. But he wouldn't document them as the same hand. He did say they were of similar style, and both might have been taught to write by the same person."

"Like a teacher?"

"Possibly."

A whole new avenue, Cilla realized. "So it might have been someone who went to school with Andrew. A friend. A close friend. Or someone who went to the same school, with the same teacher later. And that really narrows the field."

"I could look into that, or try. Talk to my grandfather. He and Andrew would be about the same age. He might remember something."

Cilla studied her four flat tires. "I think that's a good idea. If you want answers, you have to ask

questions. I have to go to work. And you have to go
to the bank." She bumped his shoulder with hers.
"Have we made up?"

"Not until we have sex."

"I'll put it on my list."

FORD PULLED UP in front of the little suburban
house. He heard the purr of a lawn mower as he
stepped out of the car, so with Spock he walked
around to the side of the house and through the
gate of the chain-link fence.

His grandfather, dressed in a polo shirt, Bermuda
shorts and Hush Puppies, pushed the power mower
across the short square of lawn between and around
the hydrangeas, the rosebushes and the maple
tree.

From the gate, Ford could see the sweat trickling
down his grandfather's temples under his Washing-
ton Redskins cap. Ford shouted, made wide arm
signals as he started over, and saw the smile spread
on his grandfather's sweaty face when Ford caught
his eye.

Charlie shut off the lawn mower. "Well, hi there.
Hi there, Spock," he added, patting his thigh
in invitation for the dog to plant his hind legs for

a head rub. "What're you doing out this way today?"

"Mowing the rest of your lawn. Granddad, it's too hot out here for you to be doing this."

"Meant to get to it earlier."

"I thought you hired a neighborhood kid to do this. That's what you told me when I said I'd come by and do it."

"I was going to." Charlie's face moved into what Ford thought of as Quint stubborn. "I like cutting my own grass. Not on my last legs yet."

"You've got plenty of legs left, but you don't have to use them working out here when it's already ninety and humid enough to drown in your own breath. I'll finish it up. Maybe you could get us a couple of cold drinks. And Spock could use some water," Ford added, knowing that would do the trick.

"All right then, all right. But you be sure you put the mower back in the shed when you're done. And don't bump into those rosebushes. Come on, Spock."

It took less than twenty minutes to finish it off— with his grandfather watching him like a hawk through the back screen door. Which meant, Ford thought, they didn't have the AC turned on inside.

By the time Ford stowed the mower, crossed over

the tiny cement patio and walked through the screen door, he was dripping. "It's August, Granddad."

"I know what month it is. Think I'm senile?"

"No, just crazy. Let me assure you, air-conditioning is not a tool of Satan."

"Not hot enough for air-conditioning."

"It's hot enough to boil internal organs."

"We got a nice cross breeze coming through."

"Yeah, from hell." Ford dropped down at the kitchen table and gulped the iced tea Charlie set out while Spock lay snoring. Probably in a heat-induced coma, Ford thought. "Where's Grandma?"

"Your aunt Ceecee picked her up, for the book club gab session at your mother's bookstore."

"Oh. If she was here, she'd give me cookies. I know damn well you gave Spock some before he passed out."

Charlie snorted out a laugh, but rose to get a box of thin lemon snaps off the counter where he'd left them after treating Spock. He shook some onto a plate, set it in front of Ford.

"Thanks. I bought a house."

"You've got a house already."

"Yeah, but this one's an investment. Cilla's going to fix it up, perform major miracles, then I'll sell it and be a rich man. Or I'll lose my shirt and have to move in with you and Grandma, and suffer from heat prostration. I'm banking on the miracle after seeing what she's done with her place."

"I hear she's done some fancy work over there. Changed a lot."

"For the better, I think."

"Guess I'll see for myself at the Labor Day shindig she's having. Your grandmother's already been out shopping for a new outfit. It'll be strange going to a party there, after all these years."

"I guess a lot of people who'll go would have been to parties there when Janet Hardy was alive." Perfect opening, Ford thought. "Mom and Dad, Brian's parents. You knew Bri's grandfather, right?"

"Everybody around here knew Andrew Morrow."

"Were you friendly?"

"With Drew Morrow?" Charlie shook his head. "Wasn't unfriendly, but I can't say we ran in the same circles. He was older, maybe six, eight years."

"So you didn't go to school with him?"

"We went to the same school. Back then, there was only the one. Andrew Morrow, he had the golden touch. Golden tongue, too," Charlie said and wet his throat. "He sure could talk anybody into fronting him money, but by God, he lined the pockets of the ones who did. Buying up land, putting up houses, buying up more, putting up the stores, the office buildings. Built the whole damn village, served as mayor. Talk was he'd be governor of Virginia. Never did run though. Talk was maybe he had some dealings that weren't up-and-up."

"Who did he hang with, when you were boys?"

"Oh, let's see." Charlie rattled off some names that meant nothing to Ford. "Some of them didn't come back from the war. He ran some with Hennessy, the one's in the loony bin now."

"Really?"

"Went around with Hennessy's sister Margie for a time, then broke it off when he met Jane Drake, the one he married. She came from money." With a smirk, Charlie rubbed his thumb and fingers together. "Old money. Man needs money to buy up land and build houses. She was a looker, too. Snooty with it."

"I remember her. She always looked pissed off. I guess money can't buy happiness if you shop in the wrong places. Maybe Morrow looked for more pleasant companionship."

"Might could've done."

"And that might be why he didn't run for governor," Ford speculated. "Sticky affair, threat of exposure, bad press. Wouldn't be the first or last time a woman killed a political career."

Charlie flicked the back of his fingers up the side of his neck. "Politicians," he said in a tone that expressed contempt for the entire breed. "Still, he was a popular man around here, with most. He gave Buddy's daddy a leg up in the plumbing business. Brought a lot of work to the valley. Buddy's doing the work over there at the farm, isn't he?"

"That's right."

"He did some back in Janet's day, he and his daddy. Buddy had more hair and less gut in those days, and about ran the business by then, I guess. Been about your age, a little more, maybe."

Ford filed that away, tried to wend his way back. "I guess back when there was only one school, all of you shared a lot of teachers. Like Brian, Matt, Shanna and I did. Mr. McGowan taught us all, and Matt's little brother, Brian's older sister. Back in elementary school, Mrs. Yates taught us to write. She always crabbed by my penmanship. I bet she'd be surprised by what I do today. Who taught you to write, Granddad?"

"God, that takes me back." He smiled now, eyes going blurry with memory. "My mama started me off. We'd sit at the table and she'd have me trace over letters she made. I was right proud when I could write my own name. We all had Mrs. Macey for penmanship, and she'd mark me down for writing the way my mama taught me. Made me stay after school to write the alphabet on the board."

"How long did she teach there?"

"Years before, years after. I thought she was old as the hills when I was six. I guess she wasn't more than forty. Sure was a hard case."

"Did you ever write her way?"

"Never did." Charlie smiled, bit into a cookie. "My mama taught me just fine."

Ford reported to Cilla under the blue umbrella, over a cold beer. "It's not much. Shared teacher in the person of the persnickety Mrs. Macey. A lot of Morrow's generation, and those coming up behind him, would've been taught to write by her. He was friendly with Hennessy, at least until he threw over Hennessy's sister for the rich and snooty Jane. He put Keystone Plumbing on the map, along with other businesses. He may or may not have had some shady dealings and/or extramarital affairs that prevented him from running for governor. He had friends in high places and you could say boosted friends into high places. Through the connection to him, some of them could have met your grandmother, and an affair could have followed."

"The who you know and how you connect doesn't run that different here than it does in Hollywood."

Or probably anywhere else, Cilla mused. "Buddy worked here when he was in his thirties? It's a little hard to see Janet tumbling madly in love with a plumber, especially Buddy. Still, he'd have only been a few years younger than she was."

"Can you picture Buddy writing phrases like 'I place my heart, my soul, in your lovely hands'?"

"Really can't. There are more connections between the then and the now than I realized, or appreciated. I may never know if there's more to then than just the continuity of the place. The way it's going, I may never know how, even if, what's been happening here connects."

"The Hennessy house is up for sale." Ford laid a hand over hers. "I drove by after I saw my grandfather. Curtains are drawn, no car in the drive. Spanking-new Century 21 sign in the front yard."

"Where is she?"

"I don't know, Cilla."

"Maybe if she's responsible for this morning, it was a final fuck-you."

It didn't play that way for Ford. The panels didn't fit, and the images in them didn't form true. He'd keep shifting them, he thought, changing, resizing, until he had not only the picture, but the whole story.

TWENTY-SEVEN

With a great deal of pleasure, Cilla hung her first kitchen cabinet.

"Looking good." Thumbs hooked in his front pockets, Matt nodded approval. "The natural cherry's going to work with the walnut trim."

"Wait until we get the doors on. Things of beauty. So worth the wait. Guy's an artist."

She laid her level on the top, adjusted.

"It's beautiful work, and a lot of it." He scanned the space. "But we'll get them in today. How long before the appliances are back?"

"Three weeks, maybe four. Maybe six. You know how it goes."

"The old-timey stuff's going to be great in here." He winked at her as she stepped down off the ladder. "Don't let Buddy tell you different."

"It'll give him something to complain about instead of my pot filler." She ran her hand, lovingly, over the next cabinet. "Let's get her up."

"One second," Matt said as his phone rang. He glanced at the display. "Hey, baby. What? When?"

The tone, the merging of the two words into one stream had Cilla looking over.

"Yeah. Yeah. Okay. I'm on my way. Josie's water broke," he said, snapping his phone off. "I gotta go." He lifted Cilla off her feet, a happy boost into the air.

"So this is what goes on around here all day," Angie said as she came into the room.

Matt just grinned like an idiot. "Josie's having the baby."

"Oh! Oh! What're you doing here?"

"Leaving." He dropped Cilla back on her feet. "Call Ford, okay? He'll pass the word. I'm sorry about—" He gestured toward the cabinets.

"Don't worry about it." Cilla gave him a two-handed shove. "Go! Go have a baby."

"We're having a girl. I'm getting me a daughter today." He grabbed Angie on the way out, dipped her, kissed her, then swung her back up as he ran out of the room.

"Boy, talk about excellent timing." With a laugh, Angie tapped her lips. "He gives good kiss. Wow, big, huge day. I need to call Suzanna, Josie's younger sister. We're friends. And another wow, look at all this!"

"Coming along. Look around if you want. I need to call Ford."

While Cilla made the call, Angie poked around the kitchen, in the utility room and back out.

"Men are odd," Cilla stated, hooking her phone back on her belt. "He said, 'Cool. Got it. See ya.'"

"A man of few words."

"Not usually."

"Well, I'll use some to say, Cilla, this all looks amazing." Angie spread her arms. "Totally amazing. And how the hell do you know where to put all these cabinets?"

"Diagram."

"Yeah, but you had to make the diagram. I have a hard time figuring out if I can move my bed from one place to the other in my room, and where the dresser could go if I did."

"I had a hard time getting through a class, much less imagining teaching one the way you're going to do. We all know what we know."

"I guess we do. Well." Angie gave a snappy salute. "Private McGowan reporting for duty."

"Sorry?"

"I'm here to paint. I could try to help you put

these up now that Matt's otherwise occupied. But I think you'll be a lot happier with my painting skills than my cabinet-hanging ones. How do you hang them, anyway?" she wondered. "I mean, what holds them up? And never mind, I'd rather use a paintbrush."

"Angie, you don't have to—"

"I want to. Dad said they've finished scraping the old paint on the front and one of the sides, and they'll be working on the back today. And if there was more help, we could get some of the primer on what's been done. It's my day off. I'm the more help."

She tugged at the leg of her baggy white painter's pants. "Look. I have the outfit."

"As fetching as it is, I don't want you to feel obligated."

Angie's face turned from teasing to solemn. "Are you ever going to think of me as a sister?"

"I do." Fumbling, Cilla picked up her level. "Of course I do. I mean . . . we are sisters."

"If that's true, then let me say: Shut up, and show me the paint." Her smile went sly. "Or I'll tell Dad you're being mean to me."

Amusement came and went, but the quiet glow remained. "You're a lot like him. The, ah, one who made us sisters."

"I have only his good qualities. You, on the other hand—"

"The paint's out in the barn. We can go out this way." Cilla opened the back door. "Maybe I don't like having a sister who's younger than I am and has a cute little cheerleader body."

"Maybe I don't like having a sister who has a yard of leg and miles of perfect hair. But I've got a better ass."

"You do not. My ass is famous."

"Yeah, you showed enough of it in *Terror at Deep Lake*."

"I did no ass work in that picture. I wore a bikini." Holding back laughter, she stopped to pull out her keys, glanced over at the house. "Oh, damn it!"

Turning to look, Angie gaped at the sight of her father, three stories up, standing on scaffolding, scraping away.

"Dad! Get down from there!" They shouted it in unison. Gavin looked around, and down, then sent them a cheerful wave.

"I told him not to go up there. No scaffolding, no extension ladders."

"He doesn't listen, not when he's decided to do something. He *pretends* to listen, then does what he was going to do anyway. Is it safe?" Angie asked, gripping Cilla's arm. "I mean, it's not going to fall over or collapse, is it?"

"No. But . . ."

"Then we're not going to look. We're going to get the paint. I'm going around to the front of the house, you're going inside. Where we can't see him up there. And we're never, never going to tell my mother."

"Okay." Cilla deliberately turned away, then stuck the key in the padlock on the barn.

OLIVIA ROSE BREWSTER came into the world at 2:25 P.M.

"Matt's floating," Ford told Cilla as they drove to the hospital. "Passing out bubble-gum cigars with this dopey smile on his face. The kid's pretty cute, got all this black hair. Ethan was bald as my uncle Edgar, but the girl, she's already got a headful."

"Uncle Ford seems pretty pleased, too."

"It's a kick. It's a pretty big kick. Josie looked pretty whipped when I saw her, right after."

"There's a surprise. She should have looked camera ready after pushing eight pounds, five ounces out of her—"

"Okay, okay. No need for details." He hunted up a parking space in the hospital's lot. "I talked with

Matt while you were cleaning up. He said they're both doing great."

"It's nice to come back here for something happy." She skimmed her gaze up to the Intensive Care floor.

"Have you talked to Shanna since she got back?"

"No, I haven't."

"She had a great time." Ford took Cilla's hand as they crossed the lot. "She said Steve's looking good. Put some of the weight back on he lost, got what she called a Roman gladiator 'do going on. He's only using the cane when he gets tired."

Ford pulled open the heavy glass door.

"I've been e-mailing him pictures of the house. I need to take some of the kitchen cabinets. Gift shop. Presents for Mommy and baby."

"I took her flowers already," Ford objected, "and a big pink teddy bear."

"Eight pounds, five ounces out of her—"

"Gift shop."

Loaded down with flowers, Mylar balloons, a plush musical lamb and a stack of coloring books for the new big brother, they walked into the birthing suite.

Josie sat up in bed, in her arms the swaddled baby, a bright pink cap over her dark hair. Josie's younger sister stood nearby, cooing over a tiny, frothy white dress, while Brian unwrapped a bubble-gum cigar and Matt snapped a picture of his wife and daughter.

"More visitors!" Josie beamed. "Cilla, you just missed your dad and Patty."

"I came to see someone else." She leaned over the bed. "Hello, Olivia. She's beautiful, Josie. You do wonderful work."

"Hey, she's got my chin, and nose," Matt claimed.

"And your big mouth. Do you want to hold her, Cilla?"

"I thought you'd never ask. Trade." She put the lamb on the bed, took the baby. "Look at you. Look how pretty you are. How are you feeling, Josie?"

"Good. Really good. Only seven and a half hours of blood, sweat and tears with this one. Ethan took twice that."

"Got some stuff here for big bro." Ford set the coloring books on the foot of the bed.

"Oh, that's so sweet! My parents just took him home for dinner. He looks so big, so sturdy. I can hardly . . . Oh, hormones still working," she managed when her eyes filled.

"It's a full house!" Cathy announced as she and Tom came in with a bouquet of pink roses and baby's breath. "Let me see that beautiful baby."

Cilla turned obligingly.

"Oh, look at all that hair. Tom, just look at this sweet thing."

"Pretty as a picture." Tom set the flowers down among the garden of others, then poked Brian in the shoulder. "When are you going to get busy making us one? Matt's got two up on you now. You, too, Ford."

"Slackers," Josie agreed, and held out her arms for Olivia.

"I have such high standards," Brian said. "I can't settle for any woman who isn't as perfect as Mom."

"That's a clever way out of it," Cathy commented, but she beamed with pleasure as she stepped over to kiss Brian's cheek. She turned and kissed Matt. "Congratulations."

"Thanks. We figured we had another week. When Josie called this morning, I figured it was to remind me to bring her home a caramel coconut sundae. She's been eating mountains of them."

"I have, too!" Josie said with a laugh.

"It was peanut brittle for me. Acres of peanut brittle. I'm lucky I have a tooth left in my head."

"Never touched it again after Brian was born," Tom commented.

"It'll probably be a good long while before I can

look at coconut." Josie stroked Olivia's cheek. "Thank God I didn't go another week."

"And now you'll be able to show off the baby at Cilla's party. We're all looking forward to that," Cathy added. "I guess you could say the house is your baby."

"Without the pink teddy bear and pretty white dresses," Cilla agreed.

Matt passed out more cigars. "I had to bail out today. We'd just started installing the kitchen cabinets. How's it going?"

"We just have to set the island, put on the doors, the hardware. We'll be ready for the counters, on schedule."

"I'm going to have a powwow with Patty and Ford's mother. And if you sweet-talk him," Cathy told Cilla, "Tom might make his special ribs."

Cilla smiled. "What makes them special?"

"It's all in the rub," Tom claimed. "Family secret."

"He won't even give *me* the recipe."

"It passes down only through the bloodline. Many have tried to unlock the secret. None have succeeded. We've got to be on our way, Cathy."

"Meeting friends for dinner. You get some rest, Josie. I'll pop in to see you and that precious baby tomorrow when I'm here."

It took several more minutes for the leave-taking,

especially when other people came in. By the time Cilla and Ford walked out, she had a bubble-gum cigar in her pocket.

"It's nice that your parents—yours, Brian's, Matt's—take such an interest in all of you. It's almost tribal."

"We grew up practically joined at the hip, along with Shanna. Her parents split about ten years ago. They both remarried and moved out of the area."

"Still, three out of four sticking with it. Well above national average. They looked so happy. Matt and Josie. Little beams of happiness shooting out of their eyes. How long have they been married?"

"About six years, I guess. But they've had a thing a lot longer. Listen, if you want to stop and have dinner, that's okay." His fingers tapped on the steering wheel. "But I'd kind of like to get home."

"No, I'm fine. Is something wrong?"

"No. Nothing's wrong." Except a rampant case of nerves, he realized. And the sudden and inescapable understanding that he needed to take the next step, make the next move.

Ready or not, he thought. Here it comes.

HE POURED two glasses of wine, brought them out to the veranda where she sat rubbing Spock with her foot and studying the house across the road.

"The coat of primer on the front of the first story, on the veranda, doesn't add style. But it's clean. And it shows care and intent. It was the oddest thing, Ford, the oddest thing. To be working with one of Matt's crew on the cabinets, knowing my father was out back scraping old paint, and Angie was out front priming for new. Then Patty shows up at lunchtime with a bunch of subs and sides. Before they were fully devoured, she has a paintbrush in her hand.

"I didn't know what to think of it, what to make of it."

"Family pitches in."

"That's just it. For basically the first half of my life, family was an illusion. A stage set. I used to dream about my mother when I was a kid. Those lucid, conversational dreams I get. But she was on that set, part of that illusion, a combination of her and Lydia—the actress who played Katie's mother."

"Seems pretty much normal to me, given the circumstances."

"My therapist said my subconscious merged them because I was unhappy with the reality. Big duh, and it was more complicated than that. I wanted pieces of both those worlds. But I was me in them, not Katie. I was Cilla. Katie had her family, for eight seasons anyway."

"And Cilla didn't."

"It was a different kind of structure." A shaky one, she thought now. "Later, I stepped away from it. I had to. And coming here, I stepped out again. It's strange trying to figure out how to blend in, or catch up, or sign on with family at this stage."

"Be mine."

"What?"

"Be my family." He set the ring box on the table between them. "Marry me."

For an instant she wasn't capable of thought or speech, as if she'd taken a sudden, shocking blow to the head. "Oh my God, Ford."

"It's not a poisonous insect," he said when she snatched her hands away. "Open it."

"Ford."

"Open it, Cilla. You're not supposed to piss a guy off when he's proposing. Thrill or crush, but not piss off."

When she hesitated, Spock grumbled at her, and bumped his head into her shin.

"Just open it."

She did, and in the soft dusk the ring gleamed like dreams. Lucid, lovely dreams.

"You don't wear jewelry much, and when you do, you don't go for the flash. You go more subtle, more classy." He felt that *thing* in his chest again, the hot rock of pressure he'd experienced with her father in the kitchen. "So I figure, you're not going to impress the girl with a big, fat rock. Plus you work with your hands, and that has to be considered. So having the diamonds set in instead of sticking up made sense. My mother helped me pick it out a few days ago."

Yet another layer of panic coated her throat. "Your mother."

"She's a woman. It's the first ring I've bought for a woman, so I wanted some input. I liked the idea of the three stones. The past, the right now, the future. We've got our yesterdays, we've got our right now. I want a future with you. I love you."

"It's beautiful, Ford. It's absolutely beautiful. And the thought behind it makes it more so. I'm such a bad bet." She reached over, took his hands. "Even the idea of marriage freezes me up. I don't have the foundation for it. Look at what we were just talking about. You have two parents, with one marriage between them. You believe. I have two parents, with seven. Seven marriages between them. How can I believe?"

Strange, he thought, that her nerves, her fears and doubts dissolved the thing in his chest. "That's bogus, Cilla. That's not you and me. Do you love me?"

"Ford—"

"It's not that hard a question. It's pretty much yes or no."

"It's simple for you. You can say yes, and it's simple. I can say yes. Yes, I love you, and it's incredibly scary. People love, and it falls apart."

"Yeah. And people love and it stays whole. It's just another step, Cilla. The next step."

"And this is meandering? Isn't that what you called it?"

"I picked up the pace. That doesn't mean I can't wait." Ford closed the box, nudged it toward her. "Take it. Keep it. Think about it."

She stared at the box. "You think I won't be able to resist opening it, looking at it. That I'll fall under its spell."

He smiled. No wonder he loved her. "Dare you."

She closed her hands over the box and, breathing slowly, pushed it into her pocket. "I'm a has-been actress with a history of alcohol, drug abuse and suicide in my family. I don't know why in hell you'd want me."

"I must be crazy." He lifted her hand, kissed it. In

the spirit of the moment, Spock kissed her ankle. "Every few days, I'm going to just say, 'Well?' When I do, you can give me your current position on my proposal."

"The key word is 'well'?"

"That's right. Otherwise, I won't bring it up. You just carry the ring around, and you think about it. Deal?"

"All right," she said after a moment. "All right."

He picked up his glass, tapped it to hers. "Why don't we call out for Chinese?"

At their feet Spock did a happy dance.

SHE DIDN'T KNOW how he did it, she honestly didn't know. The man had proposed to her. He'd presented her with a ring so utterly perfect for her, so completely right, because he'd thought of *her*. Of who and what she was when he'd chosen it. Her reaction, her reluctance—be honest, Cilla, she added, while screwing the copper knobs on her cabinets—her stuttering horror at his proposal had to have hurt him.

And yet, after he'd said his piece, after he'd made his deal, he'd ordered butterfly shrimp and kung pao chicken. He'd eaten as if his stomach hadn't been in knots—as hers had been—then had suggested unwinding with the first season of *Buffy the Vampire Slayer* (short season, summer replacement).

And sometime during episode three, just as she'd begun to relax enough to think about something other than the ring in her pocket, he'd taken her under with slow, shimmering kisses, with lazy, lingering caresses. By the time she'd come out of the sexual haze, the ring was *all* she could think about.

Nearly twelve hours later, and she still couldn't get the damn thing off her mind.

She didn't believe in marriage. Simple as that. Even living together was fraught with pitfalls. For God's sake, she'd barely gotten used to him telling her he loved her, to believing it. She hadn't finished her house, or opened her business. She'd gotten as far as she had while being harassed for months.

Didn't she have enough on her mind? Didn't she have enough to do without having an engagement ring weighing down her pocket, and the worry of not knowing when Ford might say, "Well?" preying on her mind?

"Hello?"

"Cilla?"

At the voices, Cilla simply banged her head repeatedly on the cabinet door. Perfect, she thought, just perfect. Patty and Ford's mother. Icing on her crumbling cake.

"Here you are," Patty said. "Hard at work."

Cilla watched as two pairs of eyes zoomed straight in on the third finger of her left hand. And watched two pairs of eyes cloud with disappointment. Great, now she was responsible for bringing sorrow into the lives of two middle-aged women.

"We were hoping you'd have a few minutes to talk about the menu for the party," Patty began. "We thought we could do at least some of the shopping for you, store the supplies since you don't have a place for them yet."

You were hoping for more than that, Cilla thought. "Let's get this out of the way. Yes, he asked me. Yes, the ring is absolutely beautiful. No, I'm not wearing it. I can't."

"It doesn't fit?" Penny asked.

"I don't know. I can't think about it. I can't not think about it. It was damn sneaky of him," she added with some heat. "I appreciate— No, I don't just appreciate the two of you coming here like this, but I'm trying to understand why you would. I've got enough on my mind already, enough on my head, and he adds this. I don't even know if he listened to what I said, if he's getting the reasons why . . ." She trailed off.

He doesn't listen, Angie had said of their father, *not when he's decided to do something. He* pretends *to listen, then does what he was going to do anyway.*

"Oh, God. God, isn't that perfect? He's Dad. He's Dad with a layer of nerd. Solid, steady, chipping away so patiently, you don't even know you've had your shields hacked down until you're defenseless. It's the type."

"You're not in love with a type, you're in love with a man," Penny corrected. "Or you're not."

Ford's mother, Cilla reminded herself. Be careful there. "I love him enough to give him time to consider all the reasons this won't work. I don't want to hurt him."

"Of course you'll hurt him. He'll hurt you. It's all part of being connected to someone. I wouldn't want a man I couldn't hurt. I sure as hell wouldn't marry one who couldn't hurt me."

Baffled, Cilla stared at Penny. "That makes absolutely no sense to me."

"If and when it does, I think you'll be ready to see if the ring fits. I think your cabinets are beautiful, and they're giving me cabinet lust. Why don't we find somewhere to sit down, go over this menu for a few minutes. Then we'll get out of your way."

Cilla sighed. "Maybe he's not so much my father's type. Maybe he's you."

"No, indeed. I've always been so much meaner than Ford. Let's sit out there." Penny pointed out the window. "Under that blue umbrella."

When Penny sailed out, Patty stepped closer to slip an arm around Cilla's waist. "She loves her boy. She wants him happy."

"I know. So do I."

MAYBE SHE SHOULD make a list, Cilla considered. Reasons for and reasons against taking the ring out of the box. She depended on lists, diagrams, drawings in every other area of her life. Surely it made sense to utilize one before making such a huge decision.

The against list would be the easy part, she thought as she scooped up some post-workout, pre-workday Special K. She could probably fill pages with those items. She could, in fact, write a freaking book, as many others had, on the Hardy women.

To be fair, there were a number for the pro side. But weren't they primarily, even exclusively, emotion-driven? And weren't her emotions twisted up with nerves because she was waiting—as he damn well knew—for him to stroll up to her at any point in any day and say, "Well?"

Which he hadn't, not once, in days.

So she jumped, nearly bobbled her bowl of cereal, when he strolled in.

"Too much coffee?" he suggested, and poured himself a bowl of Frosted Flakes. Spock dashed straight in to attack his dog feeder. "How do you eat that stuff? It looks like little twigs."

"As opposed to your choice, the vehicle for sugar?"

"Exactly."

Not only up at six in the morning, she thought, but cheerful and bright-eyed. And she *knew* he'd worked late. But he was up, dressed and eating Frosted Flakes because he insisted on walking her across the road, hanging out until some of the crew arrived.

Would that sort of thing go on the for or against list?

"You know I'm not going to be attacked crossing the road at six-thirty in the morning."

"Odds are against it." He smiled, ate.

"And I know you worked late last night, and find it unnatural to be up at this hour of the morning."

"Had a good run, too. You know, I'm finding that I can get a lot done by round-about noon most days with this routine. A habit which I intend to shed like a bad suit in what I hope is the near future. But right now?" He paused to shovel in more Tony the

Tiger. "It's working. I should have ten chapters fully inked by the end of today and have time to put a couple of new teaser panels up on my website."

"Happy to help, but—"

"You're looking for the negative. I like that about you because it pushes me to look on the brighter side of things—sides I might've missed or taken for granted otherwise. You remind me I love what I do. And loving what I do, it's interesting to do more of it than usual for a space of time. And to pay us both back for all this industry, I'll be taking us to the Caymans—a favorite place of mine—right about the middle of January, where we'll soak up sea and sand while our neighbors are shoveling snow."

"I'll be finishing up two flips. I—"

"You'll have to make time in your schedule. We can always bump sun and sea to February. I'm easy."

"Not nearly as much as you pretend to be." She opened the dishwasher to load in her bowl, spoon, mug. "You're a slow leak, Ford."

His eyes continued to smile as he scooped up cereal. "Is that what I am?"

"A slow leak, unchecked, eventually eats through just about anything. Stone, metal, wood. It doesn't make much noise, and it's a long way from the big gushing flood. But it gets the job done."

He shook his spoon at her. "I'm going to take that as a compliment. Kitchen counter's coming in today, right?"

"This morning. Then Buddy's on for the finish plumbing this afternoon."

He tucked his breakfast dishes in with hers. "Big day. Let's get started. Walk!" he said, lifting his voice, and Spock raced in to run in circles.

She walked out with them, then stopped just to look at the Little Farm. Summer thrived over the grounds, lushly green. The big red barn stood, its practical lines softened by the curve of the stone wall, the textures of the plantings. She could see a hint of the pond, with the last vapors of dawn still rising, with the graceful bow of a young willow dipping. Back to the fields, wild with thistle and goldenrod, back to the mountains stretched across the morning sky.

And the house, the centerpiece, rambling and sturdy, with its white veranda, and its front wall half painted in warm and dignified blue.

"I'm glad my father talked me into painting the exterior ahead of schedule. I had no idea how much satisfaction it would give me to see it. When the painting's finished, it'll be like a strong old character actress after a really good face-lift."

She laughed, the mood lightened, and she took

his hand as they walked. "One that allows her to maintain her dignity and personal style."

"I guess that's apt enough, considering all the cutting and stitching that went into it so far. But I don't get the whole face-lift thing."

"It's just another kind of maintenance."

Alarm literally vibrated out of him. "You wouldn't ever . . ."

"Who knows?" She shrugged. "I'm vain enough to want things to stay put, or have them shored up when they sag. My mother's had two already, in addition to other work." Amused by the stunned horror in his eyes, she gave him a nudge. "A lot of men have work done, too."

"You can put that one away. Deeply buried in a remote location. Are you mailing something out?" He nodded toward her mailbox and the raised red flag.

"No. That's funny. I didn't stick anything in there after yesterday's delivery. Maybe one of the guys did."

"Or someone put something in it for you. Not supposed to. Mail carrier doesn't like it." He veered over, reached for the lid.

"Wait! Don't!" She grabbed his hand while her heart leaped up to pound in her throat. Beside them, Spock quivered and growled at the alarm in her tone. "Rattlesnake in the mailbox. It's shorthand for the unexpected—an unpleasant, dangerous surprise."

"I know what it is. Code name for the season-three finale of *Lost*. Well . . . keep back some."

"Wait until I—"

But he didn't wait. Instead, he shifted his body, putting it between Cilla and the box, then yanked the lid down.

No snake coiled and hissed inside. None struck out and slithered down the pole. The doll sat, her arms lifted as if in defense. The bright blue eyes were open, and the smile frozen on Cilla's young face. The bullet left a small, scorched hole in the center of the forehead.

TWENTY-EIGHT

Enough was enough, Ford decided. The cops had the doll; the cops would investigate. And so far, the cops hadn't been able to do dick-all about stopping the threats against Cilla.

They weren't pranks, they weren't harassment. They were threats.

Dusting the damn doll and the mailbox, asking questions, even determining—if they could—what caliber of bullet had been used wasn't going to solve the problem. None of those things would prevent that look of shocked horror from covering Cilla's face the next time.

Everyone knew there'd be a next time. And the next time, at any time, it could be Cilla instead of a doll.

Yeah, enough was more than enough.

He pulled up in front of the Hennessy place. It was somewhere to start, he thought. Maybe it was somewhere to finish. He walked up, banged on the door.

"Wasting your time." A woman under an enormous straw gardening hat walked over to stand at the picket fence that formed the boundary between houses. "Nobody's in there."

"Do you know where they are?"

"Everybody knows where *he* is. Locked up." She tapped her temple under the brim of the hat, then circled it. "Tried to kill a woman over on Meadowbrook Road a couple months back. Janet Hardy's granddaughter—the one who was the little girl in that TV show? You want to talk to him, you'll have to try Central State Hospital, down in Petersburg."

"What about Mrs. Hennessy?"

"Haven't seen a sign of her the last couple weeks. Selling the place, as you can see there." She pointed to the Century 21 sign, then slipped a small pair of clippers into a pocket of her gardening belt. Settling in, Ford knew, for a little over-the-fence chat.

"She's had a hard life. Her boy was crippled back when he was a teenager. Died a year or so ago. That husband of hers never had a good word to say to anybody around here. Shouting or shaking his fist at kids for playing too loud, or telling people to mind their own if they offered a helping hand. Me, I'd've left him after the boy died, but she stuck.

Could be she's taken off now he's locked up, but more likely, she's gone down to Petersburg. Don't know if anybody's looked at the house yet. I'm going to hope somebody buys it who knows how to be neighborly."

It was a haul to Petersburg and back, Ford considered. "I guess you'd have noticed if she moved out. I mean, furniture, luggage."

"Might have, if I was home." She gave Ford a harder measure from under the wide brim of her hat. "You're not kin to them, are you?"

"No, ma'am."

"Well, I can tell you I haven't seen her or heard a peep out of the house for days now. In fact, I've taken to watering what flowers she put in. I can't stand to watch something die of neglect."

CILLA TRIED to take a page out of Ford's book and look at the bright side. The bright side could be that a defaced doll in the mailbox did no damage to her property. It cost her nothing but time and stress.

A bright side could be the police took the whole ugly business very seriously. True, they'd had no luck tracing any of the dolls so far, not when they were sold regularly on eBay or in secondhand and specialty shops, or could have been taken out of some-one's personal collection. But it brought her a measure of comfort to know the police were doing whatever the hell the police did.

And her crew was pissed off on her behalf. Having people in your corner, even if it was only to express outrage and support, was always a bright side.

Plus her new countertops and backsplash kicked serious ass. That knocked her level of stress down several notches. The streaks and specks of warm gold, flecks of black and white against rich choco-late brown set off her cabinets. And, *Jesus*, her cop-per hardware would just pop. She'd been right, so absolutely right, to go for the waterfall edging. She couldn't believe how long and hard she'd stressed over that. It gave the counters such presence, such authority.

Cilla ran her hand over the island as she might a lover's warm, naked flesh, and all but purred.

"Pretty dark, especially with this half acre of the stuff you've got in here."

Cilla merely looked over, tipped her head and spoke in the tone she'd use to a naughty little boy. "Buddy."

His lips twisted, but the attempt to defeat the smile failed. "I guess it looks all right. Cabinets are nice, anyway. Got a forest of them in here, but having the glass fronts on some breaks it up a little. I'll get your sinks mounted. Be back tomorrow after they've cured to hook up the plumbing, the dishwasher and the faucets. Don't know why anybody'd want copper for faucets."

"I'm just crazy that way."

"Crazy some way. Are you going to help me mount these sinks, or just stand around looking like the canary-eating cat?"

While they worked on the first undermount, Buddy whistled through his teeth. A few bars in, Cilla caught herself humming with him.

"'I'll Get By,'" Cilla said. "My grandmother's signature song."

"Guess the mind wanders to her in here. Got that clamp on there?"

"It's on."

"Let's test the fit then. Second time I put a sink in this place."

"Really?"

"Put in the one you're replacing for your grandmother. That's been going on forty, forty-five years, I expect. Probably time for a new. That's right, that's right," he murmured. "That's a good fit. That's a good one." He marked the location for the mounting clips.

"Let's lift her out."

Cilla gripped the two-by-four clamped to the sink. "You and your father did a lot of the work around here back then."

"Still got plenty."

"You did a lot for Andrew Morrow."

"That's a fact. We did all the plumbing for Skyline Development. Thirty-three houses," he said, taking out his drill. "That job made it so I could buy one of those houses. Lived there thirty-seven years come October. A lot of people got their homes because of Drew Morrow. I've fixed the johns in most of them."

AFTER THE TWO sinks were mounted, Cilla went outside to hunt up her father. She'd kept him off the scaffolding that morning, conning him into "doing her a favor" and painting her shutters.

It looked as if he was having as much fun running the paint sprayer as he had hanging up three stories. "Take a break?" she asked and offered a bottle of water.

"Sure can." He gave her arm a quick rub. "How're you feeling?"

"Better since I got to work. Better yet when I stand staring at my counters with a big, sloppy smile on my face. Something occurred to me when I was working with Buddy. How he and his father did some work here. Dobby did, too. I'm wondering who else who's working here now, or who I didn't hire, or who's retired, might've worked on the place when Janet had it. Maybe they're pissed off because I'm changing it. It's no crazier than Hennessy trying to run me down for something that happened before I was born."

"I'd have to think about it. I was a teenager, Cilla. I can't say I'd have paid much attention."

He took off his hat, ran a hand through his hair. "There were gardeners, of course. The grounds were a showplace. I'll ask Charlie if he remembers who she had for that. I do remember she had what you'd call caretakers. A couple who'd look after things when she wasn't here, which was more than not. They'd open the house up when she was expected, that sort of thing. Mr. and Mrs. Jorganson. They've both been gone for years."

"What about carpentry, electrical, painting?"

"Maybe Carl Kroger. He did a lot of handyman work back then. I'll ask about that, but I know he retired some years ago. Florida maybe. I only remember that because I went to school with his daughter, and I ended up teaching *her* daughter. I can't see Mary Beth Kroger—that's Marks, now—giving you this kind of trouble."

"It's probably a stupid idea. Just another straw grasped at."

"Cilla, I don't mean to make it worse, or give you more to worry about, but have you considered that whoever's doing this has a grudge directed at you? You, not Janet Hardy's granddaughter?"

"For what? I'm a former child star, a failed adult actress who recorded a couple of moderately successful CDs. My only ties to this area were to her, and you. You, Patty and Angie were literally the only people I knew when I came here. And let's be honest, I didn't know any of you that well. I've dumped a few hundred thousand into the local economy. I can't see how that would piss anyone off."

"You're right. I know you're right. It's the dolls. It's such a direct strike at you. More than the vandalism, Cilla. Mutilating those dolls, the child you were, seems so much more personal than the rest."

She studied him. "Are you here to paint, or to keep an eye on me?"

"I can do both. At least until school starts up. The summer's flown by," he said, looking past her. "I'll miss being around here, the way I've been able to. We've made a lot of progress since June."

You and I. She understood the words he didn't say.

"We have. Despite everything, it's been the best summer of my life."

FORD WATCHED WHILE Cilla hung shutters her father had painted on the front windows. The scent of the paint hung in the air, along with grass, heat and the dianthus in a big blue pot on the veranda.

"I just want to finish this off. You don't have to hover."

"I'm not hovering. I'm observing. There's something satisfying about sitting on a summer day and watching somebody else work."

She spared him a glance as he sat, at ease. "You know, I could teach you how to set a few screws."

"Why would I need to do that when I've got you?"

"I'll ignore that since you bought me that very pretty planter. And the steaks you've promised to grill—on the grill I assembled."

"Corn on the cob, too, and tomatoes fresh from the roadside stand. We'll have ourselves a feast."

She tested the shutter, checked it with her level, then moved to the next.

"Before we move to feasting," he continued, "let's get less pleasant business out of the way. I went by the Hennessy place this morning. She's not there," he added when Cilla glanced back. "Hasn't been there, according to her neighbor, for a couple of weeks. One supposition is she went down to Petersburg, to be close to the state hospital where they have him. That's proved out."

"How do you know?"

"I called the most likely hotels and motels in the area. She's registered at the Holiday Inn Express."

"Aren't you the clever detective?" she replied.

"Taught the Seeker everything he knows. Or vice versa. Anyway, I considered driving down, but it struck me as a waste of time. It's better than a hundred miles one way, Cilla. It's hard to believe she'd drive more than two hundred miles, in what had to be the middle of the night, to pose a doll she'd shot in the damn head in your mailbox. If she wanted to get at you, why move herself so far off when she's got a house twenty minutes away?"

He knew how to put things together, Cilla thought. Into panels that followed a logical line. "I hate that that's realistic, that it rings true for me. Because it would be easier, simpler, if it was her. If I can't believe that, I have to know it's someone else. That someone else hates me."

She tipped back her cap, idly watched Spock stalking one of his cats in the front yard. "I'm looking at

Buddy today because he's whistling one of my grandmother's songs, and I'm thinking, Hey, Buddy, did you happen to start a mad, passionate affair with my grandmother one night when you came by to fix a leak? Or, did she maybe reject your advances in a way that causes you to want to hurt me? I went through that same process with Dobby, who is, yes, entirely too old. But he had a son, and his son has a son. And I was just twisted up enough today to wonder if the very affable Jack was spending time shooting my plastic image because of something— anything—that went on with Janet three and a half decades ago. Or maybe my father had a point, and someone took a vicious and pathological dislike to Katie, and seeks to take revenge on me."

"Your father thinks you're being threatened by somebody who hates a TV character?"

"No. Not exactly. He suggested whoever's doing this has some grudge against me, personally. But that doesn't make any sense, either." She sighed, lowered the screwdriver. "And because it doesn't make any sense, none of it, I keep going around in circles, which leaves me dizzy and annoyed. Added to that, I'm going to have dozens of people here in a few days. And I know I'm going to be wondering, even as I pass the potato salad, if that person's the one. If the person looking at me and smiling, thanking me kindly for the potato salad, would like to shoot me in the head."

He pushed up, walked to her. "I may have gotten my ass kicked with some regularity as a boy, but that—as my mother liked to say—builds character. The kind of character that means I can say to you, and you can believe me when I say it, nobody, Cilla, nobody is going to hurt you while I'm around."

"Keeping me from being hurt hasn't been anyone's priority up till now. Because of that, I do believe you. I feel safer with you, Ford, than I ever have with anyone."

He kissed her very gently, eased back and said, "Well?"

"Oh, damn it! I walked right into it. I gave you a damn cue." She pulled away, picked up her screwdriver. "Look, it's been a really long day. I just don't want to get into this now."

He simply put a hand under her chin, lifted it until their eyes met.

"I don't know. I don't *know*. I haven't made the lists yet."

He rubbed his thumb over her jawline. "What lists would that be?"

"My lists, for and against. And if you're going to push at this point, I'll warn you that I can rattle off a ten-minute monologue of the againsts. The ones I've already given you and more."

"Give me one of the fors." He tightened his grip when she shook her head. "Just one."

"You love me. I know that you do, I know that you mean it. But they call it 'falling into' for a reason. It's the floundering around after you surface, the wondering what the hell you're doing there and looking for the escape that make the falling-out-of part so horrible. And it's not a practical for," she insisted, when he just smiled and rubbed her jawline. "One of us has to be practical. What if I said yes, yes, let's run off to Vegas—as both my grandmother and mother have done before me—and hit The Chapel of Love? What—"

"I'd say you pack, I'll book the flight."

"Oh, don't be ridiculous." She tried to be annoyed, but nerves kept jumping in the way. "You don't want some tacky Vegas fly-by. You're *serious*. You're serious about friendships, about your work, your family. You're serious about *Star Wars*, and your active dislike of Jar Jar Binks—"

"Well, God. Come on, anyone who—"

"You're serious," she continued before he went on a Jar Jar rant, "about living your life on your terms, and being easygoing doesn't negate that one bit.

You're serious about what kind of kryptonite is more lethal to Superman."

"You have to go with the classic green. I told you, the gold can strip Kryptonians' powers permanently, but—"

"*Ford.*"

"Sorry. We'll skip that and go back to Vegas."

"We're not going to Vegas. God, you make my head spin. You're not thinking of a single practicality, of the reality."

"Test the theory. Give me one."

"Fine. Fine. Where would we live? Do we flip a coin, ask your Magic 8-Ball. Or maybe we'd—"

"Well, for God's sake, Cilla, we'd live here. Here," he repeated, knocking his knuckles against the wall of the house.

His instant answer tipped her off balance. "What about your house? You love your house. It's a great house. It's tailor-made for you."

"Yeah, for me. Not for us. Sure, I love my house, and it's got a lot of me in it. But it's just a house for me, and Spock." He glanced around in time to see Spock catch and destroy the hated invisible cat. "He's happy anywhere. I haven't poured myself into my place the way you have this one. This is home for you, Cilla. I've watched you make it." Now he picked up her screwdriver. "With more than this. A lot more than tools and nails and gallons of paint. It's your place. I want it to be ours."

"But . . ." But, but, her mind was full of *buts*. "What about your studio?"

"Yeah, it's a great space. You'll think of something." He handed her back the screwdriver. "Make all the lists you want, Cilla. Love? It's green kryptonite. It powers out all the rest. I'll go out back and start the grill."

She stood, stunned, a power tool in her hand, as the screen door slapped shut behind him. And thought: *What?* Love is kryptonite? She'd think of something?

How could she understand, much less marry, a man whose mind worked that way? One who could make statements like that, then stroll off to start the grill? Where were his anger, his angst, his annoyance? And to suggest he could give up his place and move into hers without any real thought to where he'd work? It didn't make any sense. It made no sense at all.

Of course if she added the home gym off the south side of the house the way she'd been toying with, she could put on a second story, tying that into the existing house. Angle it for a little interest. Tight-winder stairs would work, and be fun to do. It would keep the work spaces entirely separate, give them both privacy. Plus the southern exposure would give a studio excellent light. Then she could . . .

Well, God, she realized. She'd thought of something. A damn good something, too, she added and put down her tool to pace the veranda. Having destroyed his quota, Spock trotted up to pace with her.

The sort of something that would not only work, not only blend in with the existing structure, Cilla realized, but enhance it. Break up the roof line, finish it off with a sweet little balcony. Jib windows for access.

Damn it, damn it, damn it! Now she could see it. Now she wanted it.

She stalked down the steps, around to the south side of the house with Spock bounding happily behind her. Oh yeah, yeah, not only doable, she thought, but it now seemed the house begged for it.

She jammed her hands into her pockets, and her fingers hit the ring box she carried there. Kryptonite, she thought, pulling it out. That was the trouble, the big trouble. She did understand him. And more terrifying, more wonderful, he understood her.

Trusted her. Loved her. Believed in her.

WHEN SHE WALKED to the patio, Ford had the grill smoking. The corn, husks in place, were submerged in a big bowl of water for reasons that eluded her. He'd brought out the wine. The scents of roses, sweet peas, jasmine tangled in the air as he poured her a glass. Sun streamed through the trees, glinted off the pond where Spock wandered to drink.

For a moment, she thought of the glamour that had once lived there, the colored lights, the beautiful people wafting like perfume over the lawns. Then she thought of him, just him, standing on stones she'd helped place with her own hands, offering her a glass of wine, and a life she'd never believed she could have.

She stood with him, one hand in her pocket, and took the first sip. "I have some questions. First, just to get it off my mind, why are you drowning the corn?"

"My mother said to."

"Okay. If I thought of something, how do you know it's something you'd want?"

"If I didn't," he said, picking up the conversation as if there had been no break, "I know how to say I don't want that. I learned how to do that at an early age, with mixed results. But the odds are, if we're talking about construction and design, whatever you thought of would work."

"Next. Could I hurt you?"

"Cilla, you could rip my heart out in bloody pieces."

She understood that, understood he could do the same to her. And wasn't that a hell of a thing? Wasn't that a miracle? "I couldn't have done that to Steve, or him to me. As much as we loved each other. As much as we still do."

"Cilla—"

"Wait. One more question. Did you ask me to carry the ring around with me because you hoped it would act as kryptonite, and weaken me over time until I agreed to marry you?"

He shifted his feet, took another drink of wine. "It might have been a factor."

With a nod, she drew her hand out of her pocket, studied the ring sparkling on it. "Apparently, it works."

His grin flashed, quicksilver delight. But when he moved to her, she slapped a hand on his chest. "Just hold on."

"That was my plan."

"Wait. Wait," she said again, softly. "Everything I said before, it's true. I'd made up my mind never to get married again. Why go through the process when the odds are so stacked for failure? I failed a lot. Some was my fault, some was just the way it was. Marriage seemed so unnecessary, so hard, so full of tangles that can never really be fully unknotted. It was easy with Steve. We were friends, and we'd always be friends. As much as I love him, it was never hard or scary. There wasn't any risk, for either of us."

Her throat filled, so much emotion rising up. But she wanted—needed—to get the rest out. "It's not like that with you because we're going to hurt each other along the way. If this screws up, we won't be friends. If this screws up, I'll hate you every day for the rest of my life."

"I'll hate you more."

"Why is that absolutely the best thing you could've said? We're not going to Vegas."

"Okay, but I think we're missing a real opportunity. How do you feel about backyard weddings?"

"I feel that's what you had in mind all along."

"You're what I had in mind all along."

She shook her head, then laid her hands on his cheeks. "I'd love a backyard wedding. I'd love to share this house with you. I don't know how anything that scares me this much can make me so happy."

He took her lips with his, soft, soft, spinning the

kiss out in the perfumed air, with the sun streaming through the trees. "I believe in us." He kissed
her again, swayed with her. "You're the one I can
dance with."

She laid her head on his shoulder, closed her
eyes.

THE LITTLE FARM
1973

"I believed in love," Janet said as she sat back on
the white silk pillows on the lipstick-pink couch.
"Why else would I have thrown myself into it so
often? It never lasted, and my heart would break,
or close. But I never stopped opening it again.
Again and again. You know that. You've read all
the books, heard all the stories, and the letters.
You have the letters so you know I loved, right to
the end."

"It never made you happy. Not the kind that
lasted." Sitting cross-legged on the floor, Cilla sorted
through photographs. "Here's one taken the day
you married Frankie Bennett. You're so young, so
happy. And it fell apart."

"He wanted the star more than the woman. That

was a lesson I had to learn. But he gave me John-nie. My beautiful boy. Johnnie's gone now. I lost my beautiful boy. It's been a year, and still I wait for him to come home. Maybe this one will be a boy."

She laid a hand on her belly, picked up a short glass, rattled the ice chilling the vodka.

"You shouldn't drink while you're pregnant."

Janet jerked a shoulder, sipped. "They didn't make such a to-do about it when I was. Besides, I'll be dead soon anyway. What will you do with all those pictures?"

"I don't know. I think I'll pick the ones I like best, have them framed. I want pictures of you in the house. Especially pictures of you at the farm. You were happy here."

"Some of my happiest moments, some of my most desolate. I gave Carlos—Chavez, my third hus-band—his walking papers right in this room. We had a vicious fight, almost passionate enough to have me consider taking him back. But I'd had enough. How he hated it here. 'Janet,' he'd say in that Spanish toreador's voice that seduced me in the first place, 'why must we camp out in the middle of nowhere? There isn't a decent restaurant for miles.' Carlos," she added and lifted her glass, "he could make love like a king. But outside of bed, he bored me brainless. The problem there was we didn't spend enough time outside of bed before I married him. Sex is no reason to get married."

"Ford never bores me. He made me a goddess, and still when he looks at me, he sees me. Too many of them didn't see you."

"I stopped seeing me."

"But in the letters, the letters you kept, he called you Trudy."

"The last love, the last chance. I couldn't know. Yet maybe some part of me did. Maybe I wanted to love and be loved by what I'd lost, or given up. For a little while, I could be Trudy again." She stroked her fingers over one of the white pillows. "But that was a lie, too. I could never get her back, and he never saw her."

"The last chance," Cilla repeated with photos spread before her, and Janet on the bright pink couch. "Why was it the last? You lost your son, and that was horrible and tragic. But you had a daughter who needed you. You had a child inside you. You left your daughter, and that's haunted her all her life—and I guess it's haunted me too. You left her, and you ended the child when you ended yourself. Why?"

Janet sipped her drink. "If there's one thing

you can do for me, it would be to answer that question."

"How?"

"You've got everything you need. It's your dream, for God's sake. Pay attention."

TWENTY-NINE

Crazy. She had to be crazy hosting a party. She didn't have any furniture, or dishes. She didn't own a serving spoon. She was at least three weeks out from delivery on her stove and refrigerator. She didn't own a goddamn rug. Her seating consisted of a single patio set, a couple of cheap plastic chairs and a collection of empty compound buckets. Her cooking tools were limited to a Weber grill, a hot plate and a microwave oven.

She had supplies, God knew. A million festive paper plates, napkins, plastic cups and forks and spoons, and enough food—which she didn't know how to prepare—stuffed into Ford's refrigerator to feed most of the county. But where were people supposed to *eat*?

"On the picnic tables my father, your father and Matt are bringing over," Ford told her. "Come back to bed."

"What if it rains?"

"Not calling for rain. There is a thirty-percent chance of hail and locusts, and a ten-percent chance of earthquakes. Cilla, it's six in the morning."

"I'm supposed to marinate the chicken."

"Now?"

"No. I don't know. I have to check my list. I wrote everything down. I said I'd make crab dip. I don't know why I said that. I've never made crab dip. Why didn't I just buy it? What am I trying to prove? And there's the pasta salad." She heard the lunacy in the rant, couldn't stop. "I took that, too. Eating pasta salad through the years doesn't mean you can make pasta salad. I've been to the doctor through the years. What's next? Am I going to start doing elective surgery?"

Though it was tempting, he didn't put the pillow over his head. "Are you going to lose your mind like this every time you give a party?"

"Yes. Yes, I am."

"Good to know. Come back to bed."

"I'm not coming back to bed. Can't you see I'm dressed? Dressed, pacing, obsessing and postponing the moment when I go downstairs and face that chicken."

"All right. All right." He pushed himself up in

bed, scooped back his hair. "Did you agree to marry me last night?"

"Apparently I did."

"Then we will go down and face the chicken together."

"Really? You'd do that?"

"I'll also face the crab dip and the pasta salad with you. Such is the depth of my love, even at six o'clock in the morning." Spock rose, yawned, stretched. "And apparently his. If we poison people, Cilla, we'll do it together."

"I feel better. I know when I'm being a maniac." She walked to him, leaned down and kissed his sleepy mouth. "And I know when I'm lucky to have someone who'll stick with me through it, right down to the crab dip."

"I don't even like crab dip. Why do people eat stuff like that?" He gave her a tug, pulling her onto the bed. And rolled on top of her. "People are always making dips out of odd things. Spinach dip, artichoke dip. Have you ever asked yourself why?"

"I can't say I have."

"Why can't they be satisfied with some Cheez Whiz on a cracker? It's simple. It's classic."

"You can't distract me with Cheez Whiz." She

shoved him off. "I'm going down." She tugged her shirt back into place. "I'm ready."

IT WASN'T ALTOGETHER horrible or intimidating, Cilla discovered. Not with a partner. Especially when the partner was as clueless as she. It was almost fun. She thought, with some repetition, and a bit more skill, boiling pasta or mincing garlic might slip past the almost and become actual fun.

"I had a Janet dream last night," she told him.

"How can the simple tomato come in so many sizes?" He held up a beefsteak and a handful of grape tomatoes. "Is it science? Is it nature? I'll have to do a study on it. What was the dream about?"

"I guess it was about love, at least on one level. And my subconscious poking around about what it means. Or what it meant to her. We were in the living room of the farm. The walls were my walls—I mean the space was mine, the color of the paint, but she was on that bright pink couch. And I had photographs spread on this glossy white coffee table. Photos I've managed to get my hands on, the photos your grandfather took, photos I think I might have just seen in books. Hundreds of them. She was drinking vodka in a short glass. She said it had been a year since Johnnie died, and how she hoped this baby was a boy. She said it was her last chance. Her last love, her last chance.

"It's so odd. She knew she was going to die soon. Because I knew. I asked her why, why did she do it? Why did she turn away from that last chance and end it all?"

"What did she say?"

"That if I could do anything for her, it would be to find that answer. That I had it all in front of me, but I wasn't paying attention. So I woke up frustrated because, as she said, it's *my* dream. If I know something, why don't I *know* it?"

Ford took up his assignment of slicing the beefsteak. "Is it too much to accept she might've been too sad, too deep in the dark, and saw it as the only way to end the pain?"

"No. But I can't quite make myself believe it. I never fully could, or never fully wanted to. And since I came here, started on the house, I believe it less—and want to believe it less," Cilla admitted. "She found something here. Look at all she took and let go of again. Men, marriages, houses, possessions. She was famous for acquiring and disposing of. But she kept this place, and more, made arrangements so it would remain in the family long after she died. She found something she needed here, something that contented her."

She looked out the window and watched Spock on his morning rounds. "She kept the dog," Cilla murmured. "And an old jeep. A stove and refrigerator that were out of date. I think, in a way, this place was real to her. The rest, it's not. For the smart ones, it's a job. It's good work. Fame can be a by-product, but it's fleeting and fickle and so much of it's an illusion. She didn't need the illusion here."

"And falling in love here made it more real?"

She looked over, grateful he followed the thread of her thoughts. "It follows, doesn't it? The worst thing in her life happened here when Johnnie was killed. An inescapable reality. But she kept coming back, facing it. She didn't close the place up, or sell it. He called her Trudy, and that's who she wanted to believe he loved. I think she wanted that last chance, desperately. I think she wanted the baby, Ford. She'd lost one child. How could she, *why* would she kill herself and end the chance for another?"

"And if she realized it wasn't Trudy this guy loved, that that was another illusion?"

"Men come and go. They always did for her. And I guess I remembered that, resolved that through the dream last night. Her one true love was Johnnie. Her work, too. She passionately loved the work. But Johnnie was hers. My mother always knew that, always knew she didn't quite hit the same spot. The last love, the last chance? I think it was the child for her. I can't believe, just can't, that she'd have killed herself over a love affair that went south."

"You said she was drinking in the dream. Vodka."

"Her standard." When the timer dinged, Cilla hefted the pot of pasta, carried it to the sink to drain into the waiting colander. "But there weren't any pills in the dream."

She stood, watching the steam rise. "Where were the pills, Ford? I keep circling back to those letters, to the anger in the last few. He didn't want her in this house. She was a threat to him, an unpredictable woman, a desperate one, pregnant with his child. But she wouldn't give it up. Not this place, not the child, not the chance. So he took it from her. I keep circling back to that."

"If you're right, proving it would be the next step. We've already tried to find out who wrote those letters. I don't know how many more avenues there might be to take."

"I feel like . . . I feel like we've already been down the right one, or close to it. And missed something that was right there. Right there. That I didn't pay attention, and it slipped by."

She turned. "This is my reality now, Ford. You, you and the farm, this life. I found that, I can take that because of her. I owe her. And I owe her more than planting roses and painting and hammering wood. More than bringing this place back as tribute. I owe her the truth."

"What you've found, and what you take may have started with her. And if you need the truth, I'll do whatever I can to help you find that. But the farm, what you've done here, it's more than a tribute to Janet Hardy. It's a tribute to you, Cilla. What you can do, what you'll work for, what you'll give. The walls were yours in the dream."

"And I haven't put anything inside it. I talk about it, but I don't take the step. Not a chair, not a table, beyond what I needed for Steve. I guess I have to fix that."

He'd been waiting for that. Waiting for that step. "I've got a house full of stuff here. It's a good start for picking and choosing."

She walked to him, linked her arms around his neck. "I pick you. I pick the guy who'll slice tomatoes with me at seven in the morning because I'm a lunatic. The guy who not only promises to help me, but does. The one who makes me understand I'm the first Hardy woman in three generations lucky enough to be in love with a man who sees me. Let's pick something, and take it across the road. We'll put it inside the house so it's not hers, it's not mine. So it's ours."

"I vote for the bed."

She grinned. "Sold."

IT WAS RIDICULOUS, of course, for two people who were preparing for a party to leave the work to break down a bed, to haul frame, headboard, footboard, mattress, box spring, bedding downstairs, out to the truck, drive it across the road with a dog in tow. Then reverse the procedure.

But Cilla found it not only symbolic, she found it therapeutic.

Still, Ford's suggestion that they try it out in its new place was going too far.

Tonight, she told him. Definitely.

Their room now, she thought, giving the pillows an extra fluff. Their room, their bed, their house. Their life.

Yes, she'd put pictures of Janet in the house, as she'd said in the dream. But there would be other pictures. Pictures of her and Ford, of friends and family. She'd ask her father if he had any of his parents, his grandparents she could copy. She'd repair and refinish the old rocker she'd found in the attic, and she'd buy cheerful, happy dishes, and put Ford's wonderful roomy couch in their living room.

She'd remember what had been, and build toward what could be. Really, hadn't that always been the purpose? And she'd keep looking for that truth. For Janet, for her mother, for herself.

At Ford's she deserted the field, ducking outside to call Dilly in New York.

"Mom."

"Cilla, it's barely nine in the morning. Don't you know I need my sleep? I have a show tonight."

"I know. I read the reviews. 'Mature and polished, Bedelia Hardy comes triumphantly into her own.' Congratulations."

"Well, I could've done without the *mature*."

"I'm awfully proud of you, and looking forward to seeing you triumphant in D.C. in a couple of weeks."

After a brief pause, Dilly said, "Thank you, Cilla. I don't know what to say."

And when her mother went on a long riff about the hard work, the three encores, the curtain calls, the *acres* of flowers in her dressing room, Cilla just smiled and listened. Dilly was never at a loss for words for long.

"Of course, I'm completely exhausted. But somehow, the energy's there when I need it most. And Mario's taking very good care of me."

"I'm glad. Mom, Ford and I are getting married."

"Who?"

"Ford, Mom. You met him when you came here."

"I can hardly be expected to remember everyone I meet. The tall one? The neighbor?"

"He's tall, and he lives across the road."

"When did all this happen?" Dilly demanded, with the first notes of petulance in her voice. "Why are you marrying him? When you come back to L.A.—"

"Mom, just listen. Just listen and don't say anything until I'm done. I'm not going back to L.A. I'm not coming back to the business."

"You—"

"Just *listen*. This is my home now, and I'm building a life here. I'm in love with an amazing man who loves me back. I'm happy. I'm as happy at this moment as you are when you step out into the lights. I want you to do one thing for me. Just this one thing, just this one time. I want you to say, whether you mean it or not, just say, 'I'm happy for you, Cilla.'"

"I'm happy for you, Cilla."

"Thanks."

"I am happy for you. I just don't understand why—"

"It's enough, Mom. Just be happy. You don't have to understand. I'll see you in a couple of weeks."

It's enough, Cilla thought again. Maybe one day there would be more, maybe there wouldn't. So it was enough.

She went back into the house, and to Ford.

REINFORCEMENT ARRIVED with platters and bowls, with tables and pounds of ice. Penny dispatched Ford to help unload at the farm before she bustled into the kitchen with Patty, where Cilla agonized over the pasta salad.

"Someone needs to taste it. Ford and I are too emotionally involved with the pasta. We have no objectivity."

"It's so pretty!" Patty exclaimed. "Isn't that a pretty salad, Pen?"

But Penny, whose eagle eyes spotted Cilla's ring in under three seconds, latched on to Cilla's hand. "When?"

"Last night."

"What? What am I missing? Oh God, oh God! Is

that what I think it is? Is that it? Oh, let me see!" Patty crowded in, peered down at the ring. "It's just beautiful. It's just so beautiful. I'm so happy. I'm so happy for both of you."

No prompting needed from the wings here, Cilla thought as Patty threw her arms around Cilla and dipped them both side to side.

"Didn't take you long to come to your senses. Let go, Patty, she's going to be my daughter-in-law." Nudging Patty aside, Penny moved in for a hug. "He's a very, very good man."

"Only the best."

"I'm pretty sure you almost deserve him." Penny leaned back, all smiles and damp eyes. "Aren't they going to make us beautiful grandbabies, Patty?"

"Oh, well . . ."

"We won't start nagging you about that yet. Much," Patty put in. "First we get to nag you about the wedding. Did you set the date?"

"No, not really. We just—"

"It's too late to take advantage of the fall season. The foliage will peak in about six weeks. And there's so much to do."

"We thought an outdoor wedding, at the farm. Simple," Cilla began.

"Perfect." Patty counted off on her fingers. "May, early May, don't you think? May's so pretty, and that gives us a comfortable time for all the details. The dress comes first. *Everything* builds around the dress. We have to go shopping. I can't wait!" Patty threw her arms around Cilla again.

"Captain Morrow reporting to the staging area," Cathy said as she came in, loaded with bags. "What's all this? Has everyone been slicing onions?"

"No." Patty dashed at tears. "Cilla and Ford. They're getting married."

"Oh!" Cathy jumbled bags onto the counter, righted one before its contents spilled. She turned, beaming smiles. "Congratulations! What happy news. When's the big day?"

"May, we think," Patty told her. "Don't we think May? Oh my God, isn't she going to be the most beautiful bride? An outdoor wedding at the farm. Isn't that perfect? Imagine the gardens next May."

"It's going to be the event of the year. Simple," Penny added with a light in her eyes that told Cilla they might have different definitions of the word. "We'll say simply the event of the year."

"You two are scaring the girl." With a laugh, Cathy put an arm around Cilla's shoulder. "She'll be running for the hills any minute."

"No. I'm staying right here. It's nice," Cilla decided. "We'll make it the event of the year. In a simple way."

"There you go." Cathy gave Cilla's shoulder a squeeze. "Now, ladies, if we don't get this particular show on the road, we're going to have a lot of hungry people, and the disaster of this year on our hands."

IT WAS so much easier than she'd imagined, and amazingly satisfying. Under the afternoon sun dozens and dozens of people spread around the grounds. They crowded at borrowed picnic tables, perched on the steps, sat at folding card tables on the veranda. They ate and drank, admired the house, the gardens. No one seemed concerned about the lack of furniture and formality.

She watched Dobby sitting in a lawn chair he'd brought himself, eating her pasta salad, and felt a ridiculous surge of pride. Her home, she thought, might not be finished, but it was more than ready to welcome people.

She joined Gavin while he flipped burgers on the grill. "How'd you earn the KP?"

"I gave Ford a break." He smiled down at Cilla. "Practicing being a father-in-law. It's a good party, Cilla. It's good to have one here again."

"I'm thinking of it as the first annual Labor Day at the farm. Next year, even better."

"I like hearing you say that. Next year."

"I'm exactly where I want to be. There's still a lot to do. Still a lot I need to know." She drew a breath. "I talked to Mom this morning."

"How is she?"

"Mature, polished and triumphant, according to the reviews. It's going to be difficult for her to come here, to the farm, for the wedding. She will, but it'll be difficult for her. Will it for you?"

"What do you mean?"

"Having her here, going through that ritual, the wedding, with her here?"

"Absolutely not." The surprise in his voice brought her comfort. "It wasn't all bad times between us, Cilla. It had to end for me to be exactly where I want to be, and, I suspect, for your mother to be mature, polished and triumphant."

"Then that's something to cross off my should-I-worry-about-this list. I want to get married here. It's our place now, Ford's and mine. And I like knowing my parents had their first kiss over there. And that my grandmother walked the gardens. That your grandfather plowed those fields. It all trickles down. I've wanted that all my life. Look at the house," she murmured.

"It's never looked more right, more real than it does now."

"That's what I want, too. The right, and the real. Did you come here after Johnnie died?"

"A few times. She seemed to like seeing me. The last was a couple of months before she died. I was doing some summer stock in Richmond. My father was ill, so I came to see him. When I learned she was here, I came by. She seemed better, or she was trying very hard to be. We talked about him, of course. I don't think he was ever out of her mind. She hadn't brought anyone with her, not like before when the house always seemed full of people. It was just the two of us for about an hour, in the living room."

"On the pink couch with the white satin pillows," Cilla added.

"Yes." He laughed a little. "How did you know about that?"

"I heard about it. Very Doris Day."

"I suppose it was. I must have commented on it, because I remember her saying she wanted bright in the house again. It was time for the new and the bright, so she'd had it shipped all the way from L.A."

He poked at the grilling chicken, flipped a burger. "She went back the next day, and I went back to Richmond for the rest of the summer. So that would've been the last time I saw her. It's a good image, really. Janet sitting on that pink, Hollywood couch with her dog snoring under the coffee table."

"I wonder if I have a picture of her on it. Ford's grandfather gave me so many pictures. I need to go through them again. If I can find one, I'll give you a copy. Here, let me have that platter." She took the dish Gavin had loaded with burgers, hot dogs, grilled chicken. "I'll deliver this to Station Meat, then go find Ford."

She wended her way through the backyard crowd, around the veranda dwellers and into the kitchen. She saw that Patty or Penny had been through by the stack of empty and freshly washed plates and bowls. Since that brought on some mild guilt, she prepared to wash the pair of serving plates she'd brought in with her instead of just putting them in the sink.

It felt good, watching through the kitchen window while she washed up, having this quick moment alone. She saw her father still at the grill, with Ford's father now, and Brian. Buddy and his wife at a picnic table with Tom and Cathy, and Patty stopping by to chat. There was Matt tossing a ball to his little boy while Josie looked on, the baby tucked in her arm.

Penny was right, Cilla realized with a quick laugh.

She and Ford would make gorgeous babies. Something to think about.

When the phone she had charging on the counter rang, she picked it up with the smile still curving her lips. "This is Cilla. Why aren't you here?"

"Ms. McGowan?"

"Yes. Sorry."

"It's Detective Wilson. I have some information."

WHEN FORD CAME IN through the front he saw her standing at the sink, looking out. "Look at us, being hosts. You washing up, me taking out the trash. I loaded a couple of bags in your truck. One of us needs to hit the dump tomorrow."

He slipped his arms around her, started to draw her back against him, and felt it immediately. "What is it?" He turned her, scanned her face. "What happened?"

"Hennessy's dead. He killed himself. He made a noose out of his own shirt, and—"

He drew her against him now, hard. She trembled first, then held on. "Oh God, Ford. Oh God."

"Some people can't be saved, Cilla. Can't be helped."

"He never got over it, got past it. What happened

to his son. All these years, he had a purpose, and he had his bitterness. But when his son died, all he had was the bitterness."

"And it killed him." He pulled her back, looking into her eyes to be sure she understood just that. "It's the hate that ended him, Cilla."

"I'm not blaming myself. I have to keep saying it, keep thinking it, so I won't. And I'm not. But there's no denying I was part of it. He made me part of it. I guess that's another kind of revenge. His poor wife, Ford. She's lost everything. And horribly, there's a part of me that's relieved."

"He hurt you, and he tried to do worse. Do you want some time? I can go out, try to wrap things up."

"No. No. He did enough." She looked back out the window, at the people on her lawn. "He's not going to ruin this."

"FORD, JUST THE MAN I wanted to see." Gavin handed over the spatula and tongs, then picked up the platter. "Your turn." With his free hand, he hefted a beer. "And mine."

"You sure this younger generation knows how to handle the grill?" Tom asked.

"We can put you guys down," Brian responded. "Anytime, anywhere."

"I feel a grill-off coming on. But before we get to that, I need to exploit my future son-in-law. I'd like you to come in and talk to my creative writing students."

"Oh. Well. Um."

"Actually, we'd like to do a three-part, possibly five-part, program on storytelling through words and art. Our art teacher is very excited by the idea."

"Oh," Ford repeated, and had Brian laughing.

"He's getting a flashback of high school, where he was president of the Nerd Club."

"Three years of being pantsed and recovering from wedgies."

"Matt, Shanna and I saved you when we could."

"Not often enough."

"I give you my word, your ass will not be exposed or abused on my watch."

Ford gave Gavin a sour look. "Can I have an armed escort?"

"We'll need to work out the details, the dates, and anything you might want or need. I can talk to you about my end of it. You should contact Sharon, the art teacher. She loves your work, by the way. Let me give you her contact information. Ah . . ." He looked at his full hands. "Got anything to write on, with?"

"No. Gee, I guess we'll have to forget the whole thing."

"I happen to have something." Grinning, Tom pulled a small leather-bound notebook and short pen out of his pocket. "Sharon, you said?"

Gavin relayed the information, cocked an eye at Ford when he passed him the sheet. "You do want to marry my daughter, don't you?"

"Yeah." Trapped, Ford stuffed the paper in his pocket.

"I'm going to deliver this, then I'll come back and give you the basic overview of what I have in mind."

"I should've known there'd be strings," Ford muttered when Gavin strolled away.

"Get used to it." Tom clamped a hand on Ford's shoulder. "And now that you're engaged, and there's Matt with his lovely family, how long before the last of the Musketeers settles down?"

"Your turn," Ford said gleefully.

Brian shook his head. "You bastard. Under the circumstances, I don't know why I'm telling you we're continuing this holiday with poker—guys only—at my place tonight. We're tapping you for leftover beer and food, Rembrandt."

"I suck at poker."

"Which is why, even under the circumstances."

"I don't know if—"

"See?" Brian pointed at his father. "She's already got him by the balls. And you ask me why I'm single."

"She doesn't have me—"

"Still getting pantsed. Only now by a woman."

"Jesus. Remind me why I'm friends with you."

"Nine o'clock. Bring beer."

WITH CONSIDERABLE HELP from friends, cleanup went quickly. Trash was bagged, leftovers tubbed, recyclables binned. A small convoy of the faithful hauled what needed to be hauled back to Ford's.

"Two households," Angie commented, "and still not quite enough room. What should I do with this pie?"

"Ford can take it to Brian's."

"I don't think I'm—"

Cilla cut him off with a look. "Go, be a man. Get out of my two households for a few hours. I'm fine."

"Of course she's fine." Patty sealed a small bowl of

leftover three-bean salad. "Why wouldn't she be fine? Has something else happened?" she said when she saw the way Ford glanced at Cilla. "Is something wrong?"

"Hennessy killed himself last night. Ford's worried I've taken it too much to heart."

"Oh, honey!"

"It's that, plus I don't like leaving you alone."

"We'll stay," Patty said immediately.

"We'll all stay," Penny put in. "We'll have our own—all women—party."

"You will not stay. I don't need babysitters. I'm going to work on the photos your father gave me," she said as she handed a bowl to Ford's mother. "A couple of hours of quiet is just what I need. No offense."

"But—"

"And I want to draw up some ideas for the gym and studio addition without you hanging over my shoulder. Go away. I'll stay here until you get back," she added when she saw more arguments in his eyes. "Brid, Warrior Goddess, requires no bodyguards. Now leave."

"Fine. It won't take me more than a couple hours to lose anyway."

"That's the spirit."

"All right, girls, let's claim our dishes and load it up. I'll give everyone a ride home since the men have deserted us." Penny put her hands on Cilla's shoulders. "I'm going to call you tomorrow, and we're going to set the time and place for you, Patty and me to hold our first Wedding of the Year strategy session."

"Should I be afraid?"

"Very." Penny kissed her cheek. "You're a good girl."

Watching the way Penny herded everyone out the door told Cilla she would have a very interesting, and very compatible, mother-in-law.

"Now you," she told Ford.

"I can probably lose in an hour."

"Stop. I'm tucked in here. No one's going to bother me. No one has bothered me for some time now. The fact is, Hennessy's dead, and the media is going to pick up on that. Some of it will start again. I could use a quiet, normal evening before the circus comes to town. And I'm not going to have either of us live worrying about me spending a quiet, normal evening alone. Besides . . ." She bent down to scratch Spock. "I have a bodyguard."

"Keep the door locked anyway."

"I'll keep the door locked anyway." She gave him a last kiss, then a shove out the door. "Don't bet on an inside straight." Then shut it, locked it at his back.

She turned around, let out a long sigh, then grinned at Spock. "I thought they'd never leave."

Content, she walked upstairs for the box of photos.

THIRTY

It gave her such pleasure to look through them. It occurred to Cilla that Ford might like to choose some of the photos they'd frame and display. The group shot, for instance. Her father, his mother, her uncle, Janet, and . . . that had to be a young and handsome Tom Morrow. Brian certainly took after him.

She began to sort them by type, then the types in a loose chronological order.

She watched her own mother grow, from child to girl to young woman. Amazing, Cilla mused, how much better they got along with distance. Not so amazing, she added with a dash of cynicism, how much better they got along when her mother collected strong reviews.

No sour notes, Cilla warned herself, topping her to-be-framed pile with the photo of Janet in the farmhouse doorway.

Had someone in one of these group shots been her lover? she wondered. Had they been careful not to be photographed together? Or had they played it cool and casual on the surface, with all that passion simmering beneath?

No sour notes, she reminded herself. But she couldn't resist speculating, studying. Would it show? It seemed to Cilla that every man photographed with Janet looked half in love with her. She'd had that power.

God, even Buddy looked spellbound—and skinny—in the shot of them on the veranda, and Janet mugging by pretending to brain him with his own pipe wrench.

She'd been irresistible, in baggy jeans or couture. Spectacular, she mused, in a red dress against the white piano. Christmas, she thought, lifting the shot, scanning it. Red candles and holly on the glossy piano, the sparkle of lights in the window.

That last Christmas before Johnnie's death. Her last party. Too painful, she decided, to frame that one. Or any from that night. It twisted her heart a little to see one of her parents, framed together in front of the tree. And the doomed Johnnie grinning as he held mistletoe over his head.

And all the young people—Gavin, Johnnie, Dilly, Ford's mother, and what she knew had to be Jimmy Hennessy and the boy who died with Johnnie that night, crowded together on the sofa in their party best. Smiling forever.

No, she could never frame that one, either.

She set it aside and picked up one of Tom. It took her a moment to recognize the woman beside him as Cathy. Her hair had been mouse brown then, and awkwardly styled in a kind of poofy ball. She looked so shy, so nervous and self-conscious. Baby weight, Cilla remembered, which the dress and the hairstyle only accentuated. Good pearls, the flash of diamonds said money, but she had certainly not yet come out of her cocoon.

Still, she might enjoy having a copy of the shot.

She continued sorting, pausing again when she came to one of Janet perched on the arm of the couch, Cathy sitting, and both women laughing. Cathy looked prettier in the candid, Cilla decided. More at ease, and with the hint of the woman she'd become in that natural smile.

She started to set it on the pile, then frowned as she studied it again. Something nagged at the edge of her mind. As she began to spread out what she thought of as Last Christmas shots, the doorbell rang.

Spock's terrified barking joined the bell.

FORD PUNCHED the button for a Coke on Brian's Sky Box. He was pitiful enough at poker without adding alcohol to the mix. In the pregame hang-out portion of the evening, men who would soon take his money gathered around the bar Matt had built in what Brian called his Real Man room.

Bar, pool table, poker table, big-ass flat screen—virtually always tuned to ESPN—leather recliners, sofa. A lot of sports decor. And, of course, the secondary TV earmarked for video games.

He needed one of those in his new studio, he decided. A guy had to have his space. He could tell Cilla he wanted it sort of sectioned off from the work area.

Maybe he should call her. He dug in his pocket for his cell, and as he pulled it out the paper he'd stuffed in the same pocket fluttered to the floor.

"No women." Brian shook his head. "Which includes calling one. Hand it over."

"I'm not giving you my phone." Ford stooped, picked up the note.

"Pussy-whipped. Hey, Matt, Ford's already calling home to check in with Cilla."

"Jesus, even I'm not that bad."

"Phones, both of you. In fact, everybody," Brian announced. "No phones at the table. House rules. Lay 'em on the bar. Hand it over," he told Ford.

"Christ, you're a pain in the ass. Remind me why I like you?"

"You can still beat me at Grand Theft Auto."

"Oh yeah, that's the reason." He passed over his phone, immediately felt naked and bereft. Phone-less, he thought, poker and, with a glance at the note, soon to be traumatized by a return to high school.

What a man did for love and friendship.

He started to stuff the note back into his pocket, then stopped, took a closer look.

His heart took a hard slam in his chest, dropped to his belly.

The handwriting was a little shaky, a little sloppy. After all, Tom had been standing up, using a stubby pen when he'd written out the information.

The urge to deny pushed at him. He couldn't be sure. It wasn't possible to be sure. At least not until he'd compared the note with the letters, side by side. Or sent them to the graphologist. It didn't make any sense anyway.

It was Brian's father. It just couldn't be.

And it made all the sense in the world.

He stared across the room at Tom standing with his own father, with Cilla's, grinning at Brian as they tapped bottles of Rolling Rock. He thought of how Tom had once helped him fly a kite on a vacation they'd all taken together at Virginia Beach. Pitched a tent for them to camp in overnight in the Mor-rows' big backyard.

And he thought of Steve in the hospital. Of Cilla staring at broken tiles. And a doll in a pink party dress hanging from a red maple tree Brian had planted.

Walking over, Ford tapped Tom on the shoulder. "I need to talk to you a minute."

"Sure. Looking for poker tips?"

"Maybe we could walk outside."

Tom's eyebrows raised. "Sure. A little fresh air before your father starts lighting those cigars. Ford and I are stepping outside so I can give him a few pointers."

"Lots of luck," Brian called out. "Make it quick. We'll be anteing up shortly."

No point in wasting time, Ford thought. No point in putting it off. And no way he could sit at a poker table with this tightness in his chest.

"Nights are cooling off again," Tom commented as they stepped out onto Brian's deck. "Another summer at our backs."

"You had an affair with Janet Hardy."

"What?" Tom's head jerked around. "For God's sake, Ford."

"She kept your letters. But you knew that. One of the guys on Cilla's job heard her telling Gavin. Most of them work for you, too. It's good juice. Too good not to spread around."

"I barely knew Janet Hardy. This is a ridiculous thing to—"

"Don't. The handwriting matches." He drew out the note. "I've got a good eye for that kind of thing. Shapes, style, form. I bet your father taught you to write. He'd have wanted you to get a leg up."

Tom's face hardened, the lines around his mouth digging deep. "Not only is this an insulting accusation, but frankly, none of your business."

There was a coldness inside Ford he hadn't known he possessed. A hard and icy rage. "Cilla's my business. What happened to her grandmother, and what's been happening to her, that's my business."

"Her grandmother killed herself. And Hennessy is responsible for what happened at the farm. I'm surprised at you, Ford. And disappointed. Now I'm going back inside. I don't want to hear any more about this."

"I always respected you, and I love Brian." It might have been the tone, very cool, very quiet, that had Tom stopping. "That's why I'm standing here with you. That's why I'm talking to you before I go to the police with this."

"With what? With a stack of unsigned letters written more than thirty years ago and a note I scribbled this afternoon?"

"I didn't say they were unsigned." Ford turned away.

"Wait. Now wait." With the first hint of panic, Tom gripped his shoulder. "This isn't a matter for the police, Ford. It won't do anyone any good for this to come out. Do you need me to admit the affair? All right, all right. I was mesmerized by her, and I betrayed my wife. I'm not the first man to slip. I'm not proud of it. And I ended it; I ended it before you were born, for God's sake. When I came to my senses, when I realized what I was doing, I ended it. Why would you punish me, hurt and embarrass Brian and Cathy, over a mistake I made when I was younger than you are now?"

"You tried to get them back, and put a man in the hospital."

"I panicked." He held up his hands. "I only wanted to find the letters and destroy them. I panicked when I heard him coming in. There was no way for me to get out. I never meant to hit him that hard. It was instinct, just instinct. My God, I thought I'd killed him."

"So you shoved the bike on top of him, what, to be sure of it?"

"I tell you, I was in shock. I thought he was dead, what else could I do? I could only think it had to look like an accident. He's fine now. He's all right now," Tom insisted in a tone of quiet reason. "What point is there in making an issue out of any of it?"

Ford could only stare. This man he'd respected, even loved, one he'd thought of all his life as a kind of second father, was shifting in front of his eyes. "He nearly died, Tom. He could have died. And you did that for what, to save your reputation over a *slip*? To cover up something you thought was already buried?"

"I did it to spare my family."

"Really? What else have you done to 'spare your family'? Let's go back. Let's go all the way back. Did you kill Janet Hardy?"

MILDLY IRRITATED by the interruption, Cilla went to the door, peeked through the sidelight. Irritation turned to puzzlement as she opened it for Cathy.

"It's okay, Spock. See?"

He stopped quivering to prance forward and bump Cathy's legs in greeting.

"I'm so sorry. Not five minutes after Penny dropped me off, I realized I'd left my rings at your place." Cathy pressed her ringless hand to her breast. "I always take them off at the kitchen sink. At least I hope I did. God, if I lost them . . . No they're there. I'm just a little frantic."

"I'd be, too. I'm sure they're there. We'll go get them right now."

"Thank you. Cilla, I feel so stupid. I don't know what I'd do if I lost them."

"Just let me grab my keys." She snagged them off the little table by the door. "Come on, Spock, let's take a walk."

The *walk* word had him shooting through the door to dance on the veranda.

"They'll be there," Cathy reassured herself. "I'm sure they'll be right there. I lost my wedding and engagement rings down the drain years ago. I'd lost weight, hadn't had them resized. I was terrified until Buddy—whom I called in hysterics—took the pipes apart and found them. So I always take them off before I shower or do dishes, or . . . I'm babbling."

They crossed the road in the moonlight. "Don't worry. I'm sure they're right where you left them."

"Of course they are." But the strain in her voice had Spock making concerned whines. "I put them in a little glass—I remember—at your sink. If someone didn't see them in there, and—"

"We'll find them." Cilla put a hand on Cathy's trembling arm.

"You must think I'm an idiot."

"I don't. I've only had my ring for a day, and I'd be a basket case if I thought I'd lost it." She unlocked the door.

"I'm just going to—" Cathy made a dash for the kitchen, and, hopeful, Spock raced behind her.

Cilla closed the door, plugged in the security code to offset the alarm, then followed.

Cathy stood in the kitchen, tears streaming down her cheeks with Spock rubbing against her legs in comfort. "Right where I left them. Right by the sink. I'm sorry."

"It's all right. It's okay." Moving fast, Cilla got an old stool out of the utility room. "Just sit down a minute."

"God, thank you. Now I do feel like an idiot. They're insured, I know, but—"

"It's not about insurance."

"No, it's not. Look at me. I'm a mess." She pulled a tissue out of her purse to dry her cheeks. "Cilla, could I have a glass of that?" She gestured to the bottle of wine on the counter. "And an aspirin."

"Sure. Aspirin's upstairs. I'll be right back."

When she came back, Cathy sat at the counter, her head propped in her hand, and two glasses of wine poured. "I know I'm taking up some of that quiet time you were after, but I just need a few minutes to calm down."

"It's no problem, Cathy." Cilla set down the aspirin.

"To wedding rings—engagement rings—and all they represent." Cathy lifted her glass, held it expectantly, then tapped it to Cilla's when Cilla picked hers up.

"And I hope that's the last time you find me knocking hysterically on your door."

"I thought you held it together pretty well. They're beautiful. I've admired them before."

"Tom wanted to buy me a new wedding ring for our twenty-fifth. I wouldn't have it." Her eyes sparkled as she sipped. "So he gave me a diamond bracelet instead. I've got a weakness for diamonds. I'm surprised I haven't seen you wear any, other than your spanking-new ring. Your grandmother had some fabulous jewelry."

"My mother has it. And the kind of work I do?" Cilla shrugged, drank a little more wine. "Doesn't lend to glitters."

"You don't need them with your looks. Neither did she. It's us lesser mortals who require the enhancements. Of course, beauty fades if you live long enough. Hers didn't. She didn't."

"I was just looking through some old photographs and thinking . . ." Cilla pressed a hand to her temple. "Sorry. I didn't realize I was so tired. The wine must've topped it off."

"You'll need to drink the rest of that. And one more, I think, to finish the job."

"I'd better not. I'm sorry, Cathy, but I feel a little off. I need to—"

"Finish your wine." Cathy opened her purse, drew out a small revolver. "I insist," she said as Spock began to grumble.

"JANET COMMITTED SUICIDE. I've regretted whatever part I might have played in that for more than thirty years."

"She was pregnant."

"She claimed . . ." Something in Ford's eyes had Tom pausing, nodding. "Yes. I didn't believe her, not until we spoke face-to-face. After, after she died, the day she died, in fact, I went to my father. Confessed everything. He was furious with me. He had no tolerance for mistakes, not when they affected the family name. He handled it. We never spoke of it again. I assume he paid off the medical examiner to omit the pregnancy."

And his political career, Ford thought, had gone down the toilet.

"It was the only thing to do, Ford. Imagine what the public would've done to her if it had come out? Imagine what might have become of my family if I was named the father?"

"You spoke, face-to-face."

"I went to the farm. I wanted her to leave it alone, to move on, but she persisted. So I went to see her, as she demanded. She'd been drinking. Not drunk, not yet, but she'd been drinking. She had the results of the pregnancy test."

"She had them with her?" Ford prompted. "The paperwork."

"Yes. She'd used her real name, went to a doctor who didn't know her. Personally, that is. She said she'd worn a wig and used makeup. She often did when we'd meet somewhere. She knew how to hide when she wanted to. I believed her then, and I believed her when she told me she intended to have the baby. But she was done with me. I didn't deserve her, or the child."

Ford's eyes narrowed. "She dumped *you?*"

"I'd already ended it. I suppose she wanted the last word on that. We argued; I won't deny it. But she was alive when I left."

"What happened to the doctor's report?"

"I have no idea. I'm telling you, she was alive when I went home, and looked in on my daughter. I thought of all I'd risked, all I might have destroyed. I thought of Cathy, and the child she carried. How I'd nearly asked her for a divorce only months before so I could be, openly, with a woman who didn't really exist. I might have done that. I nearly did that."

He leaned heavily on the deck rail, closed his eyes. "It was Cathy telling me she was pregnant that helped me begin to break the spell. I lay down on the cot in the nursery with my daughter, thought of the baby Cathy would have in the fall. Thought of Cathy and our life together. I never saw Janet again. I never risked my family again. Thirty-five years, Ford. What would it accomplish to bring it out now?"

"You terrorized Cilla. You nearly killed a man, and when that wasn't enough, you terrorized her. Breaking into her house, writing obscenities on her truck, her wall, threatening her."

"I broke in. I admit that, too. To look for the letters. And I lost control when I couldn't find them. It was the anger, the impulse that had me smashing the tiles. But the rest? I had nothing to do with it. It was Hennessy. I realized the letters didn't matter. They didn't matter. No one would connect me."

"Hennessy couldn't have done all the rest. He was locked up."

"I'm telling you, it wasn't me. Why would I lie about a stone wall, the dolls?" Tom demanded. "You know the worst of it."

"Your wife knew. Janet called her. You said so in the letter, the last letter."

"Janet was drunk, and raving. I convinced Cathy that it wasn't true. That it was alcohol, pills and grief. She was upset, of course, but she believed me. She . . ."

"If you could live a lie this long, why couldn't she? You claim you slept in the nursery the night Janet died."

"Yes, I . . . I fell asleep. I woke when Cathy came in to get the baby. She looked so tired. I asked if she was all right. She said she was fine. We were all fine now." In the moonlight, the flush of shame died to shock white. "My God."

Ford didn't wait for more reasons, more excuses. He ran. Cilla was alone. And Cathy Morrow knew it.

"YOU PUT SOMETHING IN THE WINE."

"Seconal. Just like your whore of a grandmother. But it was vodka for her."

Queasiness rose up to her throat. Fear, knowledge, the mix of drugs and wine. "The couch wasn't pink; the dress wasn't blue."

"Drink some more wine, Cilla. You're babbling now."

"You saw the couch, the dress the night . . . the night you killed her. That's what you remember—that night, not the Christmas party. Tom wrote the letters, is that it? Tom was her lover, the father of the child she carried."

"He was *my* husband, and the father of my child, and the child *I* carried. Did she care about that?" Fury blasted across her face. Not madness, Cilla thought, not like Hennessy. Sheer burning fury.

"Did she give one thought to what marriage and family meant before she tried to take what was mine? She had everything. Everything. But it wasn't enough. It never is for women like her. She was nearly ten *years* older than he was. She made a fool of me, and even that wasn't enough. He went to her, left me to go to her that night while I rocked our daughter to sleep, while our baby kicked in my womb. He went to her, and to the bastard she made with him. Drink the wine, Cilla."

"Did you hold a gun on her, too?"

"I didn't have to. She'd been drinking already. I slipped the pills into her glass. My pills," she added.

"Ones I thought I needed when I first learned she had her hooks in him."

"How long? How long did you know?"

"Months. He came home and I smelled her perfume. Soir de Paris. Her scent. I saw her in his eyes. I knew he went to her, again and again. And only touched me when I *begged*. But it changed, it started to change when I got pregnant. When I made sure I did. He was coming back to me. She wouldn't allow it. Kept luring him back. I would not be pitied. I would not see myself compared to her and laughed at.

"I'll shoot you if you don't drink. They'll call it another break-in. A tragic one this time." She reached back into her purse, pulled out the large plastic bag, and the doll trapped inside it. "In case you'd rather go with the bullet, I'll leave this behind. I bought several of them years ago. I couldn't resist. I never knew why until you came here."

Struggling against the dizziness, Cilla lifted the glass, wet her lips. "You staged her suicide."

"She made it easy. She invited me in, like an old friend. Apologized for what she'd done. She was *sorry* she'd hurt me, or caused me any pain. She couldn't undo it, wouldn't if she could. Because that would undo the baby. All she wanted now was the baby and a chance to make up for past mistakes. Of course, she'd never reveal the name of the father. Lying bitch."

"You drugged her."

"When she started to slide, I helped her upstairs. I felt so strong then. I nearly had to carry her, but I was strong. I undressed her. I wanted her naked, exposed. And I gave her more pills, gave her more vodka. And I sat and I watched her die. I sat and I watched until she stopped breathing. Then I left.

"I'd drive by here. After they'd taken her away to where she never belonged, I'd drive by. I liked watching it decay while I . . . emerged. I starved myself. I exercised until every muscle trembled. Beauty salons, spas, liposuction, face-lifts. He would never look at me and want her. No one would ever look at me with pity."

An image, Cilla thought. An illusion. "I've done nothing to you."

"You came here." With her free hand, Cathy added more pills to Cilla's glass, topped it off with wine. "Cheers!"

"I was wrong," Cilla mumbled. "You're as crazy as Hennessy after all."

"No, just a lot more focused. This house deserved to die its slow, miserable death. She only went to sleep. That was my mistake. You brought her back by coming here, shoved it all in my face again. You had my own son plant roses for her. You seduced Ford, who deserves so much better. I'd have let you live if you'd gone away. If you'd let this house die. But you kept throwing it in my face. I won't have that, Cilla. I see what you are. Hennessy and I are the only ones."

"I'm not Janet. They'll never believe I killed myself."

"She did. Your mother attempted it—or pretended to—twice. You're fruit from the tree." Casually, Cathy tucked back her swing of hair with her free hand. "Pressured into becoming engaged, distraught over causing the death of a man whose life your grandmother ruined. I'll be able to testify how anxious you were for everyone to leave you alone. If only we'd known."

"I'm not Janet," she stated, and tossed the remaining contents in her glass into Cathy's face.

The action had Spock leaping up, the grumbling going to a snarl. As his head rammed against Cathy, Cilla grabbed for the bottle, *saw* herself smash it against Cathy's head. But, impaired by the pills, she swung wide and barely grazed her temple.

It was enough to have Cathy tipping in the stool. Cilla lurched forward, shoved while the dog jumped against the teetering stool. The gun went off, plowing a bullet into the ceiling as the stool toppled.

Fight or flight. She feared she had little of either in her. As her knees buckled, she let herself fall on Cathy, raked her nails down Cathy's face. The scream was satisfying, but more was the certainty that even if she died, they'd know. She had Cathy Morrow under her nails. She grabbed Cathy's hair, yanked, twisted for good measure. Plenty of DNA, she thought vaguely as her vision dimmed at the edges. And Spock's snarling barks went tinny in her ears.

She swung out blindly. She heard shouting, another scream. Another shot. And simply slid away.

FORD'S HEART SKIDDED when he saw Cathy's car in his drive. He wouldn't be too late. He couldn't be. He slammed to a stop behind the Volvo and ran halfway to his door before his instincts stopped him.

Not here. The farm. He spun around, began to run. It had to be at the farm. He cursed, as he'd cursed for miles, the fact that his phone sat on Brian's bar.

When he heard the shot, the fear he thought he knew, the fear he thought he tasted, paled against a wild and mindless terror.

He threw himself against the door, shouting for Cilla as he heard Spock's manic barks. Someone screamed like an animal. He flew into the kitchen. It flashed in front of him, etched itself forever in his memory.

Cilla sprawled over Cathy, fists flailing as if they were almost too heavy to lift. Cathy with blood running down her face, her eyes mad with pain and hate as Spock snapped and growled. The gun in her hand. Turning, turning toward Cilla.

He leaped, grabbing Cathy's wrist with one hand, shoving Cilla clear with the other. He felt something, a quick bee sting at his biceps, before he wrenched the gun from Cathy's hand.

"Ford! Thank God!" Cathy reached for him. "She went crazy. I don't know what happened. I don't know what she's on. She had the gun, and I tried—"

"Shut up," he said coldly, clearly. "If you move, I swear to God, for the first time in my life, I'll hit a woman. Spock, knock it off! And I'll make it count," he told Cathy. "So shut the fuck up." He aimed the gun at her as he edged toward Cilla. "Or I may do worse than knock you out. Cilla. Cilla."

He checked for wounds, then lifted her eyelid as Spock bathed her face frantically with his tongue. "Wake up!" He slapped her, lightly at first. "Move one more inch," he warned Cathy in a voice he barely recognized himself. "Just one more. Cilla!"

He slapped her again, harder, and watched her lids flutter. "Sit up. Wake up." One-handed, he pulled her up to sit. "I'm calling for an ambulance, and the cops. You're all right. Do you hear me?"

"Seconal," she managed, then braced herself with one hand. And shoved her fingers ruthlessly down her throat.

LATER, A LONG TIME LATER, Cilla sat under the blue umbrella. Spring had gone, and summer nearly, she thought. She'd be here when the leaves changed and burned across the mountains. And when the first snow of the season fell, and the last. She'd be here, she thought, in all the springs to come, and the seasons to follow.

She'd be home. With Ford. And with Spock. Her heroes.

"You're still pale," he said. "Lying down might be a better idea than fresh air."

"You're still pale," she countered. "You were shot."

He glanced down at his bandaged arm. "Grazed" was the more accurate word. "Yeah. Eventually, that'll be cool. I got shot once, I'll say, rushing in—just a little too late again—to save the love of my life before she saved herself."

"You did save me. I'd lost it. I CSI'd her," she added, wiggling her fingers. "But I was done. You and Spock—fierce doggie," she murmured as she bent down to nuzzle him. "You saved my life. Now you have to keep it."

He reached over, took her hand. "That's the plan. I nearly went in the wrong house. That's it, Cilla. No more two households for us. I nearly went to the wrong one. Then I would've been too late."

"You figured it out, and you came for me. You can draw all the heroes you want. You're mine."

"Hero, goddess and superdog. We're pretty lucky, you and me."

"I guess we are. Ford, I'm so sorry, I'm so sorry for Brian."

"We'll help him get through it." No question there, Ford thought, no choice. "We'll find a way to help him get through it."

"She carried that betrayal with her all these years. And couldn't stand what I came here to do. In a way, this house was a symbol for both of us." She studied it—her pretty home, the fresh paint, the windows glinting in the early morning sun.

"I needed to bring it back; she needed to watch it die. Every fresh board, every coat of paint, a slap in the face to her. The party? Can you imagine how that must have gnawed at her? Music and laughter, food and drink. And wedding talk. How could she stand it?"

"I knew them both all my life and never saw through it. So much for the writer's power of observation."

"They put it away. Locked it in a closet. She watched Janet die." That still twisted in her heart. "She had it in her to watch. And she had it in her to put it away, to remake herself. To raise her family, to shop with her friends, to bake cookies and make the beds. And to drive by here, every once in a while, so she could let it out."

"Like a pressure valve."

"I'd say so. And I locked down the valve. My grandmother didn't commit suicide. That's going to be major news. Cameras, print, movie of the week—perhaps a major motion picture. More books, talk shows. Much."

"I think I've got the picture by now. No warning necessary. Your grandmother didn't commit suicide," he repeated.

"No, she didn't." When her eyes filled, the tears felt like redemption. "She didn't leave my mother, not in the way Mom always thought. She bought a lipstick-pink couch with white satin cushions. She grieved for a lost child and prepared for another.

"Not a saint," Cilla continued. "She slept with another woman's husband, and would have broken up his family without a qualm. Or much of one."

"Cheating's a two-way street. Tom betrayed his wife, his family. And even when he claimed he'd broken it off, he slept with Janet again. He had a pregnant wife and a child at home, and slept with the image—and refused to take responsibility for the consequences."

"I wonder if it was the brutality of that last letter that snapped Janet's feeling for him, had her come back, face him down with the facts. 'I'm pregnant, the baby's yours, but we don't want or need you.'"

She let out a breath. "I like to think so."

"Plays, doesn't it? Sure jibes with what Tom told me. Cathy took and destroyed the pregnancy results, but she didn't know about the letters. She didn't know about *Gatsby*."

"Janet kept the letters, I think, to remind her that the child was conceived in at least the illusion of love. And to remind herself why it would belong to only her. I think, too, she made certain the farm couldn't be sold because she wanted the child to have it one day. Johnnie was gone, and she knew my mother had no real ties to it. But she had another chance.

"And maybe there will always be questions, but I have the answers I needed. I wonder if I'll still dream of her, the way I always have."

"Do you want to?"

"Maybe. Sometimes. But I think I'd like to start dreaming about what might happen, about what I hope for, rather than what used to be." She smiled when he brushed his lips over her fingers.

"Take a walk with me." He got to his feet, drew her to hers. "Just you. Just me." He looked down at Spock as the dog did his happy dance. "Just us."

She walked with him across the stones, over the grass still damp with dew, with roses madly blooming and the last of the summer's flowers unfolded like jewels. Walked with him while the sweet, ugly dog chased his invisible cats around the pond strung with lily pads.

With her hand in his, she thought this was dream enough for her. Right now. With the three of them happy and safe and together.

And home.